KU-440-168

The
Playground
Mafia

The Playground Mafia

Sarah Tucker

ISIS
LARGE PRINT
Oxford

Copyright © Sarah Tucker, 2006

First published in Great Britain 2006
by
Arrow Books, one of the publishers in the
Random House Group Ltd.

Published in Large Print 2007 by ISIS Publishing Ltd.,
7 Centremead, Osney Mead, Oxford OX2 0ES
by arrangement with the
Random House Group Ltd.

All rights reserved

The moral right of the author has been asserted

British Library Cataloguing in Publication Data
Tucker, Sarah
    The playground mafia. – Large print ed.
    1. Divorced mothers – Fiction
    2. Large type books
    I. Title
    823.9'12 [F]

ISBN 978–0–7531–7812–6 (hb)
ISBN 978–0–7531–7813–3 (pb)

Printed and bound in Great Britain by
T. J. International Ltd., Padstow, Cornwall

To my darling Tom . . .
And to my mum and dad. I hope you approve.

Buckinghamshire Libraries
and Heritage

506606

ULVERSCROFT 26-2-10

19-95.

Acknowledgements

A huge thank you to Nikola and Emma, and all at Random House, and to my agent Jacqs.

Thanks also to Doreen and Hazel, who are so special to everyone, not just to me, to my friends, the lovely Caroline, Claire, Amanda, Kim, Jo, Linda, Gina, Coline, Clare, Nim, Helen and Christine, and the excellent ski / summer crowd. And to Jeremy, Duncan and Mrs Ellison of Gearies School. Thank you all in your own way for helping me find my voice.

CHAPTER
ONE

First Day

"Don't be nervous, Mummy."

My four-year-old is telling me not to worry. It's Ben's first day at school, in a new town, and he's brimming with excitement. I'm so nervous I want to throw up.

I lie.

"I'm not worried, just excited about your first day at school, making new friends and all that."

I'm not sure he's really buying it, but he just says encouragingly, "Yes, and you'll make lots of new friends as well, right? And Harry's mummy and Jennifer's mummy will be there too."

I look at Ben and laugh, because that's the kind of thing I'm supposed to say to *him*. He grins back at me, giving me a little wink, or his lopsided attempt at one.

It's seven o'clock on a bright September morning. We're still in our pyjamas, slouching over cereal and orange juice (Ben) and toast and double espresso (me) and Ben is about to start his first day at The Sycamore. Leafy, sprawling and highly sought after, The Sycamore is one of the best state schools in the country. It also happens to be a mere four hundred yards from my

1

front door, which, thankfully, is situated within the school's ridiculously small and highly controversial five-hundred-yard catchment area.

Ruthless strategic thinking has led Caroline Gray & Son to the riverside town of Frencham. After an acrimonious divorce (in truth, are they ever anything else?) from City trader John, I decided to leave behind the past and my oversized matrimonial home in Chetley. A house which said nothing about me, my character or taste, other than the obvious fact that I had married a control freak who didn't have much of either.

I spent almost an entire year looking for the right property in the right location. My initial plan after the divorce was to bury myself in some sleepy village in the middle of nowhere and dissolve into obscurity, avoiding all outside contact, especially with the opposite sex. But I quickly and regretfully had to abandon that plan. I'm a townie and like being with people and I wanted Ben to have a stimulating, lively environment to grow up in. Not the total inner-city experience, which would inevitably prove *too* stimulating for both of us, but a happy and healthy medium. Frencham seemed to have everything we needed. A glorious park up the hill, a river inviting long and leisurely walks, two cinemas (the mainstream one showing American crap and a smaller one for obscure European arty stuff), two theatres and a shopping centre with a balance of chain stores and independent shops. And the high street had a Waitrose, which, according to my mum, is a must-have. But what finally did it for me was the fact that my two best friends, Eva and Heather, live here. And their children go to The Sycamore.

So after leaving Chetley and my now ex-husband, I rented a two-bedroom flat in Frencham for a little while to find Ben and myself a home, somewhere that would be perfect for us but still doable on my income. Graphology and freelance writing — Editorial Services on my home-made but very classy business card — make me comfortably off, but obviously don't come with a huge salary. While everyone else was enjoying their summer holidays — Eva in Morocco and Heather in the Seychelles — I must have gone through more than a hundred high-maintenance cottages with too much garden, low-maintenance characterless apartments with none, four-bedroom houses with potential, and two-bedroom houses with planning permission. Eventually, after much deliberation and discussion with the bloody-minded estate agents (and a feng-shui expert who told me only a south-west facing house would mean true "happiness"), I bought a two-bedroom mid-terrace south-west facing Victorian house in a little cul-de-sac, in walking distance of local amenities and the school.

Other than Ben, who is all testosterone, a noisy and messy and aggressive four-year-old, there isn't a man in my life right now. A lot of my romantic belief in humanity was used up when I discovered John in our bed with his secretary. The devastatingly vulgar cliché of it all, the sense of utter betrayal by a man I thought I loved, the destruction of a relationship that I thought had been working just fine and the helpless grief at having to take Ben away from his father, all of those have sapped my energy for looking at men and engaging with them in an emotional way for the time being, not to mention for entering into something approximating a relationship with them.

I'd be lying if I said I wasn't keeping my eyes open for someone who doesn't show arsehole tendencies in his handwriting or erratic abnormalities in his behaviour, but I've not really felt up to being out and about on the dating scene a whole lot since my divorce. It's just too much work right now, with all that's been going on, and I've only started to discover the challenges of being a newly single mother. Just getting us organised on a day-to-day basis, co-ordinating my job with Ben's schedule, and now school, is a task in and of itself that requires the same kind of organisational skills, time management and delegating needed to run a full-scale company. A precarious balance at the best of times and getting involved with another person, bringing that person into our lives, would tip that balance and potentially invite so much trouble that it almost doesn't really justify the effort. Plus, whoever manages to weasel his way into my life would have to get past Ben first. (His latest trick is to start a play sword fight and then go straight for the balls.)

I catch Ben peacefully playing shoot-the-cornflakes with his spoon, hitting table and floor more often than his bowl, but today's not the day to argue. I down my espresso and get up to make another one. Or would a cup of herbal tea be wiser? I hold out my hands and scrutinise them for any telltale jitters. I sigh and put the kettle on, reaching for the jar of tea bags. We've been gearing up for this day for so long, I'd better keep my wits about me. I can't arrive at the school gates shaking with caffeine and nerves. Especially when I think of the terrifying Mrs Kathleen Ellison, headmistress extraordinaire. I blush, thinking back to the school's Open Day.

I was still in the rented flat, sifting through the memories of a marriage gone wrong, throwing away anything and everything that reminded me of unhappier times. I threw away a lot. The day at The Sycamore was a welcome change from plastic bin bags and trips to the communal dump. Although I almost backed out again when I entered the classroom building behind a gaggle of other mums, all of whom clearly as nervous and twitchy as me, and caught sight of a formidable figure. Tall, lean and attractive, in her early fifties and in top-to-toe brown and navy Jaeger, Mrs Ellison didn't look as though she suffered fools lightly. Not a person to cross. I'd already drawn attention to myself by knocking over a chair and half tumbling to the floor. And then I mistakenly entered through the wrong door of the music room, not noticing the "In" and "Out" stickers which were stuck, rather unhelpfully I thought, at crutch level — probably by someone no taller than Ben.

"Come through the wrong door?" she admonished me, brows almost disappearing into her hairline. "We've got to go through there and out here. Now off we go." She wagged a long finger.

I had felt four again and strangely disobedient. Another mum shot me a sympathetic look, trying to remain inconspicuous at the same time. I didn't blame her. But despite Mrs Ellison, I noticed the coloured artwork taped neatly on the walls, the short handwritten stories and accompanying crayon drawings, and had a good feeling about The Sycamore.

And I'm sure he will be absolutely fine there, but all of a sudden I'm second-guessing everything. Is this really the right set-up for us? Will it be too posh, too competitive, too hard-core? Have I missed something? Forgotten to tick a box somewhere? Dinner money, PE kit, book bag, the correct uniform?

Ben is happily munching his way through the remnants of his breakfast, now engaged in a war between a mini Obi-wan and Darth Vader, and completely oblivious to his mum's mild panic attack. Extraordinary to think how far we've come. In a year, as well as selling a house and buying another, I've researched more than twenty schools around Frencham and put Ben's name down on ten waiting lists, spending £400 before he's even been accepted by any of them. I've been interviewed by several headmasters and one headmistress, all of whom wanted to know much more about me than they did about Ben, and one who didn't ask anything about me or Ben, just talked about himself all the time. When he found out I was a graphologist, he asked me to look at a sample of his handwriting. Ready to do anything that would help get Ben into the school — the same desperation that drives any mum of under-fives — I analysed him as self-absorbed and a tad dishonest, with the potential to be cruel with intent. This obviously wasn't the time for honesty, so I told him he was single-minded, determined, creative and could be ruthless. Ben was offered a place.

After the endless hassle with the waiting lists — the energy spent on belatedly entering the rat race to get in and compete with mums who had had their children on those damn lists for the better part of the last five years, enduring the fake smiles during interviews and nervously waiting for the unassuming white envelope to plop through my front door — I declined all of them the moment Ben got a place at The Sycamore. I called John to tell him the news but he paid scant attention, although, admittedly, he seemed delighted not to have to pay the twelve-grand-plus annual fees of some of the alternatives I had recommended.

Still, he had always been hoping we'd stay in Chetley, especially since I had already researched all the schools there when I was pregnant. The girls at the local gym had warned me to put the baby's name down early as competition was fierce. For one school, I signed Ben up when he was no more than a two-month-old foetus. I didn't even know if he was a Ben then (I put his name down as *M Brio Gray*), but the school was one of the best in the country.

He got a place, but when John and I divorced I wanted to leave Chetley as soon as possible. I just didn't have a support network around me. His parents were round the corner but largely ignored me, thanks to John making me out as the scarlet woman. They're not hugely into children, so have never shown an avid interest in Ben, which suits me just fine. And my mum was still in a state of purdah about the divorce and unable to speak to me without screaming or, alternatively, sobbing. Eva suggested it was more to do with the fact she now couldn't face her coterie of tennis-club friends. Her only daughter a divorcée and, worse still, a single mum. Lowest of the low.

My reverie is interrupted by a loud slurping noise from my son. "I'm done, Mummy," he says, plonking his spoon down decisively on the table.

Ben is cornflaked out. He hops off the chair and carries his bowl and cup to the sink and drops them in with a loud clatter. He turns to smile at me apologetically, a wide-eyed, innocent grin that Eva tells me will quickly disappear the more time he spends at school. His blond hair, freshly washed and carefully combed, is already sticking up at the back.

As we go to dress, I wish I had a uniform today as well. Ben's in grey trousers, white shirt and navy jumper with everything named. I always dress more hippy-chic than conservative and I love bold colours, but perhaps I should take the lead from Mrs Ellison and go more Jaeger today? I wouldn't normally be seen dead in that stuff, so as a compromise I wear a flowery dress from Red Dawn, my favourite shop in Chetley and the only worthwhile thing I left behind.

Right, eight fifteen and I said I would meet Heather and Eva at the gates at eight thirty. A ten-minute walk or a five-minute drive? A walk will do us good.

"Have you been to the toilet?" I ask for Ben the nth time, bending down to straighten his tie and tuck his shirt in more securely, handing him his jacket. Other kids at his age are still just a touch soft and rounded from their toddler years, but Ben's all bones, sticky-out elbows and knobbly knees. He seems to repel clothes, too, shirts mysteriously untucking themselves, new trousers immediately getting scuff marks and any buttons popping off upon contact with his body.

"Yes, Mummy," he answers me for the nth time, sounding bored. In my head, I ask myself the same question. I've been five times in the last forty-five minutes.

Time for a final check in the mirror. Ben is gorgeous, as always. I look ill. I start fiddling with my hair. It's long and hideously straight and needs more than its fair share of attention before looking anything like presentable. Now. Book bag — check. Cap — check. Letters saying what Ben's allergic to (nuts and bullies) — check. Letters saying what clubs he's taking part in — check. Forms for the PTA — check. Gym kit — check. Jumper round the right way — check. All labels in all clothes including coat labelled BENJAMIN GRAY — check.

"OK, let's go." I breathe out slowly.

CHAPTER
TWO

Meeting the Mafia

I spy Heather and Eva, elegant in pink and purple amidst a scrum of mums in front of The Sycamore's black iron gates. God, there are a lot of people here this morning. Women in all shades from cappuccino to coffee, Mrs Ellison lookalikes with freshly scrubbed faces and brown highlighted hair neatly brushed into tight bobs. Women in designer tracksuits with immaculate make-up; expensively suited women on the way to work; and tired-looking mums dragging toddlers, some carrying a baby as well. Most of them look as if they've walked this path many times before and could do it with their eyes shut. As I come closer I notice some *do* still seem to have their eyes closed, with children running in front and behind them not looking where they're going either.

Dotted among the sea of mothers buttoning jackets, brushing hair and pulling apart little knots of rowdy boys, I also see quite a few nervy, black- and blue-suited men furtively fumbling with camcorders, looking awkward and threatened by the noise of female shouting and chattering. Those must be the fathers who've taken the morning off to be with their children for the first day of school and want to record the moment for posterity. Which reminds me — John said he would meet me at the school gates, too. I can't see him yet, but I know he wouldn't let Ben down. Not today.

Eva spots me and grins encouragingly. She waits for me to pick my way through the throng and then says ceremoniously, "First day at school, Caroline Gray. You nervous?"

"It's perfectly natural," says Heather, clipping her son, Philip, round the ear for tripping his younger sister, Jennifer, and giving her a bloody nose on the first day back.

Both hug me for support, while the children — Eva's twins Harry and Maddy and Heather's two — all scrubbed clean in grey and blue, ask each other what they've got for lunch, what they did over the school holidays and which teachers they've got this year. As I try to help stem the flow of blood from Jennifer's nose, I can hear Philip tell Ben that his teacher, Ms Silver, is a cannibal and eats fingers if she doesn't like the look of you. Since Ben doesn't know what a cannibal is, he thinks Philip means chocolate fingers so he is more concerned that she'll eat something from his packed lunch than bite his hands off.

Children taken care of and now running wild around us, we smile at each other and I finally have a chance to take in the scene in front of the school gates properly. More people have arrived while I was greeting the girls and I hardly recognise the school now, besieged by an onslaught of parents, and kids chasing each other. Over

11

by the trees next to the gates, I notice a few women who look as though they belong on a Page Three spread rather than outside a suburban school. Cleavages heavy and high, cheekbones taut, hair peroxided, expressions startled, skirts short, and vowels, when they speak, decidedly flat.

"God, they look like they've been bussed in here straight from Chetley." I nudge Heather delightedly.

She follows my gaze. "No, no, we get them here too," she says casually, wadding up bloody tissues and stuffing them in her bag. The children have scampered further and further away and I look wistfully after Ben, running off from his mother so happily, but I'm distracted now by the social strata at the gates.

Eva points over to another group, standing alone, whether through choice or circumstance, I can't work out. Averaging about five foot nothing, painted, manicured and highly polished, they are doll-like creatures who look strangely out of place in this Land of Suburban Giants. "Those are second wives," Eva whispers to me, more quietly than Heather. "Second-time rounders and clearly seen as predators by some of the other mums." Hence the distance. "They wear conspicuous designer labels, usually arrive in the obligatory four-wheel drives and look only marginally taller than their offspring."

Then, there's a group of women who look a few inches taller and leaner than the second wives and a lot more chilled and fresh-faced than everyone else. Dressed in sweatpants and shirts, iPods sticking out their pockets, as though they've just come or are just about to run round the park once their parental duties are done, they're smiling and chatting and gesturing to each other with big, bold arm movements. From Australia or New Zealand, Eva explains to me.

And in the corner by the side gate, three graceful Japanese women stand with their children, silent and still, although it's hard to tell whether they're dignified or terrified, whether they're gazing at everyone in amazement or amusement. Clearly startled by the noise and size of the crowd, they vice-grip their children, who stand equally immaculate and inscrutable, stunned into silence.

Heather tugs my sleeve impatiently, having asked me the same questions twice now.

"Did you drive or walk?"

"We walked, it's so close and I didn't want to have to drive around endlessly to park and get a ticket and stuff," I say. "But it seems I needn't have bothered." I point to the large number of cars parked illegally and in some cases downright dangerously around the school entrance.

Loads of second-hand Golf GTIs and new Minis, but mostly variations on four-wheel drives bursting with at least three children per car. I'm glad I didn't drive — we've got a ratty old Golf in dire need of servicing, which would be fairly out of place here. Despite the school-run mums' utter disregard for single- and double-yellow lines, parking-permit limitations and the ruthless way with which parking tickets are usually slammed on anything that so much as approaches a yellow line in the greater Frencham area, there are no parking attendants in sight.

"I should come here more often," I say appreciatively. "I get ticketed outside my own house if I'm not parked within my designated square."

Heather smiles. "I know, I have a whole wad of tickets I still need to pay off. I seem to collect them these days and Harvey gets so irritated." She flicks her long hair out of her eyes and draws herself up to her whole impressive six feet. I'm fairly tall myself, but she's the only one I know who can pull off six feet and heels and still look stunning.

"It's different in the mornings, though. The parking attendants wouldn't dare incur the wrath of the school mums. There is one group in particular which practically owns this school. I think one young guy tried to curb the wild parking several years back. He must have been new on the job and gave out over sixty tickets in half an hour. Poor bugger thought he'd hit the jackpot and made his quota for the year. Unfortunately, he didn't reckon on one of the mums knowing his boss's boss, and he got the sack that same day for being dressed incorrectly. Or something innocuous like that. Anyway, the tickets were forgotten and put down as an administrative error."

I'm intrigued. "Really? Those would be handy to have as friends around here." I'm thinking guiltily of my own collection of parking fines. "Which ones are they?" I look around, expecting to see a group wearing storm-trooper type outfits, dark glasses and pointy shoes. Heather snorts and points across the playground to a small group next to the entrance. "I wouldn't hold my breath if I were you. There're a couple of them now, a woman called Sarah Flint, and a few others. We call them the playground mafia."

I can't make out many details from here, but they seem harmless enough. Heather sees my shrug and shakes her head. "They have power in Frencham." She's always been a bit of a drama queen, I guess.

Just as Heather's about to speak again the bell rings and the scrum pours through the gates into a large concrete playground. We follow.

The Sycamore has the feeling of a rural school despite being in the centre of town. Perched at the top of Frencham Hill, the school grounds cover more than four acres of land, three of which are grass playing fields, bordered by huge hundred-year-old oaks. The drive up to the school is tree-lined and the main buildings are surrounded by a mass of green, giving the whole area a very lush, wholesome and spacious feel, like a vast meadow. Eva tells me the local council has been offered millions for the land, but has consistently refused — mostly because the land backs onto the gardens of some of the wealthiest people in the country paying millions in local taxes as well as backhanders each year to the local councillors. I'm glad. The school is like an oasis, right in the middle of town.

The school is split into two main buildings. The smaller, single-storey building to the left is for the infants — the four- to seven-year-olds. This has a little play area with slides and swings and climbing frames, towered over by a large plaque marked *With thanks to*

Sarah Flint and the PTA. There is also a sandpit, and the play area is fenced round with a large gate on which sits another large notice: *For Reception Only*. For the other children there is a large concrete playground, about the size of half a football pitch with markings for hopscotch and other games I'm sure I played but am now too old to remember. The mob slowly propels us forward and I can see the two doors into the school. I'm tugging Ben in their general direction when Heather says we have to walk round the corner to another one.

"If you don't arrive before nine, Ms Lockier, Mrs Ellison's deputy, locks the door and you have to go in the main entrance. The walk of shame. I had to do it so many times with this one," she points to Philip, "I used to give up on walking round to the infant side altogether. If you're late you have to put your name as well as your child's in the Late Book. It's ridiculous, but apparently 'disruptions from latecomers pose a serious threat to the children's concentration'." She stabs the air, putting irritated quote marks around the last bit.

"Right." I pull Ben alongside Jennifer, glad the two are going to be classmates. I don't think I could negotiate the plethora of rules, dos and don'ts, on my own. Eva's twins are a year above Ben, so close enough as well. "And juniors, do they have the same rules?" I ask, slightly bewildered but determined to avoid the walk of shame at all costs.

"No, those parents aren't allowed to say goodbye to their children at the door any more, they have to stay back. Mind you, by that age the kids think it's uncool to be seen kissing and hugging Mummy, but I must admit I'll miss it when Jennifer goes up." She looks over at her daughter who has torn herself away and is playing what looks like kiss chase with a boy who seems utterly terrified of being caught.

"Me too," says Eva, lovingly surveying Harry and Maddy, who are bashing each other quite viciously on the heads with their book bags.

"They caught a bit of *Kill Bill* last night before bedtime."

I look shocked.

"I know, I know." Eva grins ashamedly. "I was horrified too, but at least it was *Part I*. *Part II* is even worse, apparently. And it wasn't the bit where she had her head cut off," she adds reassuringly.

Ben and I stand back a bit as we wait for the infants door to open. He's still clutching my hand and seems both bemused and amused by the throng of children milling around him, as though mentally totting up the number of playmates he will have and the fact that he may have to share his precious toys. He'll be in the "system" now for at least twelve years, much longer if he wants to become an academic, although I haven't detected any nerdy or anorak qualities in him yet. But a lot could happen. This is only the first day.

"Is Daddy going to come, too?" Ben says, looking up at me expectantly. "I can't see him anywhere."

"Yes, he is. He's probably got caught up in traffic, but he will definitely be here," I say, trying to convince myself as much as reassure him. I crane my neck, hoping to see a flash of John's carefully greying hair, but all I can see is women talking to each other, embracing small children, helping to carry book bags and straightening collars.

It's time to go already and, still looking around anxiously, I line up with the other mums for Ben's class. The Kangaroo Class. I like the idea of my boy as a mini marsupial, and bend down to hug him, bringing his little face close to mine. His blue eyes look back at me solemnly.

"OK?" I finally manage to say.

Ben smiles back. "Philip says my teacher is Ms Silver," he points over to the woman herding children together at the door. "We saw her in the playground. I'm sure she's very nice and won't eat my lunch." He nods vigorously.

I let go of him and ruffle his hair, then surreptitiously try to smooth down that tuft at the back. When I stand up I find Ms Silver in front of us, looking nothing like a cannibal, not that I would recognise one if I met one, but a tall, slim woman, with brown hair and smiling eyes. She beams at me, asking if I'm Ben's mum.

I beam back. "Yes," pushing him forward a bit.

"Hi, Ben," she says. "Pleased to meet you." And to me: "Would you like to help him find his peg for his PE kit and put his lunch on the shelf? We don't allow this after the first few weeks but at the beginning we find it's quite good. And then you can look through the window and wave at them. They like that. The mums and dads as much as the children. Is your husband here?" She looks behind me.

"No, but we're expecting him," I say, trying to sound confident again. Scanning the crowd. John's last chance. *Where the fuck are you?*

Ms Silver bends down to Ben's level. "Ready for your first day?"

Ben nods enthusiastically, swinging his bag. "I think so, Ms Silver, are you?"

She smiles. "Yes, I hope so, but let me know how I'm doing, OK?"

Ben frowns, clearly liking the responsibility.

Heather and Jennifer are already in the classroom and we're one of the last to go in. We follow Ms Silver's lead and when I see Ben's peg clearly marked BENJAMIN with a little picture of a blue kangaroo underneath, I suddenly want to cry. I felt so emotional when he started nursery that I thought I'd got all that out of the way then, but here I am, furtively wiping at my eyes. I help him with the packed lunch (grilled chicken sandwich, strawberry yoghurt with no bits, apple and banana) and bend down for a final hug.

"I'll wave at you through the window, OK? And I'll pick you up at twenty-past three," I say reassuringly.

"That's big hand on the three and little hand on the four?"

"No, other way round. Big hand on the four and little on the three, but almost right."

And there he goes, he walks away and all I can think about is the first time I held him in my arms, so light and delicate. How I got up every two hours to feed him in the quiet of the night, rocking in my chair. I remember him sucking his thumb for the first time (and he still does sometimes when he's tired), taking his first steps and his first word. All those benchmark moments. I start blotting my eyes again, cursing my expensive but clearly not waterproof mascara. If I am to have any chance of surviving this, I need some support. As if I'd spoken aloud, I feel a tap on my shoulder and turn to see John staring at me, red-faced and out of breath.

"Sorry I'm late. Fucking trains. Ben in there already?" I shove him forward into the corridor, no time for anything.

"Go quickly and give him a hug. He so wants you to be there on his first day."

It's probably fairly obvious by now that I don't really like John. If it weren't for Ben, who made everything worthwhile, I would rather not ever have met him in the first place, but today I'm happy to see him because it's important for Ben that both of us are here, I think. So with an unusual amount of benevolence, I watch my little boy's face light up when he sees John standing uncertainly in the door. Ben runs to him and wraps his arms around his neck. And I'm pleased to see that John fares no better than I have, looking quite choked up as he squeezes his son and picks him up. In that split second, that squeeze, I think John knows just what he had and what he's lost. And, despite everything, in my heart of hearts I feel for him.

John gets shooed out with the last stragglers and joins me at the window. I ignore him, my momentary sympathy already largely forgotten, and continue to peer through, pressing my nose hard against the glass like some school-girl coveting a doll in a toyshop window. I watch as the class quickly settles down and Ms Silver starts playing the guitar. I can hear clapping, singing, excited chattering. Suddenly I feel very old.

After a few minutes I break the silence, grudgingly thanking John for being there. He looks contrite. "Sorry I'm late. I have to run, though, get to the office."

"I'll call and get Ben to tell you how his first day went, OK?" I offer generously.

"Yes, thank you." He already starts down the drive. Eva and Heather join me as I watch him take his mobile from his pocket and start dialling, running his hand through his closely cropped hair, straightening his thinly rimmed spectacles which, he believes, hide his rather narrowly set eyes. He always looks so hunched these days, I notice. I'm able to look at him quite dispassionately now. Not too long ago I would have either ground my teeth trying not to bash in his head or dissolved into helpless weeping. He's pretty much a stranger to me at this point, though, belonging to another world, and although I still loathe him (no point beating around the bush here) we have reached a point of cool civility.

Noticing my smudgy mascara, Eva hugs me. "I always get weepy on the first day too," she says kindly.

"Makes you feel too damn old, doesn't it?" Heather agrees, trying to find her mobile in a bag which seems crammed with everything from lipsticks to soft toys.

I nod mutely.

"Fancy a coffee?" suggests Eva.

Heather looks up from her rummaging. "God, not in the Sycamore Café, Eva, you know the mafia have their coffee mornings there. You don't want to expose Caroline to them this early on, do you?"

"I'm suggesting coffee, not initiation," Eva retorts dryly, nodding to me. "Let's go." She buttons her jacket around her small frame and pushes back her short brown hair. If Heather's the beautiful, tall one, then Eva's enviably petite, to the point of being elfin. "I could do with a large shot of caffeine."

All around us other mums disperse into the surrounding streets, some walking in groups of twos and threes, others driving off defiantly past traffic wardens who look as though they're patiently waiting for everyone to leave before they start their trawl. Eva points out the café, just down the hill, and I watch as a couple of small figures enter. Everyone has seemed pretty harmless so far. Not storm-trooper types at all. I see two mums deep in conversation turning off into a side street. I recognise the red hair, big sunglasses. I think I ran into her at the supermarket the other day; Ben and her little girl had quietly emptied the entire biscuit shelf into our carts. Nice to see a familiar face. My spirits are lifting and as we follow the rest of the mums drifting down the hill, I'm beginning to enjoy the morning sun bouncing off trees just starting to change colour.

Approaching the café, Heather obviously feels compelled to prep me for what lies ahead. "You know, Caroline, you might have to watch your back a little at The Sycamore."

"Why?" I say distractedly, admiring the hanging baskets that mark the beginning of Frencham's pretty high street. I'm glad this part of the morning is over.

Undeterred, Heather goes on. "Some of those women, the more, shall we say, high-maintenance mums. I saw them watching you today when you were saying goodbye to Ben. I think they're suspicious."

Now she has my attention. "What? Why?"

"You're single, you're attractive. There's a lot of talk about reputation and morals among them and they might consider you a lose cannon. And you're bound to be after their husbands."

I laugh. "What? I'm sure there are loads of other single mums in the playground each morning who go about their business completely innocently. And it's not my fault my husband screwed his secretary behind my back. *Ex*-husband."

"Yeah, but you look too good, and you're obviously happy." I refrain from pointing out the emotional roller-coaster of the past year. "Nothing like genuine happiness to piss off women who spend thousands on themselves and their family and are still fucking miserable. You give being a single mum too good a press. And you're over forty, for God's sake."

"Thanks," I say dryly, but a little flattered as well, although I'm not sure in what way all of this really is a compliment. She's lost the plot a little this morning. I'm sure there is the same kind of politics at this school as there is in every playground in every school in the country. A pecking order, gossip, petty jealousies. But I'm equally sure that no one at The Sycamore cares that much about the others to waste any real time on worrying about that kind of stuff.

"God, Heather, you're so paranoid." Eva pulls me along. "Let's just go and have a nice, relaxing cup of coffee."

"You just wait, Caroline," Heather says sagely. "Put a foot wrong and that's it. You'll be on their radar for life."

I end the discussion by walking into the Sycamore Café, the door heralding our arrival with a quiet ping. I expect to see a polished room full of feisty, vicious-looking women clinging to mobiles, scheming about nicking each other's nannies and grinding their teeth behind *Daily Mails* and café lattes. But the café is almost empty.

CHAPTER
THREE

The Sycamore Cafe

To be honest, I'm a little disappointed. I had expected much more of this coffee-morning mafia meeting place. The Sycamore Café is no bigger than my sitting room, with polished wooden floors and old-fashioned wall lamps. At the back there is a mezzanine with a large round oak table and chairs that look as if they are ready and waiting for the bums of noble knights rather than school-run mums. The large window behind the table looks out on to a small courtyard full of bins — not the most aesthetically pleasing of views, but it brightens the café and floods the top table with a natural spotlight effect. On the lower level a long, gleaming glass cabinet with various scrumptious-looking cakes and biscuits towers over a number of smaller tables and a coffee machine which seems inordinately noisy for something so small.

We head for a bigger table right by the door, next to the bulging magazine rack. A copy of *Harpers & Queen*, as well as *Tatler* and, for some inexplicable reason, *Nuts*. A dog-eared *Telegraph* and *The Times* and six copies of the *Daily Mail*, two of which look as though they've been put through a mangle. Behind the counter there are shelves of tins of herbal and normal teas, and a black-board announcing lemon cake as the special of the day. If you buy a tuna-and-cucumber baguette and slice of lemon cake for £7, you get a coffee free. Sounds like a steal to me.

"Right," says Eva. "I'll get us some coffees. Does everyone want black?"

"Yes, please," says Heather, already scouring the room for any sign of the enemy. She really is crazy, I think, watching her duck and sway, hair flying. And there's no one here either, just a few women sitting in the back, chatting amiably, reading the papers, working. I recognise one of the women who lives in my street, Claire, I think, and wave to her. She smiles back, nodding, and says a few words to her companion, who smiles as well. We had a quick chat over her front fence the other day, about the pitfalls of first days at school. She has two girls, but a few classes up from Ben.

"I'll have a peppermint tea, thanks," I call over to Eva, remembering my espresso excess this morning.

I see her relaying the order to the people crowding behind the counter. A sparky young girl who looks no older than eighteen and has the posture of a dancer, perhaps a drama student, making up the extra pennies. Then an older man who seems cheerful enough, and a young guy who looks as if he's going to stab anyone who asks for anything. He probably explains the copy of *Nuts* in the magazine rack.

It's all very nice, but I had expected something slightly more edgy, polished, after Heather's remarks about the politics and disputes and power plays that

26

regularly go on within these walls, but it's like any other café, a bit scruffy by Frencham standards maybe, but obviously convenient for Sycamore mums and the mafia.

"So where are they?" I ask, looking around the little square tables, noticing a few more women at the cabinet behind Eva now, ordering coffee and lemon cake.

"The mafia? Not here yet, but you just wait. They'll be here soon. And you can smell them a mile off."

According to Heather, the playground mafia meet for coffee from about nine fifteen till half ten, then again two thirty to three twenty every Monday to Friday, monopolising the top table, where they bitch and scheme about anyone and anything alien to their petty-minded sensibilities (obviously I'm quoting Heather here). For a variety of reasons, she's convinced they talk mainly about her. From what she says, she's most likely not far off the mark, but it seems she has no one to blame but herself. She admits as much. When Philip first started at The Sycamore a few years back, Heather was enthusiastic about school activities and desperate to make friends, anything to perk up her new life as a stay-at-home mum with one at school and one at home. But she soon found out that they bored her even more than the endless, aimless hours between the school runs. And to liven up everyone's days, she started telling them about her and Harvey's rocky marriage. Every emotionally raw, haemorrhaging detail was lapped up by her eager audience and now that the tide has turned and Heather would rather bite off her hand than join them in running the school, this is something she now deeply regrets.

"I'm telling you," Heather told us, "listening to them prattle on day in day out about the most inane stuff on the planet would drive anyone to distraction. I don't expect them to discuss world peace every morning, but these women are bright, they've got brains, motivation and imagination. Or they used to. Now they only talk about their kids — or the other mums. One day they'd all gone to the pottery café, you know the place where kids can paint their own plates for twice what you'd pay for Doulton bone china. Apparently most chose to paint plates with dinosaurs. Boys and girls neatly divided into brown and pink ones, with the exception of one little boy who did a pink one with brown polka dots. Clearly gay tendencies, they all immediately agreed. And do you think we should mention it to his mother or not? Is the father perhaps a bit too much in touch with his feminine side? Please discuss.

"And then another one started on about her builder making a botch job of their extension to the back of the house and how their interior designer was coming in next week to discuss how to make best use of floor space. Now really, where can you even get a good builder these days? And then we talked about the price of broccoli in Waitrose and how it's more expensive than in M&S but easier to get to and did I know that and do I really give a fuck. Do I really look as though I give a fuck? So I started to tell them about Harvey and they loved that. Well, at least they stopped talking broccoli, so maybe it was worth it in the end."

Not one to hide her opinions of anyone, Heather's snide comments didn't go unnoticed by the other members of the mafia, neither did her waning passion for all things Sycamore. From what she tells me, and this time I'm the eager audience lapping it all up, they didn't part on amiable terms, Heather and the mafia. But Heather always has things to hide (at this she smiles enigmatically and winks, and it's true, of all my friends she has the most complicated love life and is forever doing things she's not supposed to). And, she sighs, she knows the power of the mafia's tongues and the far reach of their arms so, teeth grinding, she goes about her business much more quietly these days, trying to stay below their radar. She brightens considerably when she tells me about her role at the PTA. She snatched up the position of school treasurer years ago — a Cambridge grad and trained as an architect, she's excellent with numbers — and has stubbornly refused to relinquish it so, with a deep mistrust verging on pathological loathing mixed with a gleeful determination to rile up her enemies, she attends PTA meetings once a month.

"You've got to keep your friends close but your enemies closer," she now leans in with an evil grin. I fear for the PTA's account books.

Eva finally returns with our drinks, and just as she carefully unloads an armful of teas and coffees, the door opens slowly. A trail of women, eight or so, weave into the room like a slow, silent serpent, picking their way between the small tables up to the mezzanine to sit down in a carefully orchestrated manoeuvre.

I watch them, trying not to be too obvious, but I needn't have bothered. As they pass our table some stare pointedly at Heather and then at me, scowling and smiling in turn — both equally frightening. I can't quite work out what they're doing, but it's a bit unnerving and I quickly take a sip of my scalding peppermint tea. Although, between Heather's ominous warnings and these strangely silent, grimacing women, I feel more like a drink than this herbal soup.

The first few women I didn't notice in the playground. They are all wearing shades of beige, although I hadn't realised until this moment that beige even came in shades. Most of them wear their hair in neatly cropped bobs, but a couple of them are sporting tight perms, which remind me horribly of my mum's signature hairdo. Lots of very tight ringlets that only got marginally less rigid with time. They can't be older than their late thirties but each looks about fifty. And then I recognise a few of the second wives I saw at the school gates. They are younger-looking, early thirties perhaps, immaculate hair and skin, and up close their doll-like features are even more pronounced, their mouths tightly clenched. I reel a bit from their sour look but they completely ignore our table as they pass.

And Heather was right about the smell. These women reek of perfume. I can't quite make it out, but I think it could be E'spa, a brand they sell at the health club I joined when I moved here. A lot of the high-maintenance women who work out there wear it. It's the scent of money and massage and manicure and now it's the scent of the *mafia*.

Bringing up the serpent's tail, just behind the dolls, there's an emaciated girl with long blonde hair in a ponytail, wearing lemon-yellow cotton yoga pants and a top. I can see her hips and shoulder blades pierce through her T-shirt emblazoned with *Yoga vs Pilates?* although I doubt she has the strength to do either by the look of her. She skips through the room and nods at Heather as she passes, smiling almost genuinely at both of us. I'm surprised to see Heather return her smile. Waiting until she, too, has passed, Heather leans over to me.

"That's Helen, she's a yoga instructor over at the country club," Heather whispers furtively. "She's the only one not to get her hair done at La Coiffeuse, that chichi hairdresser on the High Street." She gestures at the row of neatly glossy bobs now moving around the table at the top.

I'm about to reply that I thought her cut suited her when three more women come in, the bell over the door chiming gently. Heather and Eva tense slightly and huddle closer.

"That's them," Heather hisses, as she looks down into her coffee, studying the foam and chocolate swirl.

Eva draws her brows together and nudges Heather. "She's got new colours again. God, that woman must be swimming in money."

Finally. Here we go. The three, all dramatically different shapes and sizes, are heading for our table. I wonder where they fit into the pecking order, but, judging from Eva and Heather's reaction, it must be somewhere high. One looks like a second wife, one like a witch gone bad, with masses of untidy black hair, and one like a high-powered, expensively dressed PA.

The witch catches my eye first. She's about five foot six, slightly overweight, with hair everywhere and piercing blue eyes that are so small they seem like pinpricks in a face that looks as though it's seen too much late-night eating (which, according to the *Cosmopolitan* I read at the dentist last week, can make you puffy). Her cheeks wouldn't look out of place on a hamster and she carries a half-smoked cigarette in her left hand and a large black handbag in the other. She's wearing top-to-toe black, from her purse-lipped face to her pointy shoes, and looks as mean as shit.

The second wife is so petite I wonder if she's wearing children's clothes. Where Eva is proportionally petite and still grown-up, this woman looks like a rat with boobs, especially following the black witch's tail, but I have to give it to her — she's dressed absolutely immaculately, her black bob tight around her face and her collar and cuffs matching pink with red trimming. She's so diminutive, like something out of a curiosity shop or even a freak show, that I'm having trouble not openly staring. But we're not done yet, it seems. I feel someone stop at our table.

"Hello," a soft voice says. "My name is Sarah. Sarah Flint." I look around quickly, guilty at having been caught gaping at her friend. I smile, slightly flustered.

The woman hesitates for effect, perhaps expecting me to recognise her. She's got presence, not in an imposing, forbidding way, but quietly controlling, and I falter, just a touch, under her direct gaze. All I can think of is traffic wardens, storm troopers, Waitrose, so I keep quiet. Looking a little disappointed at my lack of response, she continues.

"I'm one of the school governors and chairwoman of the PTA. You're a new face round here, aren't you? So nice to meet you. We always need new blood at the school, don't we, Heather?"

Heather still has her head in her coffee cup, although I don't think there's anything left. At Sarah's words she looks up, unsmiling, and her "Good morning" has an icy ring to it. She mutters something else under her breath, while Eva nods regally. Sarah has already turned back to me.

If this is the godmother of the mafia, I'm surprised. It's the black witch who looks more the part, like a female Marlon Brando who could give you a good thump in the playground and send you flying if you forgot your dinner money. This Sarah woman looks almost ordinary, insignificant even, albeit in a very polished, designer way, as though she's been made over by someone else, someone who has an understanding of clothes but not of Sarah. She's wearing a green skirt, cream blouse and lime-green cardigan, cashmere I think, and two very large diamond stud earrings that make mine look like Christmas-cracker toys. She's immaculately turned out, everything screaming money and not a hair out of place, but she looks uneasy in her clothes. As though they are wearing *her* rather than she's wearing *them*. And she has the strongest whiff of E'spa out of the group.

I've finally got myself together, kick Heather under the table as much in admonishment as for support, then smile, trying to look as natural and unstrained as possible. "Hi Sarah, I'm Caroline. My son joined the school today. He's in Kangaroo Class."

Sarah gives me another one of her soft smiles. "Ah, Ms Silver. My youngest is also in Ms Silver's class this year: Edward, short brown hair, glasses?"

I nod vaguely, having absolutely no recollection of any of the children filing into the classroom.

"Great with the children, Ms Silver. Well, we must get you involved with the PTA. We can always use a new pair of hands. And I think I saw your husband there today, too?" she says, studying me intently.

I touch my cheeks, feeling weirdly as though she's looking at each and every one of my wrinkles. This woman is more than a little disorientating. I'm just about to start explaining my marital status, but Eva grabs hold of my knee. I stop immediately, finishing lamely with, "Yes, he was there too. Important day. Wouldn't miss it for the world."

Sarah looks at me encouragingly, clearly eager for more information. When nothing is forthcoming, she sighs regretfully. "Yes, quite. Well, we always need a lot of help with our activities at The Sycamore. We pride ourselves on being very involved, organising a lot of charity and social events. Bonfire Night, the Christmas Fair . . ." She looks at each of my friends, who nod silently, their mouths tight with painful-looking smiles.

"And then there's the sponsorship, the charity-card sale, the plant-a-tree day. Plus, we're trying to get the school to change its attitude on homework. So lots to do. Perhaps you would like to join us?" She gestures to their table at the back. "There's room for one more and I can introduce you to the rest of the group? I'm sure they would all like to meet you."

Heather's had about as much provocation as she can reasonably stand. Her mouth hardens, no hint of a smile now. Eva has a hold of my leg again as though she's physically restraining me. I'm going to refuse anyway; under no circumstances can I endure another ten minutes of this woman's soft, hypnotic voice. I'm beginning to get Heather's drift about the mafia, silently apologising for calling her a drama queen.

"Thank you very much, Sarah, that's very kind of you, but I've got an appointment today that I simply cannot miss."

Sarah Flint looks both disappointed and miffed and I can see her buddies craning their necks at the back.

"You do? Anything interesting?"

That I didn't expect. I want to tell her to mind her own fucking business, but she's a school governor and the chair of the PTA, she's more than a little terrifying and if she's the one to get traffic wardens to bypass the law, she'd make mincemeat of me and Ben. Don't piss her off. Think on feet, Caroline, think on feet.

I humour her.

"Well, I'm a graphologist, among other things, and I've been commissioned to do some work for a company today. But I would love to meet everyone at the PTA some time soon. I'm sure there are meetings I can attend with Eva and Heather."

Heather nearly chokes on her dregs.

Sarah looks equally revolted at the suggestion but seems mollified by my explanation. "Yes, well, there's a weekly newsletter that will be put in book bags. It's not the best way of getting messages out to the parents, but until we get a school magazine I'm afraid it's all we can do. Your job" — am I imagining a tiny sneer in the corner of her mouth? — "sounds absolutely fascinating. We must get you to analyse the PTA's handwriting. I'm sure they'd find that a scream."

I smile graciously. "Yes, I'm sure they would. Very nice to meet you, Sarah. And now, ladies, perhaps we should make a move?"

I stand up quickly, all of a sudden dying to get away. I'm eyeballing Sarah, who's as tall as me and looks a bit taken aback at my sudden departure. I think she expected me to be shorter, too. Heather and Eva get up just as quickly, half smiling, half grimacing at Sarah.

She steps back and offers me her small, manicured hand. Her handshake is fairly strong and she tries to manoeuvre her hand on top of mine, but I hold firm, making eye contact to establish, I hope, that I'm willing to be friendly but not a pushover.

Sarah is still standing by our table as we walk past her and out into the street.

"Thank fuck for that. I thought I was going to puke on all that perfume," sighs Heather when we're safely out of sight. "And what was all that about work? Do you have anything much going on today?"

I breathe in the fresh early-autumn air, trying to rid myself of the faintly claustrophobic feel of the café.

Around us women are going in and coming out of the café, some smiling and waving at Heather and Eva, pausing to exchange a few words. We walk back up the hill.

"Not today, no, but I wanted to use the time with Ben out of the house to finish a few things in his bedroom. We still have so many unpacked boxes and stuff lying around and I have quite a few deadlines coming up next week." I look at my watch. "Did you park up by the school, Heather?"

She nods, tugging Eva away from her conversation with a small, tired-looking mother who has a small baby in a sling. "I have to go too, actually, and I picked up Eva because she's had to take her car into the garage."

"Heather, you're so damn rude. I just wanted to check with Laura whether the twins and Charlotte are still on for tomorrow after school. Look at her, she's a shadow of herself with the new baby and all." She turns to wave an apologetic goodbye.

"So those were the mafia, huh?" I'm a little hesitant to open the subject again. I don't think I have the patience for more tirades from Heather. But curiosity prevails. "Who were the last three women?"

"Kind of a creepy parade, isn't it?" grins Heather. "Don't say I didn't warn you. The first lot are really only the hangers-on of the mafia, the crowd surrounding Karin, Felicity and Sarah." I give her a questioning look. "Karin Blunt and Felicity Sackville, the munchkin and the heavy, they're Sarah's henchmen, or henchwomen, whether you want to call them. They're as fucking vicious as she is."

"I would say more so," says Eva darkly. "I've seen Karin make Mrs Ellison cry."

I am shocked. A little impressed, perhaps, but largely shocked.

"Bloody hell. Is that legal?"

"She seemed to get away with it all right. Can't remember exactly what it was about. I think about where funds were to go for the school. Mrs Ellison wanted the children to see *Chitty Chitty Bang Bang* in the West End. The PTA wanted the money to go towards redesigning the school logo. The PTA won. You saw us in the café. If they succeed in getting Heather to shut up," she moves swiftly out of Heather's reach, "the teachers have no chance. A lot of mums who used to be MDs or run their own companies have turned mafia, real movers and shakers at heart. Now they want to move and shake the school about, to have some outlet for their energy. Honestly, I'm not being a wimp or anything, but it's best to keep them on your side, if at all possible. Or stay neutral."

"So what about you, Heather?" After I've seen Sarah and co in action, I'm a bit worried for my friend.

"We've come to a weird truce," Heather says with a sigh. "They don't approve of my behaviour and know that I hate their fucking guts, but as treasurer of the PTA I know too much about what goes on in that group. Information is power and they don't like that at all. They try to provoke me into resigning, hence the false flattery and smiles and '*Have a nice day, Heather*'. It's not working but I don't trust them, so I'm trying not to be too obvious in my loathing. But hell'll freeze over before I'll be bullied or tricked out of anything, even if it does mean regular interaction with them."

I smile, reassured that I won't have to fish her out of the river with concrete shoes on any time soon.

"And here I thought I'd left politics behind for good, but this seems just as bad."

Even Eva nods her head at that.

"It's worse, Caroline. Really," says Heather, beeping open her car. "No matter how fragrant and harmless they may seem."

CHAPTER
FOUR

Red Dawn

The remainder of the week passes swiftly and uneventfully. When I pick up Ben that first afternoon he is full of stories as usual, half of which (about cannibals and lions in a cage and strange new toys everyone else plays with and he just has to have) are blatant fantasies and the other half a hilarious kaleidoscope of kids meeting new kids. I swear, they gossip even more than we grown-ups do and all week I keep getting updates on Tom (great at drawing) and Edward (can walk on his hands, Mummy!) and Yoshi (he brought in a RoboCop monster, can I have one too?).

I have to finish one paper for a particularly finicky client, so beyond the seeing-off procedure at the window, I don't have time to linger too much before and after school runs. Several times I see Sarah smiling at me and she stops to say a few words after we pick up our respective sons. Even Karin and Felicity seemed to acknowledge me in a decidedly friendlier manner than before while managing blatantly to ignore Heather and Eva.

Ben seems at first to be settling in well. He has the added bonus of having as a classmate Heather's

Jennifer, who has fiercely taken him under her wing despite being in exactly the same boat, but he takes her take-no-prisoners bossiness in his stride with his customary uncomplicated outlook on life. By the end of the week, though, it's clear that the unusually disciplined schedules and, for small children unused to the daily grind of life, long days have taken their toll on energy levels and emotional stamina. By eight forty-five on Friday morning we have stood through two tantrums and a teary farewell from the younger ones and feel decidedly weary ourselves.

"Tell you what, why don't we take the day off? Give ourselves a bit of a treat?" I stayed up until one the previous night to email my project and I am in desperate need of a break and some normal conversation. "Hey, I know. Let's go to Chetley. I think we could all use a Red Dawn fix."

"Red Dawn? I haven't been there for ages," Eva says excitedly. "I can't believe it's still there."

"God yes. I usually can't afford it but occasionally it's my special treat when I've managed to sit through one of my mum's interminable Sunday lunches. A Power Ranger for Ben and a Red Dawn outfit for myself. Jessica, the new owner, has such great taste. Come on, let's do it. It'd be the best way to end a week that started with too much brown and beige Jaeger."

"I got an earful from Harvey this morning about our credit-card bill, but what the hell! It's hard work raising two kids." Heather's already at the gates and shouts back, "And you need to look good doing so."

The journey in Heather's blue four-wheel drive takes about an hour round the M25 but it gives us time to catch up properly on our respective summers and gossip about the first week at school. Eva's been back for two weeks now, but Heather and her family only just flew in a couple of days before school started. Because of his workload, Harvey can't take a holiday when normal people do, so they always have to cut it a bit close.

Heather, Eva and I go back all the way to our own first day at school in Chetley and we've been pretty much inseparable ever since. We sometimes refer to ourselves as the Witches of Essex. Actually, it was Ben who came up with it one day, when we were all nattering in Heather's back garden. Nice witches, of course, he added quickly and diplomatically. I still don't quite know what prompted him to say it, an excess of dragon books perhaps, but we thought it was funny at the time, and it's stuck. We tend to cackle with laughter a lot and Heather and I at least have the obligatory long hair. Plus, we're all on the slim side (through an unhealthy over-abundance of nervous energy more than anything else) and we pride ourselves in possessing a sixth sense about life and love and stuff (although a fat lot of good it's done us so far).

And we all adore the film *The Witches of Eastwick* — although I'm the only one that technically qualifies, as the witches in the film have all been divorced, deserted or widowed. Heather lives on the hill in a five-bedroom multi-million-pound house with her two kids, both of whom have their mother's large eyes, shiny hair, quick wits and loud voices and have learnt to manipulate her to perfection. Harvey is handsome in a chiselled, classic sort of way (he looks like a giant Action Man), a successful IT consultant, a man's man and rugby coach to under-tens on Saturday mornings. I like him but Heather does seem to have a lot to complain about. Hell, what do I know — she's the one who has to live with him. It's not the only issue our opinions diverge on. Heather is different to me in so many ways that I'm sometimes surprised we're as close as we are. Or maybe that's the reason we get on so well.

I was the quiet one at school, with straight brown shoulder-length hair, no curves and no confidence. I took refuge in the fifth-form library to avoid confrontation in the playground. Heather was the confident, tall, curvy, feisty one, who strutted boobs-out-stomach-in and treated the school corridor like her own personal catwalk. She got top grades without trying and seduced any boy she wanted, all of them inevitably lusting after her. I left school after A levels, with four B grades, two novels hidden in my underwear drawer, blossoming anorexia and a mistrust of my mother which I still haven't managed to quite shake, although we reached a tentative truce a few years back (Ben's birth, to be exact, and that of the uber-grandmother) and only occasionally revert to our old open animosities.

For years I flitted from job to job, trying everything from banking to journalism — both utterly soulless professions in their own way — and settling on marketing as a compromise for the better part of my working life. Only in my late thirties did I at last find my vocation. I love being a graphologist, looking at people's handwriting and finding out what makes them tick, separating the psychotic from the genius. It doesn't put much bread on the table, though, hence the income from other general freelance stuff to supplement my ex-husband's child payments.

Eva was always a pretty, feisty little girl at school, enthusiastic and determined and incredibly grounded considering, or perhaps because, her parents split when she was nine. She lived with her mum but saw her dad regularly and somehow both parents seemed to remain friends — albeit on a superficial level and mostly only when Eva was in hearing distance. My favourite memory of Eva is her playing centre at netball, fighting for the ball as if it was gold dust whenever Ms Bocking, the sports teacher, threw it in the air. What she lacked in size, she made up for in determination. She had a five-year plan at the age of ten, and then again at fifteen and at twenty, whether it was going out with a boy, winning a school competition or getting into the university of her choice. She did everything she planned: got a first in English and French, travelled the world for a year, and was about to start working in marketing for some commercial company that would eventually pay her hundreds of thousands and make her the skirt on the board. Then she was going to marry the MD, buy a big house, have no mortgage and two gorgeous kids. Well, it all did work out OK, but not quite as planned.

She met Gordon Thompson in Thailand — the fourth stop on her world tour — on the back of an elephant (the wedding speeches included jibes about Gordon having a big trunk, or too big a trunk). He was an investment banker and troubleshooter who travelled around the world for work and so every time Gordon uprooted, Eva went with him. She lived in New York (loved it), Hong Kong (loathed it), Manila (so boring she sort of secretly fell in love with one of her bodyguards but didn't do anything about it because, at the end of the day, Gordon is her soulmate, she says), and Fiji (too many hurricanes). So Eva was never really able to establish her own career while supporting his.

Eva had the twins during a storm in Fiji and vowed never to give birth again, storm or no storm. Finally, thankfully, Gordon was sent to Frencham, and they ended up in a gorgeous four-bedroom apartment with a roof terrace overlooking the river. Eva now works as a part-time marketing consultant for a local advertising company but I've always felt that her talents and enthusiasm for life have yet to be fully challenged. She never once expressed any feelings of resentment for giving up her five-year plan to support Gordon; she is always smiling, bubbly and selfless, with enough bite not be dull, but still not quite as feisty as the little girl I remember at school. Perhaps maturity or experience tempers enthusiasm.

Eva is still very happily married, which mocks Heather's eternal claim that, deep down, every woman is unhappy in the married state. In that, and in pretty much everything else, Eva and Heather are total opposites. Heather is fire, her anger tangible, her reactions always extreme, but her enthusiasm and her love of life incredibly infectious. Eva is earth — grounded and balanced and strong and gentle. And, apparently, the girls tell me I'm a bit of both — but frequently at the wrong times. We've rescued each other from ourselves at various stages of our lives, and I feel, witch that I am, that I ended up in Frencham for a reason other than strategically moving for Ben's school. I was meant to be with these girls.

As the landscape flies past my window, way too fast but with Heather driving always a given, I tune back into the conversation. They're talking about the competitive try-outs for the nativity play (what? It's September for crying out loud) and the fact that Felicity Sackville is furiously trying to wrestle back some control over the casting. "I'm not having it," Eva says emphatically. "Mrs Ellison asked me to be in charge and I'm going to run the show. Only over my dead body will that hideous Patrick be one of the wise men."

This reminds me. "I've been seeing Sarah and co everywhere this week and they've taken to smiling at me and stopping to chat. Is that a bad sign?"

Heather and Eva exchange a significant glance. "Who knows what they're up to these days," says Eva. "But I would watch them like a hawk if I were you."

Heather is blunter. "You should tell them to stick it. I think they're trying to weasel their way in, bring you over to the other side."

I laugh, uneasily. Something similar had occurred to me, but I didn't really put it in so many words.

Heather is watching me in the rear-view mirror. I'm worried for the other drivers, so I say quickly, "I haven't had much time to talk to them anyway. Who's the small woman again?"

"Karin Blunt," Eva says. "She's the PTA secretary, handles all the notes and administration and newsletters. Her husband always introduces her as his '*current*' wife, so don't know if that makes her the first, second or transitional model. She's got three at The Sycamore, but they're all having extra tuition before and after school so the poor buggers look exhausted most of the time. She wants to get them all into Sutherlands, you know that grammar school up in Kingston? The best in the area, actually the only good one really, so she's politicking like crazy, hobnobbing with everyone on the board."

"She's such a nasty little bully," Heather puts in. "Always reminds me of Rose Johnson at school, remember her?"

Who wouldn't. Arrogant, selfish little cow but everyone thought she was as cute as a button with her blonde curly hair and butter-wouldn't-melt-in-her-mouth smile. It was only my father giving me permission to whack her if she ever whacked me that made me stand up to someone who was about four inches shorter than me but the more spiteful for it. Seeing my face, Heather nods. "Karin's a bit like that. She's little so everyone thinks she's a delicate, fragile flower but she's more like a fucking wasp." She cackles and swerves to the right to pass a line of cars.

"How about the one with the piggy eyes?"

"Felicity?" Heather pauses to flip off the truck refusing to get out of her way. "I don't really know why Sarah and Karin mix with her, she seems a bit too downmarket for them. She didn't move to Frencham until after I got myself kicked out of the group, so I don't have much dirt on her, unfortunately. She's the sponsorship manager, the one that asks for the money when we have the Christmas Fair, Fireworks Evening, basically anything that requires funding. She has to go round the local companies with Sarah and we always get hundreds, probably because they all think she's going to slosh them one if they don't pay up. She's once divorced, lives on the outskirts of Frencham and has a huge chip about both."

"A bit of a She-Devil if you ask me," adds Eva helpfully. "She'd make a much more attractive man than a woman."

"God, they sound lovely." Why on earth would they be interested in me? "And the others?" I ask.

"Oh, they're just hangers-on. Without Sarah and her two stooges, they wouldn't have a leg to stand on, no structure at all. And the advantage for Sarah, Karin and Felicity, well there is strength in numbers, right?"

"I suppose so, but at least with me here now we've evened things out a little," I say hopefully. "But seriously, this is pretty London suburbia, not some Sicilian back alley — what can they really do to people that makes everyone so afraid?" I look at Eva, who hasn't said nearly as much as Heather on the subject.

"What can they do?" Eva looks out of the window. "They can make life very difficult. We've been looking for a house since we moved to Frencham. The apartment we've got is lovely, but I've always wanted a house, somewhere for us to put down roots. Well, there was one, just-up the road from the school in Rose Avenue. Backs on to the school land? Absolutely lovely. Large garden for Harry and Maddy to play in, lots of natural light, perfect. It needed work doing to it, but nothing I couldn't manage. It would have been ideal. But it seems that the Flints were also looking, they saw the house and they gazumped us. We offered more and more again, but they still managed to get the property, I had no idea why. Gordon wanted to complain but I told him to just leave it. I thought we would find another home, but we're still looking for something as nice, if you can believe it.

"Anyway, I later found out that it looks like Sarah Flint knows the estate agent's MD. The school gets a lot of sponsorship money from them, so there must be some Devil's pact in there somewhere. I didn't find that out until recently, but since Rose Avenue — and I drove the price way up for the Flints, too — there is no love lost between me and the mafia either. I think I'm just marginally better at hiding it than Heather. And, Heather, since we're on the subject, *again*," Eva adds, looking at Heather, "I think that thing with Nick has a lot to do with this too. If you ask me, that's really tipped the scale. They weren't quite so blatantly disapproving of us before."

I know about Nick. Heather has told me a lot about him. Nick is Heather's emotional crutch. Nick is her lover and lapdog and younger man — by five years. Six foot two, broad and toned and tanned, he is all white teeth and sparkling eyes. He reminds me of a fresh-faced, well-hung cocker spaniel, wagging his tail enthusiastically, especially when he is around Heather, which he tries to be as much as possible. They met at a school dance a year ago. Danced and kissed behind the shed on the first night and it's been non-stop sex ever since. But despite Nick's sexual prowess, he has never managed to get Heather to leave Harvey, while he himself left his long-term girlfriend of fourteen years, Alicia, a couple of months before the summer.

Inconveniently for Heather, Alicia works in a toyshop down the hill from The Sycamore. Heather needs to pass it almost every day, on the way to and from school, under the threatening glare of Alicia. And one of Alicia's confidantes, Eva now says with a meaningful nod, is Sarah Flint. Her cousin. Ah, so there's the centrepiece of their mutual loathing. Finally, the whole puzzle falls into place. A couple of points are still unclear, like why Heather is still alive, but I'm sure we'll get to that in a minute. So Heather is convinced that Alicia knows nothing about her and Nick, not yet at least, but Alicia certainly watches Heather fairly closely, uncomfortably closely, ready to pounce at the first sign of an indiscretion. And she's got enough spies that Heather needs to watch her back constantly.

Meanwhile, Nick clandestinely follows Heather about, believing they are destined to be together and are deeply in love, and that one day Heather will leave Harvey. He sends her roses, cards, beautiful presents he can't afford. It's all bollocks, of course. She won't leave Harvey. Why should she? Heather has great sex, while Harvey is blissfully ignorant that his wife is being serviced elsewhere. Harvey is bathing in an orgasm-induced afterglow he has nothing to do with — mentally, emotionally or physically.

It's such a pity, and although it's really none of my business, it's a sore subject between us. For one, because she talks incessantly about her complex love life, alternating between gleefully detailing every one of her sexual escapades and endlessly bemoaning the boredom of her life with Harvey, without ever getting her act together. It's enough to drive anyone up the wall. For another, I like Harvey. He's a nice guy and they seem well matched. She has ambition, brains and beauty and he has money, brains and potential. Ideal really. But neither of them seem to have any tolerance for each other's little foibles, which have become more annoying as the years have progressed until not stacking the dishwasher the right way, or putting unworn clothes in the laundry basket, or leaving the toilet seat up, have taken on the proportion of having an affair in both their eyes. We've been over this ground many times, though, so there's nothing really new for me to say.

Heather notices the expressive silence that has fallen over the car and she says exasperatedly, "Oh, I know, I know. I will leave Harvey. You know I will." She shakes her fist at a Mini that refuses to budge from the middle lane.

"I don't think you'll ever leave him," Eva says. She's so family-conscious, she gets even more annoyed at Heather than I do. "You said that this time last year, and the year before that, and you're still with him."

"Harvey is a good dad and a good provider," Heather protests feebly, as if quoting from a relationship manual. "And I don't want to break up the family."

"You're doing a pretty good job of that as it is." Eva bangs Heather's seat for emphasis. "Tell Nick you're not going to leave Harvey and let him get on with his own life."

"But I love him."

"If you love him, you'll let him go."

"That's bullshit. That's the advice you give losers."

"No, that's being fair," I finally say, forgetting that I vowed to keep my mouth shut. "You're leading Nick on. You have been for a year and it's not fair on the man. Ironically, I doubt your marriage to Harvey would last at all without Nick to fall into bed with. So deal with it. Put up or shut up."

Heather scowls and puts her foot on the accelerator, going at 100 mph down the A12, ruthlessly passing anything that gets in our way. I don't care. If fewer people treated Heather like a spoilt little girl, she would have gotten her act together sooner. I understand how affairs start. I understand why she doesn't want to give up her doting, lapdog, fuck-buddy, always-buys-her-roses-on-Fridays Nick, but it's bound to go sour. Too many times Heather and Nick have been indiscreet. Too many people have spotted them together in however innocent environments. No one knows anything for sure, but with the mafia nipping at Heather's heels, something will eventually have to give.

After a long silence, only punctuated by Heather's cursing at the other drivers, we arrive and Heather parks the car in the multi-storey adjacent to Red Dawn. She slams the door shut, cursing again when she sees her coat caught in it. I've had enough for the moment and start walking towards the stairs.

"Hey, Caroline, wait up." Eva catches up with me, giving me a sympathetic sideways glance. "You know how she is."

I grimace wryly. "Yes, and you'd think I'd learn not to get involved. And I wanted this to be a nice thing for us today." I hear the clicking of Heather's high heels coming closer and shut up. We troop silently down to the high street, the tension still lingering in the air. Eva is the first to break the mood. As always, she is not one for confrontations or arguments.

"Oh come on, girls, let's make up. We've got a lovely day ahead, the three of us together at last, like old times, buying clothes and spending money we don't have." She grabs us both round the shoulders and pulls us to her like she would a pair of sulking kids.

"She's right, let's not spoil it." That's the beauty with Heather — she's quick to ignite but never holds a grudge. At least not with us. We quicken our pace as we approach the shop.

The town of Chetley is a wannabee of a city, desperately trying to be cosmopolitan and sophisticated when it's merely overcrowded and overdeveloped. Despite its ornate cathedral, river, thriving university and successful annual pop concert, it remains resolutely on town status (having been passed over in favour of sexier places like Preston and Newport). Frencham is the antithesis of Chetley. I suppose you could say that we have all risen in the world, from provincial, commuter-belt Chetley to the relative suburban snobbery of Frencham, where properties are twice the price for half the size. Weirdly, though, for all the wealth and four-wheel drives, Frencham still makes a point of behaving like a village. People smile in the street and say hello even if they don't know who you are. In Chetley people don't smile and don't say hello even if they do. But Chetley has one redeeming factor and that is Red Dawn.

Red Dawn was my retail therapy during the disintegration of my marriage and I've kept coming back. The girls who work there call a spade a fucking shovel and if I look like mutton dressed as lamb, they tell me. In Frencham's designer-clothes shops, if I looked like shit, they would still reassure me that I "look wonderful, madam".

The Red Dawn girls welcome us with cups of cappuccino and the latest ranges from Ghost, Chine, Paul Smith and Lovely Hearts, all personal favourites. No-bullshit Jessica, the owner, who used to be something high-powered in the City, and still buys and sells with as much grit as she did on the dealing-room floor, immediately runs to organise clothes for each of us. Scrutinising our sizes and shapes, she comes back with, as she puts it, "things that are very you". Things that are very me are tight, sexy short skirts, long skirts, trousers and sheep-skin, and are always expensive. But I haven't been here in absolute ages, so fuck it, I'm going to buy at least one thing.

Heather and Eva hog two changing rooms with the piles of clothes they've obligingly accepted from Jessica. The other one is taken so I change outside. At forty-something, I'm past caring.

"So, how are things, Caroline?"

Jessica has a way of asking how you are while sounding completely disinterested in the answer, but I go along, partly because I want the 10 per cent discount she gave me when I still lived here.

"Fine, thanks."

"Boyfriend?"

"No."

"Oh dear."

"No worries, I'm happy just by myself." I sort through a stack of tops while Jessica continues to watch me critically.

"How's Ben?"

"Wonderful."

"What age now?"

"Four."

"Oh good. They are delicious at that age, aren't they?"

I nod as I try to squeeze myself into a pair of jeans. "I remember when I came with him last time and he told a woman who was trying on one of your skirts that she looked horrible. I think you lost a sale."

"I expect we sold her something else. Probably more expensive."

I smile, abandoning buttoning the damn jeans.

Heather comes out wearing something tight and pink which she says she'll buy and Eva is in a pair of cerise cords which make her look fat. Do I tell her?

"What do you think of these?"

"They make you look fat," Jessica says unblinkingly. "Try the brown suede."

The brown suede look fabulous. Double the price but at least Jessica's honest about it.

Heather's buying the tight pink outfit and Eva's sold on the brown suede while I'm still half out of my jeans, trying on a top by Chine and a barely there thingy by Jocanda which I want but couldn't possibly afford on any credit or debit card of mine. The girls are chatting with the girl at the cash register and I pull on a Paul Smith stripy jumper. It's funky and would look good with these jeans but I am having difficulty getting it over my head. Losing my balance, I fall down like some overweight butterfly trying to get out of a too-tight chrysalis. Jessica helps me up. Wait, this doesn't look like Jessica!

My head finally pops out of the neck of the sweater with an audible plop, and I see a man in his fifties leering at me. I recoil, trying to pull down the sweater. I may be in my forties and all, but enough is enough.

What the hell is this guy doing here? Buying women's under-wear? He has a huge red nose as though he's been too heavy on the port for decades, and wide-set eyes that make him look like a psychopathic Gummi Bear. And he's been manhandling me. I let out an indignant squeal.

"Sorry dear, you looked like you were in trouble. I didn't mean to scare you."

His voice is clipped, not the flat Essex vowel at all. From the other cubicle I can hear a shrill voice.

"Jeremy, what are you doing? Where are you? Can you tell me what these look like?"

A woman in her forties walks out in a pair of trousers two sizes too small and ready to burst.

"They look lovely on you, darling."

Jessica tells the truth.

"They're too tight, I think, but if I may suggest this skirt?"

She hands her a Chine skirt. A long brown suede thing which I think would look wonderful and complement any figure. The woman takes one look at the garment as though it's a dishcloth and hands it back to Jessica.

"No, no, these will be fine. I'll take the trousers, thank you."

Jessica smiles, a bit like Sarah Flint this morning, turns and takes back the trousers, whispering under her breath, "Some people never learn."

I'm still standing half-naked, with Gummi Bear Jeremy grinning at me, and I notice Eva and Heather almost wetting themselves over at the register. The cows. But at least we've stopped fighting.

Eva and Heather have pushed their credit cards to the limit. Their clothes now wrapped beautifully in sky-blue carrier bags with little terracotta ladybirds on red ribbons, they are finally coming to help me.

I end up buying the Paul Smith stripy top, the barely there Jocanda thingy and a Chine skirt, and Jessica talks me into a Ghost outfit which is a short skirt with a matching little black top with shoestring ties under a barely there throw. I'm pushing any thoughts of John's alimony payments out of my head. Visa will be pleased.

CHAPTER
FIVE

Absent Dads,
Reluctant Mums

"Shall we go and see our old houses?"

It's Heather who unexpectedly makes the suggestion as we buckle ourselves, Red Dawn bags piled high, back into her car.

"We so rarely come back here and it'd be fun — lay some demons to rest. How's about it, you two?" She grins eagerly.

Eva looks at her watch. "Can we do it in an hour?" she says nervously.

"I'll put my foot down," Heather says, already turning out of the parking space in one swift move.

I haven't been back to my childhood home for ages now, not since my mum moved into one of the new developments on the other side of town after my dad died. Horsham Avenue, number seventy-eight, that's where my parents lived with my grandfather — Eva was three roads away in Beattyville Gardens, and Heather lived in a house with a willow tree and a vicious sausage dog.

This time I sit in the back and lean forward. "What if they've been turned into supermarkets?"

"Then hope it's M&S." Heather grins. "I'm reliably informed their broccoli is cheaper than at Waitrose. And anyway, I've heard from my mum that one of our old schoolmates has bought my place. Do you remember Toby Shepherd?"

Do I remember Toby Shepherd? The tall dark handsome hunk of our class, the boy to date, the boy to be seen with. He used to bully me incessantly. He and Rose Johnson were a nasty double act. I remember him setting fire to my hair in chemistry, pushing me in the boys' toilets and asking me if I was a virgin in front of the class. I only knew the kind of virgin that gave birth to baby Jesus. So, of course, I replied I wasn't a virgin. How the class roared at that one. Not that it still bugs me, obviously. I've moved on with my life. "He was an arsehole," I say, trying not to sound too aggrieved.

Heather looks amused. "We don't have to say hi or have tea or anything. Let's just have a look at the houses and then go, OK?"

I sit back, contemplating a face-to-face with my old school bully. I wish Ben was here. A four-year-old could whack him with a lightsabre and kick him in the shins and get away with it, pretending he was playing *Star Wars*.

We talk very little as Heather drives, my mind buzzing with what I'll find, what it'll be like to go back. Perhaps it will do all of us good to put *our* stuff, what we consider important, into perspective.

My mum was a reluctant mum but she worked hard at working hard at it. I think my dad wanted a family more than she did. To make matters more complicated, they wanted a boy, and when I was born it was a bit like a child who wants a dog and gets a cat. My mum was someone who always wore red lipstick and had beehive hairdos from Clive's, the La Coiffeuse of its day, who liked hosting and going to dinner parties and felt that having a child didn't quite fit into her world of grown-ups. My mum and I have grown into a love-hate relationship, or a love-put-up-with-each-other relationship. It's true for some reason we're closer now than we were when I was little, but I suspect that Ben's the glue that holds us together.

If my mum was a reluctant mum, my dad was an absent dad, mainly because he played sport and worked late and wanted to avoid confrontation with my mum about playing sport and working late. He always failed to live up to my mum's standards of excellence. He never quite made headmaster but he was brilliant at sport, playing for his county — tennis, badminton, squash, anything with a racquet. He was playing tennis when Mum gave birth (the local paper said he won the match). Now that I have something to compare it to, I think my arrival made as much impact on his life as Ben's did on John's — very little. But despite my dad's long absences, he was my stalwart ally. He died years ago and I miss him terribly.

Eva's mum and dad were divorced, which was a rare and somewhat sinful thing in those days, and I remember children avoiding her in the playground as though it were contagious. Heather and I didn't care. We loved Eva from the first day of school, when we found ourselves squashed in a corner of the playground trying to avoid running into Rose Johnson and Eva managed to trip her up as she came flying around the wall.

Heather's mum and dad were quite bohemian, with a very large, very messy house. They always seemed to be arguing, but Heather says they just talked to each other very loudly so it was hard to tell the difference. They had a sausage dog called Rachette who looked cute but who used to systematically kill off the local cats and had to be put down eventually because some of them were pedigree. Heather's mum was a true "yummy mummy" of her day. Slim and blonde, she always went topless during the summer holidays. She had nipples the size of corks, and, horror of all horrors, always went without a bra. I thought she was great. She was full of life and ever so slightly naughty. She would buy shop cakes, which Heather and I used to play games with. We'd make the cakes dance and talk to each other: the cream cakes would be in love with the profiteroles and the profiteroles would fight each other (that was always the messy bit with lots of bloodshed). We never had cream cakes, bought or home-made, in my house. Everyone thought my mum was amazing because she made her own cakes. No one seemed to realise that they were always rock cakes. I can't, hand on heart, remember her making anything else but rock cakes for the entire duration of my childhood. It's a little thing, but it matters when you're a child.

Horsham Avenue has changed. It looks like something out of Mr Benn's Festive Road. All the houses look the same, with their large bay windows and oversized porches, but the front gardens, which once boasted huge smiling pink hydrangea bushes and daffodils in symmetrical, neatly cut, round flowerbeds, are now plastered over in flat black tarmac. Japanese cars and motorbikes park there, finding space which isn't charged for by the day or hour. Net curtains still hang in some of the windows, but now there are more blinds letting oversized plasma TV screens beam their light out into the street. There are obviously a lot of daytime-TV watchers round here. We stop at the curb.

"Do you want to get out, Caroline?" Heather asks hesitantly.

"They'd probably think I was staking out the house if I did. I can't just knock and say, 'Hi, I lived here when I was a little girl.'"

"Don't see why not," Heather says, buzzing down her window and peering at the house. "Bring back any old memories?"

As I look up at the house I shiver, as much from the chilly air as anything else. The house is still the same shades of yellow and white I remember; in the front garden the hydrangea bush remains, squeezed into a small, squished square patch of earth next to a parked car. "The curtains are different, ours were green. And see that window at the corner up there? That was my granddad's. He used to give me Maltesers in exchange for reading the paper to him." I never thought much about my grandfather, but looking at the house makes me miss him and my dad all over again. I think I've seen enough. "Let's go."

Heather closes the window. "Sure?" She doesn't say any more, though, and I sit back gratefully as we drive to Beattyville Gardens. We sit and stare for a few moments. I don't remember a lot about Eva's mum, but she was a funny woman, as in funny strange, not funny ha-ha. Eva never really speaks about her childhood much.

Then Heather says, "Oh come on, you two, isn't anyone going to get out and see if they can have a look round their old house?"

"Not me," says Eva. "Why don't you?"

We head towards Frencham Avenue.

"The house looks smaller than I remember," says Heather, looking critically at the front door.

Eva laughs. "You were a child then, of course it looks smaller now."

"I want to see that willow tree," says Heather, clapping her hands excitedly.

I'm annoyed. Heather said she wouldn't do this.

"You want to see Toby Shepherd, that's what you want. Come back. We've got to get back to school."

Heather ignores me and is up the front path before we can react. The front gardens look well cared for. No tarmac here.

Eva calls after her, impatiently. "Heather, come on."

Heather is already knocking on the door. She turns round and smiles. "I can and I will," she says, knocking once more.

No answer.

She waits. We wait, too, watching from the car as if she's going to ring and play Knock Down Ginger. Any moment she'll start running.

The door opens. I presume this is Toby, although I can't get a close enough look. It's impossible to hear the conversation, but he's grinning at her and she's grinning at him. What is going on?

Eva echoes my thoughts. "What *is* going on?"

Toby steps to one side, and Heather turns and waves for us to follow.

Now we're annoyed and curious. The latter wins, and Eva and I can't get out quickly enough, locking the car and running up the path.

We walk into the hallway I remember so well. Striking white, with a large tropical fish tank to the left as we walk in and angel fish peering at us with wide black eyes.

Then the kitchen. I sigh and smile. I remember this kitchen as if it was only yesterday I was lining up the cream cakes for attack. The table in the middle of the room would be laid out with small packets of breakfast cereals, which I always coveted, but we only ever had the large ones at home. Now, children's paintings of dogs and cats and what look like green and purple dragons are stuck all over the walls. (Toby's got kids?) I think I'm going to cry. If I had gone into my own house I would already have been in floods of tears, standing in my kitchen where Dad taught me how to waltz, my small feet balanced precariously on his large ones.

Toby and Heather are in the kitchen, smiling and talking animatedly. Toby is still tall, with black curly hair. Shit. He's still handsome.

"Caroline Scrope. Remember me?" Toby says, gazing at me with the most stunning green eyes I've ever seen. I recoil a little, hearing my maiden name. It's clear why I've hung on to my married name, despite getting rid of everything else to do with it. No way Ben will grow up as a "Scrope".

"Vaguely." My tone is unmistakable.

He laughs, his eyes sparkling. "Serves me right. Sorry about all that, Caroline. We were kids then. Some people grow out of it, others don't. If you want to set fire to my hair, you can."

"I'll think about it," I say, but I'm already ahead of him, going out into the garden. *Our* willow tree is still there. I'd forgotten how magnificent it was. This is where we played hide-and-seek endlessly and took turns on the tree swing that used to get tangled up in the branches. Heather skips as if she is eleven again and still lives here, then disappears among the branches. I hear whoops of delight.

"It's still here. The swing is still here."

Eva and I try to follow her as gracefully as we can but practically throw ourselves through the branches. There is Heather, swinging away, half laughing and half crying.

It's too much. I burst into tears too because I suddenly remember those sunshine days with piercing longing. The sun would come through the tree branches and warm our faces, creating mad patterns on the grass around us and we would play hopscotch with the light and the shadows and nick food from the fridge and have picnics. Heather would do her most brilliant handstands in the privacy of the hanging branches and I would watch her enviously and wish I could be as wild as her.

For what seems like ages we sit and cry and laugh and talk about the gymnastics and the fridge thieving and the time Eva found a naughty magazine in a neighbour's bin and brought it round and we saw some photographs and God, there was actually one with a woman putting, oh my God, is that really what she's doing, putting *that* in her mouth? Oh my God.

And we take turns on the swing. I loved that swing, although you could only go so high otherwise the leaves would whip you in the face. So many times I would return home with cuts and red patches on my face, and my mum would get cross because she was certain the other mums at school would say that she'd been hitting me.

"Hello in there. Are you all OK?" The voice of Toby Shepherd comes through the leaves. It takes us a moment to get back to reality. Toby tries again. "Would you like some tea or something stronger? Wine? Champagne?"

"Yes, please!" shouts Heather.

"We can't, I don't think, we've got to get back," I say, scrambling out after Heather, who's still skipping. "And I want to get home in one piece."

Toby laughs. "Still the sensible one."

What? Prat.

"I have rebelled a little," I say defensively. And obviously he hasn't seen Heather's driving.

Heather laughs at me.

"Rebelled? No drink, no drugs, no teenage pregnancies. You are totally conformist. You stopped eating for a bit, married a banker, divorced a banker, have a kid and live in suburbia with all the other single mums with wealthy ex-husbands and the wannabe single mums still with their wealthy husbands. Wild child you are not."

"God, I hope I don't turn into my mother," I plead. "If I ever start to wear red lipstick or bake rock cakes, slap me, won't you?"

"Of course, girl," Heather says. "That's what friends are for."

CHAPTER
SIX

Ben

After leaving Toby Shepherd waving and grinning at us from his front door and screeching back to Frencham, we're standing among a mass of mums dutifully waiting for our children to come out into the playground. We're in our customary spot, close to a cluster of trees on the left (mainly, I suspect, so Heather can be as far away as possible from the mafia, who are usually grouped around a couple of benches just to the other side of the door, ready to corral their children the moment they emerge). Sarah gives me a wave and a smile, as if to invite me over to join them, but I just nod courteously and scrutinise the classroom window in an ostentatiously absent-minded way. Heather gives me a nudge and points to one of the Antipodeans, who looks as though she's just done five miles round the park and, dripping with sweat, is completely unaware that she could be a contender for a wet T-shirt competition. I personally think she looks rather spectacular in her pink Sweaty Betty gear, but I notice Karin and some of the other mafia mums looking on disapprovingly.

"Well," I say, looking at my watch and then at the Sweaty Betty girl. "At least it will give the mafia someone other than you to talk about for a change. Be grateful for small mercies."

We stand idly around the playground, chatting about Toby, how well he looked. And rather nice, I admit grudgingly. I look over towards Ben's classroom to check whether we're getting close and I see the mum I met at the school tour coming towards us. "Hi," she says. "Caroline, right? I'm Marie."

Thank God. I couldn't, for the life of me, remember her name. "Nice to see you," I say, smiling back at her, jeans, untidy curls, glasses and all. Someone normal, at last. "How are you getting on with your first week? This is Eva and Heather, by the way."

They shake hands as she says, "All right, although it's both wonderful and weird to have the house to myself for the first time in what, five years?"

I open my mouth to agree, but just then the bell rings.

Ben emerges from Ms Silver's classroom bounding with kangaroo energy, book bag in one hand and clutching six or seven sheets of paper in the other. I snatch them before the wind blows them away and the urgent messages are lost for ever.

"Hi darling, all done?" I smile, glad to have him back, looking forward to the weekend. All around me mothers wait. Marie's small son comes running and throws himself into her arms.

"Good," Ben says now. "That's Tom, Mummy, remember I told you?" I smile at Marie. "And Ms Silver is still really nice. She played the guitar again this morning. I don't think she's very good, but I don't want to hurt her feelings so I don't tell her."

Wise, even at his age. I hide a grin. "What's this then, homework already?" I look at the bunch of papers I grabbed from him.

"Don't know, some stuff for you, I think."

A piece of A4 paper headed neatly with *The Sycamore PTA Newsletter*. So this is the paper Sarah mentioned. The 3N class cake sale and the chess tournament in which "Jack" — in inverted commas, no surname or year, but I am sure he knows who he is — did "very well" (again in inverted commas). The barn dance and the Harvest Festival assembly (would parents like to attend). The Christmas Fair preparations, the nativity play (try-outs next week), the fireworks-display sponsorship money and the coffee morning for Year 6 parents. The dyslexia advice session. A small paragraph on the new school logo. Then, there's a separate page headed:

Being Part of The Sycamore

All parents are invited to attend our regular public meetings on school issues and PTA plans and results. It is also a discussion forum to invite new ideas and raise suggestions and concerns. Meet second Thursday of the month in Junior Hall, 1 p.m. The first meeting will be about *School: How to Fit into a New Environment*, to be followed by *Sports vs Music: Extra-curricular Activities at The Sycamore* in October and *Being Part of the PTA: Roles and Responsibilities* in November. A further schedule will be posted for the New Year, *Making Decisions. About Homework — What the Evidence Can Tell Us* being one of the issues. Everyone welcome from Reception to Year 6.

It ends with a few bold signatures, some I recognise (Karin Blunt, Sarah Flint) and then, more towards the bottom of the page and much smaller, Ms Silver's.

I look up to catch Eva's eye over the throng of screeching kids. She's buttoning up Maddy's jacket and has the same wad of papers under her arm. Seeing my glance, she straightens and rifles through them, then shrugs as if to say I told you so.

I leaf through the pages and at the end there's a photocopied, handwritten note by some of the year representatives, The PTA chair Sarah Flint, blah blah blah, outlines her support and main concerns for The Sycamore, blah blah blah. Now this is interesting. The note has been photocopied, but it's clear as anything, just on initial inspection, that this is a woman who has real issues. Complete control freak. Look at the tight loops on the "o"s and "g"s. There is loads of suppressed anger here and possibly some narcissistic, if not slightly schizophrenic, tendencies. Perhaps Heather has a point being so worried about Sarah. I wonder how hard she was pushing into the paper when she wrote it. It's difficult to tell on a photocopied piece of paper, looks like the pen nearly cut through to the other side in some places.

"Anything the matter, Mummy?" Ben is still standing next to me, looking a bit tired.

I quickly wipe the smirk off my face. "No, no, just reading this, but I'll take it home to look at it again. Are you ready?"

"Yes, let's go, Mummy, I'm starving. Bye, Tom." He tugs my hand, at the same time punching Jennifer playfully in the side. "Race you to the gate." They tear off, Maddy and Harry following suit.

I look at Eva and Heather. "Are either of you two going to these meetings?"

"I can't, working a full day on Wednesdays and Thursdays for the next two months, which makes it impossible to organise myself for the evenings," says Eva.

"I'm seeing Ni —" Heather looks at Philip standing talking to a friend a few feet away. "A friend then. Always on Thursday evenings." Heather smiles and goes to a smug, warm fuzzy place only women in lust frequent.

I wave goodbye to Marie and we follow the kids, who have run ahead, hiding behind trees and parked cars just starting up their engines, and shout words of caution they gaily ignore. Heather has seen one of her acquaintances from the gym and disappears to chat, leaving us in charge of her brood. Eva and I walk in companionable silence.

"Does Ben miss his dad ever?" Eva asks suddenly. Clearly I'm not the only one with ambivalent Chetley memories.

"Probably, but they speak regularly. To tell you the truth, I think he misses having a family, which isn't quite the same. And he misses the male company. I see

73

him clinging to his swimming instructor and karate teacher at the end of each lesson as though he needs that kind of masculine energy. And I occasionally overhear conversations with his friends about where his daddy is and why he only sees him every other weekend and on some holidays. He always says the same thing: 'Mummy and Daddy are separated. They don't like each other, that's why they don't live together, but Mummy loves Daddy. And they both love me a lot, which is all that matters.' "

Eva smiles affectionately. "Smart kid."

"I feel a bit for him, because he shouldn't have that responsibility at his age — to explain away his parents' lack of responsibility and inability to talk and listen and get on." I realise what I've just said and stop myself. "God, Eva, I'm sorry, I didn't mean it like that."

Eva shakes her head wistfully. "Oh, don't worry. Your Ben will be more balanced than a lot of the children round here. Some parents stay together and should break up, others should work at it and don't. Things never change from generation to generation, we only think they do."

I look at my wise friend and smile.

"You should go out more, go on a few dates," she adds, quickly changing gear.

I'm dismissive. "Not really in the mood for it. Heather set me up just before the summer and we went out a couple of times." I can see Eva's ears perking up and hurriedly add, "Don't ask, it was a disaster. Point is, it's difficult enough finding a man *I* love and respect, let alone finding one *both* Ben and I would love and respect. He'd need to be someone very special. Second time round, I wouldn't go for someone who would just do."

"Not even if you got really lonely?" Eva asks, putting her arm round me.

"Sometimes I do get lonely. But I haven't found anyone who would really work. And Ben is the most wonderful, entertaining company."

The most wonderful, entertaining company is now covering himself head to foot in dust from a sandpit some builders have inadvertently left on the side of the road. It has become a honeypot for Ben, Maddy and Harry, and I can also see Heather's three leaping on and off the sand as though they'd never seen the stuff before.

I grab my son firmly by the neck and wave goodbye to Eva, who starts loading her kids into the car, still patiently waiting for Heather to come back and collect hers.

"What are we doing now?" Ben asks excitedly as he climbs in our car and fumbles for the seat belt.

"Let's go home and have a drink, then maybe go for a walk around the green?"

"And after that?"

My son, even at four, wants a programme of events for his day, as though he's managing his expectations even at his age. I can only try to keep up with him.

"Bath or shower, which would you like?"

"Shower."

"And then you can have tea."

"What's for tea? Chicken or fish?"

I think I've turned my son into believing there are only two kinds of meat in life. At least he'll feel at home with aeroplane meals.

"Chicken."

"And after tea?" he asks eagerly. Skipping to keep up with me.

"We'll see how it goes. Maybe a movie?"

Finally, home again. Our house, or "George" as Ben likes to call it for some inexplicable reason, is a true haven for the weary. For once the estate-agent hyperbole was accurate. It's delightful: bright and airy, with a fifty-foot back garden including a mature cherry tree, no detectable structural problems, quiet and eclectic neighbours, and lots and lots of light.

For the past few months Ben and I have been busy making it into a home, going so far as to visit the Ideal Home Show for the first time, which wasn't as depressing as I thought it was going to be. Now large, colourful and dramatic paintings of flowers hang on the walls, while oversized round mirrors give more space and light to the darker corners. The sitting room has yellow sofas and all the wooden floors upstairs and down have been polished. My bedroom is feminine without being chintzy: light lilac walls and more flower paintings, two large white chests of drawers and a massive white bed, a job lot I bought from John Lewis, except the bedside tables, which came from a shop that was closing down just off Chetley High Street and were a tenner each.

Of all the rooms, though, Ben's is by far the nicest, or will be once we have finished painting it. Walls and furniture are blue (I'm not a terribly PC sort of person, and he likes blue, so that's that) and there's a rug on the floor with his face on it grinning up at everyone which I commissioned from a company at the Ideal Home Show. It's not as weird as I thought it was going to be, but you do have to choose the photo carefully or else your child can look strangely wired and anaemic.

I run my hand appreciatively over the banister gleaming softly in the late afternoon sunlight as we troop through to the kitchen to wash hands and clean the worst grime off Ben before he flops down at the table and is handed a steaming mug of cocoa and some of his favourite biscuits. In honour of his first week of school, I tell myself. It looks like he's taken to the whole thing like a fish to water, chattering away about circle time and everyone loving his stories, about Edward and Tom and awful Patrick, about the ter-ah-ri-um and the class fish and Ms Silver playing guitar. Finally he runs out of steam and for a few minutes nothing is heard but the rustling of the trees in the garden and the tick-tock of the kitchen clock.

"Want to see if Fiona is in, and go and visit Tubby and Telly?" I say finally.

Fiona is our neighbour on one side, forty-something and a bit vague about the second digit. She has two miniature pedigree Scottie dogs called Telly and Tubby, whom she treats like children, and a cute squeaky voice that sounds as though she's just had a whiff of helium but belies the fact she's a top-grade Cambridge graduate and is all the way there and back again. She has a string of energetic boyfriends, most of them on average ten years younger than her, but they need to be to keep up. I know, because my bedroom backs on to hers. Fiona is brilliant with Ben and Ben is brilliant with her dogs, which helps me with the everlasting "Why can't we have a dog" argument. (Instead I've got two tortoises, called Flip and Flop. They eat a cucumber a fortnight, like wriggling their tummies in warm water and pooh neatly. And they will probably live long enough for Ben's children to see them as well.)

He nods excitedly, and I can hear him run out, knock next door and ask if he can play with the dogs.

Fiona squeaks back worriedly, "Tubby's got to go the vet, darling. He's got a sprain. His cruciate ligament."

I smile to myself, imagining Ben looking confused as to what a cruciate ligament is. Or a sprain for that matter.

"Oh, can I have one too? Can I have a sprain? Can I have a crucial ligament?"

"No darling, he's not very well. But perhaps when he comes back from the vet you can see them tomorrow. How about that then?"

"That would be lovely. Thank you very much."

That's it. Always polite, my boy.

Ben's still in need of some entertainment, though, so we get our bikes and head for the green. Circling round and round, following and chasing each other. There's still the last warmth of an Indian summer in the air. It's only early September, so perhaps we've got a few more weeks of fair weather left. On this sunny late afternoon, it's just him and me and the cycles and I'm convinced I don't need anyone else in my life.

Finally, Ben is tired out and we head back. No sooner have I put the bikes away than I hear a knock. Before I can shout anything parental about asking who it is Ben has opened the door.

"Mummy, it's Lady Macbeth Macbeth Macbeth."

It must be our day for visiting neighbours. Mrs Hartnell lives on our other side. She looks like she's fifty, dresses as though she mourns the passing of the sixties and must be in her seventies. She has perfect skin, wears lots of velvet, scarves and layers even in the height of the summer, and boasts at least fifteen rings (Ben counted them) at any one time on her long spindly and expressive fingers. She was formerly an actor in the Royal Shakespeare Company where everyone loved her Lady Macbeth. From what I hear, I don't think her bedroom sees as much action as Fiona's, but I could be wrong.

I find her charmingly eccentric but Ben doesn't warm to her as much as he does to Fiona because she only has a ginger cat called Bruno who isn't as much fun. Ben hasn't endeared himself to Mrs Hartnell either. He keeps shouting "Macbeth Macbeth Macbeth" every time he sees her after overhearing her pronounce that it was bad luck to say that word three times in a row.

Mrs Hartnell wafts into the house with a bunch of large black bin liners, her long green velvet skirt and jacket looking slightly overdone in the September sunshine. Her rings glisten in the sun's rays beaming through the skylight of the living room.

"I noticed you putting the thin white ones in your big green bin the other day, and the way those men throw the bins about, they'll soon split and get all the rubbish into your bin. We get foxes round here who love that and, well, they make an awful noise at night, especially when they're mating."

I sneak a sideways glance at Ben, who looks excited and bemused, probably wondering whether he should ask about the foxes first or the mating.

Mrs Hartnell continues, oblivious to a four-year-old's curiosity. "Anyway, are you settling in nicely?"

"Yes, thank you," I say, taking the liners. I am halfway to the kitchen before I realise she's following close behind me, Ben close behind her. "We just have to put the finishing touches to Ben's bedroom and that's about it. Not much to do now. And we're celebrating Ben's first week at school." I gesture to the empty cocoa mugs and the last two lonely biscuits.

"Wonderful," she says excitedly, clapping her hands together as if she's about to start applauding in our kitchen. Looking at the mugs, I wonder if she expects some tea.

Ben now feels he can speak. "What is mating?"

Mrs Hartnell smiles a little nervously. As she's the one who brought it up, I think I'll let her do the explaining.

"Oh, it's when two foxes want to be friends with each other," she says, lacking conviction, but Ben seems happy with the explanation.

Right. Must remember to introduce him to more programmes on Animal Planet, and explain that it's a bit more complicated than that. I can just imagine him going up to some little boy or girl in his class tomorrow and asking if they would like to mate with him. Good start to the term.

Mrs Hartnell regains her composure, deciding to steer back into safer waters. "Well, not to worry about the decorating. I've lived here for twenty years and I've still got loads of things I'd like to take care of. But too much to do, if you know what I mean, my dear."

She laughs at her own joke. I join her obediently. Ben stares. I know he wants to ask what is so funny, but he doesn't. He's probably still thinking about the foxes.

"Well, if there's anything I can do, dear, let me know. I'm just next door. And if you fancy going to the cinema or the local theatre any time, they have some absolutely wonderful productions on at the moment."

"Thank you, Mrs Hartnell, that's kind of you. Would you like some tea?" I decide it couldn't hurt to be hospitable.

Thank God, she doesn't take me up on it. "I would love to, but I'm out tonight. Going to see something at the National. Wonderful play," she says, then swirls and goes. Ben and I watch her leave the room as if it were a stage. I like her flair and as I look down at Ben, I think he has decided after all that he likes her too.

It's getting quite late, actually, weekend or not, so I put Ben in the shower, firmly ordering him to get rid of the day's grime. I watch him play chase the soap for a few minutes, then I leave him to dry himself (with his extra-fluffy towel that is twice as big as he is) and go downstairs to get dinner ready.

Ben comes back downstairs, pyjama bottoms on, towel dragging behind him, but I let it slide and then we sit down for grilled chicken with carrots and broccoli and smashed potato. Chicken is his favourite. Broccoli he eats for me.

"What did you do today, Mummy?" he says, tucking into the chicken. I move his glass of milk out of the way as he energetically spears potatoes and broccoli.

"I had a good day. It was busy. Eva and Heather and I went back to where we grew up."

"Where's that?" He is intrigued. "Did you live in this country?"

"Yes, in Chetley, actually."

"Why did you leave your mummy's house?" He swigs half his milk and sprays some across the table. I duck.

"I wanted to have my own home when I started to go out to work. I wanted to be independent."

Ben thinks and munches broccoli. I can see his little brain mulling over what I've said, bits and pieces going round and round in his mind. What to ask first? What does independent mean? When can he leave this house? When can he go out to work?

Instead he says, "I remember Chetley. We had a big garden there."

We had half an acre of garden that a part-time gardener and John couldn't even look after, so yes, it was nice, but impractical.

"But we can play on the green and in the park and you have a back garden here."

He nods, trying to convince himself that the green and the garden make up for the fact that he doesn't have his own private green as his back lawn. Then another question.

"Do you want Daddy to live with us again?"

This has only come up once before. I had been able to tell Ben, quite composedly I remember, that it would be nice. But that was a year ago and a lot has happened. These days, I wouldn't want John back for anything. I don't like the idea of him loving anyone as much as he loved me, especially as it looks like annoying Suzanne, number four after the secretary, is here to stay. They've been together for a few months, she practically lives at his place, and he seems to have an awful lot of commitments involving her. But that's a pride thing, and has nothing to do with rekindling a relationship.

I don't mention any of this to Ben, just say quietly and kindly that I don't think it will happen again. He climbs down and comes around to give me a hug. After a few minutes, I spill him back on to the floor, gently, and we make our way upstairs to read for a little while before he goes to bed. A few chapters of *Horrid Henry*, which dispels any last lingering sombreness for now and makes him laugh so much in places he starts to hiccup. I sing him "Hush little baby, don't you cry" (very badly), kiss him goodnight, rub noses and tell him to have sweet dreams. Just as I'm about to leave, he whispers in my ear.

"Mummy, in case you were worried, I do know what mating is."

CHAPTER
SEVEN

The Play Date From Hell

The bell goes. It's pick-up time and we're waiting, once again, in the playground, doing our usual ritual of smiling, greeting, waving. Some of the parents are peering through the classroom windows to see if their children are still there. Ms Silver has strategically stuck the children's artwork on the lower part of the window to try and curb this practice. Consequently those parents who still can't quite resist a peek look ridiculous, on their tiptoes and craning their necks to peer through the cracks.

Finally, children start to spill from the classrooms. Ben is one of the first to emerge, and while Heather and Eva disperse to gather their various offspring, he races towards me, knocking a little Japanese boy out of the way and lunging at me, headbutting me in the stomach.

"Mummy, Mummy, I want to go to Edward's on a play date."

"Who?" I ask, as Ben bombards me with his daily paraphernalia of book bag and lunch box. He points to a harassed-looking boy who is trailing a little behind him. The poor child is weighed down by a violin case and bulging book bag, and looks set to topple at any moment.

"He's in my class, remember, I told you?" He shakes his head and I swear I can hear him tutting. "He wants me to come round for tea after school tomorrow. Can I go, Mummy? Pleeease?"

"It's fine with me, but it would be even better if you stop hitting me and making that whining sound."

I'm about to suggest looking for Edward's mum to check with her when said child finally catches Ben up.

"Hi, you must be Edward." I smile at him and he steps forward to shake my hand politely. I'm gobsmacked, and automatically shake it back, muttering how do you do and nice to meet you for all the world as though we are at a ladies' lunch.

"It would be so nice if Ben could come and play, Mrs Gray, if it's not too much of an inconvenience," he says, gingerly relinquishing his hand, which in my astonishment I've obliviously continued to shake.

"Not at all," I reply, still reeling from his textbook manners. "Where's your mum?"

"She's over there." He points across the area in front of Reception. I can only see Sarah Flint and a few of her cronies, huddling and chatting around their benches.

"Where?"

Ben sighs again, shrugs to his new mate as if to indicate that I'm sometimes a bit slow on the uptake, and then starts tugging me across the playground. Moments later I find myself in front of Sarah Flint. She smiles at me graciously, at the same time bending down to straighten her son's tie. For the second time in ten minutes, I'm gob-smacked. While my mouth automatically dispenses a few niceties, I'm trying to work out whether this is really a coincidence or more of a strategic ploy to get me away from my trees and on to the mafia bench. I look back helplessly towards Eva and Heather, but I'm on my own, nodding around the little group, grimacing in what I hope is a friendly way at Karin, Felicity and co.

"I see our two boys have become fast friends," Sarah says pleasantly, drawing me to the side a little while her eyes give me a quick critical once-over. She purses her lips. My skirt is from Red Dawn, it can't be *that* bad! "Edward, please don't swing your violin case like that and stand up properly. What must Mrs Gray be thinking of you?" I tactfully decide to not correct her on the "Mrs".

"It sounds like the boys would like to meet up tomorrow after school, Sarah. That would be fine with me, as long as it works for you?" I'm hoping against hope that she's got a jam-packed schedule for Edward, with orchestra recitals, poetry readings and chess tournaments lined up for the next two months.

Ben grips my hand at this and looks up at me, unhelpfully reiterating, "Mummy, can I, can I, pleeease?"

Enough already, I get the message. Still recoiling a bit from the idea of Ben making friends with someone Heather would consider the Son of Satan, I give Sarah a wide smile.

"Actually, tomorrow isn't good for us, but we'd love to have you and little Benjamin around for a play date next week." Ben *and* me? But Sarah doesn't even falter at my barely concealed look of horror. "Say Tuesday after school? I'm inviting a few others and I'm making something simple for the children and some nibbles for us. Edward would absolutely love for Benjamin to come, wouldn't you, darling?"

She bends down and squeezes Edward's cheek so tightly it leaves fingerprints when she removes her hand. I step back a little, slightly shocked, but he just grimaces, obviously used to the habit. He hasn't said much, his eyes darting back and forth between us while Ben is still chanting his mantra of "Can I, pleeease?" which quickly has me wanting to give him the kind of cheek-squeeze Sarah has just demonstrated. I'm trying to think on my feet. Edward does seem nice, with an open smile and kind eyes, and luckily a laissez-faire attitude to his mum's constant ministrations, and Ben has been talking about him a lot. On the other hand, Heather will kill me if she finds out I'm fraternising with the other side. This is ridiculous. Sarah *is* a bit creepy and I don't much fancy spending two hours getting to know each other over Victoria sponge à la Delia, but refusing her now *would* seem churlish. After all, it's only a play date and I can always make excuses to leave early. I'll be fine. Heather need never find out. And I can snoop on what Sarah is really like. Plus there will be other mums there, which will help dilute Sarah's inquisition. Mind you, seeing the company she keeps, that might not be all that helpful. Decision time. Big breath. OK.

"We'd be happy to come, thank you. Can I bring anything?" I say, trying to sound as sociable as possible while drowning out my squealing son. I must speak to him about that when we get home. Edward and Ben smile delightedly.

Sarah waves dismissively "Not at all, just yourselves. Edward has plenty of toys and we have a Labrador puppy called Herbert, whom I'm sure Benjamin will love."

Ben is now almost paralytic with excitement. "Oh Mummy, a puppy, a puppy, can we have a —"

"No, Ben, we're not going to get a puppy." I cut him off in midsentence, starting to get annoyed at his constant efforts to undermine my attempts at calm and composed parenting. I don't want Sarah to think I can't control my own son, although I'm not doing a very good job of showing her.

Sarah laughs benignly at Ben's antics, and I bridle as she gives him an ever so slightly patronising pat on the head.

"See you tomorrow, and I look forward to next week." She tugs her son along, back to her mob of mafia mums, who have now been joined by an assortment of equally immaculate miniature versions of themselves.

I nod and smile and walk off as serenely as I can, knowing I've just as good as signed my own death certificate. Ben skips happily behind me, obliviously — oh, to be four again. It just goes to show, keeping distance from Sarah doesn't really work, but I'm not sure how I can explain that to Heather and Eva. They'll understand, I'm sure they will.

"You're fucking what?" gasps Heather in horror.

It's the morning after my fateful run-in with Sarah and it's five minutes before the start of school and the rush of surprisingly keen children. To think I'll be doing the school run for the next seven years. My life seems to stretch ahead of me endlessly. The mood isn't great. I've just mentioned the play date to Heather and Eva, with what I thought was quite a sensible, brisk rationale, but Heather clearly doesn't understand. Mums who are passing by with their children bristle at her language.

"Calm down, Heather," Eva says, trying to pull her away to our corner, aware that a few mums are hovering nearby, drawn by Heather's foul-mouthing, waiting for a potential argument. "Caroline can do whatever she wants. You know very well that Sarah did exactly the same to both of us when we first met her. Don't you remember the vile spinach balls she served?" What, no Victoria sponge? "And her eldest, what's his name, Charles? hitting Philip over the head with a Spiderman?"

"Ugh, don't remind me. But Caroline has no excuse. She already knows what Sarah's like. Haven't we been warning you about her since day one?" Heather is directing her exasperation straight at me now, oblivious to the gathering crowd of bored mums creeping closer to listen in, desperate for a bit of scandal to brighten their day. "And now you've gone and accepted the silly cow's Lady Muck invite to tea!"

Heather takes a brief moment from her tirade, kicking up bits of gravel, muttering under her breath. "I'm still convinced she tried to poison us with those spinach things. They really were foul. Just watch your back, Caroline, I mean *really* watch your back."

"I know it's not going to be fun, but I felt obliged because of Ben. I promise, I will be going into the whole thing with my eyes wide open," I explain, trying to reassure us all.

"OK, OK. It's just that we don't want to lose you as a friend."

"Oh don't be silly," I laugh, relieved the storm is over. "This is a play date, it's not an indoctrination class. Don't worry, Heather, I won't tell them anything they don't already know, and I'll report back with all the juicy gossip, if you're interested that is."

The lure of insider gossip isn't enough to calm Heather's fears. She still looks unconvinced.

"Sarah has a way of weaselling things out of you. She did it with me and look where that got us. And I think that's how she got wind of Rose Avenue, too. Just innocently asking Eva about their property search."

Eva frowns and, seeing more objections, I hastily add, "OK, OK, don't worry. I've got it."

"And be careful what you say about the mafia in front of Ben, too, kids are like little sponges, pick up everything. Last week I was in the playground and just as Sarah came up to me about some treasury stuff, Jennifer came out with a classic, perfectly mimicking me by saying, 'Is that the *cow* you always talk about, Mummy?' "

Eva laughs. "Nice one. What did you say?"

"Just mumbled something about meaning someone else. It was quite funny, actually. Sarah turned red, but couldn't really do anything in front of her kids either, so we just kind of glowered at each other."

"Mind you," adds Eva, smiling knowingly, "it'll be the poshest house in the larger Frencham area. Sarah has always been good at keeping up appearances."

Tuesday afternoon, three twenty. Eva and Heather have offered not to wait with me today, so that the meeting and greeting with Sarah is easier. It had seemed a good idea at the time, but standing here alone now I feel in dire need of some support. I walk slowly over to the mafia's benches, wondering with a growing sense of unease who the other mums are going to be.

The bell rings and Ben comes charging out of the classroom, with Edward and another little boy I vaguely recognise, and after unceremoniously dumping their bags at my feet, they immediately tear off for a game of bulldog. I shout feebly after him to come back as soon as he's called.

I watch them run off and I find myself, very selfishly, hoping that Ben doesn't actually become best friends with Edward. I'm pretty sure I can't face an endless string of reciprocal play dates. But Ben looks so happy that I have to promise myself I will be the epitome of motherhood at Sarah's, for his sake at least. I've even spent a couple of hours trying to make cutesy cupcakes.

Failing miserably, of course, despite my best efforts to follow the Nigella-I-just-let-the-kids-decorate-them school of thought. So I ended up in Waitrose this morning, scouring the cookie shelf for the most battered home-made-looking pack and feeling as though I was buying contraband.

I'm jolted back into reality by Karin's approach. She's not smiling, but then again the woman very rarely smiles, when she does the effect is terrifying, so it's just as well. Trailing morosely behind her stern mother is a mini-me of Karin who is now being formally introduced as Sophia. Unbelievably, both give me the same kind of once-over as Sarah did last week. We exchange a couple of words and Karin stands so close I feel like she's there mainly to ensure I don't make a run for it.

With some relief, I spot a tall blonde girl approaching us, the skinny one who trailed in with the mafia that first time I went to the Sycamore Café. I remember thinking then that she didn't look as if she really fitted into the group, mainly because she seemed genuinely friendly to all three of us, and I get the same sense now. Perhaps she's just kind of fallen in with the group through the kids, which is, after all, why I'm here, or maybe, intriguing idea, she's a double agent?

I don't have time to follow that line of thought right now though.

"Hi there. I'm Helen," she says, offering her hand for a firm shake. "You must be the new girl. Caroline, isn't it?" As she says my name I notice that she has a twang of an American accent. I consciously store that in the things-to-ask-about-when-I'm-trapped-at-Sarah's-and-have-run-out-of-conversation bank.

"Yes, that's right," I reply, grateful for the friendly face.

"Yeah, well, welcome to the club." She laughs at her own joke, which isn't really all that funny but perhaps she's as nervous as I am. Sarah is just bustling up to us and Helen takes the opportunity to add in an undertone, "We're not as anal as we look, trust me." She gives me a wink. "Well," she looks around, "not all of us anyway."

I laugh now.

"This is my son, Georgie." She points to the ruddy-faced, fair-haired little boy, slightly taller than my son, who is now vigorously trying to catch Ben. He must be a year or so older than Ben. Next to us, Karin has greeted Sarah, exchanging what can only be a secret handshake. I roll my eyes, but quickly compose my features into a welcoming smile.

"Right, is everyone here?" asks Sarah, firmly calling Edward and the others to attention. I'm astonished to see that even my unruly son immediately scampers over. "Karin, Meg is having Patrick and Charles over after swimming and will bring them back at around six, if that's OK with you?" Karin isn't given time to reply.

"Now, if you'd like to follow me." Sarah turns and wafts past the other mums. Dressed in a long, very expensive-looking cream sheepskin coat, she looks polished and expensive, reeking of E'spa as usual. I think even Jessica at Red Dawn would approve of this outfit, although I doubt she'd stock it. The playground crowd parts silently, like the sea for Moses, and we trail in Sarah's fragrant wake like hypnotised kids following the Pied Piper. I can see Marie at the back, with her little boy, and her jaw drops when she sees me pass. I'm acutely uncomfortable, my face burning, and I can only hope Eva and Heather haven't spotted me. They'd be booing loudly and throwing rotten eggs by now.

I walk with Helen, who is chatting to me about wanting to lose weight she doesn't have, while Karin and Sarah occasionally look back to see if we're still following. Why the fuck did I agree to this? Now, my plan of action is this: I'll be boring. If I've got nothing to offer her in terms of information on the girls, then she won't bother again. And I might throw in that I have no connections, emphasise the struggling single-mum image and make sure she knows I'm poor, living in a less desirable part of town.

Rose Avenue is the millionaire's row of Frencham. In an already affluent area, those who live in Rose Avenue are the cherries on the icing on the cake. My mum would probably take one look and frown at the horrendous cost of maintenance, but the sheer magnificence of these houses is not without an effect on me. I'm in awe. And it's not just the buildings themselves. The gardens are immaculate, the lawns looking combed not just mown, and no leaves anywhere. In fact, I can see a tanned guy seated on what looks like a rather grand miniature tractor mowing his vast front lawn in perfect vertical strips. I'm so distracted by him, and visions of *Desperate Housewives*-style affairs with the gardener, that I almost walk into the back of Sarah as she stops outside a large, wide house that looks like a fairy-tale birthday cake.

"We're here, ladies. Welcome to 'Chez Sarah'," she says, dramatically turning and pointing to a large wrought-iron sign on a stone wall.

Initially I think she said "Que Sera", but I quickly realise that she has indeed called her house "Sarah's Place". What a weirdo.

Helen looks at me as we pass through the gates, smiles and rolls her eyes as if to say, "Yes, I know, silly isn't it?"

My first impression of Chez Sarah is that it's very, very pink. From the paint on the walls to the curtains peeping through the sparkling windows to the hundreds of red and pink pansies in the front garden. One big, pink meringue.

As we reach the front porch, I say, trying to sound genuine, "What a lovely house, Sarah. Was it this colour when you bought it?"

She looks at me, obviously proud, but not quite sure if I'm being sarcastic or not. "Yes, I thought it set such a lovely first impression. Pink is so very positive and cheerful, don't you think?"

"Yes," I say lamely, thinking I might have to shoot myself before the day is over, and knowing that Eva would have repainted it before you could say "pink elephant".

"A lot of people were interested in this property, but we knew the family who were living here, used to have dinner here every so often, actually, and when we heard they were selling we made them an offer they couldn't refuse." She must know that Eva would have mentioned the story to me, but she just smiles blithely and opens the door to reveal a long, spacious hallway plastered with some dramatic and bright abstract art, which, I hate to say it, I like. Although it clashes horribly with all the pink.

"I absolutely love looking round art galleries when I have time. It's a little hobby of mine, Caroline. Jeremy says I spend far too much money on art, but everyone has their weakness," she says in a confiding manner, most likely trying to set the tone for more girly confidences to come.

There are three rooms leading off the hallway and I have a quick peek as I pass. I can see beige and brown sofas, with freshly puffed powder-pink cushions, and a huge glass vase full of lilies in one room, and in another a heavy mahogany table that wouldn't look out of place in one of those banquet scenes in an Errol Flynn *Robin Hood* epic.

Everything looks like something out of *House & Garden*. The kids scamper ahead of us now and I catch up quickly, realising I'm trailing behind, joining the others in the kitchen. This is nice, actually. Cupboards all along one side and, surprise surprise, a commanding pink Smeg fridge on the other. On the endless, seamless granite work surface every conceivable gadget and cooking accessory is lined up neatly beside a small bookstand, which contains Delia's, Rick's, Gary's and Jamie's best works. I recognise the usual suspects — toaster, kettle, knife block — but there's also a shiny bread machine, a sandwich maker (God, I didn't know anyone still used them) and what looks like, I think, a pasta maker. She's got a George Foreman grill, which is, of course, a larger version of mine. A Philippe Starck lemon squeezer, which I've always hated, and two more contraptions I don't have a clue about. I nudge Helen.

"What are they?" I whisper, pointing with my chin while Sarah bustles ahead.

"The one on the left is a sushi maker. The one on the right is a ravioli maker," she whispers back. "What, you don't have either of these? No home should be without them." She chuckles softly. I'm warming to my new comrade-in-arms.

Edward and Ben fly past, heading towards a large kitchen table set out with what looks like a feast to feed the forty thousand.

"Can we take something to eat upstairs, Mummy? I want to show Ben my bedroom." Edward looks hopeful.

"Now, Edward," Sarah replies. "You know we don't allow food in the bedrooms. It creates a mess and Mrs Hopkins doesn't like messes, does she?"

"She's the cleaner, Mummy. That's why you pay her," Edward answers, rather logically in my opinion.

"No backchat, Edward. Please set the table." Sarah nudges her son over to the pile of plates and novelty napkins, which he gamely picks up and distributes around the table, followed by Ben, who's fascinated by the procedure. Perhaps he will pick up a few homemaking tips.

I hand my coat to Karin, who seems to be acting as the cloakroom guardian, and take a moment to consider the offerings on the table, clutching my bag and the Tupperware hiding the bashed-about Waitrose cookies. Tiny neat wholemeal sandwiches cut into dinosaur shapes and filled with egg and cress, tuna and cucumber or salmon and rocket are stacked neatly on dainty white plates with mini serviettes. There's a fruit cake *and* a plate of gingerbread cookies, definitely home-made. But I've spotted these too late. I already have my box of cookies in hand, and Sarah has clocked them.

"Can I put these anywhere?" I ask, shamelessly offering the biscuits to Sarah.

"Oh, what's that?" she says, taking the box from my hands and peeking underneath the lid. "Oh, how charming. They look lovely. The Waitrose bakery is so good these days, isn't it?"

I smile and say nothing, feeling utterly and totally inadequate.

"Oh, nothing to be ashamed of, Caroline," Sarah says magnanimously, clearly wanting to make the most of my embarrassment. "I don't know how you manage to juggle both a job and a family. Baking cookies is the last thing you want to do at the end of the day." I nod, relieved. "Does your husband help out a lot? Jeremy's so wonderful with the children, but his job keeps him on his toes most of the week," she twinkles. "But your husband works in the City too, doesn't he? John Gray, is it? Jeremy says he was on a project with him a few years ago and he was so impressed with his talent and get-up-and-go."

I'm momentarily distracted from the cookie debacle. It sounds as if — surely she'd know that John and I are divorced? I know we still have the same last name and all, but this is the queen of gossip we're talking about, the doyenne of hoarding nuggets of information to throw into the mix whenever appropriate. I can't see how on earth she'd labour under the false impression that John and I are one big, happy family? She did see him at the gates and, if I remember correctly, asked me about him later in the café. Hmm. How to correct this graciously? Sarah's voice is still droning on in the background.

"Err, Sarah —" Wait, she seems to have moved on to the much more interesting subject of organic groceries.

"By the way," she says, nodding at her gingerbread, "these are made with organic fruit juice, and the cake is sweetened with fructose — that's fruit sugar — which is much sweeter than sucrose so you don't need to use as much." I make some noises, I think I say something about the recipe and she just shrugs gracefully, a tad smugly, perhaps. From her expression, you'd think she was running a country, reinventing the wheel and writing the next great British novel while whipping up batches of sugar-free cookies in her spare time.

"Yes," she sighs, clearly misreading my expression of contempt as barely disguised admiration. "I don't quite know where we all find the time, but there you go."

The children have been dancing around the table with silverware, occasionally stealing a nibble. Out of the corner of my eye I see Sophia, free from her mum's icy clutches, spit something into the big plant holder by the window. Clearly, the absence of sugar and all things nice isn't going down well so far.

I bite my lip as I want to ask how much Mrs Hopkins helps out, but I don't think that would help the atmosphere and I've still got a couple of hours of this, so I keep my mouth shut and my eyes open.

For a brief moment the mums are bustling around, getting kids seated and plates filled, while I meander around the kitchen, confident that Ben will be able to look after himself. I glance around for anything else I can brief the girls on tomorrow. There's a large cork noticeboard with names and telephone numbers on it. I look surreptitiously at the table, then quickly scan the list, but none look familiar. There are notes like "cake stall" and "plant stall" — must be the Christmas Fair — and on the wall she has photographs of her, Edward, what must be his bigger brother, the infamous Charles, and, I presume, Jeremy, all posing for happy-family shots. Jeremy is quite short and tired-looking, but perhaps he's just decomposed in Sarah's company.

There's also a stereo and mini CD rack. *How to Learn French in Eight Weeks*. *How to Learn Italian in Eight Weeks*. *How to Learn German in Ten Weeks*. Obviously German must be more difficult. Are they planning to emigrate? There's a lot of classical music, some Sting, Coldplay and U2 — huh? — and, perhaps unsurprisingly, Cliff Richard. And the Best of Abba, which makes sense, and the Best of Boney M, which doesn't. I wonder if there are any other people living in this house. Maybe Mrs Hopkins brought her music to listen to while she's ironing the Flints' underwear?

I move on to the fridge, where she's taped some of Edward's "gold star" awards for being kind and helpful in class. Ben hasn't got any of these yet, but I'm sure he will. I'll try to steer the conversation away from that, I think. Sarah probably already thinks Ben is in dire need of some reining in. She's also got some magnetic poetry up on the fridge door, which is unexpected. Some long words, like tremendous, others shorter like "pinch", and there's been an attempt to make a few quirky sentences, one of which is "huge dirty clock looks happy" — amusing . . .

I hear footsteps behind me. "Can I help, Sarah?" I ask quickly, but she just smiles. "No, just see if Ben's settled, would you?" She makes it sound like a mammoth task when all that's involved is sitting on a chair and waiting for the food to be heaped on your plate. No wonder she keeps herself so busy. When she opens the fridge I manage to glance in. You can tell a lot by what people have in their fridge. If it's full but not crammed, with a wide variety of food, it's someone who's organised but not anal (Eva's is always like that). Heather's is always full of organic vegetables that go off and bottles of wine and those full-fat, high-sugar yoghurts her kids love. I've moved on from my bachelor fridge before Ben — beer, champagne, white and red wine, olives, bread, milk, margarine and some Minstrels — to a slightly healthier variety. But the Minstrels and champagne (when I can afford it) are still in residence.

Sarah's fridge is full of organic food and only those ranges you have to actively seek out at organic grocery stores. The salad and vegetable crispers are full. Then there is an organic chicken, organic chicken pieces, some quails' eggs, organic hens' eggs, elderflower and apple juice, and some Duchy Original jams. Probably for a withered loaf of wholemeal in her fancy, stainless-steel bread bin. I can't see anything "naughty" in here, nothing resembling sweets or chocolate. There are a few bottles of champagne, but much classier brands than I buy. Sarah finally notices me looking and says, "I buy all my vegetables from Borough Market. It's wonderful there. You can get some amazing tofu. And all the vegetables and fruits are organic. We occasionally stop and have some oysters, don't we, Edward?"

"Yes, Mummy," he says without looking up. Sophia and Georgie are giggling over biting off the heads of all the dinosaur sandwiches, although I'm sure they're not allowed to start eating yet. Ben's head is swivelling madly back and forth, as fascinated by the family dynamic here as I am.

I help Sarah carry over some of the elderflower pressés and pour a round for the adults while the kids are fobbed off with organic whole milk or filtered water. Ben looks longingly at my drink and I give him a sip when Sarah's not looking. For a moment all you can hear are forks clattering quietly and plates being passed back and forth. Helen smiles at me encouragingly. So far, so good, she seems to be saying.

I cast around for something to break the silence with and have finally settled on asking Sarah about the languages when a golden Labrador puppy bounds up to the table, jumping up and down like a child wanting attention. For a second I forget where I am and laugh out loud, bending down to stroke and tickle the furry little creature. He's absolutely gorgeous.

"Don't touch him," Sarah snaps. "Sorry," she then says. "We're trying to get Herbert not to jump up at people and it's important not to encourage him. Please, just ignore him."

I look down and put my hands behind my back, but it's such a shame. The little dog's shiny black eyes are looking at me playfully, and he's jumping from side to side.

"He's beautiful," I say, giving Sarah my first genuine smile of the afternoon.

"Yes, he's a pedigree, rather special, in fact. Not that he will be much use as a guard dog. Labradors are quite submissive in nature."

"That's a good thing then. Sounds as if he's exactly what you're looking for." Oops. I'm not sure where that came from. Well, I guess I'm only stating the obvious, but I think Sarah takes it as a slight on her character.

"Would you like to wash your hands now?" she says with just a hint of frost as she passes round the roasted cherry-tomato crostini, some marinated olives and a cheeseboard with at least six varieties of cheese, two of which I can't identify.

"I'll be fine, thanks," I say cheerfully. I'm sure the dog is clean enough, especially in a house like this.

"Ben is always asking for a dog, but it would be a tie in my situation," I say conversationally, nibbling at an olive. "My work takes me out of the house a lot and we're always busy at the weekends."

"Yes, well." Sarah's tone is still brittle. "Mrs Hopkins is here when I'm not, and Jeremy is here when Mrs Hopkins isn't, so Herbert is never alone." This might actually be a good time to clear up that John confusion.

"John isn't really around much," I confess, trying to think of a way to say the word "divorce" without sounding as though I need to share some big emotional issue with my new friends. Already, they're clucking and nodding and tut-tutting around the table. Are they pitying me? I realise they still don't quite get it.

"But Ben is always excited when he comes back from his weekends with John, and, actually, John's new girl-friend also has a dog, so at least he 'owns' one once a month." There, that should do it.

Sarah still looks confused "But where are they going? He doesn't — Oh." You can see her recalibrating the situation, jigging pieces around in her head, until she finally gets the picture. "I hadn't realised you were divorced," she says slightly stiffly and almost accusingly. Like I'd kept it from her on purpose. Helen is chuckling into her crostinis, earning a baleful glance from Sarah, and Karin just observes us all, her face blank and expressionless. This is like dinner with the Addams family. But the worst is still to come.

"Mummy, Edward says he's got a mi-kros-kop, and a labrotarory that is brilliant. And he's got a thing that makes stones shiny and a crystal maker and a thing that makes goo glow in the dark and he's got lots and lots of Lego." Is there anything this child doesn't have? But yes, I would definitely have put Sarah down for Leapfrog toys and mini versions of the language tapes in the kitchen, so a fully fledged science lab in his bedroom isn't a revelation. Ben is positively gagging at the thought of these amazing toys. Wait and see, dear. "Mummy, Mummy, can we go up and play?"

No no no! Don't leave me here with these freaks!

"Have you finished eating?" I say desperately. "Surely you must still be hungry?"

No, he isn't. OK. No worries. I can cope. I look at Sarah, hoping she won't see this as yet another display of unruly behaviour. Although, come to think of it, why do I even care?

Edward is standing to attention by the table as though waiting for the next order.

"Yes, if you're all finished." She looks at Sophia's untouched food, Ben's mashed-up sandwiches and, more approvingly, at Edward's tidy plate. "Why don't you go upstairs and show the children your toys." The three boys race upstairs with grumpy Sophia hot on their heels.

"Now, would anyone like anything else to drink? A glass of champagne perhaps?"

I'm just about to open my mouth and enthusiastically proffer my glass when I notice everyone shaking their heads. This is going to be one long afternoon. Sarah seems to agree with me, though, because she gets a bottle of champagne out of the fridge, deftly uncorks it and pours us all a sparkling round. My heart lifts.

"Do you allow Ben to watch much television, Caroline?" Sarah offers me a glass and an opportunity to show off my mothering skills. But it takes more than that to get me to slip up. I'm a pro at this kind of thing, after years of fielding trick questions at my ex-husband's dinner parties.

"No, not during the week. Only at weekends, really, and just an hour or so. And only Animal Planet."

Complete bollocks, but I'm not telling someone as anal as Sarah that I regularly find Ben in front of the TV at seven thirty, glued to Power Rangers or the Disney Channel. Sarah smiles, looking suitably impressed; Karin is less so, fixing me with narrowed eyes. Helen's still giggling.

"Karin doesn't either," Sarah says, nodding over to Karin as if she can't talk for herself, "but we occasionally allow Edward a pre-selected show during the week. Although we're so busy, he usually doesn't even think about it." We all mull this over and sip our champagne. Oh God. Jaw-aching boredom. I can hear Edward, Ben and Georgie laughing and shouting upstairs and fervently wish I was with them. Anywhere else but around this table, in this appalling company.

"So, how do you feel Ben is doing at school?" Karin asks abruptly, popping an olive into her mouth. She always makes me jump. She's so quiet and so petite, I often forget she's there, which, I suppose, makes her almost more frightening than Sarah.

"I think he's settled in very well, thank you." I drink the last of my champagne. Sarah tops up my glass without asking. Is she trying to get me drunk? Must be careful now, Gray.

"Ms Silver is a nice teacher. Utterly capable. And you, Caroline, have you settled in well?" This is probably the most she's ever spoken to me.

"Yes, thank you. Everyone made me feel very welcome," I say, easily parrying her questions.

"Where do you live exactly?"

I describe my road and the house I bought. "Very sweet, just two bedrooms, but a really large downstairs and a nice garden." I see Karin and Sarah exchanging a quick look.

"Is that over by the big estate?"

"Not sure, Karin, I have only been there for a few months." My voice is measured. I can see where this is going now.

"And you find a two-bedroom house enough for you and an active, growing boy?"

I redden a little at her attempt to pry into my financials. God, she is such a cow. "Yes, it's perfectly adequate," I reply with as much dignity as I can muster. "And in any case, I simply couldn't afford a bigger house when we moved here after the divorce."

Sarah looks faintly embarrassed but Helen clears her throat. "I agree. Lance and I have a sweet two-bedroom cottage over on the other side of the park from you, Caroline, and it's perfect. Wonderful garden, too, lovely for Georgie in the summer." I shoot her a grateful look, but Sarah isn't pleased to be provoked.

"That's nice, Helen. By the way, I've been meaning to ask how Georgie is doing with his reading and writing? Is he progressing well with all that extra tuition you're giving him? Is he out of the remedial group yet?"

Helen recoils and reddens slightly, clearly feeling unfairly put in her place.

"The group is called special needs, Sarah, and he is making steady progress." To me, "He's dyslexic, Caroline." I nod, trying to show both empathy towards Helen and disapproval towards Sarah.

Sarah makes sympathetic noises, flashing her a weak smile. "All the fund-raising we do at the PTA has been a tremendous help to those children with learning difficulties." She must have given speeches on this many times over, it sounds so practised and glib. Quickly changing gear, she turns to me. "Does Ben have learning difficulties?"

"Not to my knowledge," I reply, now really trying not to sound annoyed.

"What plans do you have for Ben when he leaves school?"

"Plans?" I say, not sure if she means "leave school" as in this term, this year, or altogether.

"Yes, plans. What do you want him to be when he grows up?"

Helen excuses herself to go the toilet and see how the children are getting on. Great. I'm left alone with two hard-core mafia members and a question I've barely contemplated myself.

"He's four," I say stupidly, but I stumble on. "I thought I'd wait a bit. At the moment I think he wants to be a Power Ranger, but I suspect that will change. He wanted to be Bob the Builder when he was three. At least a builder has greater earning potential than a Power Ranger, don't you think? Especially around Frencham, with all its extension madness." I giggle at my own — admittedly quite lame — joke, but Sarah and Karin remain poker-faced and I quickly realise I've just committed a huge faux pas. I wipe the smile off my face and try to look earnest.

"You can never plan too far ahead, Caroline." Sarah sighs deeply and Karin nods in agreement, sighing alongside her. "It's so important to think long term. Good grammar and private schools are incredibly competitive everywhere in the country, but particularly so in this area, so you need to set your targets early on. What are Ben's academic strengths? That might help to pinpoint which school would suit him best. I plan to send Edward to the international boarding school in Angleside to do the Baccalaureate — he's very good at languages." I remember the CDs lined up. Preparation for this school has started frighteningly early, I guess.

"Well, Ben's very good at building Lego spaceships," I say, trying to keep the conversation light, but that's not the right route to go. They're appalled by my flippant attitude — I don't think I'll ever make the grade as a mafia member. I just can't take this übermum thing seriously.

"Does Ben do any sport?" Karin asks, popping another olive into her mouth. I'm starting to wish she would choke on one of the bloody things.

"Yes, he does tennis and swimming and karate at the health club," I say, resenting the interrogation and feeling as if my capabilities as a mum are being measured by how many after-school activities I've got him involved in.

"Anything else?" Karin looks dismissive. I'm determined not to be bulldozed on this, though.

"Well, I want him to have some days when he can have friends over, and I don't want to tire him out too much either," I explain, trying to sound defiant rather than defensive. "A lot of the time we just hang out, read, watch movies —" Bugger, that wasn't supposed to slip out. I must refresh my conversational skills after all. "Plus I want him in bed at a decent time." Phew, good finish!

"Edward is always in bed at seven thirty on school nights," Sarah says proudly. "Private tuition for tennis on Mondays, swimming on Tuesdays, French on Wednesdays, karate and guitar lessons on Thursdays and a reading tutor on Fridays. Tea, bath, teeth, story and lights out at seven thirty sharp." Really, too much detail, Sarah. I'm exhausted just listening to Edward's schedule, the poor lad must be permanently shattered. But I try to look impressed.

As if on cue, I hear laughter from upstairs and shouts of "Me now, me now, please!" At least Ben is having fun. And where the hell is Helen?

"Sophia has been learning French since she was a baby. Stephen, my husband, is half French so naturally she will be bilingual," says Karin smugly.

"I think this is all incredibly impressive" — more smug smiles — "but I personally think that they shouldn't do too much outside of school. I like Ben to socialise with other kids and let off a bit of energy in the evenings, but I really think they need free time as well. Plus, a lot of these clubs are very pricey, aren't they?" I'm aware that I'm being scrutinised closely by both women now, but I don't care any more.

"What price education, Caroline?" tuts Sarah in horror, shaking her head at me. "This is your son's future, and it is the most important investment you'll ever make. You can't seriously think about saving here?"

"But I don't want to overburden Ben. Ms Silver says children this age learn a lot through play and I think too much hothousing just leads to burnout." I'm shocked by my own assertiveness, but secretly proud. I sit back in my seat, hoping that Ben will come downstairs, demanding to go home, before his mother shoots herself.

But he doesn't. All I can hear is laughter and there's another awkward short silence, then Karin coughs.

"So when did you and your husband divorce? Was it a friendly split? Did he find someone else?"

I'm more than a little taken aback by the outrageous rudeness of the question. These are women who blush at the word "afford" around the table and then try to prise open my private life?

Before I can splutter a response, Sarah interrupts: "More champagne, anyone?" So she is trying to get me talking. Helen chooses this moment to come back and I'm relieved to see her — I need someone to cover my back when I tell Karin to mind her own bloody business.

"What are we talking about?" she says brightly, clearly having recovered after a snoop and a go on the microscope upstairs.

"Caroline was just telling us about her divorce, the poor girl," Karin replies, equally brightly.

Gently now, Gray. Even if I'm not going to be bosom buddies with the inner circle of the mafia, which, thank God, is looking increasingly likely seeing that Sarah doesn't have a place in her heart for a struggling single mum, I do still have to share the playground with them. For the next seven years I'll have to be courteous and polite, make small talk, and try not to incur their wrath unnecessarily.

So I say, "Ben's dad works in the City and we split about a year ago. We're on good terms and he takes a keen interest in Ben's development." Two hours in these women's company and I'm sounding like I've swallowed a parenting manual myself.

Sarah and Karin look at me pityingly, and I bite my lip so hard I think I've made it bleed.

"Ah yes," sighs Karin. "My husband works in the City. Extremely stressful job. He's always back late and flying off here and there. He spends a lot of time in the Far East, in Thailand in particular. There's a lot going on there at the moment."

I look down, trying to stifle a smile. Who knows, Mr Karin may be going to Thailand for more than business. Better change the subject altogether. This conversation is becoming increasingly uncomfortable.

"John was delighted when I chose The Sycamore for Ben. The Ofsted report for the school is absolutely glowing. I think it must be one of the best in the area."

"It *is* the best in the area," Sarah corrects me immediately. "And we try to keep it that way. We have a very close eye on how The Sycamore performs, term on term — it's easy to get to the top, it's harder to stay there. And if the children stand a fighting chance of moving on to the best secondary education, we need to maintain the standards. That means keeping an eye on the school's academic progress, being a pro-active parent, and ensuring our kids are model examples of our educational principles. And very occasionally, we have to keep an eye on whom they let into the school." She laughs unpleasantly. "There are some very undesirable types, to say the least, who want to send their children to The Sycamore, and since it's still a state school, with an official catchment area, they can slip through and inevitably this just lowers the school's tone and reputation."

Shock. Horror.

"I don't know if you saw that man on the lawnmower as we were walking here? I'm sure he's a very sweet chap, so noble of him to do his own lawn, don't you think? But he's a builder from over the other side of London. Jumped-up money, probably dodges paying his taxes, and couldn't pronounce a vowel correctly if you paid him to. I tried to get the estate agent to stop him from buying in this road but it seems he offered well over the asking price, so now his son is in the same class as Edward and Benjamin. Such a shame. Really, I feel that there's a certain quality — an attitude if you will — that marks Sycamore parents. After all, when it comes to higher education, the parents will be interviewed as much as their children."

I'm at a loss as to what to say to this. Obviously Eva and Heather haven't made that cut. And it looks like I'm also rapidly sliding down the ladder of moral integrity, academic ambition and general parenting perfection myself.

"So, you don't yet have *any* schools in mind for Ben?"

Is she kidding? I'm all for planning ahead, but seven years seems excessive even to me. I don't even know how to answer that, other than simply "No" and/or "Sod off," but help comes from an unexpected corner.

"So, do you go to a gym round here, Caroline?" Helen has surreptitiously finished her champagne as well as the rest of the bottle and looks considerably more relaxed than any of us around the table. I pounce on the subject enthusiastically, like Herbert, who is still sniffing around the kitchen every now and then, eyed disapprovingly by Sarah.

"Yes, I go to Go For Gold, down by the river. It's got those fabulous flower arrangements in reception and quite friendly staff, but some of the members seem very much up their own arses." Again, did I just say that out loud? "I mean, all those women who spend more time ogling the tennis coaches and looking at themselves in the mirror than working out."

That didn't really make things better, although at least Helen seems amused.

"Sarah and I are members as well, but we've never seen you there, have we?" Karin asks innocently.

"No, but I'm sure it's not because I spend all my time looking in the mirror," Sarah says, tight-lipped.

I reach for my glass and drain it in one gulp. Sarah doesn't get up to offer me any more, so I'm assuming I've just slipped one more step down to "entirely undesirable". How ironic that at this point we're probably both thinking of ways to get me out of Chez Sarah. But there's nothing to do but sit it out until Ben bounces back downstairs, or Edward's sent to bed.

Thankfully Helen breaks the silence again.

"So what's been happening with the rubbish around the school, Sarah? Have you sorted that out? Last I heard they couldn't do anything about it until Christmas."

"Have you heard about the rubbish bins?" Sarah says to me, almost whispering.

I want to laugh, but I answer back gamely, adopting the same hushed tones while desperately trying to keep a straight face. "No, I haven't heard about the rubbish bins."

"All rubbish bags must be kept in bins at all times, and home owners have been asked by the council to keep the bins either in their back yards or with the lids firmly closed until the morning of collection. We've got a real problem with foxes around here. They come out at night foraging for food and spread the rubbish out on the street. It's unhygienic and disgusting and I really don't want our children walking to and from school stepping over other people's trash. The school raised it

115

with the council, but there didn't seem to be too much they would do about it. The people living around the school simply didn't want to keep their rubbish indoors. But you'll be pleased to hear, Helen," Helen nods obediently, "that I did speak to my cousin, he's on the council, you know, and he's agreed that something should be done and is pushing it through for us."

Just as I'm starting to think that I've walked into a parallel universe of nutty mums who've completely lost the plot and are taking everything, including their own opinions, far too seriously, a wicked laugh comes from Sarah's mobile.

"Unusual ring tone," I say, impressed despite myself.

"Isn't it? It's actually called a wicked laugh. Very me, don't you think?"

I'm surprised by Sarah's astute self-mocking comment. Sarah picks up the phone, mouthing us an apology, and I pour us some more elderflower pressé. I'm on my fifth crostini, now fairly wilted and soggy, and am determined to find out more about these women, as they now clearly know all they want to about me. I start by asking Karin what she did before she became a full-time mafia mum.

"I worked in the City and met Stephen there. He was married at the time, but that quickly fell apart, and we've been together for over six years now. Unfortunately he still has to pay maintenance, which is quite substantial, so our home is, well," she looks around the kitchen swiftly, "more modest than this. Sarah had her own public-relations consultancy and was very successful. She specialised in designer fabrics and exclusive housewares, which is probably why everything in this house is exquisite. And Jeremy is very generous with his money. They've just had a large extension to the back of the house which must have cost an absolute fortune." Karin sighs briefly. Do I detect a sign of jealousy in one of Sarah's closest allies?

"Right. And what about Felicity? I saw you in the café with her on the first day of school. Does she work?"

"Yes, she works in the accounts department of a major insurance company, but only two days a week. Apparently, they've become quite dependent on her and she's charging them a day what she used to get in a week. But she's extremely good at fund-raising, tells all the companies how donating to the school lowers their tax bill. Very useful."

"Ah, right," I say, disappointed not to get something juicier. Better try to listen to Sarah's phone conversation instead.

"And Sarah tells me you're a graphologist? That's interesting. I don't suppose you'd like to read my handwriting?" she says, already going for her handbag and a pen.

"No, I never do outside work hours," I say curtly. There's no way I want be here all night, reading everyone's handwriting and lying through my teeth.

In the silence, I can hear Sarah say, "No, no, don't come home quite yet. I've got guests. The new one is here, you know, I was telling you about her the other evening? John Gray's, yes, no, well, turns out, well, anyway, aren't you working late tonight? . . . Right . . .

Right. OK. Well, give it another half-hour, and Charles should be back then as well, but not before. Good, that's good. Yes, you too, dear."

Sarah hangs up the phone without even a fond farewell and turns to us, smiling through her teeth.

"That was Jeremy, he'll be back in half an hour. I just didn't want him to disturb us having our fun."

For someone working in the City, five thirty seems pretty early to be knocking off from work — maybe he's a conscientious father after all. I look at my watch, gagging to escape. I've been here for nearly two hours, but it feels like a lifetime.

"Well, actually, I think we really must be heading off. Ben needs to get home and I wouldn't want to impose any longer. I'm sure Edward still has things to catch up on as well."

I get up, half-heartedly starting to clear the table, but Sarah stops me. "No, no, Mrs Hopkins will do it, don't worry."

Helen and Karin are up like a shot, calling the children, getting jackets and coats.

I turn round to Sarah and give her a hug, because that's what people do when they spend time with each other. Sarah stiffens, but I'm not bothered. I won't have to do it again, and at least it shows an immense amount of goodwill. Karin is another matter. I don't have to hug her in return for hospitality or anything. I like her even less than I do Sarah.

There's a brief moment of chaos when the children tear down the stairs, running around in circles, the puppy barking, coats flying, but Sarah restores order with a few choice barks herself. She does run a tight ship, I have to say. Ben's not impressed, but I usher him out quickly, leaving Chez Sarah for what I devoutly hope will be a very long time.

I turn out of Rose Avenue hand in hand with Ben, who is happy but still gently whingeing about wanting a puppy called Herbert. He also wants the "labroratory", which was fun but weird, the seven dwarfs as neighbours, the puppy again and a richer mummy. Is that all? I mull over the afternoon. In a way, I'm pleased that I accepted the play date. Not only because I've got something to report back to Heather and Eva, but, more importantly, because it's now completely and utterly clear why Heather and Eva would never get on with these women and why it would be absolutely pointless for me to try to be friends with them. We're just not on the same wavelength. I still think, and I'll have to reiterate this position with Heather tomorrow, that we've got to be civil. Not only because of our children playing together — although, sorry Ben, it might not be happening all that often — but also because the mafia do wield power at The Sycamore. Real power.

CHAPTER
EIGHT

The Day Job

Nightmare. I got my period. A week early. And I'm unprepared. Damn. And I've got a meeting with Jack Stone, CEO of one of the world's largest advertising companies. And I'm stuck in the ladies, in the anaemically clean, orange-blossom-smelling executive loo, trying to sort myself out without looking as though I have a nappy on. Where is that machine for tampons? Or is that just in nightclubs? Or is that just for condoms? Don't know, haven't been to a nightclub for ages. There, that should work. Must remember: first stop after the meeting, Boots.

It's not surprising I'm flustered after my typically manic morning. Up at seven. Get Ben's clothes ready. Weetabix in bowl and milk shoved in the microwave. No time to faff about with pans of hot milk. Persuade him to eat the mushy mess. Double-check his book bag and make sure I've signed everything I need to and that all invitations to parties have been accepted or rejected. I can't quite believe the social life of four-year-olds these days. The most recent birthday party invite is from a boy called Frank, but Ben says he doesn't like him so I'll make excuses. God, party politics even at this age. A nicely written thank-you note to Sarah for the play date from hell. Make sure toothbrush and toothpaste are by the door so Ben doesn't forget — I don't want him having teeth like mine. Plus, this morning I had to make an effort with myself for once. I need to be suited and booted, polished and buffed, not so much for the business meeting, which is more like a half-hour catch-up, but because of my slight obsession with looking good for Jack. It's silly, really, but he has that scrutinising gaze and I feel much better about myself if my outfit stands up to it. So, my favourite skirt and jumper, with nice, sheer tights (and, of course, it took three tries to locate a pair without horrendous ladders).

What with moving and Ben starting school I've had a lot of balls in the air recently: Ben, work, handling the mortgage on my own, finishing the decorating, keeping friends out of trouble and discouraging potential mafia enemies from keeping me on their radar. And none of the balls are the same, each needs handling with special care, like cricket versus tennis balls, with newly laid eggs and the odd bowling ball thrown in for good measure, or like unexpected tax bills or calls from my mum just when I don't need them.

I've been asked by Jack to check out two potential directors for his company, looking at their handwriting, and he wants to discuss several other things for the rest of the year. I used to work at Jack's company full-time ages ago, when I was still in marketing, but left just after I had Ben. My last assignment at Universe International was to write and research the company's history (colourful, mainly because the founders were all French and drank most of the time, racing horses the rest), but Jack regularly brings me in to detect bullshitters and arseholes, as he scientifically calls them, who want to work for him.

Jack is a particularly dynamic, extremely smart, flirtatious kind of guy. He's tapped so many female colleagues' bottoms in his time that, really, it's a surprise he hasn't been locked away for sexual harassment by now. When I returned from holidays he would always ask if I sunbathed naked. *Not a stitch*, I would say in my bolder, less responsible days. But he's the only man I know who can get away with it; he is absolutely amazing and quite inspirational to work with. I wouldn't have put up with half the amount of professional crap he's given me over the years if it wasn't for his irresistible blend of brilliance and genuine warmth.

It sounds as though I quite fancy him, which I both do and don't. We've never actually had a thing, although we've always flirted madly. There's always been this energy, this buzz between us, but, sadly, it never goes any further than that. I haven't quite given up trying, enjoying the challenge in a competitive kind of way (and generally succumbing very easily to his charm and flattery), but it's probably better that we're not involved, given his relationship with womankind in general. Plus, there's Delilah.

Delilah Kashmir is as exotic-sounding as her name. Forty next year, always immaculate, happily, ostentatiously single, generally quite manic and a bit aggressive, rumour has it she's been happily sleeping with Jack for the last few years. I'd already left the company when she started, so have never seen them together for any lengthy period of time. I still find it hard to believe that Jack would keep anything going for more than a few weeks. He's a confirmed bachelor, never in a real relationship but rarely seen without a woman hanging on his arm, a different one each time, mostly taller than him, all beautiful, and only a very few as bright. If the rumours are true, which, seeing that media people like nothing better than gossip, isn't a given, then Delilah has lasted the longest and it's probably because she sits outside his office all day and can vet those walking through his door.

So here I am, smart and stylish and stuffed with toilet tissues, waiting in his PA's office hoping this will be the quickest meeting in history while talking puffy rubbish to Delilah.

"How are things?" she says, sounding genuinely interested. God, she's good.

"Oh fine, Ben is well, only just started school but enjoying it."

"Time goes by too fast," she says brightly. "I remember when you had to bring him with you when he was just a baby. You left him on the boardroom table during the meeting and talked over him. And then you had to breastfeed in front of Jack because he started to cry."

"Breastfeed Ben, you mean, not Jack." I might be intimidated, but I'm not above the occasional little jibe, however disgusting it may be.

Delilah laughs raucously, not thrown by my comment, but before she has a chance to speak Jack walks out, looking more tired than the last time I saw him, a bit plumper and balder. His face is serious — what's this? Am I imagining more lines? — but when he sees me, he breaks into a grin.

"Caroline Gray. And what do you want?"

Jack likes to appear scatty to make the other person talk. Eventually, they slip up to make a point and Jack swoops in. Sort of shakes their foundations a bit. But it's not working with me, I know how to play him by now. Never sycophantic but always polite. Don't flatter him needlessly but flirt like mad and you'll get his respect. It's always a bit of a mental salsa when we first meet. Today he seems a little quieter, though, not up to his usual tricks.

"How are things, Ms Gray?" he says, showing me into his oversized glass and chrome office with a five-foot plasma screen, a huge glass-top desk and oversized executive black leather chair, which he likes to swivel on very fast, especially when he gets angry or excited or both. One day he swivelled the chair right out if its socket, fell over and cracked a rib. I can't help giggling at the memory. One of these days he'll go flying out the window. The walls are plastered with photos of him skiing, surfing, paragliding, snow-kiting, sailing, snowboarding and free-falling. Still no pictures of any women in his life, past or present, I'm pleased to see.

"I'm fine, thanks, Ben too. Everything's going well," I say. On a day like today and a week like this one, I have to lie. I don't have time to go into all that *and* cram in a visit to Boots. So, I'm fine.

Jack looks at me curiously.

"Have you got a man in your life, Ms Gray?" he says, tilting his head slightly to the side as though sizing up my mood as well as my outfit.

"Apart from Ben, no." I mirror his head tilt and smile back innocently.

Jack leans across the desk, almost eyeballing me, and asks me pointedly but more quietly, "Miss the sex?" There's the old Jack now, I note with relief.

"Terribly," I reply mockingly.

"Is it true divorced women are the best lays?" he asks, almost laughing now.

"I don't know. I've never slept with one. You tell me."

He leans back. He thinks he's made me nervous talking about sex, but no. Well done, Caroline.

"OK. Right. Here's the brief," he says, handing me a pile of paperwork. "There are two directors we potentially want on the board. They are both qualified up to the eyeballs. Cambridge and Yale. Masters degrees, diplomas, multilingual, references from heads of states."

"They look pretty good on paper," I say, looking in awe at the glowing references.

"Quite. But I want to know if I can work with them. After the guy we almost hired last year until you said he was hiding something — I can't have that happening again. He's working for our competitor."

I flash him a modest smile, but secretly I'm thrilled. Not everyone takes that side of my profession seriously, and it's nice that Jack — a businessman down to the core — always puts such faith in my reports.

"I'm not always right, but there was something strange that time, yes," I say, finally putting down the papers and giving Jack my undivided attention. "I need the usual — samples of their handwriting, in pencil, something relatively lengthy. Ideally I need more than one or two sentences."

"Not much handwriting going on these days, unfortunately." He spins round to point briefly at his computer as if to emphasise the comment, then does another 180 degrees to face me again. "But we got them to fill something in to get their security badges." He hands me another folder. I sneak a peek at my watch. Business over for now, Jack smiles at me thoughtfully and leans back in his chair.

"You know, I don't think you've ever checked out my writing, have you?" he asks conversationally.

"I dread to think what it would reveal. And you've never given me anything to look at — so perhaps you have something to hide. Plus, I'd have to charge you for an analysis."

"I'll pay you."

"You really want me to?" I'm not keen.

"Yes, why not? Mind you, I may have to pay you more to keep it quiet."

I laugh obediently. I'm getting a bit antsy now. I should really be going soon.

"OK, forget the paying, I was just kidding. It's got to be a complete sentence. Preferably two," I say.

126

Jack grabs a pencil and starts to swivel. Pencil in mouth, he looks pensively up at the portraits of himself skiing, sailing, windsurfing, looking manically happy. Suddenly he starts to scribble.

"Do doodles tell you anything?" he asks absentmindedly as he writes. "There, see what you make of that," he says, looking up and handing over the piece of paper: *Ms Gray. You are my favourite yummy mummy, the most delightful creature. It's always been a considerable pleasure seeing you in my office. But you look ever so slightly frazzled today. Everything OK?*

I smile, salivating at the compliments, but I don't think I'll go into the details about time of the month and the one hundred and one errands I've got to run today. If only I had a Delilah in my life.

"Oh, I'm fine." Again. "Just a lot going on at the moment, with friends and family," I explain, trying to sound convincing.

"How about your ex? Can he help with Ben?"

What planet does he live on?

"He's the last person I'd talk to, or my mother, for that matter," I say, slightly more emphatically than I intended.

He leans over and reaches for my hand, patting it in an uncharacteristic gesture of comfort rather than sexually infused flirtation. "So it's still fairly awkward, is it?"

I smile noncommittally and look down at his note, absent-mindedly circling letters, ticking off boxes. The

Jack Stone warmth always comes out when you least expect it.

"So? What do you see?" Another Jack Stone smile. His letters are rounded and loose and flowing, but a bit jerky in places. Inconsistent in style. His "g"s and "y"s have very elongated tails. Pressure is firm and even, but in places he looks as though he has lost control of the pencil.

I look up.

"That bad, eh?" he says worriedly.

"No. No. You're creative and imaginative, but you like to put on a front, are more reserved than you would naturally be. To some people you may come across as cold, when really you're not."

"Can you tell that from the writing or are you just saying that because you know me?"

"Admittedly it's more difficult to be objective in this case, but on a first meeting I'd say you come across as a bit of an arrogant, up-your-own arse, intellectual snob, so the handwriting makes a much better first impression than the man."

He laughs.

"The pressure you have on the pencil is even, except in some places, where you seem to lose control of the structure of the letters altogether. Have you been drinking or something?"

He laughs again.

"Anything else?"

I evaluate his "r"s thoughtfully.

"You're not into men are you?" I say jokingly. I look up to catch Jack's horrified expression.

"Calm down, Jack, just a joke." So you *can* get a rise out of him after all. Good to know there's a button to push. And I hadn't known Jack had a homophobic streak. Those "r"s are a bit flowery, but that could also be a sign of issues with his mother.

Jack clears his throat and jogs me out of my rumination. He stands up. "Well, I think that's enough. I'm creative, imaginative and analytical and you think I have some gay tendencies. What a morning, thanks."

God, Gray, must learn to engage brain before opening mouth. But sometimes I just go into work mode and it comes out.

"Call Del when you have details of those two regional directors. And put in a date for lunch in November, December, would you? Just the two of us, catching up?" A slight pause, then: "Have you ever read your own handwriting, Caroline?"

I laugh, trying to dispel the last remnants of awkwardness. "No, I haven't actually, but it's changed a lot over the years."

"Like you," he agrees. "You seem much more confident, happier and calmer in yourself, with yourself, since you divorced."

I'm a bit irritated. "You're the second person who's said that to me recently. That I'm happy." Did it really have to take a divorce to get me there?

"I've seen you unhappy, blistering emotionally, so I know what you're like. You're good to have around these days."

He doesn't seem 100 per cent himself today, but before I can insist that he tell me what's wrong, he hugs

129

me, holding on to me not in a sexual or flirtatious way. More fatherly, which I find rather touching. He pats my back a bit like I pat Ben's when he's been sobbing hard and needs to know he's loved. I think, but I'm not sure, I feel him gently nuzzle my neck as though he wants to kiss me. Now that, as welcome as it might be ordinarily, freaks me out a bit. All our flirting aside, we've never crossed that line and it's never wise to mix business and pleasure. Also, I'm sure Delilah will find out one day. Sarah, Karin and Rose Johnson pale next to her, in the nicest possible way.

He gently disentangles himself.

I pull away quickly. "Good to see you, Jack."

As I leave the office, I kiss Delilah on both cheeks. I'm sure she, if anyone, can cure Jack of his dark moods. Me, I've got to get home and do today's action list of shopping, cleaning, phoning, cooking, ironing, more phoning, organising and bill paying before I collect Ben and take him to karate, or is it tennis or swimming today? And I think Jennifer is coming round for tea after that. Or is it Emma from swimming class? Can't remember. I hope I will by the time I get home.

As I'm leaving the building I notice that traffic is particularly bad this morning. A warm September has turned into October drizzle and it's raining and grey. I'm so pleased I don't have to commute to Jack's office every day any more. Getting up at six in the morning, waiting like some automaton at the train station for a train I could never get a seat on, pressed up against armpits that smelt as though they hadn't seen a shower in weeks. And the points failures and the derailed trains and the bankers with flatulence and ego and girth problems and the bundle to get off the other side, trying not to look at anyone in the face for fear he would snarl or, even worse, smile at you. Which inevitably meant he had to be a pervert. That early in the morning no one smiles.

I used to work until eleven some evenings just to avoid the rush and Jack would get his chauffeur to drive me home, all the way to Chetley. He always said if I worked beyond eight I could order a cab to take me home and he never reneged on that agreement. That's the kind of nice boss he is, and I've always, beneath our banter, had a soft spot for Jack. He's seen me single, married, pregnant and divorced; he was kind and thoughtful pre-Ben and post-Ben. When I started to have contractions in one of the board meetings he demanded I go to the hospital straight away, and when I said no, I would be fine, he asked his secretary to at least put the kettle on, just in case. Thinking of that makes me smile.

Lost in thought, I turn the corner rather more energetically then I wanted to and am blinded by what looks like a huge sunbed lamp, those extra-strong ones that are supposed to make your face browner than the rest of your body — although I've never understood the logic of this myself. For a second I flail, seeing stars and I trip up over something. I take a few stumbling steps forward and land flat on my face, letting out a yelp. Not loud enough to be a full-blown scream and not insignificant enough to be a sigh either. Just a yelp. Why would someone leave ropes in the middle of the pavement?

I can hear someone shouting.

"Who let a punter through? Who let the fucking punter through?"

As I try to get to my feet, I feel a hand on my arm lifting me up. A tanned face with bright blue eyes and pushed-through-a-bush-backwards, light brown hair stares at me, slightly bemused, slightly concerned, and grins. I have a hard time focusing through the spots in my vision. But definitely male.

"I hope you don't mind, you seem to be having difficulties."

The man, he must be in his late thirties, continues to smile at me, surveying my face, perhaps looking for injuries.

I try to be gracious, despite the humiliating situation.

"Thank you. Do you often have strange women falling at your feet?"

I'm blushing, I think, but perhaps it's just early menopause or the fact that I remember all of a sudden that I'm still in search of a Boots.

He ignores my question.

"My pleasure."

I find his direct look disconcerting and I'm still slightly unclear about the ropes, which I can see now are a mass of thick black and brown cables. The huge sunbed lamp still looks like a huge sunbed lamp, but there are about six of them all over this part of the pavement. Hmm. Several people are standing around, looking at me, some smiling, others scowling, but all of them looking at their watches, back at me, then at their watches again. There's a girl, almost as petite as Karin Blunt but much younger, with a clipboard and a cigarette. The man next to her seems stressed and angry and is smoking vigorously while staring me down, his expression more of a grimace than anything else.

He's standing behind a large camera and it suddenly dawns on me, shit, I'm on TV. I'm in one of those live documentaries, a reality TV show, perhaps a crimewatch show, and they've been stalking someone and I've literally just burst in on them and screwed up the whole thing. I feel mortified. I turn to my rescuer, who is still by my side, open my mouth to apologise, but before I can say anything, he says, "I know this sounds like an awful cliché, but do I know you from somewhere?"

My rescuer is a creep. I take one step backwards, wanting to regain some composure. We're standing very close together and according to that *Cosmopolitan* I read at the dentist last week (I was in there for ages), we should have either hit or kissed each other by now.

"I don't think so," I say, feeling myself go red.

"Aren't you Caroline Scrope?"

Who the hell is this guy?

"Err, yes."

"Did you go to Greenwood High?"

"Yes." What is this? It's a small world after all?

"I'm Peter Bishop. I was in your year."

I'm trying to think. Peter Bishop. Peter Bishop. No clue. Bugger, and slightly embarrassing because he so clearly remembers me and I'm equally certain I've never laid eyes on the man. What is it with me recently? Between meeting Toby Shepherd and now this guy, I'll probably turn a corner and Rose bitch Johnson will turn up selling the *Big Issue*.

"Were you always called Peter Bishop?" I finally say, wanting to be polite and dispel the awkwardness, but needing to clarify a few things first.

He smiles, slightly confused.

I feel stupid.

"Of course you were, yes, well, I'm really sorry, I would love to say I remember but honestly I'm blanking."

"Pete!" The grimacing chain-smoker gestures for him to get back to the set now that the main show is over. "Will you stop chatting up the pretty lady and get on with the shoot? The client isn't paying us a lot of money for this kind of thing, you know." The girl with the clipboard follows him, both of them puffing furiously.

Chain-smoker turns to me and attempts to change the grimace to a smile. No such luck.

"Hi, I'm Matt Diamond. This is Lizzie."

He introduces the chain-smoking girl next to him, who at least manages a real smile. I'm still recoiling at the memory of my ungraceful fall but before I can say anything to repair the situation, he continues.

"We're shooting a commercial. I'm so sorry, were you hurt? Our insurance will cover it if need be. Lizzie," he barks. "Call the insurance."

Lizzie is now smoking even faster than she was a few seconds ago. Managing to get a "yes" out between puffs, she looks at me critically, trying to gauge the extent of my injury. "Yes, yes, yes, yes, yes." She spits out the affirmatives like rifle shots.

"Good, good, good, good, good," Matt Diamond replies, as though responding in kind or code. Weird lot these advertising types.

They're both surveying me now, expecting an introduction. Thank God I always make such an effort when I see Jack. I hope there's still a smidgen of eye make-up in place after running around today.

"This is Caroline Scrope, we knew each other at school," says Peter Bishop, still valiantly trying to get me to remember the name, the face, anything.

"School, huh?" says Matt, still looking me up and down.

"Well, I don't really remember him, actually," I say, all innocent honesty. I did try to spare Peter Bishop the embarrassment, but he doesn't seem to want it any other way.

"Trying to pull again, Pete?" Matt laughs derisively and Peter turns red. "Honestly, these cameramen. They have one on every shoot, you know. Every shoot. Just didn't expect you to pick up a punter."

In a last effort, Peter asks, "Do you remember Mr Boniface? Biology?"

"Yes, course I do. God, you really were at Greenwood High."

He smiles, a hint of triumph in his eyes as he shoots Matt a glance.

"And do you remember Toby Shepherd?"

This makes me go cold. What did he say? Toby was already a not-too-welcome blast from the past and only a few weeks ago I was walking through his house. And now this guy turns up mentioning Toby? Weird. All I say is, albeit a bit feebly, "You know Toby Shepherd?"

"I work with him back at the agency. He's in creative."

"Right. Right. Right," I say, realising I'm starting to repeat myself like the chain-smoker. "And we were all at school together."

He looks hopeful.

OK, this has gone on for way too long. I'm done with this conversation. I brush myself down and smile around the group. Perhaps I'm having a brainstorm or got knocked on my head when I fell over. Better not say that, though. Lizzie will have a fit.

"Right, let's move. Jerry's waiting to do his bit," says Matt, tapping his watch and turning to nod at a man standing a few yards from us. The man who must be Jerry has big hair, a face bright orange with make-up and is dressed in a green and pink flowery shirt paired with tight cream jeans and, for some reason, what look like riding boots. He looks very cold and very cross and very effeminate. Matt turns back to us.

"Fucking ego-tripper. Him and an injury suit," he waves his hands at me, "that's all I fucking need today. This Jerry is nothing more than a has-been TV presenter who hasn't even done soap. Try to do the best you can, Pete. His eyes are too close together and his skin is crap. We need more powder." He suddenly shouts over to a diminutive woman, the make-up assistant. He points to Jerry's cheeks and forehead, mouthing "Too shiny." She hustles to fix him up.

"Great, we've got a shiny pink presenter. We've got a shiny, big-haired, pink presenter. Why am I always the one who gets them? Why? Why? Why? Why? Why?"

I want to laugh. I've never met anyone quite so manic as this man. Not even Heather at her most irritable or Jack at his most stressed or Ben at his most needy. I don't think Matt wants an answer and, in any case, I absolutely must get to Boots before the school run. And Jack's uncharacteristic sombreness is still niggling at me, and now there's Peter Bishop with his warm smile still playing around his mouth. He seems nice. But who the fuck is Peter Bishop?

"Sorry about that. Matt is under a lot of pressure today," Peter now says apologetically.

I take a last good look at him. He's dressed in jeans, T-shirt and cord jacket, all slightly baggy and stylishly scruffy. He wears them well, looking masculine rather than macho, confident rather than arrogant. His voice is soft — gentle but not timid. Husbands in Frencham dress either in suits, ready for the office, or smart casual, ready for any sailing or golf weekend that might come along. I've kind of forgotten that men are actually able to look normal. He's got bracelets of coloured cotton around his wrists, which I think are friendship bracelets. I had them when I was ten, but grew out of them by eleven. Perhaps he's a hippy? I sniff for a hint of joss stick, but nothing.

He looks at me curiously and I'm aware that he's waiting for me to say something.

"What's the commercial for?" I say hurriedly. Why am I lingering here? I need to go, have things to do.

"Life insurance, would you believe it." He smiles towards Lizzie. "Well, she was supposed to be keeping the street cleared."

"Oh right," I say, looking round at Lizzie, who is lighting cigarettes for both her and her boss. "I'm fine, though, ego just a bit bruised."

"Oh, we've got more than enough of those around here." More hesitantly: "Well, good to see you again. If you want to meet over a coffee to catch up, let me know."

Poor guy. But how can I possibly reminisce with someone I can't remember? He must have been completely innocuous at school, invisible. But why would he have hung out with Toby Shepherd? I don't really care any more, but out of politeness I say, "Yes, that would be lovely."

He smiles and starts patting his pockets. His face drops.

"Shit, I forgot my cards. Have you got a pen? I'll give you my number."

I feel ever so slightly on show here. Matt and Lizzie are furiously smoking just a few yards away and Jerry, hair starting to visibly frizz in the drizzle, looks as though he's going to burst into tears any second. Everyone in the crew — cameramen, sound men, director, Lizzie, presenter — is now waiting for me to leave the shoot and I'm scrabbling about to get this guy's number. I find pen and paper. Well, one of Ben's crayons and the back of one of The Sycamore's PTA notes.

Peter Bishop 07769 69696.

I look at the paper and laugh. "Good number. Bet no one forgets that," I say, my good humour somewhat restored.

"Yeah, believe it or not — I didn't choose it. Anyway, I have to go. See you around."

"Yes, bye."

As I walk away I sneak a look over my shoulder. Peter has joined the others and is heaving a large camera on to his shoulder. Absent-mindedly, just before I pop down into the tube station, I admire the effortless way he's shouldering the enormous thing. Surely he isn't gay? Media types can be, I'm told. Wonder if he lives in London or commutes, if he's married or single, or has a girlfriend? Damn, I know Heather would have had all that information out of him by now. What he did, where he lived, favourite colour, music, films, country, car, whether he's married, divorced, separated, single. She'd know the lot. Me? All I do is fall all over the place, have an inane conversation with a chain-smoking wanker called Matt and I can't for the life of me even remember a Peter Bishop in Mr Boniface's class.

Now, Boots.

CHAPTER NINE

A Date on Thursday

"Go for it!"

I've made the huge mistake of telling Heather and Eva about my meeting with Jack on Wednesday, and then about bumping into Peter Bishop. We're drinking cappuccinos at the Sycamore Café, waiting for the school bell with the other mums. We've got the usual suspects up at the top table and a smattering of others sitting and chatting peacefully. Whispering furiously to keep the details from the mafia's big ears, we have started dissecting my love life.

Or lack of it, I should say. Which, I think is just fine, thank you very much, but the girls don't go for that. Heather is adamant that Jack fancies me but is fighting against it and she is convinced that if Peter works in the media he must be gay. Eva thinks Jack's gorgeous, so should be the priority, but if I decide against it I should definitely call Peter. Unlike myself, they *do* seem to remember him, though, so they're a step ahead of me.

"Wasn't he the one hanging around with Toby Shepherd?" says Eva, frowning into her cup as if she could divine any more information from the dregs.

"Yes, he was," replies Heather, licking off the froth from her top lip. Out of the corner of my eye I see Karin frown, delicately so as not to ruin her latest injections, at Heather's table manners. Heather goes on blithely. "He was really quiet, but kind of cute too if you were generously inclined, and very clever. Sort of creative and strong. Bit too quiet for me, but if he wasn't gay he might have suited you down to the ground, Caroline."

"Heather, not *all* media types are gay," I say, aware that the last part of Heather's sentence has caused a few more ears to prick up in the café. My statement doesn't help, though.

"You'd be surprised. I'm telling you."

"Toby Shepherd is married with kids, Heather," Eva puts in.

"Don't be so bloody naive. Marriage is a perfect smoke-screen. Secretly, most men want to be fucked up the arse."

Fucked up the arse wafts across the café like a bad smell. Silence descends on the café and all mafia heads slowly turn round. The buzz of chatter from the non-mafia mums on the premises becomes a careful hum, pitched at just the right level not to miss any more of this. I narrow my eyes at Heather.

"Keep your voice down. Do you want to drag us all down with you?"

She does this kind of thing just for show, I'm absolutely convinced of that, and she loves shockers.

"Well they do. I've made up my mind. Forget Peter. He's a poof."

"You're so weird, Heather. In any case, I can't 'forget' him when I haven't even been thinking about him. That's the whole point. I can't remember the guy. Apart from that, he seemed genuine and nice, and, well, straight."

"Forget him." Heather was dismissive. "He's cute and creative but probably poor to boot. Jack sounds much more your type. Successful, rich, determined, rich, single, no kids, rich, sexy, rich, has known and worked with you and liked you a long time. Ideal. He's not divorced? Never married. He could be gay, too, of course. Does he look damaged? People who've just got divorced look damaged."

Heather has gone completely off her mind. Gleeful at having successfully shocked the mafia out of their complacency, she's holding forth without giving her audience — Eva and me — another thought. I leave her to it and try to continue a normal conversation with Eva.

"Jack just didn't seem quite himself. And thanks for the information on divorced people looking damaged." I throw Heather an indignant look. "Didn't know I did."

Eva is soothing.

"Oh, you don't look damaged now, Caroline. Honest you don't. Anyway, if Jack's not gay, maybe you *should* go for him. He's a known quantity and you need someone uncomplicated in your life. He sounds perfect for that."

He's always charmed the trousers off both Heather and Eva, so I don't think they are objective enough to seriously evaluate Jack's relationship potential. And now isn't a good time to bring up Delilah either. Heather would probably start offering advice about how to get rid of her and the mafia ears are already on red alert. I think they have enough gossip to survive the week.

Across the table, Heather seems to have simmered down and now rejoins our whispered discussion. "And he's so bloody gorgeous." They both sigh. Heather gets businesslike again. "Apart from all this, find someone who will put you first and won't dump on you."

"You're one to talk — look at that blind date you set me up on. If my best friend can't get it right, who can?"

"Oh yes, Michael — but that's ages ago now." Heather is evasive.

Now I'm on a roll. "Yes, ages — thanks for reminding me that my love life is complete shit — and that guy, I've been meaning to tell you, was a prat. He was a prat. A prat," I say, realising belatedly that I'm starting to sound like the manic director.

Heather is apologetic. "Well, he can be a bit tactless perhaps, that's all."

"Tactless? He said I *didn't meet his expectations*. He used those exact words. I felt as though I was some employee being dressed down in one of his bloody board meetings. Wish I'd read his handwriting before I'd accepted the date. Prat."

Eva cuts in. "I'm confused. Who is this Michael?"

"He's someone Harvey works with." Heather is dismissive. "Charming, good-looking. Nice eyes. And he took Caroline to La Marque over in Balham."

Eva whistles.

"Food was nice?" Heather enquires conversationally.

"Mostly fish and stuff."

"But you hate fish."

"Yes I do."

"You told him?"

"Yes I did. He forgot."

She's making me lose focus. "Point is, Heather, a) I don't want to have a relationship, really, and b) if I did, I've got too little time to weed through potential guys, and c) you can't bully me into meeting someone even you haven't vetted properly." She looks sheepish, so I soften. I need to keep my voice down as well. Mafia heads are craning again. Should we ask them to join our table so they won't need physio for their neck strain?

"I agree, this Michael seemed perfect on the outset, Heather. And the date started out fine. I dropped off Ben with John — by the way, Suzanne has now opened the door to me for the fifth time running." I make a face. "OK, so we took a long walk around town and he kept looking into my eyes and saying how beautiful I was. Inevitably we drank a lot and ate very little, you know, when it makes you feel decidedly faint all evening. And then," I pause a little for dramatic effect, "we had sex, which, in hindsight, was just as well, as the conversation had rapidly deteriorated. A bit weird, my first time after John, but I was buzzed and feeling romantic and it just happened."

Heather perks back up at that. "Good?" she enquires, in much the same tone she'd asked about the food.

"Well, you spend so much time looking at each other that everything comes under intense scrutiny and he was a perfectionist — I felt I was on a mission to keep up appearances in and out of my clothes. And sex was like the Olympics, one big gymnastics display."

"Prat," says Eva.

"Exactly," I say.

"I think that sounds fun," says Heather excitedly. "So what went wrong?"

"Well, what really freaked me out was that he seemed to be thinking long term before we'd even got past the first weekend. Told me about his work and his mum and his hopes for the next five years."

"Nothing wrong with having a five-year plan," Eva interrupts.

"Well, maybe not, but it didn't turn out to include me anyway. At first, he showered me with flowers and gifts, which was nice, if a bit heavy, and we went out for another date, but his interest waned pretty quickly when he saw my normal life, the one where you don't constantly wear party clothes and can't always jump into bed with each other at the end of the night. The third night, a couple of weeks later, he finally started to come out with it — that I didn't really meet his expectations after all, it looked like we had separate lives, etc."

"Prat," Eva says again. "What did you do then?"

I lower my voice even further, aware the mafia have fallen silent, staring into mid-air as though in a semi-trance-like state.

"I invited him back home for a coffee and changed into something Paul Smith — a sexy and transparent number. Lit scented candles, doused myself in oils, opened some champagne and had the fire blazing, you know, the works. And then I dropped him like a brick."

"And then?" Heather leans forward eagerly.

"What did he say?" Eva whispers.

"Nothing, he wasn't really able to speak. I told him I was sorry, and if he stayed I would just be using him for sex and it wouldn't be fair on him." The girls are impressed. We huddle close and the café is now so quiet I can hear myself breathe. "Then he said, 'Why don't we give all this another try?'"

"What a wanker," Heather interrupts loudly. "Try indeed."

The café hums briefly at Heather's *wanker*, as though bees have been disturbed in their hive, but all quietens again.

"And I smile and say, 'I'm sorry, but this is for the best. I would just be using you. And you're worth more than that and so am I.'"

Eva claps her hands in delight.

It wasn't quite so funny at the time, but re-enacting it for Heather and Eva makes me laugh myself, thinking about it again.

Heather offers to get more coffee. I decline, I feel too jacked up as it is. Eva says yes to just one more. Black this time.

With Heather safely out of the way, Eva leans over.

"Why don't you call Peter Bishop? What's the harm? You haven't been out with anyone properly for ages." I cringe, as she pats my hand. "No time like the present," she assures me. "Why don't you do it now?" Her voice has a bit of a hypnotic undertone, it must have, there is no other explanation for why I find myself agreeing with her.

She's right. He was nice. It wouldn't do me any harm to go on another date. And if I don't do it now, I won't do it at all. And no place like the present: the Sycamore Café, enemy territory full of busybody mafia mums, and I'm about to call Peter Bishop. Great. This is the mafia's lucky day.

I find the piece of paper with my crayon scrawl. 07769 69696. That's the number. Now do I text or call?

"Texting will look cowardly," suggests Eva, "but it might be safer and doesn't give as much away. Calling is more, well, more adult, but also more risky. I think you should call."

OK. Call. Call. 07769 69696.

Ring. Ring. Ring.

No answer, great. This voicemail will click in any moment. And then what?

Ring. Ring. Ring.

"No answer," I say with a huge sense of relief, pulling the phone away from my ear.

"Wait till the machine clicks in," says Eva, pressing the phone to my ear again.

Damn, she can be quite forceful if she puts her mind to it.

Perhaps he doesn't have a voicemail and I'll be sitting here waiting endlessly. Perhaps he remembers me and won't pick up. Ridiculous, he wouldn't recognise my number. Perhaps he's on a shoot with the wanker Matt and I've just disturbed his concentration. Perhaps he's with the girlfriend. Or the boyfriend. Having sex, precoital or post-coital, with or without strawberries in hand. Perhaps he's died or is dying somewhere and can't reach the phone, it's just out of hand's reach. Perhaps he's stranded on a —

Someone answers.

"Hello?"

Oh good, he's alive. But now that he's answered, some reply is required immediately. I feel myself blushing. Heather returns with coffees, crowding around me curiously until Eva ushers her to another table to give me some privacy. We're creating quite a stir again, especially since Heather is looking furious, clearly saying, "But I want to listen."

I see Eva whispering heatedly as she restrains Heather on a small chair which looks like it's about to collapse. The hum restarts and I silently thank Eva for diverting the attention away from me.

The kind voice on the phone says, for the third time I think, "Hello?"

Now, whatever I do, I mustn't start off with "I don't know if you remember me, but . . ." It sounds weak and entirely inappropriate, given the circumstances.

"Hi, it's Caroline. Remember me?" I say, trying desperately to sound confident and natural at the same time.

"Caroline Scrope. Yes, of course. Do you finally know who I am?"

"No, I still don't," I say lamely, casting around for anything else to say, something clever and sparkly to add to what promises to be another humiliating scene involving Peter Bishop. "But I'm intrigued." Well done. I think.

"Intrigued, huh?" I can almost hear him smiling on the other end, can picture that warm grin. This is going uncharacteristically well. "I could be an axe murderer or a psychopath."

"No, no, I'd recognise a psychopath. My ex was one — albeit a functional one. By the way, I'm now Caroline Gray." Maybe that was too much? I laugh. Brief nervous pause. I better say something else. Before I do, though, he speaks.

"So, do you fancy a drink some time?"

There's no harm in just having a drink. I'll choose home territory, just in case I need to make a quick getaway, and I'm sure my mum will babysit Ben, although I don't want her knowing that I'm going out on a date. Or is this even a date in the true definition of the term? Not really, actually. It's just a drink with an old school chum. A trip down memory lane.

"That would be lovely. Can you come to me? I live in Frencham."

"Yeah, sure. I'm only in Hammersmith, so not too far. How about Thursday?"

"This Thursday?"

"Yes, this Thursday."

"Wow, that's soon," I say, inanely. You wouldn't believe I was a thriving businesswoman by day, juggling

149

career and kid with an expert, organised hand. Maybe this was a bad idea. But no chance to turn back now.

"Do you know The Chestnut, on the top of Frencham Hill? About seven? I'll wear a red carnation just in case you don't recognise me," I say jokingly.

Brief pause again. Then he says, "Sounds good, see you then."

"Bye."

I click off. Almost immediately, Heather and Eva sit down on either side of me, coffees in hand.

I take a few deep breaths, click my phone on and off again, just to make sure. That seems to have gone well. At least I've got a date. Well, not a date, strictly speaking. More a reunion? Perhaps I should log on to that website Friends Together to see if he's on there or if anyone else can remember him. At least I might be able to find out if he's married, although not that he'd put it on if he was a philanderer.

"*Well*?" says Heather, looking at me as though expecting me to give gory details of phone sex.

"We're meeting this Thursday in The Chestnut."

She looks hopeful. "And?"

"And what?"

"And do you know anything about him? Like is he married, unhappily married, single, with girlfriend, single dad, rich? Did you talk about school, what he's doing now, where he lives, anything?"

"I'm not you, Heather," I say defensively, although she does have a point. "We're meeting this Thursday at the pub and all I know is that he lives in Hammersmith and that's it."

Heather is just about to speak when Karin Blunt walks up to the table in a cloud of sweet-smelling perfume and coughs to draw our attention.

"Hello, ladies. How are you all?" she says, managing to barely move her lips and still give off the smallest hint of smile. "Everything all right?" She gives me an encouraging look, as if to invite an explanation about our hissed conversation and game of musical chairs.

"The ladies are fine," says Heather, reciprocating the superficial smile.

I still haven't forgotten her interrogating me about John and the divorce at Sarah Flint's play date. What bad taste. Sarah isn't as strong as she makes out and there's a vulnerability about her and an insecurity that make her more human. Not more likeable, perhaps even less so, but more normal in a way. Karin, on the other hand, makes me nervous and guarded. She is all spite and manipulation, hovering at the back like a menacing presence, and the fact that even when standing up her face is just about level with mine sitting down is simply freaky. In a few years time Ben will be as tall as she is.

"I know it's only October, ladies, but we're already organising the Christmas Fair, which as you know makes the school thousands of pounds each year." She smiles brightly around the room.

Heather nods reluctantly. Although the careful money management is something she's secretly immensely proud of, she doesn't want to be caught in a conversation with the mafia any longer than absolutely necessary.

151

"Right, well, we need volunteers. I doubt if you will have time to help out, ladies, but if you see anything you would like to do, just put your names down." Will she stop with the avuncular *ladies*? It's making me grind my teeth and I can see Eva's smile showing signs of strain.

Karin clearly notices that she's overstaying her welcome and without further ado she hands me a clipboard with three sheets of paper and what looks like a timetable. Underneath a list of jobs, all typed, in bold and underlined — cake stand, drinks, toy stand, Father Christmas, gnomes, elves, pixies, tombola, hot-dogs and hamburgers and so on — there are time slots from three to six. A few names have been handwritten in the boxes but most are empty.

"We've only just started approaching volunteers today," she adds, "and I know you never participate in things like these, but I thought before I hit the playground in earnest this afternoon I'd just double-check. I'm sure you're far too busy with designer shopping and entertaining your men friends to worry about insignificant things like the school's activities, but you never know." Next to me, Eva and Heather rear up in silent fury. I'm a bit stunned myself, unprepared for this full-frontal mafia assault after Sarah and Felicity and their cronies have always been quite friendly to me — even Karin has grimaced at me across the playground.

Smiling sweetly, Karin hands me the pen and I stare at her, my mouth slightly open. Is this *lady* for real?

Karin ignores my sharp intake of breath and just says, "I'll leave that with you, shall I, and you can just give it back to me in a second?" Triumphantly, she turns and heads for the round table, sitting down daintily next to ogreish Felicity and frowning Sarah. I expect Sarah to flash me her usual friendly smile, but she just looks over at us briefly, then huddles back into Karin, as though she was sent over to spy on enemy activity and is now reporting back. I think Sarah's gone off me. She hasn't really been talking to me at all these past few days. She usually waves at me, we exchange a few words, vague promises of our children playing together, but that all seems to have come to a grinding halt since the play date from hell. And Karin's performance just now seems to corroborate this. Which is absolutely fine by me, but it *is* slightly worrying to think what they might be up to now.

"They are nuts," I say, staring after her. "You were right, they're crazy."

Eva, who has now taken the clipboard from me and is busily surveying the list, grins mischievously. "Do you know what? Now that there's the three of us, why don't we actually do something this year?"

Heather is looking horrified. "Have you switched camps? It's enough that Caroline is on a play-date basis with them." That's not quite fair — she and Eva had the full low-down the same night and know perfectly well that I'd do anything never to have to do that again. "And it's enough that I have to endure their company during our PTA meetings. I'm not working with those women on a regular basis, Eva."

"But that's exactly what they expect, Heather. That's the only reason she came over here to needle us. She thinks we'd never do it. I think it depends on what we're doing — it could actually be fun."

She looks speculatively at the list. I can see her mind working and find myself relax. If Eva is taking matters in hand, it'll all work out fine.

"Anyone want to be an elf?"

Heather and I just look at Eva, who holds up her hands in appeasement.

"OK, OK, how about we work on the hot-dog and hamburger stall? If it's cold, we'll have the warmest place. Let's sign up for the whole event so we can really *own* the stall." Her eyes are sparkling. I shudder to think what Eva comes up with when she puts her mind to mischief. "Strength in numbers," Eva adds encouragingly.

Heather doesn't look convinced.

"In your own words, *fuck 'em*," Eva says.

We both look shocked because Eva doesn't say fuck much. Heather says it enough for the three of us.

"OK, here we go. Across the board, in ink so they can't erase us."

Eva is just finishing writing when I feel the hairs on my back prickle. I turn to find myself nose to nose with Karin again. She's crept up so quietly that I involuntarily jump.

"Have you finished with the clipboard?" she asks, looking slightly worried now that we may have actually offered to do something.

I regain my composure and smile warmly, pretending that Karin is Ben. I look her straight in the eyes, which takes her aback a bit. She must not be used to people staring her in the eye and smiling warmly.

I speak.

"Yes, we have, Karin, thank you. We are going to be running the hot-dog and hamburger stall for the duration of the fair."

Ridicule, dismissal, boredom. But *this*, this she had not expected. Karin looks shocked, verging on horrified. I see her glancing helplessly at Sarah and Felicity, who are practically hanging over the balustrade to hear what's going on.

"Really," she finally says feebly, "are you sure? The smells and all on your clothes, and —"

"Oh, we won't come in our nice stuff," Heather interrupts. "We'll wear what everyone else here usually does. That will be just fine."

I can't but reel slightly at Heather's brazen rudeness. How does she do it? Karin scowls at Heather, snatches the clipboard from Eva and returns to base. Furious whispers. Then I see her making her way over to some of the other tables. Eileen, the mum I met at the supermarket and seem to run into on a daily basis these days, has taken it all in with one glance and gives me a secret thumbs-up, pointing to the clipboard behind Karin's back and waggling two fingers in a barely perceptible salute.

I nod and roll my eyes, hiding a triumphant smile.

With a feeling of immense accomplishment — a call to Peter Bishop and a date, plus a put-down for the mafia — we leave the café. That's what you would call a successful day.

We slowly make our way up the hill, past a beady-eyed Alicia in her toyshop (I can see her picking up the phone as we walk by, but it might be entirely unrelated), and through the gates. Walking into the playground, I watch the other mums and a few dads, a lot of them standing restless and irritable, impatient to see their children, or perhaps just impatient to collect them and make the football, rugby, tennis, karate, mini musketeers, swimming or dancing clubs or the French, Italian or Spanish lessons that they need to play chauffeur for that day. My own mum greeted me very similarly when I left Ms Bocking's class each afternoon, looking similarly restless and irritable in her red lipstick.

Now I see Ben come out in a sea of others, I give him a huge smile and hug him tightly as he rushes into my arms, talking fast about needing tinned soup for the Harvest Festival and no, packet soup won't do, it must be tinned, and that Frank's just being horrid and will I never make him play with Patrick either, please. But could we invite Jennifer and Tom back with us? Edward's busy, otherwise he said he'd come too. (Thank God.) And he proudly shows me his grazed knee and tells me how Mrs Cox, the school secretary, put a huge plaster on his knee and said he was very brave. And how he helped with the register today and got a star, and that the caretaker, Mr Henry, doesn't just look after the school. Otto told him that the caretaker actually bought the school and the teachers are just allowed to live there while they teach.

I wave goodbye to Eva and Heather, giving them a final thumbs-up about our day, and then go back to listening to my son. On and on he chatters as we walk towards the car, all the things he's doing this moment and all the things he wants to do that evening and that week and this lifetime. I squeeze his hands and smile, because it makes everything — the juggling, the struggling, the putting up with Mum as a babysitter, facing the mafia, rushing around — worthwhile.

CHAPTER
TEN

Grandma

"I don't feel well," says Ben, looking at me as though he is mortally wounded and I'm making him carry his cross for five miles across the desert. "I don't feel well and you're leaving me."

"Ben, you're absolutely fine. Don't think I'm falling for this now."

It's Thursday, half-past five, and I've just picked Ben up from karate. He's still in his white suit and looks cute and lethal and very happy, practising his kicks in the living room, but once he hears that I'm going out tonight he changes tack so fast it's hard to keep up.

"I've got a tummy ache, Mummy." Big eyes blinking at me in anguish.

"You didn't have one a minute ago."

"I don't feel well."

I look at him for any signs of smirking or smiling or even the slightest glint of mischief in his face. Is he telling the truth? Shit. My first outing with a man since Michael the prat seems in danger already. Instinct tells me he's putting it on. A bit more subtly than last week, when he told me that he had cancer of the ankle and rabies as well and was going to die before teatime. And that his head would probably explode all over his bedroom and there would be a lot of blood and guts and I would have to clean it all up and then I'd be sorry.

Sighing, I send him to bathe and change, ignoring further protestations for the moment. I'm expecting Mum any moment now. She's late, probably delayed on the trains, which is just as well, giving me the chance for a quick tidy up, just to nip the inevitable conversation about the state of my house in the bud. I rifle through Ben's book bag, cleaning out an old banana peel and a smuggled Bay Blade toy. His bag always seems to bulge considerably more at the end of the day than when we leave the house in the morning because of the reams of paperwork the PTA sends back. Sarah seriously needs another outlet for her energy other than keeping that scarily immaculate house of hers, and terrorising the school with her Sisyphean search for perfection.

There's another note about the monthly meetings, which I think I will have to attend at some point when Ben and I have settled in. Sarah mentioned it once at the very beginning, but she hasn't asked me again. A blessing if anything, but her silence and newly cool stance make me both relieved and a bit uneasy. My eyes fall on paperwork about the Christmas Fair, Bonfire Night, the library, the petition to save our playing fields and the sponsored walk for saving the South American rain-forests, although I think sending out less paperwork would already be a small contribution.

I smile as I pull out a drawing Ben must have inadvertently taken from Marie's Tom, as it says both their names at the bottom. Quite handy with a pen, Tom. I squint at the complicated megastructure, trying to work out what tentacles reach out to grab which part of the monster. Ben has done some speech balloons with various roars to explain. Marie and Tom have turned out to be such a nice part of our social calendar, coming round regularly for playtime (which usually results in all sorts of wild adventures and colourful stories behind closed doors) and clandestine drinks (although we tend to start with tea).

I tip everything back in his bag, including the drawing. Must remind Ben to return that to Tom. Enough school stuff for today, though. So should I stay in, be a good mum, or go out and worry sick all evening? I want to look forward to my evening out. The doorbell goes. It's my mother. I shove a few things into the chest of drawers, straighten the sofa cushions and call for Ben to come downstairs. I make a quick decision. Even if he is unwell, at least he'll be with his grandmother. She's good with him. Still lousy with me, but good with him, and she will have a present for him which usually perks him up even when he thinks he is on his deathbed.

As I walk towards the door I'm bracing myself mentally. What mood will she be in? If she's had a good week, she will be funny and friendly and kiss me on both cheeks. If she's had a bad week, she will be morose and distracted and irritable. I haven't told her I'm going out on a date, or said anything much about

Peter at all, because she would ask even more questions about him than Heather did. Instead, I told her I have a work event with Jack, which I knew would make her say yes. She adores her grandson, of course, but she is also very much part of the Jack Stone fan club, dropping hint after hint that he is single and rich and available. On the odd occasion when we were all three in the same room, some Christmas do or other, she immediately sniffed out the on-and-off office flirtation. And was delighted.

If there's a possibility, however slim, that her daughter will marry someone even richer and more suitable second time round, Mum will do anything to support it. Plus, she's desperate to be able to talk about her offspring the way her tennis friends talk about theirs, all of whom, she tells me, are doing "well in the City". She'll say things like, "Charlie just got another promotion" and "Bella from next door married a banker", then sigh deeply and look as though she's about to burst into tears. Clearly, I'm still a major disappointment to her. Bless. And, inevitably, hopefully, she will ask how that nice Jack Stone is doing or if there is a "young man" in my life. I always tell her yes. His name is Ben.

I open the door, uttering one last quick prayer for a funny and friendly face. I can't deal with morose today. My mum is fidgeting on the doorstep, smiling at me expectantly. Thank God for that.

"Hello, darling." She peers round me for Ben, who is slowly shuffling down the stairs in his dressing gown.

From the pained look on his face I can tell he's mutinously keeping to his story.

I see my mum has a new red lipstick, which looks a bit dry. When she goes for my cheek, as though she's about to bite into it, the effect is a little like being brushed with a crusty loaf of bread.

I hug her back, a small price to pay for an evening out.

She quickly pulls back and looks me up and down critically. She's immaculate as ever, in a skirt and top that probably came from Marks & Spencer, hair neat — the beehive replaced by a neat loose bob — hmm, I wonder what made her change — and the same shrill, red mouth.

"Darling, you're not going out like that, are you? Is that what you're wearing? No tights? I always think tights are a must, otherwise one can look very slovenly. And Jack's always so perfectly turned out. And such a gentleman." She sighs.

I'm forty-one. Why the fuck, every time I am in my mum's company, do I suddenly feel fourteen? I turn my grimace into a contorted smile.

"I'm going to get ready in a minute. Ben's only just come back from karate. By the way, he says he's not feeling well, bit of a tummy ache, but I don't think it's too serious, so I thought I'd go anyway. Is that OK?"

My mum seems to completely ignore what I'm saying and walks past me, dropping her small suitcase and a plastic bag just inside the door.

"Where's my best boy then?" she trills. "Where's the best little boy in the whole wide world?"

The best little boy in the whole wide world comes out from behind me, grinning like the Cheshire cat. It's Granny and Granny means only one thing. Well, two actually. Granny means a long tight squeeze and a kiss on both cheeks, lasting for about thirty seconds. And then — a *present*. The body lock is worth the present and Ben endures it with good grace. Thirty seconds later, he looks up at his granny expectantly.

"Guess what? Grandma has bought you a present."

I have to laugh as Ben affects a look of complete surprise worthy of an Oscar. I think Mrs Hartnell could really do something with him. His eyes are wide open and hands up in the air in a gesture of overwhelmed bewilderment.

"Oh really, Granny? Thank you so much." Then a quick, "Where is it?"

I give him a look. *Don't push it.*

He adds a "Where is it, *please*, Granny?"

I hide a smile as my mum starts rifling through the plastic bag, giving me a brief look as if to say "You haven't picked up my suitcase yet?"

She emerges with a large oblong box and I can already see a Power Ranger figure, a black one. My first thought is shit, he's got the black one already, we'll have to exchange it at the local toyshop. My second thought is how to communicate that to Ben? My mum places much importance on things like gratitude and appreciation and I couldn't stand the funny and friendly woman turning morose after all. I give him a stern look as Mum hands it to him.

"Here you are, darling. I think you like these, don't you?"

Ben looks at it with a lot less enthusiasm than a few seconds earlier, but thank God for the nativity plays and drama clubs we've had to endure together since he was able to walk and talk. He puts on a look of sheer delight and hugs his granny again. Over her shoulder he mouths to me silently, "I've got this one already."

"I know," I mouth back. "We'll get you another one in the toyshop."

He smiles. Mum smiles. I smile. Great. Everyone happy.

Mum, delighted that her gift has now guaranteed her Ben's devoted love for at least the rest of the evening, proceeds into the sitting room, the two of us trailing behind her like groupies. Looking Ben firmly in the eyes, she says, "Now what is it I hear about a tummy ache? Now if I make you a nice shepherd's pie with lovely fresh organic lamb mince and some nice apple pie for afterwards, do you think that will make it better?"

Thinking back to the rock cakes of my childhood, I'm indignant. Somewhere, certainly not in the family home I was reared in, she seems to have picked up a few tricks of the mothering trade after all. Ben has forgotten his tummy ache already.

"Yes, please."

The ice lady melts under the warmth of this little ray of sunshine.

"Well, I'd better put the oven on then."

I leave Mum and Ben to chat and take her small yet remarkably heavy suitcase upstairs — my God, how long is she staying? — to get ready and look marginally less slovenly.

I go into my bedroom and put Mum's bag next to the bed. She'll be using my room tonight and I'll sleep on the downstairs sofa. I make a mental note to tidy up here as well and lock away any and all incriminating things. A delicious smell begins to waft up and I close the door on the intergenerational idyll downstairs, putting rock cakes versus apple pie firmly out of my mind. *Now*. I need to take a quick inventory of myself in the mirror. I want to look casual but gorgeous. Sort of thrown-together chic. Effortless. As if gorgeous was my everyday look and I just freshened up a bit for the evening.

As usual I have just about fifteen minutes for the date makeover, which is fourteen more than I usually have in the morning, so it'll have to do. Shower first. Loads of Jo Malone. Shit, I should have gone to the gym. Must try to tone the bits that I don't look at much. If I do have sex again, I will need to tone fast because the guy will certainly be looking at them a lot. Right. Hair. Shampoo, ten strokes, fast. Wash out. Then conditioner. Leave in for ten minutes it says. Fuck that. I've got thirty seconds tops. Will have to do.

Face pack. Leave that on for twenty minutes. Obviously not designed for single mums. Then cleanse, tone and moisturise (CTM). Somehow I've perfected the art of CTM in one go. I don't know if one on top of the other all at once works, I usually end up with a bit of a gooey mess, but it shaves a few minutes off my beauty routine so I hope for the best.

Now, what shall I wear? When I fell into the photo shoot I had on my favourite Chine skirt, so that's out. A very short black Paul Smith skirt with a slouchy jumper, which make me look like a rock chick? Or jeans with the loose brown blouson top, which make me look like a hippy chick? I swivel madly back and forth in front of my wardrobe, wet towels in a heap around me. Sixty seconds to decide. I wear the skirt with the blouson so I look like a hippy rock chick.

On to make-up. It has to be natural but strong round the eyes. Emphasise your best feature, the magazines always say, and my eyes aren't half bad even if much of the rest of me is in dire need of a makeover that goes beyond fifteen minutes.

I smooth and powder and tweak and blot and tidy and finally I walk down the stairs smelling gorgeous and hopefully looking half decent. Fuck, didn't have time to look at old school photos. Don't have time to search now, it would also make my mum suspicious, but must try to find those this weekend. Perhaps he'll bring some. Look at watch.

It's already gone seven. I have to go.

In the kitchen I find Ben sitting at the table, waiting patiently for his shepherd's pie and chatting companionably to his granny. I look in the downstairs mirror for the last time, hoping that it will make me look more beautiful, thinner, more radiant and younger, listening absent-mindedly to their chat. I think my mum is on one of her favourite subjects, the toilet wartime story.

She can make that relevant in absolutely any conversational situation, it's amazing to watch her do it. In brief, when she was about Ben's age, she was in the loo one day when her older brother scared her with a Halloween mask on the end of a broomstick through the bathroom window. She raced downstairs in terror, skirt tucked into her knickers, and a few minutes later a bomb landed on the house next door and the ceiling fell in on the bathroom where she had just been sitting. If it hadn't been for her brother, she would have been a "goner", as she puts it.

Ben, who's listened to this story millions of times and still loves the idea of his grandma running into the street with her knickers showing, is laughing now, tummy ache all but forgotten as he tells her about his karate moves and she potters around the kitchen and tells him he's brilliant and will be better than Hong Kong Phooey. He's very pleased about that. I watch them quietly for another few seconds, not wanting to disturb the moment. But I'm already a bit late so reluctantly I break into the cosy scene.

"I've got to go now, Ben. You take care of Granny, OK?"

"Yes, Mummy." I'm still not entirely forgiven, but we're getting there. I give him a kiss and half hug my mum in the process.

"Thanks for watching him, Mum. I shouldn't be back late."

She looks me up and down and although she doesn't say anything, I think I don't look too bad for forty-one.

All she says is, "That's OK, darling. Have a nice time with Jack. Do give him my best, won't you?"

She's got this inflated notion that Jack knows and cares about her well-being every time I see him. But "Yes," I say automatically, then cringe. Shit, I've actually had to lie to my mum repeatedly now, instead of simply getting away with implied information. I feel like a fourteen-year-old again. Like when I went out with a boy on the back of his bike and told her I was going round to Eva's instead. Got found out and was grounded for weeks. She can't do that now, of course, she would just sulk and disown me as her daughter, but I still feel guilty all the same. So I keep it short.

"Yes. See you later. Bye."

CHAPTER
ELEVEN

Meeting at The Chestnut

The Chestnut is less than five hundred yards from the Sycamore Café and the school and I make up most of my delay on the drive there. I want to be sure I don't drink too much and it's a good, quick getaway if the date turns out to be disastrous.

The Chestnut is a large, comfortable, sprawling pub, with floor-to-ceiling oak panelling and impressionist paintings of the local park, though for some inexplicable reason they are in shades of red and purple. It's got inviting black and brown leather sofas grouped around low tables and discreet corner cubicles for courting couples. There's a large beer garden at the back with a playground at the far end. Several playgrounds, actually: one for toddlers, one for seven- to ten-year-olds (although a lot of the dads and some of the mums have a go on that one when they have had too much to drink) and a hang-out area for teenagers. And, because it's Frencham and mostly frequented by millionaires and mafia, and millionaire mafia, there is a wooden climbing frame so large and imaginative that it wouldn't look out of place on an army assault course.

I park in The Chestnut's lot in the back and walk through the playground, dispassionately eyeing the preposterously ostentatious equipment. And, sure enough, on one of the benches overlooking the playground a modest sign announces that it has been "Kindly donated by The Sycamore PTA". There's no such thing as neutral ground, I realise.

I shouldn't have expected anything less, though, as it's one of the few really nice pubs around and pretty much everyone in town, pretentious and normal, is a regular here. The girls and I came a couple of times before the summer, Eva sometimes uses it for her marketing lunches, and I've seen both Fiona, sitting with Tubby and Telly in the garden, and, separately, Mrs Hartnell, who is inevitably accompanied by someone who looks vaguely famous.

The mafia frequent this place quite often as well, but as they tend to come here more for date nights with their husbands, Heather and Nick have made this one of their daytime haunts, tucked away discreetly in one of the booths. Both know Eric, the owner, quite well. Eric doesn't smile a lot even when business is good. He was the bass guitarist in a rock band, then became a Hell's Angel. He's been bound over once before because allegedly (well, according to Heather) a guy cut him up on the A1 and he beat the shit out of him. He made a lot of money in the band, most of which he put up his nose, and once he was clean the rest went into The Chestnut.

I walk into the warm, dimly lit bar. It's crowded already, but I can't see Peter Bishop or anyone wearing a red carnation. I thought ten minutes late would be enough to guarantee being the one to make the entrance, not the one to watch it. Oh well, I'll get myself a drink first. Craning my head to read the wine list on the blackboard, I look round to find Eric waiting for my order.

"Caroline. How are things?"

I smile at him brightly. Heather, Eva and I have a bet going, who will make Eric smile first.

"Can I have a house white?"

He nods in a friendly enough way, but doesn't oblige with a smile.

"Here by yourself? I haven't seen Heather or Eva yet."

"No, no, waiting for someone. An old schoolfriend."

He snorts dismissively. "Old schoolfriend, eh? Don't have any of those."

"Well, girls are probably better at keeping in touch than men."

"Probably right. Well," handing me a glass of white and waving away my cash, "there you are. That'll be nothing to you."

Still no smile, but a free glass of wine isn't a bad substitute. I'm absurdly flattered.

"Thanks, Eric."

"No problem," he nods, already moving away to pick up some empty glasses from the counter. "Your friend can pay double. OK?"

I smile. "OK."

Now, choosing a table. I don't want to sit at the courting corners or on the sofas which fart as you sit down, and it's too cold for the garden. Then I spy the table against the wall, close to the door. Not too much direct light and a bit out of people's way so I won't have to constantly say hello and chit-chat with acquaintances. Perfect. It's already occupied, though, bugger. Wait. I look more closely. Great. Peter Bishop is already sitting there, quietly watching me. So much for making an entrance. I blush but manage to smile graciously in greeting. He watches me quite openly as I pick my way through the crowd, still clutching my wine. I feel his eyes on me, almost as if he's trying to film me and he's observing closely how I walk and move and tilt my head. Looking how to light me, how to frame my face. It's a little intimidating but rather sexy at the same time.

"Hi, I didn't see you there for a moment," I say rather unnecessarily, trying to sound natural. "Did you find this place easily?"

"Yes, no problem." He smiles, standing up and politely drawing back the other chair for me. My mother would be in raptures.

"Have you been here long?" I ask, sinking gratefully on to a seat.

"No, no, I saw you come in and go up to the bar and order. I really must work on that invisibility problem. Anything come back from days of yore?"

"I'm working on it. My friends Eva and Heather remember, though."

"God, you're still in contact with Eva Mills and Heather Buck. What are they doing now?"

"Eva is now Eva Thompson and works part-time as a marketing consultant, Heather is now Heather Charles and is a full-time mum and they both live in Frencham."

"God, I knew you were close at school but I didn't think you would follow each other through life. Bet Heather is happy to get rid of the name 'Buck'. Some ribbing she took for that one."

The door opens and a small group of people bursts into the room. One of the women gives me a small wave and I recognise her as a mum from Ben's class.

"I think she took it in her stride. If ever there was a girl to pull that off it was Heather."

But I'm not making the same mistake twice. I need to find out more about him this time than his job and address. "You've managed to keep in contact with Toby Shepherd?"

"Yeah, that wasn't by design, though. We're both interested in similar things and it's a small industry. It works for us."

I nod and smile, sneaking a closer look at him. He's dressed in almost the same shabby chic as he was in the street, looking relaxed and comfortable. I surprise myself by being nervous all of a sudden. I don't say anything, so he does.

"So where do you want to start?" He smiles.

"We've got, let's think, about twenty-five years to catch up on."

"You go first," he says.

"OK." I take a sip of wine. "Not that much to tell, really. A levels, uni, career stuff. Did you stay on in the sixth form?"

"Yes, but I screwed up the exams. I was never very good under pressure. And in college I did badly because I discovered girls. One in particular. Whom I wanted to marry but who didn't want to marry me."

Finally we're getting somewhere. "Bit young, no?"

"Yes, I know, but it was the first time I'd got laid so, well, anyway, I was hooked. I remember screaming at her across the college common room when she dumped me '*I would have married you*,' which probably sounded more like a threat than a missed opportunity, poor girl. Then I bummed out for about a year. Lived in Brighton selling doughnuts on the beach. Shared a flat with three other friends. Smoked a lot of pot. Then eventually decided to go back home to live with my parents. Found a job. Paid back some debts. Moved out. And here I am."

He laughs. I know that laugh. I remember that laugh.

Then . . . all of sudden . . . the penny drops. I remember Peter Bishop. Arty, longish hair, good at drawing and painting. Toby was the loud, sporty one. Peter was quiet. Cute but quiet. I don't think we ever spoke during the five years we were in the same class. Perhaps we did, you know, like "Excuse me," or "I've dropped my pencil," or something like that. But we never really spoke. Not once.

I realise all of a sudden that no one has said anything for a minute or so and find Peter staring at me curiously. "Anything?" He's not bad at this. I've decided to make him sweat a little, though.

"No," I say, shaking my head, "I still can't quite place you. Was there anything spectacular you did at school that I would remember?"

"No, I was rather quiet, I think. I always was a bit of an observer on life. That's why I became a cameraman, I suppose. Ideal profession for someone like me really. I still prefer being behind the camera rather than in front of it, while your friends always struck me as people who would grow up in some kind of limelight. Especially Heather. You were pretty much always in the library, if I remember rightly?"

I laugh.

"Believe it or not, I had my aspirations. Be on TV, write a book, star in the film of my book, present my own relationship radio show, star in a Broadway musical, make my fortune without marrying one. You know, the usual."

"Not having a family, babies and large house on Frencham Hill, then?"

He's fishing. Time to put the boot on the other foot.

"No, that wasn't on my hit list of things to do before I'm forty. So who do you work for?"

"For myself, but I mostly do projects for advertising companies and shoot commercials. I've worked on a few independent films, but it's mainly advertising that makes the money."

"No TV?"

"No money in it."

"Married?" (Might as well come straight out with it.)

175

"No, you?"

My head shake elicits an immediate positive reaction. Good, keep the momentum going.

"Divorced."

"Right." (Sounds disappointed — perhaps he's met a lot of damaged divorcees? Not quite as good.)

"Children?"

"Yes, a little boy, Ben. He's four." Best to be honest here. One of my friends decided that she wouldn't tell her new boyfriend she had a little girl and they went out for three months without him knowing. How the hell she managed to keep her child a secret or why she chose to do it, I don't know. She wanted to keep her life simple, but I always thought that if he loved her he would be buying into the whole package. They're still going out, though, so maybe I'm wrong, but at the time it seemed an odd way of doing it.

"Still in touch with the father?"

"Yes, he's quite busy, works in the City, so usually Ben sees him one weekend a month, sometimes two." And, actually, this Christmas too, which is a sensitive issue, but I won't go into that. Similarly, I won't mention the hows, whys and wherefores of the divorce, too boring and too complicated. And too much potential for awkward nodding and hemming and hawing on his part.

"I never imagined you as a corporate wife." He laughs again. Raucous laughter rings over from the bar and for a moment the hum of voices rises a few decibels. I have to lean in closer across the candle to hear what he says.

"No, neither did I and it didn't work anyway. But hey, live and learn."

Could asking about a girlfriend at this point be considered too much?

"Do you work?" He's taking control of the conversation.

Bugger, I wasn't going to tell him until I saw his handwriting first. I once went out with a psychologist and could almost see him analyse my body language every time I crossed my legs and arms — when really I was just cold and didn't want him to see my nipples. I say, "Yes, I provide editorial work — editing, writing, etc. — and I also do quite a bit of freelance stuff for, ironically, an advertising company I used to work for. Universe International, do you know it?"

Of course, it's a small world once again. "Yes, I've done some corporate jobs for them. I've filmed some of the top bods."

He must know Jack Stone, then, but probably best to wait till he mentions him. Although he tends to have the same magnetic effect on guys as well, as most of my men friends confirm.

He pauses, looking at me, doing the cameraman thing again. It's a little disconcerting, but he's still smiling so perhaps he likes what he sees. I drink a bit more wine. I want him to continue talking.

"What about your parents? Do they still live in Chetley?" I finally ask. Lame question, Gray.

"My dad was in the merchant navy so I didn't see much of him when I was growing up. It was tough on my mum, especially round family holidays. I spent a lot of Christmases handing my mum tissues. I'm still close to her and I've got to know my dad more since he had a heart attack a few years back."

We pause again and stare at each other, both trying to remember how we looked all those years ago and if we can still see anything of the child, the innocence, the vulnerable teenager in each other. Eventually I ask, "Did you bring any photos?"

"No, I've been working since we last met and didn't make time. I will though. And you?"

"No, I was going to, but I didn't have time either."

Slight pause again. It's a tad stilted, our date, and a bit bumpy on the conversational front. The pub has filled up, is noisy and warm, and around us small knots of people are chattering animatedly. Maybe I should get more drinks?

Just as I'm starting to get up, he asks, "Want to get something to eat?"

I'm surprised at the sudden speed of things, pleasantly so, actually, but I try not to show it. "This place doesn't do food but there's a good Indian next door."

My usual haunts are kid-friendly places like Pizza Express, Gourmet Burger Kitchen and Giraffe, and I don't eat a lot of curries, but according to the gossip in The Sycamore playground, the guys who own this place arrived from Delhi last year and set it up with the help of some local rock-star celebrity. It's simple and comfortable, with a myriad of spicy smells permeating the air. They've got a last-minute cancellation and Peter Bishop orders for us, which is fine with me. The food is good, aromatic and unexpected. After the shadowy, candle-lit atmosphere of the pub, this feels slightly less claustrophobic, less romantic but the conversation flows much more easily, to my great relief.

We sit and talk through dinner, dessert, tea. What the papers say, what we say about what the papers say. Where we've travelled and would still like to go. Our favourite restaurants, our seminal moments, our favourite smells (I say spring and autumn, he says the smell of fresh paint). Favourite animals (spiders, lions), colours (purple, red), stones (amethyst, moonstone). Famous people we've met, what we would have liked to have done with our lives. Favourite film (*The Witches of Eastwick*, of course, *Big*). From our circle of mutual acquaintances who has died, got married, moved away, done well, won the lottery. And then back to schooldays. Favourite teachers? Favourite subjects? Least favourite sports lesson. When we lost our virginity and where. Who we fancied in the class. Who we didn't. He says he fancied me. I can't quite believe that but finally admit to knowing him and tell him, as kindly as possible, that I thought he was cute but quiet and I fancied Andrew. He says Andrew fancied me but didn't have the balls to tell me.

We laugh a lot. He looks very attractive when he laughs and, involuntarily, I lean closer. He's got a tooth which slightly sticks out, as though he's a lopsided vampire. It's disconcerting when I first start talking to him but rather charming the more the evening progresses. I can feel myself mellowing and getting hazy about where I am and who I am and what I'm doing here. Moving on to a second helping of tea, I finally admit to myself that I'm starting to flirt with him. Our legs are touching. He moves closer to me, invading my space, and I let him. We lower our voices to a throaty whisper and laugh softly. In the half-light of the restaurant I see him lean closer, his face just inches from mine. He comes closer still and —

My mobile rings.

I've just left it on throb and am tempted to ignore it, but the insistent vibration jolts me back to real life. Reluctantly, I pull it out of my pocket. Maybe my mum, calling with some emergency or other?

Heather. Great timing. I ignore it and shove it back into my pocket. I'll talk to her tomorrow. Seconds later, it rings again.

I sigh.

"Excuse me, I've just got to take this." He shrugs and moves away a bit to reach for the sugar. So much for our electrical moment, the blossoming romance.

"Heather, what's going on? I'm with P —"

Before I can even finish, I have to remove the phone from my ear. Heather is shrieking into it, loud, hysterical, completely unintelligible. God, what now? Quickly, I get up and move away from the table, although I'm almost positive everyone in the restaurant is able to hear both sides of this conversation wherever I am.

"*The fucking bitches*. Shitty little human beings. Scum-of-the-earth fuckers."

"Err, Heather?"

"Yes, sorry, Caroline. Sorry, I'm calling. I know you're with Peter Bishop, but I've got to talk to someone. I'll go nuts and Eva isn't answering her phone. Can I come and see you?"

Now? No. I may have said that out loud because Peter is looking over to see if everything is all right.

Heather is crying now, big, noisy sobs punctuated by further expletives. I feel slightly ashamed for my reluctance. Clearly something is very wrong.

"OK," I say soothingly. "But I'll come and see you, OK?"

"Can you come now? It's important. Fucking hell!" I can almost hear Heather pacing. "Sorry, Caroline, I know it's a date, but please, please, come now."

"Yes, of c —"

Click.

I return to the table.

"Peter, an emergency has come up. I've got to go. I'm really sorry."

"Nothing wrong with Ben, I hope?" he says, standing up immediately.

"No, not Ben. Something else, but it sounds like an emergency. Friend in need."

"They're the best kind. Can I drive you somewhere?" I'm relieved he's not miffed but I'm a bit put out myself. I'm enjoying my time with Peter Bishop. He's sexy and funny and interesting and gentle. I like the way he talks and listens. I like his company. I like the way he watches me. I like the way I am with him. I like him. Still, we've already had most of the evening and it was lovely, so hopefully —

"Would you like to meet again?" he asks expectantly, which I find rather charming.

"That would be lovely."

I get a pen out of my bag and use the back of a napkin to write my number on while he waves over the waiter for the bill.

"Thank you." He smiles and pockets the napkin.

I can't quite think straight. I'm slightly woozy, but more from the sexual tension than the alcohol. Thank God I'm still OK to drive. Walking to my car through the chilly night, I sober rapidly. Perhaps it's all for the best. I haven't had sex in ages and my mum's back home with Ben. It's never good to sleep with the guy on the first date anyway.

CHAPTER
TWELVE

The Mafia Strikes Back

As I drive carefully across to Heather's house, I wonder, with a sense of ugly foreboding, whether this has something to do with the mafia. Only the mafia get Heather this wound up. She juggles two kids, one husband and one lover, one huge house and two cars with aplomb, she goes through life knowing exactly what she wants and mostly getting her way, but with the mafia she gets angry, emotional and thrown off her guard. And she sounded completely wired on the phone. I've called my mum to let her know that it would be a bit later after all. She sounded delighted and claimed all was in hand, no worries. I know I'm going to have to sort out that misunderstanding as soon as I get home, otherwise I will never hear the end of it.

I pull into Heather's driveway, with its nicely trimmed hedges and cleanly swept car park. For all her ditzy, loud ways, Heather can be surprisingly anal about her house. I'm always in awe when I step in here. Her house is about five times the size of my terraced place. Five bedrooms, which is very useful as she no longer sleeps in the same room as Harvey. I knock at her door. Nothing happens for a few moments. I'm just about to knock again, a little louder, when I fall forwards into her house.

Heather is standing at the door as though rooted to the spot, like some firework that's about to explode but can't make up its mind in which direction to zip off.

She makes no motion to help me get up but ushers me in quickly and impatiently, so I half stumble, half crawl into the oversized entrance hall with wood flooring and large mirrors that always make you feel as if someone is mimicking you on both sides of the room. Today I have no time to admire the gorgeous flowers on the hall table, which the gardener lovingly delivers once a week, or the new plasma-screen TV, which Heather has been railing against all week as a completely pointless purchase. (Apparently the screen moves to whatever spot you're sitting in, which means that the children have tried to break it from day one by walking off in different directions at the same time.) Instead of the living room with its oversized cream sofas, Heather leads me to the kitchen and the window seats overlooking the large back garden. I sit down by the patio window, just opposite the aquarium where a few goldfish stare at Heather and me from the corner, as though they would like to listen in to the conversation.

Heather starts to pace. It looks like she's been doing this for a while, and I'm getting worried. I've never seen her like this. Well, once, I guess. When she was in labour with Jennifer and she was taking deep breaths, in two three and out two three, and she seems to be practising the same breathing movements now. I get back up to make us both some camomile tea. I don't think she needs any more stimulants at the moment. While I'm moving around the kitchen, getting the tea things together, I stick to practicalities.

"Are the kids OK?"

"Yes, they're fine, thank goodness. Upstairs asleep. I love them more than anything, Caroline," she says, looking at me, eyes red.

My mind is spinning. Has Harvey found out about Nick and threatened to take the kids away from her?

"I know that, Heather," I say carefully.

"I'd kill anyone who'd think of hurting them." I make soothing noises. "I love Harvey too, you know."

I'm taken aback and speak normally for the first time since I've seen her. I'm gagging to find out what has happened. "God, I haven't heard you say that for a long time."

She starts pacing again. "Yes I know. I know I go on about Nick a lot. I love him and he loves me and I know what you think about everything, Caroline. That I'm handling it badly and I should make a clean break from Nick and then focus on the family or decide to divorce. I know. I know. But I love my family. I live for my family. I just want to live a little for *me* as well. You understand that, don't you?"

I nod reassuringly and Heather drifts off again, staring at the goldfish, playing with their little container of food.

When she finally speaks, she's calmer, almost quiet, as though the interminable pacing has helped her get all the facts straight.

"I've been seeing Nick for ages now; I don't know if Harvey ever knew about it. Well, he does now."

I think, Fuck, she's told him.

I say, "How does he know now? Have you told him?"

Heather doesn't answer my question, just continues to talk.

"I think he's been in denial really, but he knows I've been restless for a long time. He knows I want to keep the family together but he also knows that deep down I'm just not happy. Alicia has always suspected me, staring at me from her junky little toyshop with the overpriced wooden crap in the window and gossiping with the other mums and the mafia. But I didn't think of her as anything more than Nick's ditzy ex-girlfriend. Serves me right for being so arrogant."

Deep breaths in. Heather sips some more tea, then starts again, still staring at the fish.

"Lately, Nick and I have been taking more risks when we've been meeting each other. Almost trying to get caught. Which has been both dangerous and exciting. I can't believe I've been doing this, Caroline. Having an affair. It's all a bit, well, a bit sad really. If I'm not happy, I should just move on. It's weird, though. Both men satisfy me in different ways, but neither satisfies me completely."

She opens the fish-food container and shakes a cloud of the tiny flakes on to the water. The fish immediately make for the surface, mouths gaping.

"I understand that completely," I reassure her again, my usual irritation at her relationship mess forgotten in the face of her abject misery. Another pause, then I say

186

thoughtfully, "I don't know why you and Harvey didn't ever go to counselling."

Heather's voice changes, becoming angry and irritable. "Oh, don't give me a lecture about that, Caroline. I know I should have gone to counselling, but its pretty fucking redundant when you're already in a full-blown affair, right? I could have hardly blurted out, 'Oh and by the way, I've been having an affair.'"

"I understand that. But there's more than just you and Harvey to think about. The issue is how to resolve things without causing harm to your children. Both of you have to behave like adults, not like children yourselves. You're not in school any more."

This isn't the right way to do this at all. I'm scolding a friend who's down already. I can see she's distressed and she's right the last thing she needs is a lecture. "I'm sorry. I didn't mean to reprimand you, Heather, really. I'm sorry."

Heather shakes her head, takes it in her stride. "To tell you the truth, though, I feel almost as trapped by Nick as I am by Harvey — because Nick dotes on me as much as Harvey does. I've hooked them both and can't untangle myself from either of them. Sometimes I envy you, and think I'd be best off by myself, with time to myself. After our fight in the car the other day," she smiles at me and I shrug slightly, "I came home and thought for the first time about how I could extricate myself from Nick and see how things really stand with Harvey and if I can survive without that particular emotional crutch."

I nod carefully.

"But I was equally sure that I should put the kids first, which may not necessarily mean staying with Harvey. All a bit complicated, really." She blows her nose.

"I understand — stripping away layers to find out which one makes you feel fulfilled and which one you can live without. Taking stock. But that's all good, Heather. Why are you so upset?"

Heather finally turns away from the fish, who may never eat again after tonight, and looks me straight in the eyes. Her big blue eyes are so smudged with mascara she looks like a clown.

"Tonight, I was just cleaning up after dinner when there was a ring at the door. Harvey went and I heard some mutterings, male voices, then Harvey was shouting, slamming the door. I called out to see what was wrong but thought maybe it was just an annoying salesman or something. The kids were in such dismal form all day, squabbling like hell and really getting to me, so I didn't really pay attention. I started the usual routine, bathing, stories, hot milk, when I heard the front door slam and thought Harvey had gone to get something from the car." She breathes more normally, obviously talking herself through the scenes bit by bit. "When the kids were finally settled, I went downstairs to sort out some laundry the cleaning lady had left out. The usual evening chores."

I don't know that someone who is on a first-name basis with the dry-cleaner down the road and has both a cleaning lady *and* a gardener really does any kind of "usual evening chores", but I let it pass. Heather is still talking.

"Nick called me, he often does at night but I rarely take it because of Harvey. But he was out, so we had a rare moment to chat. Nick said he missed me and, well, let's say it was quite an explicit chat. He was so sweet and I've been feeling a bit ropy all day, and I did miss him too. Missed the sex and wished I could be with him. And we were talking about all the things we do, you know?" She gives me a long look. I don't really want to know, but I do. I have an uneasy feeling about this story and its inevitable conclusion.

"Just then, don't know why, I turn to the door. And Harvey walks in. He walks sideways into the frame, as though he's been standing just out of it, listening."

I go cold.

"I feel sick. Just utterly sick. I think I'm going to throw up. Then I think fuck, he's going to kill me. Is the iron on? Silly thing that, but do I say anything or do I just stand there and say nothing and wait for him? Can I even explain this? How much has he heard? Perhaps not enough, maybe just the end bit? The *I love you* bit. The *We will be together* bit. Fuck, what has he heard, I thought, what has he heard?"

I feel sick, too, listening to this, and although my heart goes out to Heather, who sits in a crumpled heap in front of me, confessing to me as if I can somehow absolve her, I ache for Harvey as well. He's a nice guy and he doesn't deserve to come home and find his wife having phone sex with her lover.

But I don't say anything. I still don't know what this has got to do with Heather's rage at the "fucking bitches". There must still be more to come.

"Caroline, I was terrified. He came into the room, quietly and in such a white rage, I've never seen anything like it before. He grabbed my mobile and called up the last number, thank God it said withheld so he couldn't call it back. Then he yells, 'You fucking slut. You're fucking that Nick guy, aren't you? They're right. God, I could kill you.' Something like that. Then he pushed me across the room. 'Happy now?' he asked me, bringing his face really close to mine.

"You know what I said, Caroline? I said, '*I'm stupid.*' Because I am. I've completely fucked this up. Fucked up my life, his life, my kids' life, Nick's life and Alicia's life. And I'm stupid because I've just let it happen. I didn't say I'm sorry. I'm not sorry for sleeping with Nick, I'm just sorry I made such crap decisions and didn't deal with our relationship when I needed to. We both didn't deal with it. And there are so many cracks now, I don't think it's going to work.

"And then it sank in. He said 'they said', and all of a sudden I'm wondering just who knocked on our door earlier that evening. It was them. Jeremy Flint and Stephen Blunt, Sarah's and Karin's husbands."

She can't speak for a second and I bring my chair over and put an arm around her. Heather hugs me back. I can feel her grief, just in the way she's holding me. She's sobbing, too, and my feisty beautiful friend doesn't sob. Heather shouts and gets angry, but she doesn't sob. I hold her tight, my mind buzzing. What the hell is going on?

I let her hug me and sob and then pull back. "Are you going to tell me what they've done?"

Heather tries to compose herself.

"Can I have another cup of tea?" she finally asks, her voice hoarse.

"Sure."

I take the cup and get up to make another.

"So what happened?"

"They're such wimps, completely under the thumbs of their other halves. Well, if you can believe it, those fucking bitches actually sent their husbands round to tell Harvey I was having an affair. In the interests of the community and the school, they would prefer it if I resigned my post as treasurer."

So they finally know. Their snooping and ferreting has paid off, especially if Nick and Heather have been even the tiniest bit less careful. Or did they just decide to take a punt? A good guess and see how Harvey reacts?

Heather takes a breath and looks away, trying to regain her composure. I can't tell if she's going to sob again or scream. Then she speaks.

"Harvey said he defended me. He told them that whatever I did was absolutely none of their business and had nothing to do with them."

Listening to Heather makes me feel as if I've drunk too much coffee on an empty stomach, a bit faint and a bit nauseous. But I'm also angry. Not quite the white rage that Heather is giving off, but furious at the violation of her privacy, the arrogance and elitism with which these women reign over the town. Their ridiculous moral high ground. The absolute extremes they think nothing of going to. I've only seen Jeremy and Stephen from afar but they'd always seemed harmless, A bit square, perhaps a bit conservative, bit non-entity, bit chippy — but largely harmless. What the hell did they think they were doing?

Now that the bulk of her story is over, Heather is slowly gathering steam again and, almost in front of my eyes, the sad crumpled creature is turning into a fury from hell.

"God, if I see those bitches tomorrow at school I'm going to tear their fucking hearts out. *They went for my family, Caroline.* Bullying me at meetings and in the café is one thing. It's my own fault, really, telling them about things not being great with Harvey and making myself vulnerable to their spiteful little minds, but I've been able to handle them just fine. It's almost fun, really. But coming round to my house and going for my husband? That's different. I want them to fucking die."

She looks like she means it.

"What are you going to do, beat them up?"

Heather snorts dismissively.

"Well, you could have thirty years ago perhaps, but not now," I say firmly, seeing her imagination run wild and desperately trying to put a stop to it. "The only way to deal with people like this is to walk tall, Heather. I know, it sounds easy to say and yet bloody difficult to do. Christ, I'm your friend and I want to kill them for you, but it's not the way to do it. They're little people with little lives and you've got to rise above it. The one thing they'll hate is if you're happy and can rise above this. But the problem itself won't go away, you've got to deal with Nick and Harvey. You must."

"I know."

Some of the heat has gone out of her.

"Harvey loves you so much."

"I know he does."

"That counts for a lot, Heather."

"I know. I know all this."

Heather holds my hands for a while.

"Just because I'm married to Mr Perfect doesn't mean he's Mr Right, Caroline. It's got to be two-way. I can't just love someone because they love me. It doesn't work that way."

My eye falls on the kitchen clock. God, almost one thirty. I have to go. But before I leave, I'll have to have a plan for the next day, otherwise Heather will run amok before the morning school run.

"Why don't I take your two into school with Ben tomorrow, Heather, so you won't have to meet them. Have a lie-in, take a yoga lesson or something. But chill. You've got to give yourself space until you can deal with these things."

"I know," she says, looking tired and old. "OK, I'll sort something out for myself tomorrow. I won't do kick-boxing, since I'll just be visualising Sarah and her henchwomen all the time, but I'll go and do something. Calm down. Stay away from the school gates. And from them."

"That's good. I'll pick up the kids at eight thirty. OK?" I hate to leave her, so hug her close as I say goodbye at the door.

"Will you be OK here tonight?"

"Yes, I'll be fine. Harvey will be back. I know he will."

"I'm sure he will. Are you going to see Nick again?" I ask, hoping she'll say no.

Heather looks down at her feet, like a guilty school-girl, then up again at me and sighs.

"Who the hell knows."

CHAPTER
THIRTEEN

Pummelling Sarah in the Cafe

Next morning, Ben eats his Weetabix, blissfully ignorant of all my nocturnal activities. His new Power Ranger is sitting by his bowl, ominously glowering at its mushy contents. My mum looks around when she hears me coming in.

"You look very tired, darling," she says with barely suppressed glee. "What time did you come home last night?"

Fourteen again. I wake up a grown woman and as soon as I meet my mum, I'm a teenager. And yet even that is weirdly turned on its head. My mum can't stop smiling at the thought that Jack and I got it on last night.

I bite my lip and say, "Late. I hope I didn't wake you."

"No, no, but I don't sleep well these days anyway. My back, you know. I've got an appointment to see the doctor about it, but you know what the NHS is like."

I ignore the question, if it is a question, and ask her if she wants breakfast.

"I'm fine. I've had some cereal and coffee, but can I fix you anything?"

I mutter something about tea and head for the counter.

"You need a proper breakfast, Caroline, just like Ben." Since when are Coco Pops and cornflakes — Ben's usual fare — considered a proper meal?

I can tell she is twitching to grill me about my night, but before she does I switch the kettle on and pretend I can't hear her any more. Idly, I look out of the kitchen window. There are the first signs of frost this morning and it's not as light as it used to be. Winter is drawing in and there's a nip in the air. I must wrap Ben up warmly this morning and remember his gloves as well. I keep tying them on to his sleeves with elastic but Patrick (who is, I now know, Felicity's youngest) keeps pinging them in his face and they keep coming undone. My mother follows me to the counter.

"So how was your evening with Jack, darling?"

I can't escape.

"Fine, Mum, just fine. Was Ben good for you?"

"Oh, he was an absolute treasure. An absolute poppet."

Mum turns round to the treasure and smiles. She leans over to brush him on the head just the way Ben does Fiona's dogs. Ben looks up and grins, his mouth full of Weetabix, which he usually loathes.

"We had a good time. He loved my shepherd's pie for dinner. And the apple pie."

"And custard," Ben pipes in.

"And custard, yes. And then bedtime story and bed. Good as gold."

"Good. Ben you have to hustle a little this morning. We have to collect Philip and Jennifer from Heather's before we go to school."

"Oh brilliant!" He loves Philip, so this is enough to jolt him into action. He shoves the rest of his cereal into his mouth, perfunctorily wipes his face on the napkin and jumps off the chair to get his things. Good, one happy person then. And I have successfully managed to distract my mother from asking questions about last night. Or so I think.

"So where did he take you?" she asks pointedly.

"Where did who take me?"

"Jack, of course."

"Oh, to an advertising awards do," I reply, trying to sound dismissive, blushing again at the lie.

"Really? Aren't they quite grand affairs? But they must be dressing down these days, you barely left the house in tights last night." Mum looks at me innocently.

"No one's dressing down," I say through gritted teeth. "Just me. Right, would you like me to drive you to the station or would you like to walk?"

"You take Ben to school, I'll walk, Caroline. I'll be fine."

She stands up, her hand on her back, looking for all the world like a weary pregnant woman. I'm not the only one acting this morning. I wonder if it's possible to grind one's teeth straight into one's brain.

"If you can hold on for half an hour, I'll take you after I run Ben to school. Your suitcase is way too heavy."

My mum disappears upstairs and Ben and I hurry to pick up Philip and Jennifer, both of whom look, perhaps unsurprisingly, a bit subdued. Philip, who's eight, is pensive; he's a bit quieter in general these days. Not the happy-go-lucky child I knew BN — Before Nick. Harvey brings them to the door looking tired.

"Caroline." He manages a smile.

"Harvey. How are you?" I ask, shooing the kids into the back of my small car and slamming the door.

"Could be better. Thanks for taking them in."

Silly question really. Engage brain, Gray. Engage brain.

"I'm off to work. I've just come back to collect some clothes and stuff. I spent last night in a hotel. I expect Heather's told you?"

Oh God, what do I say? Yes, I know about last night, or yes, I know and have known about the affair with Nick, or yes I know about you overhearing the phone sex? Or do I deny everything? Heather hasn't briefed me, so I say, "A little. If there's anything I can do, have the kids over sometime, let me know."

I give him a smile but I really don't want to chat any longer. Sensing my imminent departure, Harvey reaches out and grabs hold of my arm, his face a desperate question.

"Did you know?"

This I was dreading. Heather is my friend. Harvey is my friend. But I've got nothing to do with their

198

relationship and I don't have any answers for either of them.

"The older I get, the less I think I know about anything, Harvey."

He looks down, perhaps not wanting to probe further.

"Yeah, me too."

I walk away from a man who looks more lost than wounded. As long as I've known Harvey, he's always been a reliable husband, the good father, the rock, the man everyone's liked and respected. He adored Heather from the first moment he met her. But Heather was never meant to be a homemaker. She was never meant to be a competitive housewife. It's something that works for some but not for others and with her personality something was bound to happen. I don't agree that having an affair should be the answer but I understand why she's done it. I just wish that Harvey was cruel or boorish or selfish, then I could hate him and tell her to just go and fuck him and take all his money, but I can't — because he's none of these things. He's a nice guy, a bit square for Heather, safe and solid. Maybe he really isn't the one for her. But then again I don't think Nick is either. But what do I know? I've resorted to reading handwriting to see if I can get it right. Or get Mr Right.

The playground is full this morning. Trailing a line of children behind me, I try to find Eva so I can tell her quickly, before anyone else does. The grapevine at The Sycamore works fast. And maybe she's heard something useful. The children run off to see their respective friends and I see Eva holding Harry's book bag while he's tying his shoelaces.

"So how did it go?" She looks rested and happy, in marked contrast to my tired face.

"How did what go?"

"The date with Peter Bishop?" She smiles at my confusion.

"Oh, fine, that went fine." It seems like ages ago.

"You don't sound very enamoured about it. I thought you two would get on." She looks at her watch, drops kisses on her twins' heads and makes a move towards the doors.

"Oh we did, actually, really lovely." I smile for the first time this morning, recalling the spicy air and the low lights, the throaty whispers. "But the evening was curtailed somewhat by Heather phoning me halfway through."

"She didn't! Unbelievable. She knows you haven't been on a date for ages. What did she want?"

Eva obviously hasn't heard yet.

Just then the bell rings and Ben runs back to give me a hug. Marie comes over to join us as we watch the classes above Ben enter the main building, their book bags spinning, gloves flying and hats tossed in the air as they funnel through a door that only takes two children at a time. Every morning they somehow manage to squeeze in by fours, in a lethal operation. And I'd wondered why Eva tries to send her kids in ahead of the throng. Ms Silver, looking rather splendid in peacock blue, ushers in her mini marsupials in a more civilised way, Ben walking in with Tom.

I like Ms Silver. She has an air of confidence about her and an earthiness. She bounces everywhere, sort of like an overgrown hobbit. We've got the parent-teacher afternoon coming up just before Christmas, and I have a ten-minute one-to-one with her about Ben's progress. Ten minutes isn't very long, so I hope she talks fast.

"I hear you're doing the hot-dog stand," she calls over. "Very popular that one. The warmest place in the fair."

We grin back. So they didn't manage to cross us out. My grin fades as I think about Heather pointing red-hot tongs across the grill at Sarah Flint. As if on cue, there she is now, waving at Edward. We'd vaguely said he could come and play with us tomorrow, but when she passes us on way out, she says coolly, "Oh, Caroline, about tomorrow. I'm afraid Edward can't make it, he's got quite a bit of schoolwork to catch up on." And moves on. There isn't much that stuns me after the last twenty-four hours and my overriding feeling is one of profound relief. But schoolwork?

"Don't ask," I say in answer to Marie and Eva's astonished gaze. "I'm *not* on a play-date basis with her. Or not any more at least."

Once we've finished pressing our noses against the classroom window and waving at children who have far better things to do with their time than wave back, I say a quick goodbye to Marie, with promises that we must do tea (she winks) again soon. Then I drag Eva away towards our cars.

Eva listens to my story with her mouth open. When I'm done, she says furiously, "I have never heard of anything so unnecessarily evil in my life. What business is it of either Sarah or her husband's what Heather is doing with her life? And poor Harvey, what a thing to have to go through."

"They told Harvey she was giving the school a bad name. Someone needed to watch its reputation for the sake of everyone's academic career. And so on."

"What rubbish. The way they go round behaving like prats is more likely to give the school a bad name. How ridiculous. I bet Heather is fuming."

"She is. That's why I took her kids into school today. I don't want her meeting any of the mafia. She might attack them."

"Oh." Eva blanches. "Yes, that would be absolutely terrifying, Caroline. We have to stop her."

"As long as Heather stays away from school for a few days she'll have time to calm down. But she's got to face the mafia sometime. Not only Sarah and Karin and that lot but all their other cronies who are always out and about, shopping and gossiping. She's bound to bump into them pretty soon."

Eva and I walk out of the playground in contemplative silence. I break it to say, "Let's go down to the café, though, to see if we can't glean anything from enemy territory. Maybe Claire and Eileen are there and have already picked up a rumour."

"Always good to know what the enemy is doing," Eva nods, then says, "You know, I remember working with a famous author once who almost got some really bad press from one of the tabloid newspapers. I think he was playing away from home and had been found out."

202

I'm listening but am not quite sure what it has to do with Heather's predicament.

"He told me that it didn't get into the papers because he had more dirt on the editor than the editor had on him. A lot more. And that he wasn't afraid to threaten him with it. So nothing happened. There was a stalemate. An understanding. An ungentlemanly agreement, if you like."

We've reached my car and I get some coins out for a ticket. The mafia protection only keeps the traffic wardens away for the duration of the school run, so I'd better not risk it.

"So you're saying, see what we can find out about Sarah or Karin or any of the mafia and blackmail them? Where the hell are we here, Sicily? These things always escalate, Eva, and you don't want to get caught in the middle. I know you want to protect Heather, so do I, but I think it's up to Heather to stay the hell away from them. That's the only way out of this."

We make our way down the hill. There's the usual bustle on the High Street, but as we come closer to the Sycamore Café I see someone in front of the glass, looking inside, much like we did at the school. She's very familiar: tall, slender, killer brown boots. Surely, it can't —

"What the hell are you doing here?" I whisper as loudly as I can.

Heather is so intent on the scene inside she doesn't even turn around.

"It's a free country," she snaps, her cheeks red from the wind, her breath fogging up the window.

"Not this morning it's not," I whisper back furiously. Eva kind of pats us both on the back helplessly, desperate not to create a scene in the middle of Frencham High Street.

Heather motions us closer. "Look," she gestures triumphantly.

Hesitantly I press my face to the window. How do I get roped into these things? Standing by the counter, I see Derek. The owner doesn't seem his usual cheerful self. He looks rather stern actually. He's talking to Sarah Flint, who seems agitated. I can't make out what they're saying (I wish I'd gone to that lip-reading evening class), but Derek has what looks like a credit card in one hand and some scissors in the other. Eva and I watch in awe as he starts cutting the shiny golden card in two. Heather pulls away from the window, claps her hands in glee and jumps up and down like she's hit the jackpot.

"Yessss. Got her. I knew it. She's skint. She's all front. Aghhh. Got something on the bitch. No credit allowed, not even at her headquarters now."

Gone is the miserable creature from the night before, replaced by a manic witch with a dangerous glint in her eyes. Before Eva and I have time to stop her, Heather strides into the café. The lions' den. I grab Eva's hand and race in after her.

"Heather," I whisper furiously, much like trying to summon a stubborn child, willing her to turn around. "Don't say any —" Too late. I can see Sarah look up, her anger replaced by a fleeting look of abject horror, then changing back to anger again.

Heather speaks. "Is there a problem, Sarah? Derek, is there a bill that needs paying?"

Derek looks at Heather and clearly can't decide whether to hold on to the steady custom of "Skinny latte, no foam please," and "Just a hot water with some lemon, thank you," or pay Sarah and co back for the staggering amount of drinks returned over time. Vengeance wins.

"I'm afraid I'm just following procedure, Mrs Flint. Want me to try any of the others?" He looks hopeful, clutching the scissors. His voice rings through the café and Sarah cringes.

"How embarrassing. Fancy that, the chairman of the PTA can't afford her own coffee. Mustn't let the side down, must we, Sarah? We have the school's reputation to consider and appearances are everything. Reputation is everything. Perhaps that's something we should discuss at the next monthly parenting meeting. Perhaps I can help, Sarah? Always think one good turn deserves another, don't you?" Before Sarah can answer, Heather whips out her wallet, losing a few gum wrappers and a lipstick in the process, and hands Derek some coins, her hand shaking ever so slightly.

Rage is emanating from the two women like an electric storm. Even Derek takes a step back, unsure of what's going on. The rest of the café, mafia mums and other women, look on, spellbound, as Sarah and Heather move closer to each other, fists clenched, faces contorted in a grimace. And, for some ungodly reason, I find myself in the middle. I'm in the middle of them and like some sandwich filling I'm going to get squished both ways. I don't want Heather to hit Sarah, something she's clearly more than capable of doing, and I don't want Sarah to rile Heather any more than she already has. Eva dances around us, horrified, tugging uselessly on Heather's coat. Unintentionally I've put myself in the way, as though I'm in some sort of netball game, wing defender or something. Somehow, probably simply because we're running out of space, Heather pushes me into Sarah. And I don't know why, don't ask me why, but, well, I pummel her.

Initially I can feel myself lifting up my arms to stop myself from falling into Sarah, and instead I pummel her. On the shoulders. Almost like the massages I used to get after work, in my single days. Actually, this is nothing like it. It's a bit harder and a tiny little bit more like a shove. To be exact. Sarah looks at me, more shocked than hurt. Then she starts hissing, spitting at me furiously, wordlessly. She tries to move towards me, but catches her coat on the metal edge of the countertop. There's a ripping sound and I watch in horror as, almost in slow motion, she trips, stumbles helplessly and falls backwards, hitting her elbow hard on the cabinet displaying the usual colourfully decorated cakes and muffins.

The whole room has fallen silent, except for the muffled sound of Sarah scrabbling on the floor, trying to get back up. I see the shocked-to-excited faces of the mafia, the bewildered looks from the baristas. I can see Eileen watching me helplessly, making a small move towards us as if to help.

I say nothing. Hey, what the fuck *can* I say at this point?

I see Felicity and Karin advancing to defend their fallen comrade so I quickly sidle my way out of the body sandwich, take Heather by the arm, and march her out of the café, with Eva trailing closely behind. Derek smiles nervously as Sarah slowly spins around, looking after me.

Away from the window of the café, and far, far away from Alicia's toyshop, we stop. Eva's mouth is still partially open, the look of horror not yet completely gone, but weirdly strangled now. With laughter. Tears are streaming down their faces, which gets me started, out of sheer nervousness initially and then belatedly I realise how ridiculous that must all have looked.

"What the fuck was that all about? I've never seen the like! At least if you're going to hit her, slosh her one. I don't even know what you would call that." Heather mimics me pummelling Sarah, which does, admittedly, look very funny.

"I didn't mean to touch her at all. I just wanted to keep you from hitting her. No need to stoop to their level. Who gives a fuck whether she can pay for her coffee or not? Surely you've been caught without money sometimes, Heather."

"I have. But that's just it. It *does* matter to her. This is exactly that reputation stuff she cares about. But now the boot's on the other foot. Fuck them, coming round to my house — no, not even having the balls to come round to my house themselves, sending their whimpering, toadying husbands round to my house and saying I let the reputation of the school down. Well, two can play at that game."

"You're so getting into trouble over this whole thing. It's not worth it."

"It was, just to see you pummel her."

Eva's still laughing and Heather starts again, but I'm worried now. I walk back to peek carefully inside the café. In the back I can see Felicity and Karin standing by Sarah, their arms around her as though I've just given their leader a black eye and a broken nose. Absolutely ridiculous. Eileen sees me through the window and makes flapping motions to shoo me away, tilting her head slightly over at the top table. "Call you later," she mouths. I feel a hand on my arm and jump about a mile. Eva pulls me back up the street.

"Don't worry. No use crying over spilt coffee."

"Perhaps I should have apologised, but she wasn't hurt. Just shocked, I think."

She coughs, trying not to laugh again. "I think you were more shocked than she was."

"I was. Anyway, it's done. No one was hurt and it's over. And don't ever make me do that again, Heather. OK?"

"OK karate kid."

We herd back up the hill and as I get into my car, I wonder uneasily if this is really the end of it. I've just made a sworn enemy out of Sarah Flint and it's not even half-term yet.

CHAPTER
FOURTEEN

Bullies

The day after the pummelling, I hesitantly walk into the playground and a sort of silence descends, very similar to when Al Pacino walks into the restaurant in *Scarface* and everyone knows him for the violent man he is. I smile uncertainly at a few familiar faces and ignore a smattering of mafia figures looming in the back. Where are Heather and Eva? Within a few minutes the general hum builds back up to its normal pitch and I escape to the Reception entrance and my usual spot by the trees, dodging mums buzzing about like bees, talking about the waiting list for the drama club and organising a party bus for some child's sixth birthday. When Eileen and Marie separately come to find me, I smile gratefully at both.

"So?" Eileen hisses. "Have you spoken to Sarah yet?"

"Trying to stay out of her way," I hiss back.

A futile effort, it turns out. Almost immediately Sarah walks over to *her* usual spot by the benches. Oh God. Her right arm is bulging with what looks like a thick bandage underneath her coat sleeve. What the — Did she actually hurt herself? Eileen and Marie have spotted the bandage as well, as have quite a few other people, but before the ominous *Scarface* silence can descend once more, the bell finally rings. The usual scrum of kids and mums pairing up ensues, and Eileen and Marie take off at a trot, patting my arm in a last gesture of support. I hang back a little. Ben knows where to find me. He's one of the last ones to come out of the classroom and he skips over to me happily.

"Can Edward come and play, Mummy?"

"Not today, darling. Another time, OK?" I see Edward hanging back uncertainly and come to a quick decision. "Ben, could you just go and find Marie for a second? I need to speak to Edward's mum." He scampers off, waving at Edward, and catches up with Marie at the school gate.

I march over to Sarah with a sense of purpose. This is silly. We're all adults and although she's loathsome and completely bonkers, I'll just apologise to her and we can both get on with our lives, perhaps even maintain a level of civility that will allow our children to socialise. She's watching me approach with beady eyes, Karin and Felicity closing in on her protectively, but before I actually reach her, Ms Silver steps out of the classroom, calling my name.

"Mrs Gray, oh, and Mrs Flint. I'm glad I caught you two. Would you both come in here for a moment?"

It catches us both by surprise and for a moment we're suspended in motion, like some weird tableau of cartoon characters — me caught in full strut with my arms out and Sarah with her head cocked forward aggressively. But only a couple of seconds and then we obediently follow her. I call out to Marie and gesture towards Ms Silver and the classroom. She waves, no problem.

Inside, Ms Silver looks curiously from one to the other, but we're both silent, so she shrugs and says, "I just wanted to tell you what a fabulous pair Ben and Edward were today. It was story time and Ben was telling us all a story about a puppy and a dragon, while Edward was acting alongside him, doing the puppy and roaring like the dragon, strutting across the circle. It was such a funny scene, and the kids absolutely loved them — it was a real showpiece, there's really no other word for it, and I just thought you'd like to know." She smiles encouragingly.

It is sweet, it really is, and I say so, while Sarah mutters something unintelligible. You can cut the tension with a knife at this stage and Ms Silver finally lets us go, turning to shuffle some papers around on her desk. In the corridor, I grab Sarah by the sleeve and say quickly and urgently, "Listen, I'm really sorry about what happened yesterday, Sarah. I didn't mean for all of us to get into this situation and I truly didn't mean for you to fall."

She looks at me dismissively.

"A little too late, don't you think? I always knew there was something about you that didn't quite fit in here." She brings her face close to mine and hisses, low, menacingly. "Who do you think you are? You swan in here like a queen, and yet you're nothing more than a jumped-up, discarded ex-wife struggling to bring up an unruly child. This today? You think this is cute? This is not what I want my Edward to do and it's certainly not something that will help him with life after The Sycamore. We," she points a finger at me in emphasis, which doesn't quite seem to work in the circumstances, "we take our children's education seriously, we try to maintain a calm, structured, academic life, and we would do anything to uphold the school's reputation, academic or otherwise." Her face is one ugly, twisted mass, her usual soft serenity has disappeared completely and I know without a shred of doubt that I'm finally seeing the real Sarah emerge.

The more she spits in fury, the calmer I become, and when she finally draws breath, I bring my face close to hers and look her in the eye.

"You listen to me, Sarah. Since I've come to this school you've patronised me, insulted me, and forced your opinions on to everyone. And I'm still trying to do the right thing here. Our kids want to be friends, and I'd like us to be civil for their sakes. That's what it's like to be a good parent, but that's something someone like you will never understand. All you care about is academic achievement, your ridiculous moral high ground and some inflated notion of your own importance. Well, you know what? You're nothing but a pompous, arrogant, conniving bitch and I'm actually glad you didn't accept my apology because now I can go back to loathing you in peace, you cow."

I turn on my heel and can only just keep myself from sprinting out of the classroom, the click-clack of Sarah's heels just behind me. I throw her one last look of contempt before I almost barrel into Marie, still waiting patiently by the school gate. She takes one look at my face and Sarah's figure looming in the back, and pulls me aside, sending Ben and Tom ahead to the car. "OK, here's a tissue, and let's get the hell out of here." We bolt to the car and it's not until we're safely at my house, sitting over two large glasses of wine and listening to the kids tear up the living room, that I can speak without gasping in fury. Marie listens with her mouth gaping in shock.

"You've absolutely done the right thing, Caroline, don't worry about that. And I'm glad someone finally gave her a piece of their mind. That was brave of you." We sit for a while in silence, slugging our wine.

"Oh God, what is she going to do next?" I finally say.

Marie just pats my hand.

I don't make eye contact with Sarah Flint or any of her henchwomen for the next few days. This is quite difficult as the playground isn't that large and I find myself trying to strategically drop Ben off late or time-check with Eva or Heather to make sure that at least I've got strength in numbers. I feel a little like I did at school when I was trying to avoid Rose Johnson. You'd think with a mum like mine I'd be more assertive, but unfortunately I'm like my dad in this regard. He didn't like confrontation either — more's the pity, as my mum probably wouldn't have got away with half as much if he had been firmer. So I sneak and sidle and jump at sudden noises, annoyed that I'm driven to such lengths but not quite sure what to do about it.

The scene at the Sycamore Café has made the rounds and mutated into a many-headed beast. Some mums flash me an appreciative smile, which is gratifying but weirdly inappropriate, others sidestep me furtively on the street. Eileen says she's heard one version where Sarah raked her nails across Heather's face and slapped her and another that had us all wrestling on the floor, showered by falling cakes and eclairs from the display case. As far as I know, it hasn't made the rounds among the children, although Marie says that Tom has reported tales of a fight between all the mummies circulating among the kids. And, thank God, no one has heard of my misguided apology, but still, my cheeks are burning every time I think of what Ben might pick up of all this.

Through it all, Eva, who *has* heard the story of the apology and promised to keep it from Heather, keeps intoning that it'll have simmered down in just a few weeks and we'll all patch things up over the Christmas Fair. We're bound to. Meanwhile, Ben is baffled by his mum's behaviour.

"Why are we always so late?" he complains bitterly as we trek up the hill, hurrying to make the bell. "Ms Silver doesn't like it when we come in after the bell's rung. Can we just leave a little earlier. Please?"

He's right. I look at Ben who is four, almost five, and I think, this is ridiculous. I'm the one who's behaving like a child. Grow up, Gray. What's the worst these women can do? That afternoon, four days after the unfortunate incident and three after the apology, I arrive at the school along with everyone else. Gratefully

I see Eileen hovering by the gates and I march in, more or less confidently, to wait for Ben. As soon as Ms Silver's door opens, children burst out, jumping and skipping, tearing through the playground to find their parents. I crane my head and spot Ben at the back. He walks out slowly, head down a little. I leave Eileen and elbow my way through the crowd, knocking over a little girl in the process. I can already see from here that Ben's been crying and I quickly scoop him up and give him a hug, turning away from everyone else. His little body judders as if he's trying to stop crying but failing miserably.

I put him down, pat his back soothingly and after a few minutes I pull away slightly so I can see his face. It's red and puffy but there are no bruises, no physical hurt as far as I can see. I'm oblivious to the other children and mums collecting and chatting to their kids.

"Ben, what's the matter?" I ask gently.

Ben sniffles, tears dripping from his button nose as he starts hiccupping slightly.

"Mummy, I, I . . ."

I feel the eyes of the other mums, but am grateful that everyone keeps a distance. The children are largely ignoring us, too, until Jennifer comes up and half hugs Ben and says, "Don't worry, Ben, just ignore them. They're being silly."

I stop dead and ask, "Ignore who?"

Jennifer looks at Ben questioningly.

I'm getting a little stressed now. What's going on?

Finally I see Ms Silver approaching. Her presence is reassuring and I can now hear Heather's and Eva's voices in the background as well.

"You OK there?"

I squeeze Ben once more tightly. Before I can pull myself up to Ms Silver level, she's already kneeling down, her kind, weathered face now level with Ben's red, tearstained one.

"Everything all right, Ben?"

He nods mutely. We're all huddled there for a moment and then she sighs and gets back up.

"Can I have a word with you, Ms Gray?"

"Yes, of course, of course you can."

Now I'm seriously worried. Ms Silver, the head marsupial, wants to see me in her room. Again? What has happened now? Has Ben been naughty? Is he ill? Have I done anything wrong? What? What?

I tug Ben along and follow Ms Silver, looking around helplessly at Heather and Eva. Before I close the door I see them bending down to listen to Jennifer.

I've not been inside Ben's classroom since his first day, and things were a bit blurry then, so despite the gravity of the situation I look around me in wonder. The walls are full of bright paintings of houses and stick men and ships and planes and animals of indiscernible species. There's an alphabet and then a list of "Dos and Don'ts" on the blackboard.

Don't interrupt Ms Silver when she is speaking.
    Do put your hand up when you want to leave the classroom to go to the toilet.

Do not shout.

Always be polite and never be rude.

Please queue quietly when taking your snack in the morning.

Always remember to say please and thank you.

Talk to Ms Silver if you are unhappy.

I like that list. I like the simplicity of it and the fairness. Maybe grown-ups should have a variation on it. On Ms Silver's desk there is the goldfish bowl with two fish Ben was telling me about last week, one of which seems on its last legs, and in the corner I can hear rustling from a glass cabinet with lots of twigs and leaves, which must house some sort of insect. There's a bookcase filled with lots of thin paperback books in yellow, green, pink, grey, all in order of difficulty. Ben has brought back a couple of yellow books this week, the easiest.

Ms Silver motions for me to sit down. The six miniature tables with miniature chairs around them look so endearing that I spontaneously go "Ahhhhh".

Ms Silver notices and smiles.

"Aren't they cute? Not comfortable for grown-ups, though, I'm afraid."

With both of us perching gingerly on two tiny blue chairs, Mr Silver clears her throat. I squeeze Ben who has now stopped sniffling and is hanging on to my neck not unlike he did when he was a baby.

"Right, well, where do I begin? First of all let me say that Benjamin is a lovely little boy and has settled in very well indeed. He is a delight." She gives Ben a reassuring grin. "However, some of the children in the classroom apparently told him that his mum was a nasty person and that he wouldn't be invited to anyone's birthday parties again. There was a heated discussion about not fitting in, not being right, etc."

"But why and who were these children? I think Ben's only ever had problems with Patrick before, but never really seriously, I didn't think . . ." I trail off as the full impact of the situation finally hits me. This must be it. The mafia striking back.

Ms Silver is watching me closely. "Yes, well, I think Ben obviously wanted to defend you and he punched one of the other little boys on the nose. Which is out of character for him."

"Right." This is awful. Poor Ben having to fight my battles.

"We had to keep him inside at playtime, just in case."

"Right."

My instinct is to find these boys and bash their heads together, but that's more the sort of thing Heather would do, so instead I ask Ms Silver what she suggests I do.

"Well, the reason I've asked to see you is because when the other children were asked why they had been bullying Ben, some said they'd been told by their parents to stay away from him."

I'm outraged and back to wanting to bash their heads together. Not only the children's.

"How are you dealing with these bullies?"

"Well, it's a bit tricky as the children in question don't generally tend to be real bullies. Most of them are behaving out of character too."

I can feel my blood beginning to boil. Surely the mafia wouldn't stoop so low as to intentionally hit out at Ben, would they? I breathe out deeply, aware that Ms Silver is still watching me. I pull myself together.

"I don't suppose you are in a position to tell me who these children are?" She doesn't really have to tell me, I think I know, but I'm so enraged I need to point some fingers officially.

Ms Silver shakes her head. "Unfortunately, I'm not, Ms Gray. But please be assured that they have been spoken to and know that if they gang up on Ben again, they will be put in detention. We are very strict about this kind of thing at this school. We have a zero-tolerance policy, because we know how debilitating it can be for children. Ben is to tell us immediately if this happens again. Plus he has a lot of friends in the classroom, which will help. Jennifer Charles was standing up for Ben, so were Tom and Edward Flint."

I'm stunned for a moment at the unexpected mention of Sarah's name. But I shouldn't have been surprised. Since day one, Ben has been coming home every week full of stories about Edward this and Edward that.

Despite my rage, I'm comforted by the evidence of our newly built social network, by the fact that Edward is still just a lovely little boy and by the way the school is handling the whole situation. Zero tolerance for bullying. I like that. I know school means developing a thicker skin in general, but this is entirely my fault. He's suffering because of my run-in with Sarah in the café. Nasty, spiteful, vicious bitches. Hitting out at them again won't help, will probably make things worse, but I vow right here and now that I'll find a way to get back at them for this.

Ms Silver seems to read my mind and she says, more quietly, "This happens from time to time, Ms Gray. I've been at this school for seven years and, inevitably, there will be conflicts and fights. The best thing to do is to ignore bullies. That's what I tell all my children and that's what I tell their parents. The bullying doesn't stop when you leave school, it just takes different forms, but in many ways you will have to handle it in the same way." It's a bit of homespun wisdom, but it makes me smile.

"Thank you, Ms Silver, for telling me all this. And I'm pleased to hear that Ben is doing well at school. Did you hear that, Ben?"

He's been so quiet throughout our conversation that I now nudge him gently, try to lift him away from my shoulder. But I find a deadweight. He has fallen asleep.

Ms Silver smiles at him and says, "I'm not surprised. He's had quite a full day. And you take care of yourself too. We can stop the bullying in the playground, but not outside it."

I like Ms Silver and I know Ben thinks she's wonderful. I get up, staggering a bit under the weight.

"Thanks again. I better get this one home."

"Everything will be all right," she says reassuringly as she opens the door for me.

I don't know if she is saying this about me or Ben, but I feel a bit better and walk out into the playground to find Heather and Eva waiting for me, their kids still playing.

"Finally. We were so worried about you. Jennifer said there was some fight in the playground?" Heather is agitated. She's still pale and has dark smudges under her eyes, but she's been more composed in the last few days, less nervy. The pummelling seems to have had a bit of a cathartic effect on her — I guess at least some good came of it then. I think she's also managed some sort of truce with Harvey. They're still not sleeping in the same bedroom, although I don't think either of them is sleeping much in general, but I know what little they have said to each other recently is at least more honest now.

I shift Ben in my arms, talking softly over his head. I decide on the spot not to tell Heather for now, just in case she goes and sloshes Sarah, Karin or Felicity in a rampage of revenge, which would make everything so much worse.

"Yes, there's been a bit of trouble with the other kids in the playground, but it's all sorted now." I throw Eva a meaningful look and although she has no idea what's going on, she comes to my rescue immediately.

"That's good. Ms Silver is nice, isn't she? Now, girls, we haven't yet made a plan for the Christmas Fair, and it's rapidly coming up."

Relieved, I say, "God, yes, it's already Bonfire Night next week, isn't it?"

Eva beams delightedly, shooing the children ahead of us.

"I think we should all dress up as sexy Santa's helpers."

A moment of silence as we digest this, then, "Brilliant idea," Heather giggles, almost looking like herself at that moment. "I know where to rent costumes. I'm sure we can find something good."

"Good idea, something to look forward to," I put in, staggering a bit under Ben's sleeping form.

"Should we do suspenders?" Heather muses.

I have to stop her before she goes too far.

"Bit over the top, I think. Sexy Santa outfits should be enough."

We've almost reached my car when Heather suddenly says, "With all the drama, I forgot to ask how things went with Peter Bishop the other day? What was he like?"

"It was great, actually, he was really nice. I take back some of what I've said about mankind — emphasis on *man*! He was so sweet. And, although I was there for you 100 per cent, Heather, your phone call couldn't have come at a more inopportune time." I grin like a lovesick teenager at the memory of our near kiss. Heather looks at me gleefully, as if to say, go on, dish the juicy stuff.

"He called the other day to see if I was in his area again, and since I had to go drop something off with Jack — oh stop it you two." They're simpering and Eva's doing a little dance. "We just went for coffee."

That shuts them up. Eva stops dancing and they both huddle closer around me. The kids have discovered another sandpit so are preoccupied with that while I relate the newest incident involving Peter Bishop. Amazingly, or at least amazing if you consider our history, the coffee date went without a single cringeworthy moment. I walked in, he hugged me, we got large lattes and chatted for absolute ages. The coffee shop was comfy, although it couldn't have been less romantic — nonetheless, it was a real treat to have some normal, non-school, adult conversation. Every now and then, he would touch my knee in emphasis, and every now and then I would tap his arm. There wasn't any outright romance, or sexual tension, but it was sooo good. Comfortable and familiar in the best possible way.

"And?" Heather prompts.

"He asked me out for another date. The day of the Christmas Fair."

"But you can't bail on us," Eva protests.

Heather shushes her. "Yes, she can. If she's got a date, she's got a date." I'm stunned. For someone as hell-bent on shocking the mafia as she is, that's a big statement.

"It's in the evening. He's taking me to a restaurant over in Wimbledon. Don't worry, I wouldn't miss the fair," I say quickly. Both beam at me wordlessly, delighted, and I can't help it, I just smile smugly, kiss them goodbye and open my car, loading Ben into it.

For once they've walked and I've driven, and I wave and watch their kids skip off down the road, past the Sycamore Café, demanding sweets from the newsagent. I sincerely hope they will go straight home rather than detouring into the café. I'm still worried that Heather will decide to clout Sarah after all. Not that I'm feeling any less aggressive at the moment, after all the mafia have now gone for my family as well, but I know Ms Silver's advice is as relevant to me as it is to Ben: ignore the fuckers.

I half wish John were here so we could shake our heads over Ben's first trouble at school together — which shows the extent of my aggravation — but work and/or Suzanne must be keeping him busy these days and we haven't spoken in a while. He cancelled Ben's last weekend and is generally becoming more and more of an absent, redundant father who pays the maintenance like clockwork but can barely fit Ben into his hectic schedule, take him to football or run around in the park with him. Having family obligations doesn't always fit in with his lifestyle, he told me by email a few months ago, and I almost cried. I don't mourn the loss of John one little bit for me any more, but I would like for Ben to be adored by his father just as he worships him.

I look back at Ben who is snoring away happily. All those tears must have tired him out. Secretly, I hope he gave Patrick — I'm convinced he's the ringleader, a true chip off the old block — a good whacking. Is it too early to give Ben my dad's Rose Johnson advice, about beating the crap out of the leader to get rid of the whole group? It was so uncharacteristic for him, it stuck with me ever since. Maybe not just yet. Although, ironically, that's what I'd like to do to Sarah Flint. I wonder what would happen if the mafia didn't have

Sarah, whether it would all fall apart, or whether Karin or Felicity or someone else would take over.

We're just rounding the corner to our house and I can feel myself pushing hard on the accelerator, wishing it was one of their heads underneath the pedal. Those fucking interfering women. Who the fuck do they think they are?

They must have a weak point. They must be vulnerable. No one's invincible. The problem is, these women have a wonderful reputation. But maybe that's where they are at their most vulnerable. They're perceived as the pinnacle of Frencham society when really they're just a bunch of bored, spoilt, petty-minded women who use the same politics they've practised in their offices in the playground. These people need to get a job, a life, if not another house in another country. I can feel myself winding myself up like a top. Spiteful bitches. Now, calm down, Gray. Sarah's already been taken down a notch. I smile grimly, thinking of the embarrassing credit-card scene at the café. Between the pummelling and Heather's disintegrating marriage, I haven't had much chance to relive that moment of glory. I wonder what that was all about. Maybe she's charged one too many LeapPads or Botox injections?

But more is needed to piss them off, to expose their ridiculous focus on *reputation* — I mimick Sarah's soft, condescending drawl — and *performance*. I hit the steering wheel.

No, I've got to chill. I've got to be rational or else I'll be bad-tempered when Ben wakes up and that I don't want to be. It would mean that these bitches really will have won, so stop the blood from boiling, Gray. And if they can intimidate the emotionally anorexic traffic wardens and the grounded teachers at The Sycamore, they can probably do quite a bit of harm to our life if they really put their minds to it. Probably get Ben expelled at some point. I must keep calm, but I'm starting to realise why Heather hates these women so much, yet fears, and rightly so, the awful power they wield over everyone in and out of the playground. But, God, picking on a four-year-old boy. I want to scream.

The compilation CD I made when I was splitting up with John is playing softly in the background — nothing like classical music to stir and appease the emotions — as I come to a stop in front of my house. It looks neat and cosy, with its white windows and the atmospheric bit of frost still clinging to the trees. We have to put up lights and decorations, the boxes are already sitting in the living room. I like it here, and I want to carve out a solid, safe life for us. I won't stand for being bullied, either of us. At least I have the sexy Santa outfit to focus on now. Three unwelcome splodges on the perfect canvas of Sarah's Sycamore Christmas Fair: the biggest event of the year and the school's showpiece. I can't wait to see their faces when we show up in miniskirts and sexy Santa jackets. It's only a small thing — after all I can't embarrass Ben any further — but even that tiny bit of revenge will be sweet.

CHAPTER
FIFTEEN

The Christmas Fair

"Do you think three hundred hot dogs will be enough?"

Heather bellows across the school playground, balancing a large plastic bag of baps in one hand and a tray of sausages in the other. The buzz is almost deafening, mums dragging tables, setting up stalls and stringing up paper banners announcing each stall's goods, calling questions and encouragement back and forth.

The day of the Christmas Fair has arrived. We've come early to get our stall ready while Heather's long-suffering babysitter has been paid extra to mind all of our children. A formidable task, but I think she'll be all right.

It's been a month now since the pummelling incident and all's been relatively quiet on the mafia front. The school Bonfire Night was a huge success, nothing flared other than the fabulous fireworks, and more than £2,500 was raised, Heather said proudly, much more than last year. All three of us went, plus Marie and Eileen, and nice Claire and Heather's gym friend, Katie, with their girls. Claire's two were quite taken with Ben and took him under their wings for the night, solicitously protecting him from sparks and getting him hot drinks, jealously watched over by Jennifer. It meant that I could enjoy the night, have a few drinks and talk to the girls.

Peter and I have chatted a little and texted a lot and I'm excited about having a proper date with him tonight. I've everything ready at home and Mrs Hartnell has agreed to babysit in exchange for company to a matinee next week. Ben too. No need to twist my arm on that one.

Ben has not been bullied again — although Patrick is shaping up to be a constant source of annoyance. But manageable annoyance, according to Ben, who has grouped a good posse around him. Tom and Jennifer spend quite a bit of time with us after school.

I've talked Ben through the whole incident and explained the background in the most accessible of terms. He just nodded, and all in all little seems to have changed on the surface, but now he comes out of Ms Silver's class and instead of giving me one of his detailed rundowns of the day when I ask him what he's done, he usually just says "Nothing."

And the mafia haven't spoken much to Heather or myself. Sarah and I studiously avoid even looking at each other and thankfully poor Edward has so much going on after school that the question of having him over hasn't really come up again. I did my bit, so I can't help the way things are. As far as the confrontation with Sarah goes, I don't know about Heather and I certainly don't know about Sarah and the rest, but I'm just biding my time. I'm trying to stay low, keep Ben and myself out of trouble, but I haven't forgotten anything. I clutch my bag with my outfit protectively. Tonight might be the beginning of a few tables being turned.

Sarah Flint has sent a heavily colour-coded-with-lots-of-headings-underlined note round to all stallholders on how to set up their tables. There are timetables and sketches and more details than I can bear to trawl through. For our stall, we need to have two tables in front and two at the side for ketchup, mayo and mustard bottles. Dress code: sensible. Jeans. T-Shirts. Aprons. No Jewellery. Hairnets. Hah. She won't know what hit her. More than five hundred hamburgers and sausages, together with cigar rolls and baps, have been provided free of charge by the local butcher and baker, in return for a half-page mention in the school's Christmas Fair programme. Personally I think they got a bad deal, but what do I know. Probably Felicity's work.

As I help Eva and Heather unpack boxes and boxes of food, put up our stall banner (artistically enhanced by Marie, who used to be a creative consultant for a marketing firm and has added cheeky elves dancing rings around Santa) and set up the barbecue, we decide who's doing what. Heather is the leader and there's a lot of the old sparkle back in her eyes.

"Right, I'll do the cooking first. Caroline, you serve, and Eva, you can put the meat in the buns."

We all giggle.

"Then we can rotate after an hour and take it in turns from there. See how it goes. I hope we'll sell out.

I have my heart set on making the most money today. Santa's grotto is always a real competitor, but we'll see." She rubs her hands together. "Three hundred hot dogs and two hundred and fifty hamburgers, that's a lot of meat. We need to pull out all the stops in selling this stuff."

We giggle again.

"This is the biggest event of the PTA calendar. Rumour has it that even the school governors will be here, traipsing around the stalls and spending the obligatory coins as a show of goodwill. Our chance to really shine, even out the score and come out top." Her voice rises and she has a slightly manic glint in her eyes. I throw Eva a glance and we quietly start setting out the oversized squeezy ketchup and mustard bottles.

Finally, we're done and I have a chance to survey the scene, walk up to the entrance of the hall. Maybe Heather hasn't exaggerated too much. The fair looks amazing and the detail on some of the stalls is hugely impressive. One woman is creating an enormous, hazardous-looking pyramid with wine bottles, another one has brought eight or ten house plants and is busy artistically draping vines and flowers around her tables. There are Eileen and Marie, who've teamed up on a Christmas-card stall, another cheery banner waving up high. Eva has followed me and is pointing out a mum whose daughter is in Harry and Maddy's class — she has brought a whole still life of Christmas paraphernalia and is lovingly arranging a nativity scene.

"We raised more than £3,500 all together last year," she explains, "which paid for extra library books, tuition support for Year 6 and a new PTA office. The mafia used to sell second-hand and new school uniforms as well as books in the main reception area of the school every Monday and Friday lunchtime and Mrs Ellison complained that they took over the entire place during lunch, not to mention the fire hazard. Old Elly is a tough woman. She lost her husband to, I think, throat cancer several years back, leaving her with two now grown-up children. It's fairly clear that, up until the school-uniform incident, she was on quite good terms with the PTA. After all, their projects make a lot of money for the school. But now Mrs Ellison and Sarah Flint don't exactly get on. I heard through the grapevine that Sarah even tried to get her removed, via some of the local councillors she knows, but Old Elly has got an impeccable track record and is well liked and respected by everyone. And the SATs results are some of the best in the country. When Mrs Ellison got wind of Sarah trying to get rid of her, she was absolutely furious, as you can imagine. But they both do a lot for the school in their own ways, so it's an immovable object meeting an irresistible force."

"So Mrs Ellison is an anti-mafia ally." I like this woman.

"Up to a point," replies Eva cautiously. "She's a politician more than anything else and she knows exactly how much the PTA does for the school. And some of the mums are extremely well connected — this is Frencham after all. Some of the City boys and CEO husbands wouldn't bat an eyelid at giving five grand towards their kid's education — as long as nothing more would be required of them. And thankfully, not all the PTA are as power-crazed as Sarah, Karin and Felicity, so there is a bit of a respite from the mafia every now and then." She smiles. "Hard to believe, I know. I get the feeling Elly watches a lot of what goes on and keeps note. She wouldn't have survived if she wasn't that astute. Sarah would have seen to that a long time ago."

We're just coming back to the stall, when Heather shouts from behind the grill. "Barbecue's warming up nicely. I've got a fire extinguisher just in case it gets out of hand. Everyone ready to get dressed? The fair officially opens in fifteen minutes."

"Let's have another look around first," I say, excited about Ben's first ever school Christmas Fair. I can't wait to see him later and take him to Santa's grotto. I won't tell Heather that I'm adding to their income; she's on fire today and wouldn't look kindly on me sabotaging her project in however small a way.

We enter the hall, which is also used as the school gym and has a permanent faint smell of sweat. Heather warns me that it becomes unbearably hot after a few hours of all the children and their parents walking slowly around each stall to part with their coins.

There are thirty stalls at the fair, ranging from bring-a-bottle and tombola to cake, sweet and the £5 stall, then there are our hot dogs and hamburgers. Most are in the main hall, arranged in outer and inner rings; ours, together with a fragrant mulled-wine stand, is in the playground. Thankfully it's a dry day and people will be able to mill around both areas.

As we pass a tombola stand, Eva leans over and whispers, "I saw Karin going round with a tape measure earlier today to make sure all the tables are meticulously positioned. Complete fascist that woman."

Most of the handmade banners above each stall look like they've been made by members of the upper school, with spelling only roughly accurate.

Outside the gym, in the junior school library, is Santa's grotto, which has been put together by a dad who is an interior designer, helped, coincidentally, by Nick. Personally, I think it's just a ploy to be closer to Heather, who, although she hasn't said it in so many words, seems to be slightly cooling her heels a little where Nick is concerned as she tries to figure out her situation with Harvey. But then she called me last week in that breathless, happy way that could indicate that Nick's still very much in the picture. Oh well, not my problem. At least not today.

God, this is the swankiest-looking grotto I've ever seen, with a white papier-mâché mountain and diamanté stars hung on chicken wire suspended from the ceiling at a height even the tallest child in Year 6 wouldn't be able to reach. There's a green tissue paper curtain that prevents children from looking in and allows the rota of dads dressing up as Santa to change safe from prying eyes. And the air is perfumed with aromatherapy oils of cinnamon and cloves and all things festive. The elves are some of the leggier mums in miniskirts and green make-up. After the stern directives we all have received, I recognise them as fellow subversive elements and smile appreciatively. I notice Karin approaching with one of her clipboards, though, and hurriedly move on.

Having made the rounds and seen all the stalls, we change in the infants' toilets. Looking at everything in miniature size, crouching down to peer at mirrors meant for three-foot people rather than five-foot-niners, I have the same warm, protective feeling I had in Ben's classroom.

Heather has found three perfect Santa's helpers outfits at the fancy-dress shop on the road coming into Frencham: tight-fitting Santa jackets with plunging necklines and cute little skirts trimmed with white fur, plus small, furry hats. One of my friends has loaned me three huge wigs, blonde and black.

Heather, of course, got herself the shortest outfit of all. Tall, busty and with endless legs disappearing under the red skirt, she's absolutely sensational.

Eva and I laugh. I say, looking Heather up and down, "If you serve, Heather, we'll get loads of business."

With bold make-up and new hairdos, hats perching cheekily atop masses of curls hanging down our backs, Heather lines us up in front of the mini loos. We snort and break into laughter. We each look like a cross between some X-rated version of Mrs Claus and Edina in *Absolutely Fabulous*.

"This is how you should show up at your date tonight, Caroline." Heather is half serious. Not a chance. I smile, looking forward to seeing the mafia's faces.

As we walk out and ceremoniously throw open the door to the gym, parading slowly through the hall, every head turns our way. Silence descends. Mouths are open. A few giggles escape and then I can hear some clapping. More clapping and a few whoops, Marie and Eileen whistling from behind their stall, and then, we turn round to find Ms Silver and Mrs Ellison, and a few of the other teachers, grinning and waving. Just behind them, stony-faced, Sarah, Karin and Felicity flank a small knot of quite serious-looking people, no doubt the councillors and governors coming to see how the school is doing.

"Very well done, ladies. If you don't sell all your hot dogs dressed like that, I don't know what you'll have to do." Mrs Ellison smiles and ushers us through the room. Everyone has finished their displays and most have changed into festive outfits, making a sea of reds, blacks and greens. Lots of Jaeger, some jeans, some sombre black dresses. A few horrible holiday sweaters with red baubles and bells.

Mrs Ellison coughs and silence falls once more. "Right, well, thank you for all your support. I already know this will be a very successful event. And I would like to say a special thank you to Sarah Flint and her team at the PTA for organising it so fantastically once more." She turns to her left and nods her appreciation at Sarah, who has regained some of her colour and composure and is receiving the praise with grace. Mrs Ellison continues. "I hope you all have a good time, please be sure to take advantage of the stalls yourselves." In other words: spend money! "Now, let's get to work!"

She nods at Sarah and leaves, followed by a gleeful Ms Silver, who winks at me as she passes, and the rest of the teachers. We make our way outside without looking at Sarah.

"Now," Heather says, clapping her hands together. "I couldn't have asked for a more perfect start. Let's make some money."

Buns and burgers at the ready, we're fielding a steady flow of customers. I overhear several of them saying that it was getting sweltering in the gym, and soon more people come out into the playground for fresh air. The aroma of mulled wine and burgers is tantalising. Heather is putting up quite a show with her cooking, flipping burger after burger and throwing around dazzling smiles, while Eva is slicing and dousing the fillings with mustard and ketchup for those too lazy to do it themselves. I'm taking the money. My days working in the pub after school are coming in handy here. I've brought in £50 worth of change so that we wouldn't be caught out and a money bag around my waist to keep everything separate. I'm taking the orders and serving quickly, Heather's cooking the meat so that none of it drips blood, and Eva is taking the occasional break to keep us topped up with mulled wine, which we're getting free from the neighbouring stall. It's run by two other mums from Dragon Class. Between the two stalls we've gathered quite a crowd, which is getting progressively louder and more raucous as the afternoon wears on and the wine flows.

Most dads seem to have found their way outside by now, and some mums who are fleeing the sweltering atmosphere and the heavily scented candles and flower arrangement in the main hall. I think I even see Alicia from the toyshop at some point, carrying a fistful of mulled-wine mugs into the hall. We're getting grins about our outfits from some of the mums, and appreciative jokes on the size of the hot dogs and the amount of sauce on the burgers from the dads. The mafia is curiously absent, especially considering their obsessive need for control, and the only dads that don't appear are Jeremy Flint and Stephen Blunt. We're making money hand over fist and, a couple of hours into the event, the hot dogs are flying off the barbecue.

Nick approaches the stall sometime after three, grinning deviously at Heather. He's a broad-shouldered man, with dark eyes, brownish hair and an impish smile, always carefully dressed and fit, well toned and tanned. And usually furtive as well, on the lookout to see if Harvey is round the corner. His appearance reminds me of John, which doesn't help me to warm to him, but he's got none of John's arrogance, and his childlike enthusiasm for life is infectious. I can see why Heather likes him. He's Heather's Peter Pan. Harvey is her Mr Darling.

"Hello, gorgeous," he smiles. Heather looks around, embarrassed and excited at the same time.

"Nick, what are you doing here? I thought I told you that this really isn't appropriate."

"You look wonderful." He ignores her hand motions and scuttles closer to the side of the stall. There's a small lull in the crowd and we huddle around our mugs of wine for a second. He toasts us. "You both look wonderful too. Bet you're selling lots."

Eva pretends to be indignant. "It's all in the quality of our cooking."

"Yeah, right. I hear you caused quite a storm earlier, everyone was talking about it." He leans closer to whisper conspiratorially, "No one's going to Flint's stall. She's on one of the plant tables, but it's so hot in there everything is wilting. And people aren't in the mood for plants — what a stupid idea. She looks as pathetic as her rose bushes."

Heather laughs and makes a rude hand gesture. Eva is more forgiving.

"Hey, we don't care. It's all for a good cause."

Heather and I make an incredulous noise, which has Eva throwing up her hands in defeat, laughing. "OK, OK, a point scored for us."

Nick looks at Heather as though he wants a quick word. Or perhaps a quickie.

"Can you spare her for five minutes, girls?"

I'm not keen, especially because I'm expecting Ben any moment now and would like ten minutes off myself, but Heather looks at me pleadingly. "Just for a quick word."

"Yes, but only just. Don't be too long," I say grudgingly, for all the world like a clucking mother. And Heather downs tools and brushes herself off, then saunters off innocently. She looks like some naughty school-girl and every man's wet dream going behind the bike sheds. So much for cooling her heels with Nick. I desperately need some more time to catch up with my friends. I don't want to pummel anyone else and I think a stern talking-to from Eva and me might jolt Heather into action.

Two minutes later, six hamburgers and three hot dogs on order and five more people waiting, Gordon and Harvey arrive with Harry and Maddy asking for three hot dogs, and Jennifer, Philip and Ben all clutching enormous cookies. We process the queue at top speed and Eva leans over to give her family a hug, all of them grinning broadly at her outfit. Harry and Maddy are a year older than Ben. They're a nice combination of Gordon and Eva, smiling faces with long lashes and piercing blue eyes.

"Sexy, Eva," says Gordon, giving her a peck on the lips. Gordon, in his late thirties but looking older thanks to the commuting he does to the City every day, has an open face and the twins' mischievous sparkling eyes. He dotes on Eva, and Eva dotes on him, and it's reassuring to watch the two of them together, still so lively and happy after more than fifteen years. The children don't agree.

"Urrgh, kissing," the twins say in unison.

"Kissing is nice," smiles Eva, giving her husband a kiss back and handing Maddy a hot dog. "You just wait, the girls will be wanting to kiss the boys and the boys will be wanting to kiss the girls when you're older."

"Never, never," says Philip anxiously, tugging on his dad's hand while Harvey is looking around for Heather. "I will never have a girlfriend. Daddy, do I have to? Do I?"

"Of course you don't, Philip," his dad assures him. "They can be more trouble than they're worth sometimes."

A couple come up and order three hot dogs, one each and one to share. I shove four at them and smile, pocketing their money. They leave, just in time to overhear Harry asking innocently, "Catherine Wyatt in my class says some boys like to kiss boys. Is that true, Daddy?"

Another mass urrgh, this time among the grown-ups, and somewhat curious expressions on the couple's faces.

Gordon nips the conversation in the bud. "At the end of a football match the players hug each other, but that's natural. Now more hot dogs anyone?"

As hands shoot up, Gordon takes note of who wants what.

I bend down to hug Ben, who looks flushed in the face, as if he's had too much mulled wine.

"We've tried to get into the grotto, Mummy, but there's a queue and it's very hot and Santa Claus looks awfully like Mr Matthews, the PE teacher."

"Perhaps he's related to Santa Claus in some way," I suggest.

"Oh, don't be silly, Mummy." He starts to scamper off towards some of the other stalls, but I keep hold of him.

"Are you having a nice time? Will you come to the grotto with me later?"

"Yes," comes his enthusiastic reply. "Mummy, can I have a toy too?"

240

"No, darling, you've got to wait till Christmas." We've had the same conversation at least four times this week.

"But that's such a long way away."

"It's not, darling. It's only a few weeks now. It will go very quickly."

I look at Ben's disappointed face, his concept of time so different from mine. I remember as a child the days seeming endless and the nights a waste of time. Now, in my forties, there are not enough hours in the day and sleeping, especially deep sleep, is a luxury I would love to have more of.

"Where is Heather?" Harvey has come back with five mugs of mulled wine and sets hers down by the grill. He looks around questioningly.

"She's gone to the toilet," I say, lying through my teeth but looking, I think, relatively convincing.

"Oh, right."

Harvey is a handsome man, over six foot two, with broad shoulders, and in his white shirt and chinos he looks like a trendy George Clooney today — the total antithesis of Nick, who is more of a Brad Pitt look-a -like. Philip, with his brown hair and dark eyes, is the spitting image of his father. He's into tennis, football and cricket and Ben always wishes he was his elder brother. Philip hangs on to his father's hand today; there isn't as much teasing Ben and chasing his sister across the playground. He's been subdued lately, less mischievous and cheeky, and he's now also looking around for his mum, anxiously watching his father's face. I pray that Heather won't choose this moment to come back to the stall. Heather told me that Philip met Nick a few weeks ago, under the guise of "an old friend", but Philip didn't speak to Heather for a week after that. Forget the mafia. Heather could do more damage to her family than Sarah Flint ever could.

Philip and Jennifer are fighting over the ketchup bottle, splattering the tablecloth and themselves liberally in the process. Jennifer is an absolute favourite of mine, not only because she's been such a great friend to Ben. With blonde curly hair like Shirley Temple, she looks sweet but she's got an edge to her; she has the gentleness of her father and the no-nonsense approach and fire of her mother. Ben told me that she said she would be his guardian in the playground and would punch anyone's lights out if needed. He didn't really understand that last bit, but he thought it was something to do with their bicycle lights, and generally approved of the punching.

"Where's Mummy?" Jennifer asks now, generously sharing some of her hot-dog bun with Ben.

"She's gone to do a pooh," replies Ben loudly, having heard what I said to Harvey and making everyone giggle and forget the question. Some of the people still milling around the stall smile to themselves.

I can feel myself getting increasingly nervous. Eva tries to give Gordon a meaningful side glance, but Gordon is engrossed in a conversation with another dad who has ordered about nine hot dogs.

I'm more direct.

"Harvey, can you take the kids to the lucky-dip stall? I know Ben would love to get a toy."

Harvey smiles, a bit wistfully and perhaps a little bit knowingly as well, but I can't be sure.

"Sure. Tell Heather we came round to see her. Everyone looks great."

They turn, everyone still munching. Ben is clutching his bun, with a bit of ketchup on it the way he likes it (he's not much for sausages and I won't let him eat burgers — not even the local organic stuff). The children run on ahead, Philip still next to his father and throwing me a backward glance. I feel like I'm betraying him but his look gives little away. Ben is holding his other hand. What happened to keeping life simple?

"Where the fuck have you been?"

Heather returns fifteen minutes later, looking slightly ruffled but grinning. Nick is not with her.

"Where do you think? Having a break," says Heather, looking defiant. "I thought you could cope without me."

"We could and have, but Harvey turned up with Gordon and all the kids and he wanted to know where you were." I pull her aside a little, away from the queue.

Heather looks less defiant now. "Oh, right. What did you say?"

"That you'd gone to the toilet."

"Right, well, thank you."

She has the grace to look abashed, and I want to remind her of her plan to sort out her relationships.

"I don't want to do that for you again, Heather. Neither Eva nor I like to be put in a position where we have to lie for you. And Philip looked at me as if he knew exactly what I was doing, and Harvey too. It's horrible."

"Sorry. Sorry, Caroline. Really, it won't happen again."

Heather looks deflated. As I'm handing out more hot dogs, I whisper, "Sorry, Heather, I didn't mean to ruin your mood. I just felt awkward and I'm really sorry for everyone." Also, all things considered, what do I really know about relationships? I couldn't hold on to a marriage myself, so who am I to be giving advice to anyone else?

She smiles and pats my arm. "Don't worry. Let's get on with it. The cash box looks nice and full already."

We're run off our feet for the rest of the afternoon, with no chance to nip away again for a visit to the grotto with Ben. Finally, the fair is almost over and, incredibly, all the hot dogs have gone. So have the hamburgers and we're left with about thirty cigar buns and twenty-five baps. We all feel very proud of ourselves. I clear away the tables and put the bottles of ketchup and mustard into boxes while Eva sorts out the barbecue. As Heather counts through the notes and coins, Sarah Flint and Mrs Ellison approach our stall.

Mrs Ellison is smiling, Sarah only thinly masking a scowl.

"Well, ladies, how have you done?"

Heather's finished counting up the money and stands up, a look of glee on her face.

"We've raised over £800, Mrs Ellison," she announces proudly.

Mrs Ellison claps her hands. "Very well done! I think that makes you the most successful stall today, doesn't it?" She turns to Sarah with an innocent smile. "I'm doing a list of what's been raised by all the individual stalls and will announce it in the hall in a few minutes. Make sure you're there, ladies, and congratulations! Some kind of team effort, eh, Mrs Flint?"

Ready to explode, Mrs Flint looks as though she wants to hit someone. Possibly all of us and maybe even Mrs Ellison, who seems to be enjoying this moment just as much as we are, although she does hide it much better than Heather, who is beaming as she hands over the cash.

"Thank you," we all say, feeling utterly chuffed with our efforts.

Then Sarah speaks. "I must admit, when I first saw you dressed in those outfits," she looks us up and down, "I didn't know what service you were planning to sell. Doubtless, you thought the food would get you more customers."

She lingers on the last word, her eyes boring into mine. I shiver. Thank God she turns before Heather is able to come up with some kind of retort, something, no doubt, along the lines of us getting a lot more for our services than she would for hers. But Eva holds her arm and shakes her head, whispering, "It's not worth it. Let it go."

We finish packing up. Harvey and Gordon return with the kids, who have all seen Santa Claus now and come away with promises of toys that we hope are sold at Toys R Us. I'm wistful. I didn't see much of the fair with my son, but there'll be plenty more Christmas stuff for us to do before he is whisked off to John's for the holidays. My heart lurches a little. Better not think about that quite yet. Heather hugs the children and kisses Harvey on the cheek, not unlike I do with my mother. I hug Ben close to me again.

Gordon smiles. "I hear you've done very well. Everyone's packing up in the gym and Mrs Ellison is just counting up the last of the money. Marie said she heard you made a killing?"

"I swear, word travels faster around this school than anywhere else. But yes, I think we did well. Let's go in and look around, savour our triumph. And then it's home for the lot of you," says Heather, looking down at her brood.

The chattering has grown distinctly more tired-sounding, though largely happy, and in the gym the tables are all packed away now and everything is back in boxes. I can see Sarah's stall and crates of unsold plants wilting in the heat, but Sarah is standing by Mrs Ellison, Karin and Felicity in the centre of the room.

Mrs Ellison coughs and quietness descends.

"I'm delighted to announce that the Christmas Fair this year has raised over £4,000 and, again, I would like to thank everyone here for their help, especially Sarah Flint and the members of the PTA. I would also like to give a very special mention to the fabulous mums on the hot-dog stand, who've made over £800 all on their own. They were the most successful stall today, even surpassing the money raised by individual stalls last year. There's a prize for you, ladies, if you would like to come up and collect it?" She scans the crowd and spots us, jubilantly waving us up front.

We're stunned. We didn't know there was a prize, but Mrs Ellison turns round and picks up a magnum of champagne, mouthing, "Well done," then hands Sarah the champagne. "I think you should present it, Mrs Flint, as chair of the PTA."

Sarah looks as though she'd like to throw up, but she has to hold on to the bottle when Mrs Ellison presses it into her hands.

We walk up to her, me with a slight sense of trepidation, Eva with a huge smile of pleasure and Heather with one of unchecked triumph. She tries to grab the bottle from Sarah, but Sarah isn't really letting go, preferring, most likely, to hit Heather over the head with it. Ever the peacemaker, Eva ends the tug of war by thanking Sarah graciously.

"Thank you, Sarah, for including us. We had a lot of fun."

Sarah can only nod mutely, but Karin and Felicity look like they're about to spit bile. Staring at Heather and me, it's clear that if we were in the playground this would be the moment when the hair pulling, biting and scratching would start. Perhaps that's what we need to do. Have a bloody good punch-up.

Our moment of triumph and glory passes all too quickly and we turn and head towards our families. We get "Well dones" from a lot of the mums, and a few whistles and whoops, and our kids and their dads walk ahead while we stop to chat with a few people on our way out. As we head into the playground I notice that I'm suddenly incredibly tired.

CHAPTER
SIXTEEN

A Surprise Phone Call

Back at home I've finally settled a hyperactive Ben on the sofa (the result of far too many Christmas candies from the lucky-dip stall) and start to get ready for my date with Peter. Waiting for the kettle to boil for a restorative cup of tea, I check the answerphone messages, hoping that Mrs Hartnell hasn't called to cancel and that John has called to say he will take Ben to his next football practice. No, still no message from him, the bastard, so I guess I'll be standing on the sidelines myself, cheering on my small son while his father is off gallivanting with his blonde bimbo. She's a hairdresser, according to my mother, so always keeps her platinum topped up. How my mum always knows these things is beyond me.

The answerphone beeps. I doodle absent-mindedly on the notepad by the phone, waiting for the next message to start and trying to think up excuses for our next visit with her. She promised, or threatened more like, to take us both Christmas shopping in Chetley. Maybe — Wait, did someone just say "Police"? A male voice is monotonously reeling off something, while in the background I can hear phones ringing. I jab the button to replay. A message from a PC Gerard of Frencham Police Station asking me to call back as soon as possible.

What the — ? I feel all the warmth of the day's success and Christmas cheer drain away, drowned by a wave of shock-fuelled adrenaline. My immediate thought is thank God Ben is with me, just after every worst imaginable tragedy, disaster, nightmare known to any mother has reeled through my head. Then I think, oh God, maybe *my* mother, or Heather or Eva in a car crash? Even a potential accident involving John brings on a wave of nausea and fear. Poking my head around the door frame, I check that Ben is still happily ensconced in front of the TV and quickly, hands shaking, dial the number left by the officious-sounding PC Gerard.

"Frencham Police Station, how may I help you?" answers a young and thankfully calming male voice.

"Ah, um, yes, this is Caroline Gray. I, um, was asked to call and speak to um, Mr, uh, PC Gerard."

"One moment," and I'm put on hold. After a long silence blissfully free of any chiming music, a voice returns.

"Caroline Gray of number five Frencham Hill?"

"Um, yes?" Surely they wouldn't break bad news over the phone.

"Hello, thank you for calling back. I'm PC Gerard. I've been asked to investigate a matter concerning yourself. I'm afraid I need you to come into the station to answer a few questions."

"What, has someone been in an accident? Oh God, is this about that speeding ticket? I posted the fine just this morning, I promise, and I'm terribly sorry I was just in such a rush . . . Very silly of me, err . . ." I've run out of things to say and PC Gerard has gone ominously silent. It feels like the time my dad found out I was staying over at my boyfriend's house (I was meant to be at Heather's sleepover) and I have never felt more ashamed on the phone, stuttering at my dad's silence while standing in front of my boyfriend's parents, who had, until my father's call, been completely oblivious to my presence in their son's room.

"No, Ms Gray, it's nothing to do with that, and no one has been involved in an accident. But I really would appreciate it if you could come over to the station now. It shouldn't take too long."

I'm about to nod obligingly and say I'll be right there when the sound of CBeebies blaring from the lounge reminds me of Ben's happy ignorance of his mother's brush with the law.

"Ah, yes of course, but I just need to sort out somewhere for my son to go. Can you give me an hour?"

"Yes of course, madam," and with that PC Gerard hangs up, not even leaving me time to make a nervous gag about fleeing the country. What on earth can this be about? I run through the last few weeks, ticking off potential crimes in my head. Tickets. Overdraft. Credit-card debt. Don't be ridiculous, Gray, the credit-card companies love you for every penny of interest you hand over to them. Swearing at someone on the motorway? I am always in a fairly foul mood coming back from my mother's, but I try to restrain myself for Ben's sake.

I change into a skirt and T-shirt and frantically dress a rather confused Ben in his pyjamas, the mystery and potential severity of the whole situation only now sinking in. I wonder if I'll need a solicitor. For what, though? When Ben asks, "What's a solisseeter?" I realise I've said this last thought out loud and quickly distract him with some sardines on toast, which will have to substitute as dinner. Now I'm wondering who the hell I should call for help.

John? I shudder at the thought. He'd just relish this so much. Harvey or Heather have enough on their plates. Nor can I call Eva or Gordon, because I remember Eva telling me that Gordon has a dislike of the police that stems from being pushed aggressively by one of them at a football match when he was a kid. Peter? Oh God, I'm meant to be meeting him in an hour and a half. I'll never make that, but I can't really tell him I've been summoned to the police station. It's just not the kind of second-date material you'd like to share. Hah. I've got it. I'll call Jack. There must be someone he knows who can represent me, and he won't judge me or get emotional about it all.

But first, Mrs Hartnell. I pop over to knock on her door, tapping my nails impatiently on the frame. Through the window I see that Ben has sneaked off to the couch again with his toast. Mrs Hartnell answers the door, just as I'm about to give up hope. I explain the situation as quickly as possible, hoping to avoid any awkward questions.

"I'll be there in a jiffy, don't you worry, my dear," she declares dramatically.

I leave Mrs Hartnell wrapping her boa round Ben's middle for a rendition of *Mutiny on the Bounty* (the only play she knew in answer to Ben's request to play pirates) and practically throw myself into the car. Stalling the engine only twice, I'm finally on my way to Frencham Police Station. I need to speak to someone else, so I fish my mobile out of my bag and dial Jack's number. Another illegal thing to do, if I'm not mistaken. God, it's so easy to be on the wrong side of the law these days.

A surprised "Hello?" answers. I've called Jack's personal mobile, which I don't tend to use much these days, when most things go through the lovely Delilah.

"Caroline!" I hear Jack's anxious voice. "Are you OK?"

"I think so, well not really, I've been asked to go to the police station for, well, for questioning I presume, but it's all very mysterious and I don't have a clue what it's about."

"What? I think you're breaking up a bit. I thought you just said the police station?"

I inhale deeply.

"Yes, the police station. They called to ask if I could come in. Am I being arrested, Jack?"

Moment of silence.

"God, you get yourself in some scrapes, Caroline Gray. Now don't panic yet, I'm sure it's just some minor thing they need some witness statement on. You haven't committed any crimes against humanity have you now, unless it involves that skirt you were wearing the other day — the fashion police may be after that!" Jack laughs. He's very sweet to try to lighten my mood, but I'm not amused. And since when has he been so attuned to what is and isn't stylish? Sensing my disapproving silence, he speaks again. "Anyway, yes, bad time for jokes. Do you think you need a solicitor?"

"I'm really not sure. I didn't think to ask and I don't know one anyway." I'm nearly at the station now, and slow down to look for a space while Jack's reassuring voice booms into my ear.

"They're not about to lock you up or anything, so don't worry, there'll be plenty of time to sort something out. I have some contacts I'll call once you know what this is all about." I make a half-hearted attempt to smother a sob. "Really, Caroline, it'll be OK. Do you want me to come over and hold your hand?"

"No, no, I'll be all right." I exhale deeply, trying to convince myself that I can do this without a man to prop me up. "It'll take you an hour to drive over here in the traffic and I'm parked now, so I'll call you back as soon as I can. Thanks, Jack. I just didn't know who to call. Hope I didn't interrupt anything."

"Nothing that can't wait, and call me back, no matter how late, OK?"

"OK." I press end call and scrabble around for my handbag before braving a very cold and uninviting evening.

★ ★ ★

I walk into the station, wishing I'd worn a longer skirt and less make-up. The policeman behind the counter asks me to wait one moment, pointing at the only bench in the small reception area. I obediently sit down. Unbelievably, I've never been into a police station and despite myself I'm fascinated. Where are the wanted posters on the walls and the coke heads throwing up in the waiting room? The winos waiting for the drunk tank and the mirrored walls? It's fairly quiet, with lots of notes about parking offences and lost dogs, and appears to be completely empty, which I suppose says more about the level of crime in Frencham than anything else.

After five minutes the solemn-looking police officer I spoke to earlier returns and asks me to follow him. I'm led to a desk in a more central part of the police station, behind which I can see, to my horror, the doors to what look like cells.

"What the hell is going on here?" my voice rises in panic. "I haven't done anything, you can't seriously be about to arrest me!" I'm not sure who I'm yelling this at, but an older officer, whom I haven't noticed until now, answers me.

"I'm afraid I have to arrest you on suspicion of actual bodily harm, Ms Gray. Please don't be alarmed, this is usual procedure after a complaint has been made. I'm the custody sergeant and I just need you to check in your possessions, take some details and read you your rights before we can continue with this." He holds out his hand, which I half expect to be holding handcuffs, but then realise he just wants my bag. Dutifully I give it to him, but my mouth opens to bombard him with a dozen more questions.

"But who, how, when? I don't understand. Just exactly who have I hurt?"

The sergeant looks down at a piece of paper on the desk. "A Mrs Sarah," he consults his paper, "Flint has reported that you assaulted her in the Sycamore Café. Now, I understand that this occurred some weeks ago now, but we do have to take this seriously. I'm sure we can get this all resolved this evening, and it bodes well that you've come in of your own accord." He looks at me, frowning slightly at what must be a rather unattractive picture of my mouth hanging wide open. Sarah has done *what*?

After twenty minutes of humiliation emptying the entire contents of my handbag (wish I'd left it in the car now) on to the custody desk, an assortment of tampons and Beyblades spilling everywhere, and having a DNA swab taken from my mouth, I'm shown into a small interview room. A female police officer sits in the corner and another officer who introduces himself as PC Gerard indicates the chair on which I'm supposed to sit. Again I obediently sit, still trying to rub off the ink from when my fingerprints were taken. PC Gerard introduces the woman as PC Shiffer. God, she's fierce-looking. I'd love to check out her handwriting. He then switches on what I can only presume is the modern version of a tape recorder.

"Was it really necessary to take my photo?" I ask, completely on the defensive already.

"I'm afraid it's standard procedure, madam, photograph, DNA and fingerprints." PC Gerard reels it off like it's a shopping list. He's surprisingly chipper, and I wonder whether if I wasn't feeling so degraded at this moment I might actually fancy him. But I'm fuming so much at the audacity of Sarah Flint that I can barely see straight. Nothing is left of our Christmas Fair triumph. She has certainly succeeded in making her point, and her power, known.

"Now Ms Gray, it has been brought to our attention that at approximately 10 a.m. on Tuesday 20th October you were in the Sycamore Café and did purposely attack Mrs Sarah Flint. She claims to have only just brought this to our attention because she initially believed she received no injury, but has since visited her GP who has written a letter confirming that an injury to her arm is the direct result of a fall, caused by you grabbing her . . ." PC Gerard pauses and scans the document in front of him briefly, oblivious to my look of utter disbelief. "Caused by you grabbing her right shoulder and pushing her into the counter behind her so that she fell on to the floor. She has several witnesses willing to testify to this incident. Is there anything you'd like to add?"

I want to throw up. Sarah is actually going to make sure I'm sent to court. I can't believe this is happening. PC Gerard is still looking at me expectantly.

"I, um, I did grab her shoulder, but it was in defence, or well out of protection, for my friend. And I did try to apologise, but she was still quite mad," I stutter. He nods and looks so kind that I just can't stop myself, the

257

whole lurid story of Heather's affair with Nick, of the mafia's power kick, culminating in the pummelling in the café, all comes out in a torrent of anger and frustration at this ridiculous and downright undeserved situation that I have found myself in. I just moved to this goddamned place and now I'm about to be led to court in handcuffs over a power struggle between a crazy PTA lady and my equally crazy best friend? Eventually PC Gerard manages to stop me and, slightly apologetically, says he has to charge me. All I can think of is how the hell I'm going to explain this to Ben, and, worse, to my mother and John. God, I could even lose custody of Ben.

I realise I've said this out loud as PC Shiffer, who until now has sat in silence, says, "I'm sure it won't come to that. It is your first offence, after all, and by the sound of things you and this Mrs Flint will be sipping cappuccinos in motherly peace soon enough." The prospect is so unlikely I almost chuckle. What the hell does she know? But I keep quiet and content myself with smiling weakly at both of them. I need them on my side. But rest assured, next time I see that Flint bitch I'll be more likely to chuck my cappuccino over her.

I'm finally allowed to leave the station after two hours of sitting around and being interrogated, although, admittedly, once I've pleaded not guilty to the charges I am fairly quickly bundled off with a court date and the advice to get a solicitor.

I'm back in my car again, this time stationary, just to make sure, and I'm calling Jack for an update. But it's not Jack who answers this time, it's a guy whose voice I don't recognise.

"Oh hi, sorry, Jack's just gone to the bar. Ah, here he is, I'll hand you over," the strange man stutters. Great. I'm in jail, well almost, and Jack's on the pull with his mates.

"Hi Caroline," Jack says. He sounds slightly flustered, but I guess it's a busy bar and he's just had to battle through a heaving mass of sweaty post-work bodies to get his pint.

"Well, I've been charged with actual bodily harm, would you believe it?"

"Jesus, who the hell did you attack? And when? And how bad?"

"Well to avoid a second line of questioning, because I think I've had my fill for the next century, I'll make it brief. Basically I did kind of pummel this mum, Sarah, at Ben's school, but it was an accident that she fell over, and I'm not even sure she genuinely hurt herself, and it was to protect Heather anyway, or actually to protect Sarah, ironically. And then I tried to apologise and she completely turned on me. Anyway, she's a nasty piece of work, and I've pleaded not guilty so I've got to go to court in about four weeks. Do you know someone who can represent me?" I say breathlessly. I can hear some muffled whispers, then Jack comes back on the line.

"Sure thing, I know just the person. And it all sounds pretty minor, so don't you worry. Just get home to Ben and fix yourself a strong drink. You sound exhausted."

"Thanks, Jack. I'll call tomorrow."

I sit in my car for a moment, trying to pull myself together. This is horrible. This is awful. What with all the police jargon and hemming and hawing I can't quite grasp the enormity of this. What exactly is going to happen to me? What did Jack say? "Minor?" And how public will it all be? Well, I can answer that one right away — Sarah's going to make sure everyone knows every last detail by the end of today if she can, or at least first thing on Monday at the school gates. God, Ben will find out. And my mum. And John. Oh God. Do I have a criminal record now? John must never find out, that's my number-one priority. Yes, we've come to a tentative truce these days, but our divorce was such a nasty struggle last year and we fought over Ben like crazy, pulling out all the stops even though we both knew that it would have been ridiculous for John to keep Ben full-time. Unthinkable, really. But this Sarah Flint charge wouldn't be much of a trump card for me if the custody thing was ever reopened. I'm sure John wouldn't be so mean-spirited as to pounce on this. I'm sure. And he doesn't really want custody of Ben, does he? Not with Suzanne fluttering around, demanding sex all day and night, and with his busy work schedule. And this wouldn't really be able to influence things, would it?

I shake my head, trying to gain some perspective. I'm blowing this way out of proportion. I pummelled her, I'll go to court to apologise, I'll pay a fine. Surely it can't be much more than that? But Suzanne is always trying to ensnare Ben, butting in with a sweet smile, buying him presents. She's taken such a fancy to him, it's disgusting. Surely, she couldn't — Oh this is too much. I can't believe this is happening to me. A fucking court case? Oh God. How am I going to explain this one to Ben? Or anyone at school? If people get wind of this, I won't be involved in any more school activities. And I'll be on every mum's blacklist. Ben won't have anyone to play with, to grow up with. And I'll be off that drama-club waiting list for next year for certain.

I drive away slowly, taking extra care to indicate and slow down in all the right places. On a whim, I decide to stop in at Heather's. I figure Ben will be asleep by now anyway, and I desperately want to speak to someone who was actually there when I pummelled Sarah, more than anything to reassure myself that I wasn't actually attacking her as outrageously as her statement seems to imply. After PC Gerard was through with me, I felt slightly like an American psychopath who goes around attacking defenceless PTA mums.

Harvey answers the door.

"Oh, hi, Harvey. Is Heather about?"

"Sure, come in, Caroline. Gosh, you look white as a sheet. Can I get you a drink?"

"No, thanks, I'm not stopping long. Ben's with a neighbour, so I need to get back."

"Right, come through, Heather's in the study checking her emails."

I walk across their expansive hallway, still holding my coat tightly around me. Heather starts when I come in and I guess she's been emailing Nick. I can't believe her, after all this. That woman sure knows how to walk a tightrope.

"Caroline, what's wrong?" she asks, concerned. "Something with Peter?"

Oh. My. God. I forgot to phone Peter. In the rush to leave the house, to know what was going on, I completely fucking forgot to call Peter. I can't believe it. He's sitting somewhere in a posh restaurant in Wimbledon, waiting for me. Or, presumably, sitting at home, wondering what the hell he's doing with this crazy woman. I'm somewhere between about to cry and about to scream. I quickly recount the evening's events in a whisper, desperately trying to make sure the rest of the house doesn't overhear anything. Now that I have to tell someone else, now that everything is quiet around me, I feel the true impact of this ridiculous Sarah situation. How could I have felt as though I was walking on air just a few hours ago and then this, like a smack in the face? I blurt out the story, and I'm not quite through when Harvey walks in and catches the tail end. He isn't stupid and before Heather can even say anything, he's put two and two together.

"I had no idea you'd managed to drag Caroline into this as well." He turns to Heather, dropping his voice only at Heather's warning glares and violent finger jabs in the direction of the upstairs bedrooms. He shakes his head furiously, then says more quietly to me: "I'm really sorry about all this, Caroline. You shouldn't have to be involved in our private life and problems in this way. I really am sorry. I can't believe things have got so out of hand."

Heather can't meet my eyes, she sits mutely, her face beet-red. It's such a desperate mess — puppy-dog Nick wagging his tail, suspicious Alicia narrowing her eyes at Heather, kind Harvey being confronted by Jeremy Flint, poor Philip clutching his father's hand — and nothing Heather can say now will make any difference. The awkward silence builds, and just as it's about to become unbearable, Heather pulls herself together and calmly asks Harvey to give us a moment. He sighs, the fury suddenly gone from his eyes, leaving his face tired and drawn. The true gentleman he is, he leaves, closing the door behind him.

"Caroline, I don't know what to say," Heather starts carefully. "I just can't believe she'd go this far, and after so long as well. If there is anything I can do, not that you'd want me to at this stage, just ask. Barring attacking any and all members of the PTA, of course. Anything, character references, witness testaments, anything."

I smile weakly. I've known her for so long and in all that time I have never really been able to stay mad at Heather for any period of time. She smiles at me apologetically. "I'm so sorry, Caroline." Now I really do start crying and she hugs and holds me, making soothing noises.

"I didn't even really push her, did I?" I finally say, wiping my eyes and grabbing a tissue. "I mean I'm starting to doubt what really happened."

"You did absolutely nothing wrong, it's just all a big misunderstanding, and trust me that malicious, conniving cow is going to get her come-uppance. Now, where's Ben?"

"With Mrs Hartnell, in fact I must go get him. Fuck, and I've got to call Peter and apologise." She nods vigorously at that. "I just wanted to be sure, you know. This is just all so surreal."

"I know, and I'm entirely responsible for things getting this far. But I'm here for you. I promise."

At home I smile gratefully at Mrs Hartnell, praying she won't stay for a drink, then troop wearily upstairs to change and check on Ben. But the day isn't over. I pour myself a well-deserved glass of wine in the kitchen and resolutely grab the phone. I've got to ring Peter, and apologise. But what to say? Where could I have been, instead of throwing him come-on glances over a romantic candlelit dinner? I'll just plead an illness. Not me, Ben. That's good. Bad mothering ethics, but these are dire straits. His phone rings. Five, six, seven times. No one answers. Sighing, I hang up. Shit.

I clutch my wine and sink down into the sofa, looking hopelessly at a pile of washing that needs ironing, another pile of clothes that needs washing and a pile of papers that need looking through, and I just want to tip the whole lot in the bin. I put on some music, something calming, and lean back into the sofa cushions.

If I had a man about the house, would it help? Would it have helped today, with everything that's happened? Would he have laughed at my costume, helped me with Harvey, taken Ben to the grotto? Come with me to the police? Maybe, but I think I coped OK nonetheless. If I was still married to John he would have been all jealous and sulky about the Santa suit, and Blind Date Michael would have made sleazy comments and tried to get me to nip behind the bike shed. But not all men are like John or Michael, and I should keep reminding myself of that. Harvey isn't, Jack isn't, Gordon isn't and I'm sure Peter isn't. I must stop judging all men by one bad experience. But all a serious relationship would mean for me is more work and pleasing someone, changing and having less freedom and having to compromise again with clothes and budgets and time. And I like the freedom I have. That's if I don't go to jail. But perhaps Peter would have just patted my arm and driven me to the station, waited for me outside and poured me a glass of wine afterwards? Maybe I should have given him the chance to do just that, instead of unintentionally standing him up. At the restaurant. I close my eyes at the thought. He's going to be livid.

I need to talk to someone. I can't call Peter back, it's just too embarrassing to have my name show up on his display more than once. I can't really call Jack again. Heather, no, Harvey, no, Eva. I'll call Eva.

"Hello?"

"Eva, it's me, Caroline."

"Hello darling? How are you?"

I breathe out with a great shudder and start talking, telling Eva everything, starting with getting home and driving to the police station. The call to Jack. The horrible interrogation. PCs Gerard and Shiffer. Heather and Harvey. John and our custody struggle. Standing up Peter Bishop.

Eva is a captive audience, throwing in gasps of surprise, furious mutters and the occasional "No!" and "That bitch." Already, just hearing her quiet voice, I feel myself calming down.

"And now I've offended Peter on top of everything else," I finish.

"Well, I wouldn't worry about that. If he likes you, and it sounds like he does, at least enough to call, he will call you back eventually. But all this Sarah Flint stuff, God, I could just club that woman."

I laugh. "Not you too. I don't think I can do two court cases at once. Well, I know it's late, so I'll let you go, I just wanted to talk to someone."

"Don't worry about Sarah — she's got power, but we're a match for her any day. You didn't really touch her and she won't be able to maintain the case for very long."

"Well, I hope to God you're right. She seems to know so many people in all the right places. I can't turn around these days for someone connected to her. And she wants to destroy me. If anything else happened I don't think I could look Ben in the eye. Or anyone else."

"We'll help you and we'll be able to pull all those strings too, if she starts down that route. I know for a fact that her GP is Alicia's new boyfriend, so I'm not surprised that he cooperated with a fake letter. But between the three of us, I think we can rustle up some support too. Now, listen, just to take your mind off

things, don't forget my ghastly dinner party tomorrow."
Eva and Gordon are returning a year's worth of awful
social obligations. "I desperately need some help with
awkward silences and stuff. Heather's coming too. And
who knows, it will take you out of yourself and that
might be just what you need."

I doubt it. How would the dinner party from hell
make me feel any better? But I promised her a few
months ago and she so rarely asks me for help.

"I don't feel in the mood for a dinner party, so I'm
not sure you want me, Eva," I say morosely. "But I'll
definitely be there. And don't worry, you can rely on
Heather to run the show, pretty much, as she always
does, so it'll be fine."

"That's what I'm worried about," she says darkly.
"See you tomorrow."

I put the phone down and drink my wine
thoughtfully. Hey, at least it's a chance to wear a posh
frock and dress like a grown-up. I look over at my
crumpled Santa outfit, still shoved in a plastic bag, and
think, yeah — and attempt to act like one too, Gray.

CHAPTER
SEVENTEEN

Bankers' Wives

Gordon is not really your typical banker. He has never owned a Porsche or a Beamer, and except for Manila, where they were surrounded by tropical rainforest, he's never had any sort of four-wheel drive either. He doesn't wear Church's shoes, Pink's shirts or White Stuff and Gant clothes and doesn't like sailing, port or smoking cigars, not even when he was in his twenties. And he has always utterly detested golf. He's the only one, I believe, in his building who doesn't have his children privately educated. I know, I know. I'm dredging up every single cliché about City workers and bankers here, but I've met my fair share of them in the past and, it has to be said, there's always something about these stereotypes that does ring true. Anyway, Gordon's a nice guy. Not that Eva would tell me otherwise. But whenever I see him he's invariably charming and gracious, gentle and kind, and always extremely attentive to Eva — even when he's drunk. His favourite phrase is "If you can't say something good about someone, don't say anything at all."

If Gordon is not your typical banker, Eva is certainly not your typical banker's wife (more stereotypes, I know); she never talks about make-up or designer labels, or about Pilates or yoga (either going to a class or training to teach it), she never really mentions money and refuses point-blank to be a brown-noser, even to Gordon's boss and Gordon's boss's wife.

What I love most about Eva and Gordon together is that they genuinely like each other, they are always kind to each other, and are always interested and affectionate (they have this little habit of doing Eskimos and butterflies when they see each other, which is rather sweet if a bit embarrassing). It does set them apart a little from his professional environment. When I did my brief (and admittedly entirely unsuccessful) stint as John's corporate wife, I can't remember any dinner, cocktail, themed luncheon or birthday party where I met a couple who so openly enjoyed each other's company.

I'm getting ready to go to Eva's ghastly dinner party. It's been a while since I've worn clothes from the more conservative end of my wardrobe — reserved for work stuff, mainly — and I had to drag them out from way back in the closet, ruining my carefully organised system at the front. Obviously, it's quite hard to decide what to wear when you're presented with infinite combinations of sweaters and skirts in a variety of blacks, blues and greys, all looking exactly the same, so my room looks like it has recently seen a major explosion. Clothes are strewn everywhere, make-up and jewellery is scattered across the dresser and steam from the bathroom is still hanging in the air, making everything feel quite close and damp. Ben's whining.

For some inexplicable reason, he has decided that he doesn't like Harry any more.

"They're looking forward to seeing you, Ben," I argue absent-mindedly, as I squint critically at one of my belts to see if it would make the skirt I'm wearing any less boring.

"Harry's a crybaby I don't mind Maddy, but Harry had to wait a turn on the swing the other day in the playground and he cried until Edward asked one of the other kids to get off theirs."

"I'm sure that was just a one-off. He'll be fine tonight," I assure him. He stamps his foot and storms out. I can hear him clattering down the stairs. Minutes later, the TV goes on, even though he's not allowed to just turn it on by himself. I kick the door shut. The belt's crap, so the skirt'll just have to work on its own. I start flinging on make-up, wishing already I hadn't agreed to go. I'm still reeling from my day yesterday and what I really need right now is a break. I need some food (coffee and wine gums have been my staple diet for several days now). I need some sleep (I didn't get any last night; a hundred and one visions of maiming Sarah had me staring wide-eyed at the ceiling all night). I need another twenty-four hours in each day. Peter hasn't called me back since last night and I haven't yet got my spirits up enough to call him again. Too busy worrying over what I'll look like in stripes.

Which reminds me, I must tell Ben something about the court case, some child-friendly version of why his mum went to the police and will go to court, before he goes back to school on Monday. Sarah will have already started churning the gossip machine by then and I have to get in there before someone else does it for me, much less gently no doubt. Visions of playground attacks, Mrs Ellison calling me in for a chat. And then I have to tell my mother before she has a chance to prise it out of Ben. I sigh heavily. I'm quite hard done by these days. Do they even wear stripes in prison any more? Or is it khaki or light blue? Fuck it all. I tear off the boring skirt and decide to wear what *I* want to, never mind Eva's bankers' wives. So I'm wearing the barely there Jocanda thingly and Paul Smith jumper I bought from Red Dawn.

Ben and I argue all the way through packing his little backpack, me packing my clutch and us both getting into the car, and when I finally stand in front of Eva's gates I think he's still talking in the back. It would be easier to get into Buckingham Palace than into the Cheshire Pease secured residential area, where security patrols and electric fences are included in the package. I key in the pin number, eyed beadily by the snotty security guards, who stare at both me and my beaten-up car. They're always suspicious when someone else knows the code, which is heavily frowned upon, and they've had to talk to me sternly a few times in the past when I disabled the system by putting in the wrong numbers. Now I've made my debit-card pin the same number — ridiculous, I know — so as not to have to disturb the guards from their weekly fumble at *Playboy* and *Dirty Nurses*.

Finally, most likely looking rather stressed and perhaps a bit malnourished, I ring Eva and Gordon's bell, having dragged Ben upstairs. An even more stressed and malnourished woman answers the door.

"Hello. You must be Caroline Gray? Do come in."

I nod and prod Ben forward while she introduces herself as Lavinia, one of the catering team Gordon has hired for the evening. I didn't realise it was this formal or this large. Shit, should I have gone for that skirt after all? I follow Lavinia through the hall. I can already hear people chattering and laughing.

Eva's apartment always looks like a *Interiors* apartment, sumptuous, uncluttered but somehow always cosy too. They've got masses of space, laid out over one large, generous floor, with open doors and archways, a huge eat-in kitchen, wooden floors everywhere and cream and brown rugs scattered around. Tonight, the hall looks barer than I'm used to, not as though two children frequently tear around it. Which reminds me. "Do you know where Harry and Maddy are, Lavinia?"

She points down the hall. "Mrs Thompson wanted them out of the way for a bit, so they're in their room, playing video games, I think."

I flash her an appreciative smile — that was the right thing to have said. Ben's only allowed a limited amount at home, so, his initial reluctance largely forgotten, he bounds off towards the latest Game Boy, Nintendo and PlayStation packages that Harry and Maddy have talked the indulgent Eva into buying.

Lavinia waits until the door closes behind him, then turns and leads me through to the large sitting room with its oversized sofas and oversized paintings and

272

oversized vases. The corridor walls have large photographs of Eva and family, all smiling and laughing and screaming on their various world travels, and it's difficult not to stop and look at each one at leisure. But Lavinia seems intent on getting me to the other guests as soon as possible.

Eight people are dotted around the living room, drinking cocktails and nibbling at trays of food handed out by people looking as emaciated as Lavinia. There are four large cream sofas in front of the fireplace at one end of the room, with a large oblong light cherrywood table at the other end, set for twelve. I look around quickly for Eva or Gordon, but Lavinia's on the case and marches me over to a tall, black-suited man standing by a wall. He gives me a wide, warm smile, which lights up his eyes. Lavinia introduces him, as if he doesn't have a tongue of his own.

"Henry Chambers, barrister, specialising in family law. Caroline Gray, graphologist."

He looks at Lavinia and smiles, as bemused by the formal introduction as I am, and the fact that we both seem to be immediately defined by what we do. I wonder, if I didn't do graphology, would she introduce me as Caroline Gray, single mum, or Caroline Gray, best friend to hostess?

Since there isn't a woman standing by his side, or one heading over immediately to join him, I presume he is here alone. I wonder if he's the single man Eva intended for me? I open my mouth to say something more substantial in greeting, but Lavinia already pulls me away to meet the next guy. Where did Eva find this woman? No doubt she's terribly efficient and all, the nibbles are certainly circulating rapidly and everyone has a full drink, but honestly, since when was she in charge here? I flash an apologetic smile back at Henry and allow myself to be dragged to Jamie Tyne, who manages to introduce himself before Lavinia can speak.

"Goldman Sachs, trader, name's Jamie. Jamie Tyne."

In that order. He's balding and slightly leathery in the face but probably a lot younger than he looks. I nod and smile and he goes on to explain that he's just come back from sailing one of his yachts off the Isle of Wight. "It was fucking lethal."

I'm not quite sure if this means it was very good or very bad, but I don't have time to ask.

"Sailing is in my blood. In my family's blood. About the only bloody thing me and the wife have in common." He barks a short laugh.

I turn to the wife, ready to give her a sympathetic glance. But she doesn't seem to need it.

Tracey Tyne is short and slim with shiny jet-black hair pulled back very tight into a ponytail. Looks bloody painful, but perhaps looks worse because of her very obvious facelift.

I try not to shudder and shake her hand quickly, introducing myself to both of them, then drift off in the direction of Eva, whom I've spotted at the other end of the room. Heather is nowhere to be seen. Thankfully, Lavinia has been called away on some urgent dinner issue or other. Eva is deep in conversation with two men. When she sees me, she gives me a grin while surreptitiously making shooing motions. Finally she breaks away, excusing herself politely, and comes over.

"Caroline, hi." She gives me a hug. "So pleased you're here. Sorry I didn't get you settled. Gordon's just sorting out some wine trouble or other and I had to get those two together over there, so I asked Lavinia to help with the guests. Isn't she frightening? Terribly good at what she does, though." She breaks off, looking slightly strained. I turn to see Gordon out in the hall, waving her over.

I smile reassuringly. "Nice party, Eva. Let's catch up later." She hurries off and I find myself next to another girl, who's looking critically at one of the big paintings.

"Nice, isn't it?" I say, trying to make the introduction a smooth one.

I squirm during the pause that ensues until she finally rescues me and says, although without looking at me, "Yeeeees, if you like that sort of thing. Not my style. It's an unknown."

"Yes, well most of them are at the beginning, aren't they?" I stare at the painting. "I should imagine in ten years it will be worth a lot, but it's lovely to look at now, too."

"Yeeeeees."

The woman is as warm as an ice cube, but I'm starting to enjoy the challenge. Now I'm in the mood to chat and, damn it, so I will. I've had my fill of playground politics these past few days and, anyway, the only alternatives seem to be going back to the Tynes — quite frankly I'd rather stick hot pins in my eyes —

or getting scary Lavinia to introduce me to the rest. So I offer ice cube my hand.

"Hello, I'm Caroline Gray, I'm a very good friend of Gordon and Eva's and I'm an editor and graphologist."

It sounds slightly inane, even to me, and the woman turns her head slowly, looking me up and down intently.

"A graphologist? That's interesting." She speaks very quickly and quietly, barely moving her lips.

"I'm French. I'm married to George Gateley." She points at one of the black-suited, brown-haired men Eva has just been talking to. "But I kept my name."

I'm casting around for something to say in response, but there's more. In her quiet, staccato voice, Charlotte gives me the rundown. Her husband works for UBS and she used to work for JP Morgan, but now runs a nanny agency in Chelsea. She has already received commissions worth tens of thousands of pounds from some of her friends. In her free time, she studies photography. They live in Chelsea, the nice bit, she spits, where houses don't come under a million. I didn't know there wasn't a nice bit of Chelsea, so I just smile back, trying to look informed and suitably impressed.

I'm rescued by her husband, who suddenly appears at her side.

"George. George Gateley. Nice to meet you. Bloody hot in here, don't you think? Which bank are you?" Firm handshake, glazed eyes, ruddy cheeks.

"I'm not. I don't work in a bank. I —"

Before I can finish he continues. "Oh thank fuck for that. Thought Gordon had made this a complete wanker bash. I'll sit next to you then. You'll be the only fucking interesting one here."

I have to laugh, but Charlotte doesn't find it funny. George, whom I'm warming to mainly because he's making Charlotte so cross, introduces me to Sasha and Mark. They are not married, Mark relays in a series of short, sharp sentences which sound like he's finding it difficult to breathe; he has just come out of a very expensive and messy divorce from a "fucking bitch" and he doesn't believe in marriage anyway. Both Sasha and Mark are weird and wired, I think, so I back away slightly, looking for Henry again. No sign of Heather.

I back into Lavinia, who passes by with a tray of salmon sushi and tempura.

"Do you mind if I check on the children?" I ask her, feeling ridiculously as though I need her permission to disengage myself from the social dynamics in the room.

"Yes, please do, they're still in their bedroom. We've got their snacks ready to go, if crudités with hummus and sandwiches sound good to you?"

But no answer is really required, so I quietly leave the room humming with conversation and find my way to the twins' large bedroom. It's a mess of paper and toys, the walls covered with drawings, and the three of them are hunched over the PlayStation.

"I'm winning, Mummy," Ben greets me triumphantly. Harry looks tearful, Maddy hell-bent on revenge.

I murmur encouragement all around and hug Ben, needing a fix of normal affection and unadulterated joy, a hint of watching a warm Disney film snuggled up on the sofa on a late Sunday afternoon. For a moment, icy Charlotte and annoying Tracy recede and everything is all right with the world. I have a go on the PlayStation, fail utterly to climb or shoot anything, and keel over within two minutes. The children are hooting, reunited once more in their glee at having beaten me.

Lavinia comes in with a tray, casts a disapproving glance at the joystick in my hand, and announces that supper is ready. I jump up guiltily, having been caught skiving off, and tell my son I'll be back soon.

"Don't worry, Mummy. I'm cool."

"Yes, I know you are, darling." Even Lavinia has to smile. "I know you are."

CHAPTER
EIGHTEEN

Friends Behaving Badly

I walk into the dining room just as everyone is getting up from the sofas and moving towards the table. There's plenty of wine on the sideboard, so the crisis has clearly been sorted satisfactorily. Eva is walking around the table, doing some last-minute seat arrangement. I sidle over to her.

"Everything OK?"

"Heather just called to say she's going to be late, so I have to rearrange things a bit. And I don't know who she's coming with, if anyone, so I want to put her guest at the end, in case the seat'll be empty. Bloody inconvenient," she hisses, bustling around with napkins. "I was counting on her for dinner. I wouldn't have invited awful Mark if I knew she'd bail. Did you speak to the divorce lawyer? He's nice. And the only other person here who's not a banker, so, who knows, he might be something for —"

She breaks off just as the others reach the table. I sit down on my allotted chair, slightly miffed that my friend quite obviously feels that I'm failing abysmally in the male department. Mind you, after the thing with Peter last night, she does have a point. Things improve only marginally when I discover that I sit next to Henry (good) and Mark (bad).

Mark talks about his ex-wife over the smoked-salmon starter. Or the psychotic ex, as he calls her. I get the impression that the divorce from the psychotic ex must have been pretty recent — he's still at the stage where he wishes her dead or, alternatively, for her death to be long and slow and preferably in public. I feel much less sorry for him when he tells me that Sasha, his "current squeeze", is exquisite and perfect and everything the psychotic ex wasn't.

"The world is full of psychotic exes," Henry comments, reaching for his wine glass. "But a lot of them aren't actually psychotic, in my experience, they are usually more ill-used than anything. It just suits the jilted party to put a name on it all. Does she have care of your children?"

Mark doesn't expect to be pulled up on this and turns to Henry slightly aggressively. I sit back as they hash it out. Mark's clearly still a bit unhinged himself, and I don't much care to have salmon sprayed on to my new Paul Smith jumper.

"Not that it's any of your business, but yes, she does." He draws himself up. "We have three and she has ample maintenance for them and herself. No more, no less than I would pay a live-in nanny."

"Then she can't be psychotic," Henry argues, quite sensibly in my view. "The courts wouldn't allow her to look after the children and, hopefully, neither would you."

I'm warming to Henry more. Maybe it won't matter that I've ruined any and all chances with Peter Bishop.

"That's a matter of opinion," Mark seethes, fingering the salmon hectically, "but the settlement was no more than daylight robbery. I'm penalised because I'm rich. The judge said I had an attitude problem. Bloody cheek."

The table goes quiet and he visibly controls himself. "Anyway, I have a right to my opinion and I guess you have a right to yours." He bares his teeth reassuringly around the table. I'm sitting all the way back in my chair, and just at that moment Lavinia comes in with a chicken dish with roast vegetables which look and smell wonderful.

People ooh and aah and soon the hum of conversation starts up again. I catch Eva's eye and she winks at me almost imperceptibly. Henry asks about me and I tell him about our moving to Frencham, about Ben starting school and a little about the PTA and the playground mafia. Really only a tiny bit, and the PG version at that. I'm not making the same mistake twice. He laughs, which I like.

"It goes to show, power politics finds its way into every area of life. Even somewhere as innocent as the playground becomes a battlefield, in fact maybe that's where we're taught all that strategic thinking for later in life."

He smiles warmly over the rim of his glass, tempering the effect of his slightly pompous speech.

"It's nice that you talk about your son with such genuine affection. This lot," he gestures dismissively around the table, "are all about ambitions and achievements and success, as if their offspring are more an extension of their own achievements. It's tough for a little kid to live up to all those expectations and often without much of an emotional support structure. I like hearing someone be less demanding, and more realistic perhaps, about their child's development."

I nod in agreement.

"These guys here make the mafia at my school look like sweethearts. I'd hate to be in their playgrounds."

He snorts.

"I doubt if they ever even go to the playground. They probably have nannies to do that sort of thing."

He's nice, Henry, but there's no denying he is a bit ponderous. And the way he sops up the gravy with his bread is decidedly unattractive, despite his even, white teeth. Which he does, I notice, display quite often.

As Lavinia comes in and starts pottering around the table, removing people's plates, Mark looks like he's getting ready to engage me in conversation again and I quickly excuse myself and hustle out to the loo. I know it's not the best behaviour at a dinner party, but I can't bear any more stories about the psychotic ex and, spurred on by the hideously desperate motley crew at this dinner party, I'm determined to make things right with Peter Bishop. He's a nice bloke, in sharp contrast to all the wankers here, and he deserves an explanation.

I sit on the loo for a while, pondering what to do. It's quite nice in here, quiet and warm, although the large round mirror next to the sink is set so low that I get a disconcertingly clear view of myself with my knickers around my ankles.

Call or not? Call or text? I decide to text. Less scope for saying the wrong thing. Unemotional. I pull up my knickers first, to feel slightly more together.

So sorry ab last nite. Pls call me. In loo @ dner prty. Full of b/wnkrs.

Send. Another minute goes by. I imagine Lavinia standing outside the bathroom, tapping her watch impatiently, and, reluctantly, I get up. Eva needs all the support she can with this lot, so I'd better get back.

Phone rings. I freeze, my hand on the doorknob. Then, quickly, I fumble for the phone.

"Hi there. Bankers, eh?"

I sink back on the seat. Relief washes over me.

"Yeah, it's quite gruesome."

"How on earth did you end up there?"

"Eva, you know, she's married to a City guy. A nice one. And once a year they have a ghastly party for the worst of the worst. I'm just here for support. There's one nice divorce lawyer, actually I'm sitting next to him, thank God."

"Handsome is he?"

"Very." I smile at myself across the dimly lit room.

"Right. I'm coming over," he says mockingly.

"Don't be silly." Quickly now, while the mood's good. "Listen, I'm so sorry about last night. Something came up, something huge, and I just couldn't make it. But it didn't have anything to do with you personally, just unfortunate timing." Great, Gray. So much for the family-sickness line.

Silence.

"Peter?"

"Yes, still here. Don't worry about last night. I did wait for a while, but I figured you were held up. I tried calling you at home, but you weren't there." He sounds wary, and I realise that he must be thinking that if I left the house, chances were I was out somewhere, with someone else. Now's the time to be careful. Pummelling Sarah, lurking in the corner of the playground wielding a spatula in a tight Santa's helper outfit. Being arrested. None of those seem quite the thing to come out with, so I finally say, aware that the longer the pause, the more damage will be done, "Something came up with Heather, a neighbour was watching Ben, and I drove over there." That's good. Although Heather's reputation is now completely ruined as far as Peter Bishop is concerned.

His sigh of relief is audible.

"God, I was so worried I'd somehow put you off, maybe come on too strong?"

I hold my breath. That's nice.

He says softly, "Shall we try again, Caroline?"

Suddenly, he's so nice and so reassuringly normal, I can't wait to see him again. "Yes, that would be great," I murmur into the phone.

"There's an event on next week, an awards dinner? It's a bit formal but it's advertising so there won't be too much sermonising. It'd be fun."

Just what I need, a glamorous night out. I try not to sound too enthusiastic.

"Sounds good. Text me details tomorrow?" Now I really do hear rustling on the other side of the door. Quickly I whisper into the phone, "Really sorry, I've got to go now, someone's at the door. Take care."

"OK," he whispers back. "Bye." Click.

Ha. He still likes me. Despite everything, Peter Bishop still likes me. Peter Bishop likes Caroline Gray. I haven't scared him off. And he's inviting me to a fancy dinner. Incredibly, unbelievably, I may have at long last met a straightforward, honest, lovely man. Wow, they exist. No children, no wedding ring, no girlfriend. So he may not be able to commit, but at least he is fussy. Well, sort of. The rustling turns into a discreet cough and I quickly shove open the door, nailing that dinner-party smile back on my face. One of the catering girls gives me a strange look as she hurries in. I slink back into the living room.

Judging by the babble of voices (Jamie boasting about the case of 2004 Petrus Pomerol he's just spent nearly three grand on, Tracey asking Eva the cost of the paintings, the apartment, the catering, the wine, and Henry holding forth on the subject of child support), my absence has gone largely unnoticed. Just as I'm sinking into the chair, Heather arrives. She's with Nick, who's wearing top-to-toe black and looking smart out of his usual jeans and T-shirt. Heather is flushed and almost inexcusably late by now, at the end of the main course. How she pulls it off without getting her hands slapped, I don't know.

Eva is looking more than a bit disgruntled, but gamely hugs them both and introduces them as a couple, which pleases Nick so much his chest positively swells with pride. Gordon smiles, says nothing and sits them separately at the table. Heather waves at me and sits down on the other side of Henry, where she picks at her food and asks him about divorce for the rest of the evening. Henry gives her his card.

Nick tries to flirt with Charlotte, who is singularly unimpressed with his knowledge of interior design and refuses to smile.

On my other side, Mark is now drunk, his teeth and lips stained with red wine so that he looks vaguely vampire-like. I'm not sure, but could it be possible that I feel his hand on my knee as he asks me about my job?

"Gordon tells me you're a graphologist?" He smiles ingratiatingly, slurring slightly. I shudder and quickly move my leg.

"Yes, that's right. Companies pay me when they are employing new people in higher management, for example. I get the odd spouse wanting to check out whether they're matched to their soulmate. That kind of thing."

"Get paid well?"

I ignore the question, reaching for my wine glass instead. I have no intention of ending up like him, but, clearly, fortification is needed here. He burps and grins.

"Would you like to look at mine?"

"I'm actually off duty," I decline graciously.

"I'd pay you."

"No, no. I really don't want to."

"Come on, old girl. Why not? How much. Five hundred? A thousand? Nothing to me."

Old girl? A thousand? I take another sip. Fuck it, why not. No doubt, his handwriting will prove that he's a dickhead. I look up to catch Eva's eye. She shakes her head frantically. OK, OK, I won't then.

"What do I have to do?" We now have the attention of everyone else at the table. I look at Eva and we both shrug in defeat. I guess there's no way out.

"Just write a sentence in pencil," I instruct him. Lavinia, ever attentive, hurries forward with a sheet and an assortment of pens.

Seeing all the pens, Mark says, "Perhaps I should get everyone around the table to do it. Write the same thing and you've got to guess who we are?"

Everyone nods approvingly, already reaching for the pens that Lavinia obligingly carries round. Shit, that wasn't quite how this was supposed to go. Heather beams, ever the traitor.

"Oh yes, go on, Caroline, that'll be fun."

"OK. Why don't we all write 'I think Eva is an amazing hostess'?"

I like to see what people do with their "z"s. You can tell a lot from their "z"s.

I close my eyes, like some child at a birthday party waiting for the present to arrive, and everyone duly bends down over their paper.

After a few moments, Mark whispers in my ear, "Open your eyes."

I reel a little from the closeness of his mouth. And he stinks of wine. I know it's an excellent 1997 grand Cru St Emilion Bordeaux (because he's just told me) but he manages to make it smell foul.

All eyes upon me, I look through the stack of papers. Jamie and Tracey, Mark and Sasha, Gordon and Eva, Heather and Nick, George and Charlotte, and Henry. I instantly detect Mark's and Jamie's. The third and fifth lines. Aggressive, irritable, opinionated, unbalanced and, perhaps, but I could be wrong, bisexual control freaks? This one looks determined and more creative. Probably Gordon's. Three more masculine sentences. One, quite emotional, very intelligent. Henry? Could be Nick too. One looks like it's written by a man who's determined and unemotional but quite well balanced overall. It's got something white and powdery on it, so I presume that's George. The last one I can't quite decide if it's male or female. Nick? His handwriting slopes backwards slightly, which shows signs of mental instability. Perhaps I should warn Heather. Mind you, it's probably Heather's fault.

The five feminine hands. Lighter, gentler. There's one that I recognise as Eva's. It's gentle and even, but a little more agitated and erratic than usual. Maybe it's having Nick here with Heather, and the fear that Harvey's going to knock on the door any moment. This one is Heather's. It's uneven, some words almost illegible. She's unbalanced. Almost unhinged. Not excited, more manic. The last two are Sasha and Charlotte. Both strong. Very opinionated. Very determined and very arrogant. Which one is which? I haven't spoken to Sasha enough, so don't really know, but I would think the one with the small loops on the "g"s. Right, now that I've got ideas about each, what shall I tell them? Eva is looking nervous. Well, Mark or no

Mark, the best policy tonight, with all that's going on, is to be discreet, be nice, be vague.

Expectant faces are peering back at me when I finally look up.

"Who is the first one?" Tracey asks eagerly.

I go through the lines one by one and receive a round of applause for each guest I've guessed right. I'm wrong about Sasha and Charlotte, but their writing is so similar, I didn't have much of a chance. Despite desperately wanting to blurt out that Mark has the handwriting of an arrogant and repressed homosexual and that Jamie is extremely narrow-minded and has a small dick (OK, this last one I made up), I use polite words like "strong-willed", "sensitive" and "focused".

Everyone applauds my bleach-white lies. I smile, stand and do a mini curtsy.

At about eleven o'clock I look at my watch and nod to Eva that I want to go. People are drinking coffee and brandy and I'm tired and increasingly irritated by Heather, who is nuzzling into Nick while asking Henry about divorce proceedings and giving him hypothetical scenarios, all of which involve two children and a long marriage. I say a perfunctory goodbye to everyone, while Henry offers me his card, which I accept but only because he could be someone to give me free legal advice for the court case if Jack's friend Gary can't help.

Heather is fairly drunk at this point, so Eva surreptitiously removes her car keys from her handbag and looks at me pleadingly. I shrug: OK, I'll take her. I carry a sleeping Ben downstairs, while Nick supports

Heather and we slowly amble down to my car. In the car, Heather slouches in the back beside Ben, muttering something about not having enough space to stretch her legs. "And it smells," she complains. "You should really think about upgrading your car, Caroline."

I ignore her and we drive in silence for a few minutes.

"God, those women." Heather's voice comes from the back again, slurring slightly. "I don't know how Eva stands it."

"That's why we were meant to be there, to help her," I say, not turning my head. I hear her burp quietly.

"How did the police station go?" Nick asks, nodding towards the back and rolling his eyes.

"So now you know, too? Thanks, Heather. Well, Jack, you know my old boss, he thinks it will all turn out fine, but who knows. I've been charged and have to appear in court in January. It was horrible. I felt like a common criminal, and I can't shake the feeling that I'll be punished for it all."

"God, imagining you attacking Flint — hilarious. I wish I'd been there. You're the last person I thought would have attacked anyone, Caroline." Nick grins.

"I didn't attack. I pummelled." I'm a bit irritated that they seem to think it all one big joke.

"Well, yes, pummelled." He's trying to suppress a laugh.

We've come to a stop light just down the road from Heather's and I turn to look back at her. Ben's sleeping peacefully, but she's fully awake now, trying to smooth back her hair, powder her face, get out a piece of gum.

"Well, to be honest, it isn't really all that funny. I have to go to court and Ben's being terrorised at school. I have to say, Heather, I'm fairly pissed off I got involved in this mess to start with."

"We didn't ask you to pummel Sarah," Nick says, incensed on Heather's behalf. Pathetic, I think.

"I was just trying to protect your girlfriend from herself. She'd probably have killed her. And now that we're on the subject, I think in light of what has happened, you two might want to cool it a bit."

"Why?"

They both look annoyed now, Heather pausing in her self-ministrations and Nick throwing me dark and accusatory glances. The light has changed, but I'm not moving.

"Why? Because this is all getting out of hand. The mafia, the stunt you two pulled at the fair. There's only so long Harvey can live in denial, and what about your kids? Philip already knows something's not quite right and it's not fair that he should have to watch his parents' marriage disintegrate so publicly. Kids talk just as much in the playground as mums do, don't you remember that from our own schooldays? Philip's either going to hate you for doing this to his father or he'll hate his father for putting up with your behaviour. But whatever he decides, it's not going to be healthy."

A car horn hoots behind me and I quickly move on, not wanting to wake Ben, then stop at the side of the road. Unbelievably, Heather is back to fixing her face, clearly unperturbed by anything I've said. She looks up when she realises we've stopped.

"Caroline, I really need to get home, why have we stopped?"

I look at her.

"Yes, well, Harvey has an emotion chip missing," she finally says defensively. "I don't know how much we can do about all this."

"If you're really convinced it's not working, you could always divorce him."

Nick picks up on it.

"Yeah, Heather, why don't you?"

Heather snaps her bag shut. "Because of the children," she hisses, now red in the face.

"But, as Caroline said, this situation is bad for the kids. You've got to make up your mind one way or another."

There's nothing that riles up Heather more than two people arguing the same side — the one that isn't hers. She abandons her compact and glowers at us from the back. Nick gets the message and sinks into his seat, gesturing for me to continue driving.

But I'm not done. It's late and my son needs to go to bed, hell, *I* need to go to bed. But we're having this discussion and we're having it now. I'm so fed up with Heather and her shenanigans, always getting away with what's most convenient and most amusing to her and her alone.

"Look, Heather," I say quietly. "You've got to make a decision. Harvey is a great guy," I shrug apologetically to Nick, but I've run out of polite chit-chat, "and I think you won't have a clue what you're letting go of until he's gone. I don't care if you're ruining your own life, really, I don't give a shit, but this whole *arrangement*," I gesture at Nick and in the general direction of her house, "doesn't just involve you. Think about it. Stop behaving like a spoilt brat. And whatever you do, please leave me out of it."

Her eyes are bulging now and she furiously casts around for something to say, but I've already put my foot on the accelerator and she falls backwards, out of my line of vision. We tear down the road and into her driveway, Nick cowering in his seat.

I stop abruptly in front of her house, not caring if Harvey comes out and sees us all in the car, like one happy family out for a night-time drive. I march around and open the door for her so fast she almost falls out, but she manages to right herself.

She's livid now, which is a frightening thing to behold at the best of times, and she grabs me by the arm before I can get back into the car.

"Stop interfering with my life. This is none of your business. And if you think Harvey's such a catch, why don't you have him yourself, then? After all, you're the one who thought he would be a good match for me all those years ago. Why don't you take him off my hands? You're having such a hard time finding anyone new. You didn't even get that handsome barrister to ask you out to dinner and Eva went to all that trouble to invite him. You're going to end up as Caroline no-mates and no-lovers. At least I'm getting laid."

This is the last straw. I draw myself up, wanting to hit her, kick the shit out of her, shake her until her teeth rattle. But when I look into her red, angry, miserable face, I take a step backwards. "Bye, Heather."

I get into the car and start driving without a backwards glance. Nick doesn't say a word for a few minutes, then speaks tentatively, as if he's afraid of me. Well, it's time people took me a bit more seriously anyway.

"You're right, Caroline. I'm not saying she has to decide for me, well, that's what I'd hope she would, but this can't really go on for much longer."

"I think you should walk away and see if she follows you," I say tiredly. I'm done with solving people's problems for tonight.

"That's taking a big gamble."

"I think you're taking a bigger one by staying."

It's strange, but I like Nick. He's so different from Harvey and I don't like the fact he is sleeping with a married woman, but to be fair to him, he thought Heather would have been divorced or separated by now. Really, it's Heather I'm cross with. And myself for not having taken a firm stand sooner. Before I started pummelling people.

"She's lucky to have a friend like you, Caroline," he says with a sigh as we come up to his apartment building.

"Yeah, right. You tell her that."

He gets out, waits for me to pull away. I think I'll give Heather a wide berth for the next few weeks, or at least the next few days. I've had enough excitement to last a lifetime.

CHAPTER
NINETEEN

Posh Do

Nits. I've got fucking nits. Ben, bless him, has caught nits at school and has promptly passed them on to me. I've never had head lice before so I don't discover them until they're running rampant on my scalp, the day I'm going to the TV awards with Peter. Even then, I've got no clue. It's Charmaine, my lovely hairdresser, who reluctantly gives me the news, after combing out my hair for a cut and highlights. I'm sitting in the high-back swivel chair, enjoying a cappuccino and looking forward to emerging, glamorous and sleek, from the big dryer when she whispers in my ear, "Caroline, did you know you've got lice?"

I whip around and stare at her, as though I haven't heard her right.

"I have lice?" I repeat, hoping she'll grin and say, "No, only kidding." But she doesn't.

"Don't worry about it, it's quite common. You can get something to treat it from the chemist."

"But I can't," I say disbelievingly. "I'm supposed to be going out tonight. Are you sure?" I'm desperate. My big do. My night of glamour. My evening with Peter Bishop. God, what am I going to do?

"Well, you need to get some chemicals or some special conditioner and a nit comb, or you'll be scratching all night." Charmaine is matter-of-fact. "And check your son, there seems to be a real epidemic going around right now."

"Fuck." Then I have to smile. "Oh well, his dad had him last weekend, so at least that means his dad and bimbo Suzanne will have them too."

Charmaine flashes me a conspiratorial grin. "See? There's always an upside."

I haven't been to a posh do for ages. I used to go to them all the time, in my days as John's corporate wife, but I don't have the time or the man or, really, the inclination to frequent them much these days. Come to think of it, Ben now has a social life far superior to my own. Mondays he has tennis, Tuesdays swimming lessons for half an hour, after which he has his friends round for tea (usually Tom or Harry and they discuss everything from the latest gossip about smelly Kelly in their class to the fact that Ben can ride his bike without stabilisers and Tom still can't). Wednesdays it's drama club (new, we finally got off the waiting list and into the club, despite my reputation as a criminal), Thursdays karate and Fridays we have a night in, just the two of us. He has time for three meals a day, a more or less balanced diet, a regular early bedtime and bedtime kiss, and he's learning something new each day. At the weekends he's with me, he has football Saturday morning, then a Sunday matinee followed by an early supper at Pizza Express or Giraffe, or a bicycle ride along the river if the weather is nice and he's not too tired. What he does with his father I haven't got a clue, not that he's there enough for me to have to worry. Still, I'm sincerely hoping it's something reasonably constructive. Last time I asked John what he did, he told me to "mind your own fucking business", and Ben doesn't talk much when he comes back, occasionally mentioning Suzanne's sloppy kisses. Once all this Sarah Flint crap is done with, I must sit down with John and talk about his weekends once and for all. Well, I guess I shouldn't open that can of worms, seeing that I'm about to be a convict. That'll give me a good bargaining position.

Speaking of which, I did manage to mention my situation to Ben over dinner on Sunday night. Casually, really, I laid out the basics of what happened, couching it all in quite rosy terms. I didn't actually say the word "police" as I knew his ears would have perked up immediately and the whole thing would have become a kind of adventure to him. As it was, he didn't seem particularly interested in my quite dull account of grown-ups fighting in such a boring way. Little does he know, but at least I made sure he got the gist, especially when I pointed out the parallel to him hitting Felicity's son in the playground a couple of weeks ago.

"Now, this woman will make me go into court and apologise, which is absolutely fine." The lie of the century, but there you go. How far will you go to protect your child from the evil ways of the world? "That's what you do when you hit someone. And that'll be it. I just wanted to talk to you about it in case someone mentions it, but I don't really want you talking about it in school. OK? And when someone says anything, just walk away, because it's not really anyone's business."

"Don't worry, Mummy. I won't say anything. Kind of like when you have a present for someone and you can't tell them?" I nod carefully. Kind of. "You'll be fine, just say you're sorry right away. Ms Silver always says that's the most important thing."

That's my boy. If only things were as easy as that, but we'll see.

I guess, in the large scheme of things, head lice don't seem a terribly huge problem. I expect everyone in prison has nits. But right now, waiting at a traffic light, the closeness of the car making me feel even more itchy, it seems pretty miserable. Shit, that means I can't get close to Peter tonight. The nit shampoo will stink and if I don't treat it right away, I'll pass on the bloody things to boot.

And, I've got to check if Fiona will still babysit for Ben. She may be put off by the nits and I'd have to organise a replacement quickly if she doesn't want to do it.

The moment I screech up to the kerb in front of my house, I run to knock on her door. Tubby and Telly come to the door first, barking and scratching, and I can hear Fiona's voice in the kitchen shouting, "Telly, Tubby, please be quiet. Just wait for Mummy. OK. Wait for Mummy now."

Mummy opens the door and the two bound out, sniffing and licking my ankles. If dog fleas meet head lice and do battle, who would win?

"Fiona," I blurt out, gasping to catch my breath. "Ben's got nits. Are you still OK to babysit?"

She flaps her hands in a pooh-pooh kind of gesture. "God, not a problem at all, Caroline. Have you given him anything?"

"No, but I will immediately after school, so hopefully he'll be relatively clean by the time you see him. I've got them too." I shudder again at the thought, but Fiona pats my arm reassuringly.

"Don't worry, these things happen. They do go away when you keep treating them. Right, so I'll come round at six and you can go off. What's his bedtime?"

"Seven. He'll tell you it's nine, but it's seven. He has a story or a few pages of *Horrid Henry*, then sleep. He'll come down a few times and ask for a drink or something to eat. Don't let him. He's not hungry or thirsty."

"OK, sounds good. We'll be just fine."

I've got enough time to visit Angela, who does my waxing. Half-leg, underarm and bikini. I'm half wondering if I should warn her about the lice, but knowing her, I'm sure if she found any she'd tell me.

Finally, at five fifty-five, Ben has been deloused and kissed, I've been deloused, spent thirty minutes tearing apart my wardrobe after rejecting my initial outfit, and have drenched myself in neroli, lavender and patchouli to stave off the smell of the nit conditioner. Fiona and Ben wave goodbye as I drive away, feeling fairly good given the circumstances, and excited about the evening ahead.

I manage to find a parking space around Park Lane. I'm told the parking attendants are even more zealous round here than they are in Frencham, so I look everywhere, behind bushes, on fences, on pavements, on lamp posts, for a sign to suggest that it's illegal to park here. The sign clearly says it's free after six thirty and there's no small print.

We've agreed to meet at the main entrance. I stand to the side a bit and watch as the other guests arrive and walk up the steps. The women are all wearing variations of tight satin in black, cream or deep red. I'm wearing a long brown satin dress with a very low back which I haven't had occasion to bring out in ages. It's slinky but the colour tones down the overt sexiness of it, so that I think it looks quite stylish. It's a few years old, but hey, I got it from Red Dawn, and Jessica, who never lies, told me it was timeless when I bought it.

I don't want to walk up to the door until I see Peter, but I feel a bit furtive peering up the stairs and finally decide just to wait by the door, looking as aloof as possible.

It's a cold December evening and what light there is left fades to that icy grey winter does so well. I shiver with anticipation as much as from the evening chill. Black cabs, mostly with their lights still on, move slowly down the road, searching for expectant customers, occasionally discharging fellow partygoers. I am watching one particularly stunning couple with undisguised envy when a voice makes me jump.

"Hello."

I turn quickly, expecting to see Peter.

Shit. It's Toby Shepherd. Toby Shepherd looking very dashing in his dinner jacket and beaming at me. I've totally forgotten that the two work together.

"Caroline! I didn't expect to see you again so soon. Twice in one year, in a few months even, when we haven't seen each other for about twenty years. What are you doing here?"

"I've been invited by a friend." I'm feeling a bit flustered. Should I mention that I'm here with Peter? I guess if Peter wanted him to know he would have told him himself. Better not to say any more for now.

He looks at me curiously, expectantly. "Right, well. Good to see you. I hope you enjoy the evening."

He turns, still looking slightly bemused, and walks in alone. Probably left the wife at home with the kids.

Peter Bishop, Peter Bishop where the fuck are you? I'm getting antsy and am starting to smell the nit conditioner again.

And then, as if I've spoken aloud, I hear his voice. "Caroline, I'm so sorry I'm late. Very bad traffic." He bounds up the stairs.

When he's close, he stops, stands back and looks at me. Not saying a word. Then: "You look absolutely stunning, Ms Gray. Enchanting. Quite perfect on this cold evening."

I'm not cross any more.

He offers his arm and I take it, although secretly I think it's a tad old-fashioned. But in an endearing, sweet kind of way. The reception area is full of people, all jabbering away importantly, but Peter walks past everyone, whispering in my ear, "I'm not important enough to network with and I can't offer any advice or free anything in exchange for information. So we can go straight in. Would you like some champagne?"

"I would love some. But I can only have one or two. I'm going to have to be a Cinderella tonight, I'm afraid. I've got to drive back by midnight."

"But that's when the dancing starts." His face falls. "The awards go on for so long. Everyone always wants to give an Oscar speech."

"You may win and you may want to as well."

"If I do win, I promise not to go on. I'll dedicate everything to the lovely lady I'm with."

The bar has more people in it than the reception area, men and women everywhere dressed up to the nines, sipping at champagne and giggling and laughing, the smell of E'spa overpowering. I always get the feeling at bashes like this that none of the people particularly like each other but no one wants to act aloof in case one of them happens to be useful. A bit like Eva's dinner party. No doubt a playground in its own right.

We grab two champagnes from the bar and head for the seating chart. We're on table eight, close to the stage, which I suppose means that Peter has a good chance of winning.

"What have you beeen nominated for?" I sip the cold, pearly champagne, feeling pretty good, lousy hair and all. Peter seems not to have noticed the pervasive smell of lice shampoo, which is a good start to the evening.

"Oh, an ad campaign my team did for BA. I've always thought cabin crew were naturally theatrical. You know when they do the safety regulations and point to the hatches and the emergency entrances and so on, it's like a graceful dance. So I put the safety show to Lenny Kravitz's 'Fly Away' — I know it's clichéd, but the client bought it — and, well, the airline loved it and the judges obviously loved it."

"It sounds great." I'm watching his hands as he gesticulates, punctuating his descriptions, much like a dance of his own. "I haven't seen it on TV, though," I say apologetically. "We don't watch a lot. Well, not grown-up TV, I guess."

"What?" He's incredulous.

"Yes, I know. I know more about the life of all the Power Rangers, all five Ninja Turtles and Spongebob Squarepants than I do about politics and current affairs. If *University Challenge* ever did a single mums' team I would know all there is to know about cartoons."

Before we can explore this further, a short fat man wearing red tails rings a bell and booms, "Dinner is served."

There's a brief dip in the conversational hum around the room, which rises back up again as everyone slowly makes their way to the dining room. It reminds me a bit of how Ben and his friends walk into school to the morning bell, some in a measured fashion, others pushing and shoving, all in uniform, kind of like we are now. All wanting to meet their friends and talk about their toys, and who's got the best one and what they've been doing. I smile and tuck Peter's arm in mine, old-fashioned or not. Suddenly he nudges me. All the way over to the right is Matt, the nervous chain-smoking wanker from the photo shoot. He's got an impossibly glamorous woman by his side ("Probably his sister," Peter whispers) and seems to be positively bursting with pride.

Table eight is positioned close to the left-hand side of the stage. On the stage I can see two lecterns and a large table with eight awards. They look like large metal V-signs, but Peter tells me they've been specially commissioned from the famous artist Antoine Hurnot (whom I haven't heard of — he obviously hasn't made it on to kids' TV yet), and are supposed to symbolise the unity of information and entertainment which advertising is allegedly all about. Looking at the objects, shiny and grey in the light, I wonder if I'm the only one in the room having an Emperor with No Clothes moment about the huge, shiny two-finger salute.

"Yeah, that's what I thought when I saw them too." Peter has read my mind. "But hey, if I win, tell Ben he can use it as a catapult."

The short fat man shouts at everyone again to sit down and shut up.

"Mr Toby Shepherd and Mr Tim Bryant," he intones pompously.

Toby and Tim walk on to the stage and beam around, as if they know everyone in the room intimately. After a brief round of applause, the spotlight goes to the large screen. For what seems like that ages, various ads are shown, all to music which denotes the mood. Joss Stone (angst), Coldplay (more angst),

Queen (nostalgia) and Robbie Williams (not quite sure). I can't see Peter's, but it might still be to come. Lights go on again and everyone applauds. I hope the remains of my (dead) nits don't show up in the bright lights. So far so good. I smile graciously around my table. God, I think I'm the oldest person here, closely followed by Peter Bishop. There's a guy on my left whose name I don't know because he tore up his name card as soon as he arrived. I'm the only non-blonde at the table and I'd say only about half of them have their natural boobs. Cleavages are obviously in, and I'm one of the few who doesn't have hers hanging out. Everyone else is in black or cream, so I do rather spoil the general tableau in my brown. Hey, I don't care. If any of them are rude to me, I'll just shake my head and give them nits.

As the bread rolls and smoked-salmon thingy with creamy thingy inside — between Eva's party and this, I've had my fill of salmon for the year — is put in front of us, I say to Peter, "I forgot to say, you look rather splendid this evening."

"Yes, I clean up nice." He fusses with his collar and slicks back his hair theatrically. "Not really my sort of thing," he then confesses quietly, leaning forward so only I can hear him. His collar immediately bunches up again at the back, making him look refreshingly boyish among all the starched and polished figures around us. "But, well, it's a pat on the back from an industry that rarely gives pats on the back, especially to cameramen. So, what have you been doing with yourself? Heather OK?"

I'm deliberately casual. Adding nits to my list of pummelling, jail sentences, Sarah and the Christmas Fair and my recent adventure at the police station won't do. I smile nonchalantly. Quickly, Caroline, say something, anything at all.

"You know, the usual busy run-up to the holidays. Wrapping up several projects I've been working on, helping out a bit at the school and stuff. You wouldn't believe all the things they're doing for Christmas at this school. It's unbelievable. And then organising Christmas for Ben and myself. It's John's turn to have Ben for Christmas and, well, it's going to be tough."

Damn it, I wasn't going to venture into dangerous territory again. The closer Christmas looms, the more the thought of having to be without Ben has become something I dread beyond anything. I would never do anything but smile and play nice when John's around, for Ben's sake, but it's all I can do not to blurt out just how much I begrudge him taking away my small boy for the holidays. And all without ever pulling his weight throughout the rest of the year.

I quickly shove all that to the back of my mind, but Peter's looking at me sympathetically.

"God, that is tough. Why is Christmas always such a difficult time?" I shrug wearily. Peter takes my hand. "Oh, I didn't mean to upset you. Sorry I asked."

"No, don't be silly." I want us to get back into the festive mood. "I'm OK. I've got to get used to this sort of thing, sharing Ben. Maybe I'll go somewhere hot, without snowflakes and where they've never heard of

Santa Claus. And the upside is, I will have him next year. I can look forward to that all year." I smile.

Salmon starters eaten, plates removed, white wine offered, we move on to the main course, fish, or a vegetarian option of something with couscous and nuts. Everyone on our table, with the exception of Peter and me, goes for the veggie option. Do they know something we don't?

Peter's mobile rings. He flashes me an apologetic glance and looks at a message under the table. Almost imperceptibly, his face hardens.

"Do you mind if I excuse myself for a minute?"

"No, of course not." God, what now? "Anything I can do to help?"

"No, I won't be long."

He gets up and weaves through the tables towards the exit. I am watching him leave, admiring the way his jacket fits across the small of his back, when I suddenly feel a tap on my shoulder. I jump in my seat and indignantly turn around. Toby Shepherd is beaming at me again.

"Now I get it, I didn't realise Peter had invited you. Dawn couldn't make it?"

"Dawn?" I'm confused. Who?

"Dawn, Peter's girlfriend."

Peter's girlfriend. Girlfriend of Peter. Peter Bishop has a girlfriend. A girlfriend called Dawn. I feel myself flushing, my whole face is hot and tingly, as if I've been on a sunbed for too long. My scalp feels like it's on fire and my brain is buzzing so loudly I don't really hear what Toby's saying next, but I get the last bit.

"Do you know Dawn?"

"Actually, I don't." With enormous effort, I'm pulling myself together. "And I've only just met Peter again a few weeks ago."

Toby recoils, as if he's just dropped a brick on his foot. If I weren't so stunned myself, and so fucking furious, it'd be almost amusing to watch the slow realisation dawn on his face, like an exaggerated mime performance. Only a second ago he was cool, collected and ready to go win that award and now he looks at me in sheer horror, having given away his two-timing son-of-a-bitch media buddy. I say, almost kindly and with much more composure than I feel, "Don't worry, Toby. I'm sure he was going to tell me later on in the evening."

I smile. I put on my best stage smile. The smile I did when I was tap dancing for Ms Hembry when I was ten, and my feet were bleeding with blisters from practising my wings and ball changes and time steps over and over and over again.

Toby smiles back uncertainly. There's no way to salvage this situation and he knows it.

"Well, I've got to start the announcements now, so I'd better be going."

"Yes, see you around." I wave casually and turn to the man with the place-card phobia, giving him a wide grin. He flinches and grabs his menu for protection. I nail the smile more firmly on to my face and try to decide whether to love or loathe Toby for what he's just told me. I know it's not entirely his fault and maybe Toby is simply doomed in life always to be the one to humiliate me in some way, just like he did in Mr Boniface's class all those years ago. Perhaps there are just some people I should keep away from.

I sit there for a few minutes, trying to simmer down. Peter still hasn't returned and the man next to me has obviously decided I'm now safe to talk to. He's renamed himself Darth Vader on his name card and is telling me about his Chinese horoscope sign (he's a wooden ox) and food allergies (wheat, dairy, red meat, anything solid really). I listen with half an ear and grimace occasionally, gratefully hiding behind mundane small talk about his five-snacks-a-day routine while I decide what the fuck to do now. My head is starting to itch. God, I thought this would be such a lovely evening and the perfect break from all the crap with the mafia, but the only thing it's done is made me realise that fairy tales don't happen. Princes don't marry princesses these days, they're more likely to go off with ugly stepmothers who look like their nannies.

I feel foolish — I'd been so relieved that things between us weren't irreparably wrecked, so excited in anticipation of my night of glamour, my big do. But why should I, single mum and divorcee, believe that I can actually manage to find someone nice? The drone around me hushes to a whisper, the lights go down and the spotlights pick out the table and the podium onstage. A man comes on, starts a speech, makes a few jokes, and the crowd titters. Finally, about ten minutes into it, I feel a hand on my shoulder and Peter quietly slips into the chair next to me. "Sorry, Caroline. Something came up."

This is what finally jolts me into action. I grab my clutch and say even more quietly, "I'm sorry too, Peter. I'm sorry I came."

I get up and walk away from the table as fast as I can. Behind me, I hear his name being called out, encouraging calls from the audience, more clapping. I slip out the door without a backward glance.

CHAPTER
TWENTY

Party Politics

"Mummy, look, a snowman!"

Ben has opened another door on his advent calendar. He's as excited about his snowman as he is about the fact that he's got a whole lot more chocolate Santas and stars and elves and reindeer and parcels and moulded shapes to eat over the next days. I don't think they did chocolate ones in my days, I just remember having a large A4 card covered in glitter and looking vaguely like Santa Claus's house. The twenty-four would always be the biggest, with the double-door frontage, and I would wake up each morning expectantly looking for the next picture. Today, that doesn't seem to be good enough, it has to be toys or chocolates.

Ben munches contemplatively and we put the frantic getting-ready-for-school routine on hold for a moment to peek out the front window at the frost on the small tree out front. It's all getting very festive, even the weather is doing its bit. There's only about two weeks left at school, but it seems to be the busiest since the term started. The Christmas play and other advent school activities, our Christmas party and, finally, both eagerly anticipated (Ben) and dreaded (me) — the holiday break.

We take a small detour on our way to school, to savour the holiday atmosphere. Frencham looks very pretty at Christmas. OK, some of the decorations have been up since early October, but it's in December that the town really lights up. The streets, always immaculate anyway, are now lit with silver lights, tiny Christmas trees perch on lamp posts, and the river sparkles with reflected fairy lights and silver stars. All shops are decorated. (Although Alicia has gone a bit overboard with a huge post-modern nativity scene. Apparently, the colours and shapes are good for young kids' mental development, a small sign in the window informs us. More detail inside.) There is the occasional Happy Christmas and Season's Greetings and horrible plastic Santas hanging like sacks from house fronts, but everything is largely tasteful, no tacky bits. If only the restraint could extend to the interiors as well, with tinned carols everywhere you go. If I hear Lennon singing "And now this is Christmas" once more I will fucking scream.

I've started to jog with Eva and Heather in the mornings (and, every so often, Nick too), after dropping Ben off. We collectively thought that, all things considered, we should give the café a wide berth for a few weeks and do something to balance out the numerous Christmas parties. The court case is looming and Jack says that Gary — whose last name is, unbelievably, Cooper — has agreed to take my case. Court, closely followed by prison: what a lovely way to start the season. Heather and I haven't talked about our shouting match after Eva's dinner party. I've briefly told Eva what happened and I suspect Heather has given her a version of events as well, but none of us has mentioned it since. I decided that in terms of damage control it might be better to keep a close eye on Heather rather than avoid her altogether, so we've come to an unspoken truce. She's been a bit more careful with me, a little less egomaniacal all round, and I haven't entirely forgotten everything that's been said and why I was so bloody furious with her, but we've been friends long enough for it not to get blown completely out of proportion. I'm distracted anyway by last week's scene with Peter Bishop and the revolting revelation of his girlfriend. Dawn. I mentioned it to Eva and Heather but I've tried to talk about it as little as possible, unable to bear yet another session dissecting the miserable state of my love life.

I've taken to jogging with Heather and Eva in the park a few mornings a week, in the hope that Christmas won't have any of us feeling guilty and overweight.

Frencham Park looks haunting in the crisp, cold December morning. The mist wafts in the air like huge puffs of smoke rising from the ground and the trees elegantly scar a sky that looks heavy in the early light. The birdsong is clear and sharp. I occasionally spot squirrels, some of whom are so tame they come up to me, lifting their little paws and begging for monkey nuts, like some misguided Disney animal.

We don't talk much as we run, mainly because none of us is fit enough to chat and move at the same time.

But it doesn't stop any of us from thinking, and even in the half-darkness I can tell from the frown on Heather's face that she's still see-sawing between her two alternatives: should I leave him, should I not? Although I still can't work out if it's Harvey or Nick she's thinking about.

Eva seems mostly preoccupied with organising the school nativity play. As the nominated school rep, she's at the receiving end of all the competitive mums in the school wanting the best roles for their kids and things have been spiralling out of control for the past few weeks. Already, Mrs Ellison has had to call the participating parents to order and each rehearsal, each meeting, includes at least one rowdy argument, two or three mums falling out with each other and several icy remarks to carry it all along.

I've guessed correctly.

"I'm sure Tony Blair never has this problem with his Cabinet," she suddenly puffs as we're passing the halfway mark, the uphill, will-it-ever-end bit, and are on the downhill-please-don't-let-it-stop bit. "You wouldn't believe it, but we're scheduling a separate session to vote on two of the last remaining roles. Two kids, Joseph and the Angel Gabriel, have dropped out due to changes in holiday plans and now the biggest bone of contention is who is going to be Herod this year."

"Why does everyone want to be Herod?" Heather asks, shaking hair out of her sweaty face. "I thought the Angel Gabriel would be the cool guy to be?"

"Not sure, but apparently they see Herod as some kind of Darth Vader, plus he gets to wear the biggest

315

crown. Felicity Sackville has been lobbying for her Patrick quite aggressively, but I think there are some others in the class who should have a go, some of the shyer ones."

All Heather and I can manage are indignant grunts at this point, a tribute to Felicity's impudence. Eva slows down and stops, putting her hands on her knees. Gratefully, I stop too and we walk the rest of the way. Eva speaks again.

"And Karin's sponsoring the stable, has organised the clothes for all the shepherds and made the papier-mâché crowns for the wise men. Poor Marie, who's in charge of the scenery and all the artwork, is going up the wall fielding Karin's crazy requests for the stable and the stars. Things have got so out of hand we've had to have five wise men this year."

"God, where does she find the time?" I'm incredulous. I can barely organise my Christmas party without the rest of my life falling apart.

"Her Polish nanny did most of it, actually. She runs the Blunt household like clockwork. And then Karin went and did this article for the *Frencham Gazette* last year about managing to have her own business, run a house, and look after the kids. She's got such cheek. Anyway, would Ben like to be Joseph or the Angel Gabriel?"

I have to laugh, but stop quickly, clutching the stitch in my side.

"That's brave of you, but they'd crucify you if you gave it to me. Seriously, you don't have to do that."

"I think he'd make a good Joseph, actually," Eva said. "It's quite a long speaking part but he's got a good memory and his voice would carry well across the hall. And I sure as hell won't be intimidated by Karin and her lot if I think he's the best person for the part."

Not sure if that's wise, but he'll love it and it would show those last few kids who still seem to be blowing their mother's horns that he's a force to be reckoned with. We watch a fellow jogger, tiny from up here, slowly trek up the hill. As he comes closer, Heather squints at him just before he veers off into the trees, then shakes her head.

"What?" I ask, motioning for us to up the pace again.

"I thought that was Jeremy Flint down there, but I must have been mistaken."

We're already a bit ahead, and she turns around a couple of times, but the jogger is nowhere to be seen. We finish our run in silence, sharing the path only with the odd Lycra-clad cyclist and a few more wrapped-up dog walkers.

The day passes in a flash. I finish up a big project for one of the book-publishing companies and manage to clear some other stuff off my desk in the process. I spend the rest of the afternoon and evening organising our party. I've decided to have a nice, jolly Christmas do for friends and kids, a bit of fun for everyone, a project for me to distract myself from Peter Bishop and a way to rally my support structure and cement my version of the pummelling story. Rumours about the court case still abound and the mafia is now giving me the same evil eye they have given Eva and Heather since I came to the school (which is just fine with me), but I haven't yet been subject to any seriously vicious muttering from anyone else, mostly curious glances and some hastily broken-off conversations as I pass. Still, it would be nice to find out just how much people know and what the general opinion is about me at this stage. So I plan to keep my ears open during the party while showing everyone that Caroline Gray is holding her head high and is not without her friends. A fairly big agenda for one little get-together, but worth it, considering the circumstances.

The house is quiet, only the occasional sound of a car driving by. I sift through Ben's book bag to see if there are any notes about school stuff, or, much more fun, last-minute communiqués about the party. I sent out invites early so there would be no conflict with other social engagements, parents or children alike. It's after school on a Tuesday, between three thirty and six thirty. In Ben's bag, I find some old PTA meeting notices and a note from Mrs Ellison about Reception homework after the break. That's a bit puzzling — surely it's too early for homework for Reception? — but I put it aside for later to look instead at a crumpled-up invite I unearth from the bottom of Ben's bag. They've come out really well. I got Ben to draw a lopsided tree and some angels and then photocopied it. Now I look at my "To do" list again. I've organised crackers, hats, treats, balloons, wonderful kiddie bags for £2 a pop and a party entertainer (who, I hope, has a tarantula somewhere. Ben recently watched a documentary on spiders and is now totally tarantula-mad, whether they're Christmassy or not). Lots of food, the obvious stuff for the kids and then for the adults things like vol-au-vents and sausages and cheese nibbles and smoked-salmon baskets and little chocolate cheesecakes and all sorts of good stuff that I never had at any of my parties as a child. Not a rock cake in sight. Everything's finished off with a couple of crates of champagne, wine, beer. Anything else? Probably not. I put it aside for a second and look at the guest list as it stands.

I've invited only ten children, as more than fifteen doubles the cost of the entertainer, although I don't quite see why. All underage guests have been approved by Ben, which is only fair. There are a few children that Ben wants to include but whose mothers are trying to have *his* mother arrested for ABH. I don't want Sarah, Karin or Felicity anywhere near my home, not that they'd accept anyway. Ben wanted Edward to come so badly I didn't have the heart to deny him, so I did invite him in the end, but his mother sent a curt note of refusal on his behalf. Edward took it in his stride and said manfully that they'll have Ben over again in the New Year. Uh huh. Hopefully the snakes and spiders provided by the entertainer will distract Ben from the nonsense between the grown-ups.

For myself, I've invited a diverse group of parents and other friends — the usual suspects, Eva, Heather, Marie, Claire and Eileen, then a few other mums I've become friendly with at the playground and one dad who's always seemed a bit lonely during the school run. I've also asked Jack (he's accepted, although I wouldn't have thought it'd be his kind of thing) and my mum

319

(had to, she spotted one of the invites and sneakily bribed Ben into including her), Fiona, Mrs Hartnell (I'm sure those two would love a bit of entertainment and they can't complain if it gets too raucous) and James, the handyman who sometimes helps us out around the house (it'll be nice to have a gorgeous man in the room even if he does come with his boyfriend).

Then there's Anne, a mum whose little girl has only just joined the school and is in Ben's class. The poor woman looked as nervous as I did on my first day so I introduced myself in the playground and after quite a long and bizarre chat I invited her along too. She's an intuitive therapist and yoga instructor and she tells me I should take fifteen minutes for myself each day and just "be". Apparently I'm a *human doing* rather than a human being at the moment, and should practise being a tree, imagining my roots going deep into the ground so that I can be a firm foundation for Ben. After I stopped laughing, I told her I don't have time to spare fifteen minutes each day, but I might try to get to one of her yoga classes.

I haven't invited Nick, as Harvey is going to be there with Heather. I've also invited the guy with the fast car and the fast girlfriend at number twelve but I doubt if they will come. I'm not really of their world, just thought I'd be nice. I was going to invite Peter at some point, but what with one thing and another forgot to mention it when things were going well and didn't want to when they went pear-shaped. So I don't have to uninvite him now, which is handy. It would have made things way too complicated anyway, with Ben and all my friends and Jack and so on. Better this way.

John's is the last name on the list. I'm thoughtful. He's not due to see Ben at this time, and he'll probably have work on as well, but I don't want to disappoint Ben either. If my mum comes, she'll probably say something scathing like "You're not dead yet, then?" which I'd rather avoid, for Ben's sake more than for mine.

On the spur of the moment, I decide to ring John. After ringing for ages, he finally picks up, with his familiar impatient "Hello".

"Hi, John, it's me. Just checking whether you'll make it to the Christmas party?"

"I can't make it, Caroline, I'm sorry. You know how Christmas is, so many work commitments. You would know how important they are, being on the receiving end of rather large maintenance payments."

We do play nice, I swear, but when Ben's in bed we sometimes slip up. I bite back an icy retort. "Being a dad is more than paying maintenance. They would understand. I know they would."

"Look, I'm really sorry. I'm sure he'll have a lovely time and won't really miss me."

"It would be nice to have his dad there. He only has one."

Brief pause. Got to him that time.

"I'll see what I can do," he finally says, sounding tired. I feel a twinge of remorse for blackmailing him into that, but I do really think that Ben would be crushed if John wasn't there. Although I hate it when he ingratiates himself with the other parents I introduce him to (eliciting way too many remarks of "Isn't he nice?" or "Isn't he handsome?" or "You can see where Ben gets his looks from" for my taste).

"Thanks, that's all. And there's football this weekend. I know you usually can't take him, but it's the end-of-term match and there's a chance to win medals. And don't forget about the parents' evening next week after the musical, it's just ten minutes, to meet Ms Silver?"

"I doubt we'll do the football, Caroline. It's halfway around the M25, it's such a common game, and I've got some other stuff Suzie and I want to do, with him this weekend. You know how she adores him. And there're parties going on here, too, corporate things."

So it's Suzie now? Sickening.

"What other stuff? Are you planning to take him to a corporate party? Come on, John, this is the time when it counts. There's also his nativity. Eva just told me today she wants him to be Joseph. That's a speaking part, it would be great to watch."

"For fuck's sake, Caroline, I have a life too, you know, and I live over the other fucking side of London. I can't come to everything, stop pressuring me. I've got enough going on already."

"Sorry, I know, I know. It's just that Ben so much wants you to be a part of his life." I can hear the note of desperation in my voice and can't decide who to hate more for it, him or me. "He wants nothing more than for you to watch him pass his karate exams and play

322

football and be there when he's Joseph and be proud of him."

"I am proud of him."

Click. I look at the phone. John has such a short fuse these days. Perhaps I can set the Roboraptor on him.

Two days later, the day of the party has arrived. Eva has kindly agreed to help me out a bit and we've been slaving over decorating and preparing the food, fuelled by a few sneaky glasses of champagne. The children show up all at once, promptly at three forty-five, accompanied by their adults. The rest of the guests come in dribs and drabs. The entertainer arrives at four from East London and I hustle him inside, thinking fuck, half the kids won't understand what he's saying and the other half will try to copy him.

"Hi, my name's Mick. What's yours?"

"Caroline."

"And yer son's?"

"Ben."

"And 'e's four?"

"Yes, that's right." I'm craning my head to see if everything's all right in the living room. Parents and kids are milling about, Eva's liberally dispensing champagne and lemonade and all looks under control.

"Where would yer like me to set up? 'Ere would be lovely," he answers before I can speak, pointing to the conservatory.

"Perfect." I leave him to it and escape to the sitting room.

Ten minutes later ten children are sitting cross-legged watching intently as Mick takes a snake out of a box. The snake is followed by a tarantula, a chinchilla (my favourite — the fur and the eyes, so cute) and a millipede which poohs on Ben's hand. I didn't know they could do that. And, lastly, an owl. A large white owl which is so beautiful I want to cry. And some of the girls do. I guess it's not quite the usual procedure to have an entertainer at a Christmas party, but I wanted this to be special. And the kids to be occupied.

Meanwhile, the rest of us drink champagne and eat one canapé after another, slowly getting very merry as the afternoon progresses. The entertainer finally leaves and I'm playing lots of Queen and AC/DC and Led Zeppelin, which the kids seem to love. Not a Christmas compilation in sight. I have to dig up some extra nibbles as the children run rampant, systematically wrecking the house (the boys mostly, the girls just watch and play with Ben's tortoises, Flip and Flop, insisting on giving them baths they neither want nor need).

Much to my surprise the trendy couple from number twelve turn up. Stephen and Miranda, with a magnum of Krug, matching moschino jeans and broad grins, greet me at the doorway and tell me what a lovely addition I am to the road and how they think Ben is a real sweetie. Always so polite when he sees them. I usher them into the warm, noisy living room and seriously wonder if they have him mixed up with another boy down the road.

Anne immediately seems to gather a small following of yoga wannabes among my guests, including Eva, Heather and Fiona, all of whom are desperately trying to be trees, although Heather looks like she's got a touch of Dutch elm, wobbling precariously on one leg, a bit the worse for wear after three glasses of bubbly.

Mrs Hartnell is perched on the edge of the sofa, gesturing wildly, eyes wide and full of drama. A few of the mums are listening raptly to her stories of theatrical grande dames plus old and current stars-in-the-making, which always sound like a mixture of *Hello!*, *OK!* and *Tatler*.

James, the handyman-cum-gardener, has come along without his partner and Jack has come without Delilah. The two men seem to be chatting away quite happily, although I wouldn't have put them together ordinarily. As far as I know, Jack has negligible interest in DIY or gardening.

Claire, Marie and Eileen are listening to my mum, who looks in good form and is projecting loudly in the clipped vowels she only uses when she wants to impress. She's brought her toy boy, Gerald (sixty-five and looks it), who is keeping her topped up with compliments, Martini and lemonade (light on the lemonade, Gerry) while she tells my friends about her wartime childhood experiences, which become more extreme every time I hear them. Bizarrely, the women look genuinely interested, or perhaps they're pissed as well.

For a while I feel like I'm undercover at my own party, circling with nibbles and champagne, drinking a glass with one friend, eavesdropping on another, but, strange as that sounds, it's a nice feeling, a kind of quiet sense of contentment that all my friends are gathered under one roof, mine, and seem to be thoroughly enjoying themselves. My mum has left her rapt audience and cornered Jack, who is being his usual charming self. When I top up his glass, he gives me a quick hug — "Nice party, Caroline, thanks for inviting me."

I can see my mum's eyes getting misty and quickly move on to Stephen and Miranda, who need someone to do a mural in their backyard and have discovered that Marie has a background in design. "Something tasteful to cover up the concrete of the back wall," Miranda keeps saying. "Would you show us your portfolio?"

Marie is looking distinctly flustered and drains her champagne in a hasty gulp, catching my eye. I move in smoothly, giving everyone another slug and nudge her encouragingly. "Marie does all our artwork around school, she's brilliant." Marie snatches her glass back from me and has another fortifying sip.

Further on, Eileen and some of the other mums dive into the nibbles, asking for news of the pummelling and the court case. I dispense a few, vague details in a hushed voice, furtively looking over to my mum, who is still talking to Jack. Perhaps I need to go and warn him, too? I'd totally forgotten to defuse that particular mine before the party.

But it's too late. Eva comes over to me just as I'm shoving another tray of sausage rolls into the oven and whispers, "I think Heather let slip about the court case to your mum."

"Fuck, what did Mum say?" I feel myself getting hot flushes but perhaps it's just the heat of the oven.

"Heather was talking about how busy you were and that you had even more on your plate next year, what with the court case and all."

I shut the oven door with a bang.

"It's probably better coming from Heather than from anyone else. She's even more opinionated than your mum. Sorry, Caroline." She grins sheepishly, looking flushed from several glasses of champagne. "And, I know you're not going to believe this, but she seemed to take it in her stride. In fact, she said the woman probably deserved to be whacked and she once whacked a bully with a dustbin lid on the way back from school when she was a girl." I gasp at the thought of my mum whacking anyone with a dustbin lid. "Plus Marie and the others were there, telling your mum that this woman is horrible, and Heather helpfully asked how your mum met Gerald, so she lost interest after that."

I turn round to look at my mum still flirting with Jack over by the tree, thoroughly enjoying herself, poor Gerald shuttling back and forth with drinks. I make a mental note to speak to her tonight. Suddenly my eyes fall on a large figure clad in red, with a long white beard and hair covering most of his face except for two large brown eyes that are unmistakably Harvey's. Our Santa Claus has arrived, albeit coming down my stairs rather than down the chimney.

"Ho ho ho, hello, children," says Harvey in very deep tones, jiggling his belly furiously and doing a bit of a shuffle step, like a bear dancing. I'm just about to jump in and catch the three cushions precariously held in place by a few safety pins when the kids discover Santa and mayhem ensues.

The chaos subsides only after endless repeats of "Ho ho ho" and "Please be patient, children" from Santa and "Shut up or we're going home now" from the parents. Finally, the children sit patiently round Harvey and wait in turn for their name to be called and a present to be handed to them in return for a very brief "Thank you". (Each present has been carefully labelled by mothers who covertly slipped me the wrapped packages a week before the party.) All the kids are delighted — except Isobel, Claire's little girl, who hates her fluffy slippers and repeatedly bangs her head on my sitting-room floor and eventually makes herself sick. All the parents take digitally enhanced photos of their children sitting with Santa, everyone shouting, laughing, gesturing wildly. I smile to myself. The party's a hit. I go back to the oven to tend to my sausage rolls, and as I'm about to add them to the plates of mini quiches I hear my name being called out. No, must have heard wrong.

"Caroline Gray."

No, there it is again. Santa has definitely called out my name.

Still in oven gloves, I turn and head towards the man in the red suit. Heckles and whoops from the sidelines as I gingerly perch on his knee, shaking off the giant, food-stained mitts.

"Now, I hear you've been a very good girl this year," Harvey says in the same deep voice he used for the children. "And Santa and his little elves have got you a special present," he cackles, valiantly staying in character.

Harvey reaches deep into his sack, almost knocking off his beard in the process, and brings out a large wrapped box. The children squeal at the box as Harvey plops it on my lap. It's absolutely enormous and I can barely see over the top.

"Open it then," says Heather impatiently, hovering above me, Eva, Marie, Fiona and Claire looking eagerly over her shoulder. I unwrap and open the box and laugh. Santa has bought me a pair of boxing gloves. Bless him.

"Put them on," Heather says, clapping her hands with excitement. So I do.

I stand up and mock a "one-two" punch in the air. Laughs and more whoops, clapping. Even my mum joins in, clearly pleased to be in on the joke. I'm just glad John isn't here, although it would seem innocent enough to an outsider.

"How do I look?" I say, grinning at the surrounding parents and bemused children.

"Like a pro," says Santa. "And that's not all," he says, delving into his sack and handing me an envelope. I take the glove off and open it quickly, laughing and throwing the glittering envelope aside. I'm getting into the Christmas spirit at long last! The card inside is a voucher for, oh my God, a free haircut at La Coiffeuse in Richmond.

I laugh again.

"Thank you, Santa. Now I really do feel part of the in crowd in Frencham, and," I add mischievously, eyeing my boxing gloves, "ready to take on anyone who says otherwise."

Everyone breaks into applause, the kids dancing around me with the two gloves. Heather and Eva hug me and for a moment everyone crowds around me in the small space by the tree, hugging and exclaiming. What a nice party.

As six thirty rolls on to seven, then seven thirty, the children are flagging and, eventually, so are their parents. One and a half hours after it should have ended, entertainer, animals, grown-ups, children, food and drink are gone. It's eight o'clock and Ben has already fallen asleep in bed surrounded by sweet papers and toys.

My mum is the last to leave. On the doorstep, she pulls me into a hug and kisses me on both cheeks. The mulled wine seems to have warmed even her spirits.

"What are you doing for Christmas, Caroline?" Even when slightly pissed, her scrutinising look has lost none of its sharpness.

"Oh, not sure yet. Going somewhere hot."

"Are you sure? I'm going to be with Gerald and his family, and you're very welcome. But there'll be lots of children there. Anyway, well, the offer is there if you want it."

"Thank you." I mustn't cry. I mustn't cry. I mustn't cry. My hard-as-a-rock-cake mum has just shown a kindness I've never seen in her before, and although it's probably just the champagne I want to cry. Visualise Tony Blair Tony Blair Tony Blair. He always makes me feel emotionally anaemic.

But I don't have to. Mum redresses her kindness by saying, "And darling, watch what you're wearing these days. You can't afford to wear skirts that short any more, even at Christmas. You don't have the legs."

CHAPTER
TWENTY-ONE

Dawn

It's nine and I've cleared away the last of the food and drink, roughly tidied the general mess and swept up what appear to be millipede droppings on my sofa. The tortoises look as though they've been put through the grinder. And the little girls seemed so sweet. I keep smiling to myself as I hoover the living room. Good party.

I mull over the court case. So my mum knows, and obviously my close friends know, but the other mums, the ones I like but am not close to on a daily basis, didn't really talk all that much about it. They knew about the pummelling (how could they not, with such an avid audience in the café) and one or two mentioned having heard of Sarah filing charges, but they didn't really know the full extent of things and I was deliberately vague fielding their questions. I'd rather have to explain away a jail sentence later, but if there's a chance this all might go away relatively quietly, then I don't want to blab too much now. So perhaps Sarah's rumour machine hasn't really been working at full swing. Maybe she's a little wary of being in the public eye too much herself? Worried about her *reputation*?

I'm done. Finally, I collapse on the sofa, looking at my slightly bedraggled Christmas tree and the heap of presents I've been collecting for Ben. I pour myself the last of the champagne and put up my feet. God, what a night. I idly scroll through my mobile. I already have a few post-party texts, which is lovely, and I send one to Eva, thanking her for all the help. She's the best. Looking through and deleting stuff on my mobile, I stumble over the text I sent to Peter Bishop at Eva's dinner party from hell. *So sorry ab last nite. Pls call me. In loo @ dner prty. Full of b/wnkrs.*

I smile, remembering the moment, then delete it. I sip my champagne, pour another glass. As hostess, I couldn't really indulge, but there's nothing nicer than some ice-cold champagne after a long day. With all that's been going on I had managed to push Peter Bishop to the back of my mind, along with all the other unpleasant things, like a Ben-less Christmas and what might happen *after* the court case, and so on. What a prat. I presume he spoke to Toby and knows that I know and is too ashamed to say anything. Thinking about it now, maybe I'm better off without all the complications and frustrations of a new relationship. Although it is galling that even my mother is more successful in that department, gushing and flirting with her toy boy. If *she* can find a man at her age, then I'm clearly doing something wrong.

The beeping of my phone startles me out of my reverie and I slosh a bit of champagne over my wrist. God almighty, that almost gave me a heart attack. Another text. Oh goody. Oh no. Fuck fuck fuck. From

Peter, would you believe it? That guy certainly knows his timing.

MESSAGE RECEIVED: *Cnt stp thnkng abt u. Can I call? Nd to xplain.*

I stare at the message. Do I need this in my life? I put down the champagne, get up and make myself a coffee. Back at the sofa, I look at the message again. And reply

MESSAGE SENT: *No.*

The phone goes. I snatch it up before it wakes Ben. Peter's voice.

"Can I come round? I owe you an explanation."

"What don't you understand about the word 'No'? You don't need to explain. I don't want or need you to. Toby told me and, well, I want to keep my life simple and I suggest you do the same. It's not good having two on the go at the same time, Peter. Makes life very confusing."

"It's not like that."

"Well it seems like that. Call me when you're not seeing Dawn any more and you're a single man."

"But I am a single man."

I'm getting annoyed now. Who does he think he is?

"Toby said you have a girlfriend called Dawn."

"I did. But I don't now. You're right, it is complicated and I've made it more complicated, but I would like to see you and explain. I owe you that much."

"You don't. It's fine."

He must sense that I'm about to hang up because he suddenly yells into the phone: "I need to see you."

He sounds genuine, but I don't care.

"Well that's your problem."

I hang up before he has time to say anything else. I feel a bit rude, but I've had a little too much champagne and I'm tired. I trudge upstairs, get out some comfortable clothes and step into the shower. I stand underneath the hot water for ages, letting it stream down hard on to my head, plastering my hair flat to my face, masking my tears. Why the fuck can't life be simpler?

By the time I come out my fingers are prune-like, but I feel better, more perky. I slip into my oldest dressing gown, not bothering with underwear, wrap a towel turban-like round my hair and put on some music and a face mask. I look like an old woman doing her Avon beauty routine. Tomorrow is a bit of a crazy day and I've got a few more Christmas cards and stuff to get off my desk, plus I need to put the finishing touches to Ben's Joseph costume. It's not much more than an old shirt of John's that somehow survived the clear-out and that I spent an enjoyable hour dragging through mud, adding bits of straw and a few rips to make it look more like stable-wear, but it's still a little big in the waist. I sit on my bed, humming to myself and eating the last of the chocolate cheesecakes and for a while there's no sound but the rustling of wrapping paper and the scratch of my pen as I write labels and notes. I'm just looking up an address when the bell rings.

I look at the clock on my nightstand. Ten thirty? Who's at the door at ten thirty? I trudge down the stairs, trailing some ribbon behind me. I can hear voices behind the door, someone laughing.

"Who is it?"

"It's Fiona, dear, I left my handbag at the party. And there's also" — I open the door — "a young man here to see you." A smiling, clearly tipsy Fiona steps aside to reveal a slightly shamefaced and much more sober Peter Bishop.

I mutter something under my breath, disappear behind the door and return to shove Fiona's bag at her. "Thank you, darling," she trills and gives me what she clearly thinks is a lascivious smile.

I round on Peter.

"What are you doing here?" Now I'm really annoyed. Using my neighbours as pawns in his games?

"I had to see you."

"You don't have to see me. I told you, you don't need to explain or apologise or anything. It's late, I'm tired and I don't want to see you."

"Just five minutes. Please just let me explain for five minutes. Can I come in?"

"Well, you're here, so I suppose so. Why don't you take a seat? Would you like something to drink?" My voice is frosty and clipped. I could teach Delilah a thing or two these days.

"No, I came to explain and that's what I'll do." Slight dramatic pause, then he speaks.

"I know I should have told you about Dawn, but I felt it would make things so complicated and I didn't want to stress you out. Dawn and I had been going out for over five years, but we'd been growing apart for ages and the relationship was already practically over when you and I met. I lived with her, yes —" I make an indignant noise "— but we were in the process of breaking up, selling the house, and for a while I didn't know your situation or if you were even interested in me. And if you had ever asked if I had a girlfriend, I would have told you exactly this." Well, lying by omission is just as bad in my book.

He pauses, expecting me to speak, but I stay silent, so he continues and starts to pace.

"I proposed to Dawn two years ago, in Prague. We went for a romantic break and, well, I was drunk and went down on bended knee." He looks at me again. "She said yes." Another pause. This is so awkward, it hurts. "When we came back I realised I'd done the wrong thing. I didn't want to marry her." Silence. He doesn't say anything either.

"You told her that?" I finally ask.

"No."

"So you're married?"

"No."

"Well, what then?" I'm getting annoyed with this.

"I didn't mention it again and neither did she. She only told her parents and a few friends, but I think they guessed my heart wasn't in it."

I'm stunned.

"Wait, let me get this straight. You propose to someone and then don't even have the good grace to tell her that you don't want to marry her any more? And Dawn plus friends and family allow you to get away with it? I think you deserve each other."

"I suppose so." He has the grace to look abashed. "But there's more. So you and I met and got along great and Dawn and I got an offer on the house, and all of a sudden everything seems to fall into place." I make another indignant noise. Trust men to wait until things work themselves out rather than taking action. "But then I was just about to move in with a friend until I found a place of my own when Dawn dropped the bomb. She was pregnant. It was the night I got back from Wimbledon and you'd just stood me up. I was so angry, it was all just fucked up. And I wanted to call you, but I couldn't leave her in the lurch. I just couldn't do it. And when I talked to you I was so relieved that we were still OK, and I still didn't know what to do. It was awful. For a week or so we co-existed, trying to figure out what was going on, and then she came clean. She'd been desperate for us to get back together, to try to patch things up, but it was the last straw. She called me again, the night of the advertising do, but I just couldn't do it one more day. And that's the truth."

I sit down. My turn to stare into the fire now.

"Poor girl," I finally say. "I thought I made my life complicated sometimes, but talk about a mess."

"I know, I'm not proud of it, believe me." He does look earnest in his entreaty. "Toby didn't really know Dawn and I were splitting up. We're not that close. The last he knew we were still together. I tried to call you but didn't want to leave messages and, well, I just felt I should explain and apologise."

He smiles beseechingly, looking tanned in the halflight and annoyingly handsome.

I'm not ready to give in so quickly.

"You're looking tanned. Have you been away?" I say accusingly.

"Yes, working in Tunisia doing a commercial for a holiday company. Wonderful country, but everyone got food poisoning. I was the only one who wasn't struck down."

"Did you win that award?"

"Yes, I did. But it wasn't quite the same with an empty seat next to me."

Slight pause again.

"Do you want that drink before you go, Peter?"

"Yes, I wouldn't say no to a drink now. Do you have any wine?"

"Champagne is all I've got left. It was our Christmas party today, but we had the parents over as well. Lots of mums and dads with very sore heads tomorrow."

"I wish I could have been there. Did Ben have a nice time?" He follows me into the kitchen, but retreats a bit when I start opening the bottle.

"I'm perfectly capable of opening this, had plenty of practice today, after all. Yes, Ben had a really nice time."

I give him a glass of frothy champagne and pour another one for myself, sitting down at the kitchen table. I don't think I'm quite ready for romantic, dimmed lights in the living room tonight.

"So, what've you been up to?" He takes a sip and another one. We both breathe out slightly, letting go of the tension. I grab the bowl of crisps from the counter, struggling to think how to continue the conversation.

"I've taken up running in the park with Eva and Heather, which has been good. This," I gesture with my hand full of crisps, "isn't helping much, but hey. And there's been loads going on at Ben's school, as usual."

I chatter on a bit, enjoying talking to him about mundane stuff, friends, work, school, and he nods and frowns and laughs in all the right places. He talks a bit about Tunisia and a new assignment he's going to do in January. He doesn't mention Dawn, I don't mention Sarah or John. After a while, the conversation dries up and we drink the champagne, not talking, just listening to the last few tracks of the CD. He looks at me, still smiling, which makes me a little embarrassed, then looks down into his drink.

"I don't know whether you would be interested, but you are very welcome to spend Christmas with me and my family. I know you said Ben wouldn't be with you."

I'm touched. And a tiny bit freaked out at the speed with which things are rushing along. But, beyond everything, I'm touched. That makes two people who've wanted to take care of me today.

"That's incredibly kind of you, but I don't want to be in a family setting, if you know what I mean. I was thinking of going somewhere hot, to laze around on the beach for a few days."

If I say it often enough I might just convince myself. He doesn't quite buy it, but lets it go. It's really too early in our relationship for that kind of stuff.

He gets up.

"Well, I better go now. It's late. And it's a school night, right?"

I chuckle. "Different world for you, huh? Thanks again for coming by, it was nice seeing you."

I show him to the front door and he pulls on his coat. There's a small moment of awkwardness as I open the door and he turns at the same time, bumping into me. Our faces are close and his eyes find mine for a moment. I can feel it, he wants to kiss me. I half close my eyes, just in case, but he doesn't do it. He smiles and, strangely, just pats my arm.

As I close the door behind him, I'm disappointed. I haven't been kissed for ages, well not by a male over four that is, and things seemed to be going well. I'm about to turn off the light in the hall when I catch sight of myself in the mirror.

Shit. Double shit. I'm orange. My whole face and neck are bright orange. I'm a walking Kiora. Bloody fucking face mask. That's probably why he kept smiling. He was laughing at me and all the time I thought he was flirting. Damn, the one time in months that I have a handsome man in my house and I can't even look half decent.

I go upstairs and check on Ben, who is still clenching his new green Power Ranger, express delivery from Santa, and I give him a kiss on the forehead.

"You don't mind if your mummy looks like an orange, do you, darling?" I whisper.

He snores and turns on his side, still clutching the toy.

I walk back to my bedroom and slowly undo my ragged dressing gown and let it fall to the ground. Looking at it in a crumpled heap on the floor, I feel myself going bright crimson underneath the orange mask. I'm not wearing knickers. Or a bra. Christ, how was I sitting? Did I lift my knees up or cross my legs at any time? Fuck, what did I do? Did I give him a Sharon

Stone moment? I really, really must pull myself together for next time or he'll run away.

Pushing Peter Bishop firmly out of my mind, I slide below the covers with a grateful sigh and sink into oblivion.

CHAPTER
TWENTY-TWO

Playing Happy Families

It's the week before Christmas. Everyone I meet on the streets of Frencham is supposed to be smiling, but, without exception, everyone looks as cross and bothered as I do. Looking happy is tiring, especially when you're not. And the weather is foul.

The court hearing is on 27th January. Bloody great start to the year. When I call Jack to check Gary's progress, I have a hard time not whining over the phone. He says Gary is prepared and has all the details and he'll arrange for the two of us to meet early in the New Year. He also wants to meet to talk about a few projects he's got coming up. The money would be more than welcome, but the prospect of more late nights is daunting.

Last night, Harry slept over (he and Ben have made their peace over the new green Power Ranger) and spent most of the night mashing chocolate into the £500 rug I bought at the Spirit of Bloody Christmas Exhibition last year. This is a dry-cleaning bill I could do without.

Then this morning I got a parking ticket from the fat guy who always smiles at me so graciously as he waddles down our street. "I've got a parking permit," I said, sounding as calm as I could, feverishly reciting my slightly modified mantra "May you be happy, may you be well, you mean fucker" in my head. But I was two millimetres over the yellow line or something and the shit still gave me a ticket. That's £40 down the drain and no use filling out a stupid yellow complaint form, it will just be fucking ignored and I'll end up coughing up £120 instead, wasting an hour filling out the form and calling the bloody council and feeling like a mug at the end of it all. I wouldn't mind so much but the fuckers always smile as they stick the ticket on the windscreen. It's so infuriating.

Then I lost the silver and amethyst pendant I was given in Italy last year by a friend who told me it would bring me luck. Now that really pisses me off.

And now I've forgotten my kit for the gym and with no time to drive back and still get to the spinning class I wanted to go to, I end up buying a pair of bright pink shorts that I will never wear again. And my shoes are too tight so they will go straight in the bin afterwards. The small highlight is working out with Nasima, an irritatingly perky twenty-something personal trainer whom I only ever see as a special treat, when I have the time and money (which is rarely). She gets me to sweat more than I ever do by myself and just laying eyes on her makes me lose a pound, from sheer terror alone. She's also a great listener, which comes with the profession I guess, so I offload my misery on to her as she starts stretching my right leg over as far past my head as she can reach. At each push, I gasp for breath, but she goes on, heedless of my agony.

"Don't get me wrong. I'm a glass-half-full sort of . . . argh . . . girl. Look on the bright side, see the silver lining before I see the cloud, see the trees *and* the wood, know the mantras to . . . grrr . . . improve life expectancy, wealth, health and happiness, but nothing is working today. I've played Elton John's 'Tiny Dancer' over and over again, which is the most uplifting song in the known universe, marginally beating ELO's 'Mr Blue Sky', which on a shitty day . . . err . . . in December seems inappropriate. I've gone for a run and now I'm here, and I still can't shake this grey-day feeling." I sit up, gingerly feeling my leg, sure it's broken. Nasima listens, says nothing and grabs my other leg, silently starting to push me to my physical limit.

"It's not that I have anyone or anything in particular, it's just that life's treating me like shit today. And I don't like it."

My left leg is now in excruciating pain, which Nasima calmly reassures me is good for me. I stop talking to get my breath back. Is there a doctor on the premises? I think she's seriously damaged something this time.

She smiles, tells me not to worry, that everything will be fine. That I am an amazing woman and don't need a man. Not this one anyway. She probably says that to all of us and there are hundreds of amazing women walking around Frencham.

Well, I reflect, as I hobble out of the gym, I may not be having Ben for Christmas this year but I'm making the time I do have with him as good as possible. I've taken him to see *The Snowman*, which was beautiful and sad. We both cried. How can a children's story include one of the major characters dying? OK, sort of dying — melting. It's just too upsetting for words. Then we went to see *Dick Whittington* at Frencham Theatre with my mum (instead of dinner at her house, what a coup). It's a bit different as Dick now has to be called Richard, for all the obvious reasons, but honestly, he's Dick Whittington. And I take Ben to see Disney on Ice, where he munches on popcorn and watches Woody and Buzz Lightyear beat the crap out of the Evil Emperor Zurg. I already have most of Ben's presents, mainly because I started thinking about those in early April, only scrabbling to get everyone else's around mid-December. I'm ashamed to admit that Ben will do well this year, although I was a bit taken aback when we wrote his letter to Santa.

Dear Santa

I would like this year some skates and a Power Ranger toy — the new green one which moves its head. I'd also like a Robopet and a Roboraptor and a speed bike and a Dr Dreadful Chemical Lab. (*Ben wants to poison Patrick. I sympathise, but have tried to talk him out of it. Honest.*)

Love Ben. Kiss kiss kiss.

Five things, more than £500. Gosh.

The list was sent off late November and now he waits in hope. He's already got the green Power Ranger from Santa Harvey. And when we went to New York earlier this year I secretly got him trainers that double up as roller skates from the huge Toys R Us in Times Square. They won't be available in the UK for another year and with the increased competition among school kids about who has the best toys and all, I'm glad Ben will have something special. I'm a sucker, I know, but he did really want them, so I caved in. And maybe now Yoshi can go and stuff his weird Roboscorpion that turns into a man-eating spider wherever. Ben will have his own cool toys to show off. I've texted John the list as well and asked what he wanted to get. He said none of these things. He's already got him a £400 Scalextric set, although I'm not sure who that's really for.

School slowly winds down and the nativity play goes without a hitch. Ben makes a brilliant Joseph. He is very attentive to a rather obnoxious Mary who has a wind problem and an Angel Gabriel who keeps losing his wings. He is the best Joseph that I've ever seen, and Heather and I stand and clap for about ten minutes, surreptitiously calling encore out of the sides of our mouths. Eva goes onstage, blushing and laughing, probably thanking her stars that the politics of Herod and Gabriel are now safely behind her. As we walk out, I see Sarah at the far end of the hall and quickly steer Heather to the other side, backstage. I've been successfully keeping my distance from Sarah and her cronies for weeks now. We keep to our spot by the trees and they to their place by the benches, but it's so chilly

347

out that no one really lingers in the playground all that much anyway. And thankfully I've been so busy that I haven't really been in the café much either. Eva and I sometimes go during off-peak times, but Heather has stopped going altogether. And when I see any of the mafia on Frencham High Street, I walk on the other side of the road, coward that I am. I asked Jack, though, and he's given me absolution — apparently, it's the right thing to do under the circumstances.

Heather and I go back to the dressing room (a classroom repurposed as a changing room for the whole cast) and a gleeful Ben jumps into my arms. "Did you see me, Mummy?" I smile and hug and do my "wows" and Ben scampers away happily to get his things.

As well as the nativity, The Sycamore is organising a school musical on the last Thursday of term and a charitycard sale. I swear, I'm spending more time (and money) up at that school than I could ever have dreamed I would. And then it's the parent/teachers meetings, just afterwards. I've got a five-thirty slot with Ms Silver for ten minutes, and I've talked at John for about fifteen minutes, trying to impress upon him the importance of his turning up vs not turning up. These days I spend more time talking to him than I did during our last year of being married, and most of it is about activities involving Ben and how John will participate. He hasn't made it to the nativity and he'll only just tear into the musical after a corporate do; he hasn't bought anything at the bake sale a couple of weeks ago. Even he recognises that he definitely needs to make five thirty with Ms Silver on Thursday.

But first, the musical. So at three thirty on a grey Thursday afternoon, about a hundred mums and dads are crammed into the hall, which is decorated with red and blue paper chains and a Christmas tree that touches the ceiling and is completely covered in silver baubles and tinsel courtesy of PTA funding. Everyone sits on chairs suitable for much smaller bottoms. As the Stroppy Christmas Tree Fairy enters the room, followed by a line of elves (Year 5s), baubles (Year 4s), elves again (Year 3s), stars (Year 2s), gingerbread men (Year 1s) and tinsel (Reception), both John and I are there, together with my mum who insisted on coming too, waiting to grin at Ben if he looks up. I sit at the front and John, having come in a bit late, stands at the side with the camera. Peter would have taken beautiful shots but he's caught up in a project and, anyway, we're not quite at the meeting-Ben-and-the-rest point yet.

Our silver tinsel enters and sees me and grins and then spots his daddy. He can't keep his eyes off him and then just walks out of line and hugs him, as if he hasn't seen him for years. When John is able to disentangle himself from Ben's vice-like grip round his knees, he bends down and whispers in his ear, probably encouraging him to go back and join the rest of the tinsel. Ben nods, tries to get John to come with him onstage, but finally just bolts back into place, occasionally waving at John and me. I can just see Felicity and Karin out of the corner of my eye, both narrowing their eyes and shaking their heads. Karin's face looks like it'll crack and shatter like glass under too much strain if she smiles and frowns in too quick succession.

Ben and his year sing songs about how it's wonderful being silver tinsel and John and I are the loudest and proudest parents there. There's a bit of plot, a lot of dancing and singing, and at the end of the last song everyone bows, glitter and papier mâché flying everywhere, and marches out.

When the last child has gone, Mrs Ellison takes the stage.

"Thank you, mums and dads, for coming today. The children really enjoyed performing for you. They worked hard on the project and I know you'd like to give them a very warm round of applause again when they take another bow. A particular thank you to Marie Smith, who did the design of the scenery, and all the other mums and dads who helped with the costumes. But special thanks go, as always, to Sarah Flint and her team at the PTA. Well done." She points to the back and claps.

I turn around and, of course, Sarah has joined Karin and Felicity, who flank her on either side, like bodyguards.

The lines of tinsel, stars, gingerbread men, baubles, elves and the Stroppy Fairy herself (Karin's daughter, Sophia, now that I've taken a closer look) all march back in for a final bow, some looking down as the others go up, like a colourful, sparkly, disorganised football wave. My mum is the first to clap, embarrassingly, but all parents follow suit more than enthusiastically.

Mrs Ellison comes back onstage to announce that craft projects and artwork have been put up for us all over the school. "Please feel free to go around and have a look. Apologies again for running our parent/teacher meetings right after the musical, it's just this year, because of various scheduling problems. Next year we'll go back to a week night during the first week of December. Anyway, I look forward to seeing some of you later and hope you enjoy your children's work." The lights go on and everyone starts filing out.

Eva and Gordon are there, Heather and Harvey as well, but we don't manage to get to them until we're almost into the main hallway, the throng of parents pushing and shuffling all around us, waiting around to collect their kids. I half wish we didn't have to bump into them, really, it's always exceedingly awkward when Eva and Heather are forced to engage with John. Neither of them likes him, in fact they told him in no uncertain terms that they thought he was a fuckwit the last time they actually talked to him, on the steps of Chetley court-house. Since then, they've studiously avoided each other during the few times that John has shown up at school dos. Thank God my mum has picked her way back towards the stage, to look at the decorations and things, otherwise John wouldn't survive all the glacial stares.

Harvey knows very little about John, but when it becomes apparent that the wives are less than forthcoming, he kindly enquires after John's job, his

351

car, business in general, nodding sympathetically as John makes a few comments about the market being good but changeable, you never know, and so on. Finally, with even the weather refusing to yield much in the way of subject matter, conversation dries up altogether and we gratefully crane our necks to see the children coming to rescue us.

Eva and Gordon have their teacher meeting in five minutes, but our time slot with Ms Silver isn't until five thirty, so when Ben hurtles towards us, half of his tinsel still pinned to his back, and grabs John's hands, we walk around and marvel at all the colourful bits and pieces. Ben keeps up a running commentary on the other kids milling around, on projects, his lunch boxes and any general titbit he thinks his dad might find interesting. John feels slightly anxiously for his mobile, but allows himself to be tugged along, smiling into his small son's expectant face and nodding in all the right places. I fall behind a little to walk with Heather, watching John closely in case he starts talking to any of the other parents. I can't risk him finding out too much about this court case. Already Ben has mentioned something about the police and me having to say I'm sorry and John, half laughing, commented on our son's lively imagination, but I know he could dig deeper into that at any moment. Harvey has disappeared with the kids to admire their costumes and the backstage area. My heart lurches when I look at Ben's tinselly back and his earnest face. Heather, in an uncharacteristic display of sensitivity, squeezes my arm and we walk on in companionable, slightly sombre silence as the decibel level around us rises and falls in waves.

I see Claire and Eileen waving me over; they're with their other halves, Dean and Trevor respectively, who didn't manage to make my Christmas party. I've seen Claire's husband before, washing his car and watering the front lawn, but I size up Trevor with discreet curiosity. Where Dean is short and jolly, always chasing his girls around the garden, constantly pottering around the house, putting things up, sawing things off, Trevor seems quieter, more reserved. Not at all what I'd have pictured my outgoing friend with, but there you go.

There's a few of the mafia about, as usual. I can spot their La Coiffeuse bobs sailing elegantly through the crowd. As we walk by a particularly garish display of labels arranged into some kind of recycling project, I overhear one mafia dad talking earnestly to his little son while his wife smiles upon them benignly. "Better", I catch, and "handwriting" and "grades". Is he telling him he could do better with neater handwriting and improve his grades? I spot Anne and her daughter perched on a window seat talking, scrutinised by a few beady mafia eyes who clearly disapprove of such goings-on and I see Helen, the yoga vs pilates mum from Sarah's play date, strolling through the halls with a man who looks as though he belongs on the cover of *GQ*. Toned and chiselled, not less than six three. I think he's prettier than she is.

The Japanese couples are staring up at everyone, looking as bemused in the crowds as they did on the first day of school. The second wives, make-up and hair immaculate, aren't talking to anyone, not even their husbands, who look old enough to be their fathers. The gym mums look almost unrecognisable out of their running gear. They do clean up nice. I smile at a couple of fellow spinners, reddening slightly at the memory of my unfortunate pink shorts, and move on.

Up ahead, I see John reach into his coat, no doubt pulling out his mobile phone. I quicken my step just as he gently prises Ben's fingers from his arm, showing him the phone and pointing to the corner. Ben nods and looks around for me, slightly forlorn in the crowd. John's already crouched over his phone in the corner, speaking rapidly and impatiently, probably to his long-suffering secretary, Geraldine. I gesture to him, trying to get his attention, pointing to the clock above and the corridor to the left.

He smiles and nods equally exaggeratedly, clearly thinking me a patronising bitch, but he doesn't stop talking. Meanwhile, my mum's arrived, assessed things with one shrewd look, and has taken Ben off to show her the Christmas landscape by the back wall.

"God, he'll be the end of me one of these days," I say to Heather, my head swivelling back and forth between Ben and John.

"Fuckwit," she agrees emphatically, then looks at her watch and groans. "Shit, we're due with Ms Allen now. *Harvey.*" The people next to us hastily move out of the way as she charges through the crowd. When I look back over to John's corner, he's gone. Shit, what now? I try to move through the crowd quickly, craning to see his tall, lanky frame over the sea of heads, but he's nowhere to be seen. Double shit. I make my way back to the Christmas display where I last saw my mum and Ben, but they must have moved on because they, too, are nowhere to be seen. I close my eyes for a second. My festive mood and parental pride from an hour ago have evaporated completely. I turn on my heel and march out, into the other building for my appointment with Ms Silver. Out of the corner of my eye I see Sarah coming out of a classroom with her husband, but I'm in no mood to be meek, so I flash her a pointedly cold glare, baring my teeth in a grimace. She recoils in surprise and quickly pulls Jeremy down the hall.

I pace the little space before Ms Silver's classroom impatiently, gripping my purse in one hand and Ben's school file in the other. The person before me must have a lot to say, we're already five minutes into my session. I mutter something savage under my breath and open Ben's file on the window sill. A few colourful drawings fall out, some other bits and pieces he's written, his loopy, scraggly handwriting filling the lines, almost squished on the paper. I smile at drawings of Darth Vader and other mechanical marvels. There are lots of paintings with a house and a little family of stick fingers, one with longer hair, all holding hands. There's one that's clearly Ben and myself and, I squint to see it, tortoises? They look like lion cubs, but I'd find that hard to believe. He is such a storyteller, though, so who knows. My anger melts away as I trace some of the garishly green paint swirls that are meant to be my hair.

The door opens, startling me out of my reverie. Karin Blunt walks out and her small, doll-like form immediately brings back all the irritation and resentment that I felt just moments ago. Contrary to Sarah Flint, Karin looks me in the eye. She says nothing, though, just smirks knowingly and pushes past me forcefully, brushing my arm needlessly in the process. I rear up as she does so, ready to pounce, but Ms Silver walks out and smiles at me.

"Right, Ms Gray. Sorry to keep you waiting." She looks from me to Karin, frowning, dismissing her.

I march into the classroom.

"No problem. Sorry my ex-husband isn't here yet. He's around, but had to take an urgent phone call."

"Should we wait for him?" Ms Silver asks solicitously, though looking at her watch slightly nervously.

"No, no, let's just get on with it. How is Ben doing? Any more problems with some of the maf — the other kids?"

"No, I'm pleased to say. Ben is such a lively, fun-loving boy who socialises well with the other children in the class."

I laugh. "Does that translate as 'He's a bit of a character, but can get on with most of the kids'?"

Ms Silver chuckles.

"No more accusations have been made, you'll be pleased to hear. Ben's got a really good group of friends and they seem to get along rather well with the rest of the class these days. They've been swapping lunches — a big thing around here." I'm horrified. Must talk to Ben about that before Sarah Flint gets wind of it and puts slugs or worse in her son's sandwiches. "And things seem to have simmered down. Both Edward and Jennifer are good to have in the playground, as is Tom Smith." She consults her notes, ticks off a few things with her finger, then looks up, blinking at me through her spectacles.

"He's such a delightful little boy, Ms Gray. Thoughtful and considerate, and I think the other children really benefit from his creativity and vivid imagination. He's always got interesting ideas for stories and is very good at inventing games." She pauses. "I know I'm not supposed to say this, but he's one of my favourites. He's so sweet, I could gobble him up sometimes." This isn't, strictly speaking, what I'd expected from a teacher who is supposed to remain objective, but I have to smile, thinking back to what Philip told Ben on his first day at The Sycamore. I hope Ms Silver never tells him he's edible to his face because Ben has the memory of an elephant and, as far as I know, has now realised what a cannibal really is.

The cannibal continues.

"He is doing really well with his writing and he obviously reads a lot, judging from the stories he comes up with, but he definitely needs more help with his numbers. You know, not only supervising his actual projects when he gets them but weaving in additions and subtractions throughout your daily activities with him, casually. Two apples plus one apple, that kind of thing. It's not a problem or anything, nothing that support at home wouldn't take care of, but it's just worth keeping an eye on." I nod, already making mental lists of activity books and practice routines and such.

Ms Silver speaks again. "I should point out, and a leaflet has gone home with Ben a little while ago, too, that we've decided this year for the first time to start giving Reception some homework. I know it's not usually done until Year 1, and even then they're given relatively undemanding workloads, but we've done a lot of research this year, initiated and funded by the PTA — so your hot-dog money has been well spent, really." She smiles. "The general consensus was that kids benefit from working at home in so many ways, even as early as Reception. Plus, it's become clear that the reason that some of our children are so much further behind than others is that they don't get enough support at home and we hope that with a more structured approach, i.e. giving them specific assign-ments, we can jolt some of the parents into action."

"God, Ms Silver, it makes for an incredibly long day for the little ones. And all they want after school is to run around and tire themselves out. And, I have to say, I think that's best for them."

She smiles.

"I've been getting a huge variety of reactions from Reception parents and we'll be dedicating one of our parents' meetings early next year to this issue. I think we should try it for a few weeks and then it's only fair that everyone gets a say once we've had a bit of time to see how it works out. So why don't you come along to that and we'll be able to discuss it with everyone else."

I make a mental note to find that piece of paper Ben brought home the other day. It must still be in that stack on the living-room sideboard.

"And I hope," she says pointedly, "that things are going equally smoothly for you? If you do have any issues with any of the other parents, please let us know. We need to know as it can affect the children." She looks at me sternly and I feel sheepish thinking about my face-off with Karin in the hall just now.

"Yes, Ms Silver, thank you, all is fine." I pray she hasn't heard any of the whispers about a certain court case. Which reminds me, I must get back to John and prevent him from talking to some of the other parents. Although that doesn't strike me as particularly likely, seeing that he's so busy on the phone.

I make my way back into the hall, which is considerably emptier now, and almost immediately spot my mother and Ben. They both look somewhat tired, but Ben perks up when he sees me.

"Mummy, I showed Granny my Darth Vader pictures, and she said Santa might have something else, something special for me." I smile gratefully at my mother as she hands me Ben's bag and things. Her face freezes and I quickly turn around.

"Sorry I'm late." John bolts up the stairs to the entrance hall. "I had a phone call I had to deal with. Really sorry." He picks up Ben to swing him around. I eye him reproachfully, but he does look stressed and dishevelled and out of breath and I simply can't find any more energy today to keep nagging. In the end, it's most important that he showed up for the musical, and

Ben doesn't really care that he didn't see Ms Silver. My earlier wrath seems out of proportion now. My mother has no such qualms, though, so I quickly elbow her just as she opens her mouth. She sighs with audible exasperation, gives me a look that clearly says pushover and gives him a look that would even more clearly say fuckwit if she knew the word, and hugs Ben.

"Bye, sweetie, I'll see you soon, OK? You were such great tinsel today. Granny is very proud of you."

I say feebly, "Why don't you come back home and have some tea?" but she waves me off.

"No dear, I'm meeting Gerald for a drink at The Chestnut." She's already out the door, waving goodbye to Ben one last time. God, these are dire straits indeed if my own mother is starting to frequent my dating haunts. And, to top it off, has more dates than me.

Ben is pulling John towards the gates.

"Come on, Dad, Mummy said we'd go to Pizza Express to celebrate. I'm having a Four Cheese, and you?"

John looks at me helplessly over his shoulder. "I don't know, Ben, actually, maybe your mum wants . . ." His voice trails off and I step in smoothly.

"Yes, why don't you join us, John? I'll catch you up on what Ms Silver said if you like."

"Yeah, OK." He looks surprised. And relieved. "Let me just make a quick call to Geraldine."

Pizza Express is only a five-minute walk away but John insists we take his Porsche. He's still embarrassed to be seen in my Golf. Some things never change. I climb into the back while Ben proudly sits up front. He is off again, something about Jennifer and Harry, and I tune out for a moment. Strangely, I'm cool about going out with John. Six months ago it would have freaked me out. A year ago I would have been sobbing, two and I would have been nagging and whining at him for one thing and another. Now, I'm cool. I like it, like the freedom of not caring, and, actually, not having the energy to be angry and annoyed with John is strangely liberating as well.

He parks the car (on a yellow line and within a square mile of Frencham's most vicious traffic warden, but I don't quite feel generous enough to point that out. He was the one who insisted on driving after all). Ben holds both our hands and asks us to swing him. We oblige. One two three, swing, one two three, swing, one two three, swing. We could almost pass for a happy family getting ready for a relaxed, comfortable pre-Christmas dinner.

The pizza place is buzzing with families from school who had the same idea as we did. John orders what he's always ordered since the day I met him, a Margarita with extra tuna and a fried egg on top. I laugh and say how little things change. Ben usually has the Four Cheese but has a Margarita with extra tuna to keep his dad company. I get the Four Cheese for myself, just in case Ben doesn't know what he is getting himself into.

We chat companiably, he tells me about work and some of the couples we used to socialise with. With each anecdote, I'm gladder and gladder not to be part of that world any more. I tell him about Marie's new vegan kick, which is a bit weird, and her small son being so surprisingly bullish these days, getting a new belt in karate, and so on. I talk about the gym and the success of our Christmas party. He looks slightly bewildered at what clearly is an unfamiliar world to him, but nods gamely. I relay Ms Silver's conversation to him and he proudly ruffles his son's hair.

"That's my boy."

Ben smiles and slides off his chair. "I need to go to the toilet, Mummy."

I shuffle my chair back to get up with him, but stop seeing his indignant face.

"Mum, I can go on my own, I know where it is." He gestures at me embarrassedly and says to John, "I'll be right back."

Mum?

"Are you sure?" I can't help but say. This is new.

We watch Ben weave carefully through the tables and I take the opportunity to tell John what Ms Silver said about the maths. His face falls.

"Perhaps we need to consider a tutor?" I suggest.

"Do you really think that's necessary? Can we not just agree to help him more day to day?"

"We have to do that anyway, tutor or not, but it's not really fair for me. It'll be me who has to sort it all out and I do have to work as well, if you remember."

"I would hardly call this handwriting stuff a real job. It's more of a hobby, isn't it?" He smiles indulgently. "Anyway, I know boys take longer to improve than girls, but if you think he needs more help, then he should take priority over anything like that. And perhaps we need to sort out some extra studying. At night or at the weekends."

Ah. Those weekends he keeps cancelling on Ben at the last minute? The evenings he always misses when there's a nativity play to watch? I'm about to come out with an icy retort when Ben clambers back up at his chair. "I'm back," he announces unnecessarily.

John bites into his pizza as I seethe, secretly hoping (I'm ashamed to admit) that the sanctimonious git will choke on an olive. I now remember why I don't attempt to do many of these "Let's all eat as a family" moments and I resolve yet again to try to rustle up more money from somewhere, so that I can pay for the car repairs myself, and try to be less dependent on his alimony payments.

Ben watches us, slightly anxiously, so I smile, offer him my Four Cheese pizza, but no, he likes the tuna. I make an effort to talk about something else. Enquire after his holiday plans with Ben. After Suzie. Talk about various innocuous bits and pieces. John plays along and by the end of the evening we're almost back to being a normal family, at least from the outside. As John drops us off at our car after the meal, he hugs Ben and tells him how happy he is to have him for the whole of Christmas this year. I climb into the car and watch Ben waving to his dad, reminding myself that it will get easier. John smirks at me like the cat that's got the cream before zooming off. I reassure myself that Ben will have a wonderful time with his dad, that I will be just fine, and that at least tonight John paid not only for the meal but for the £50 parking ticket as well.

CHAPTER
TWENTY-THREE

Lonely This Christmas

"Hug me tight before you go for three seconds, and then turn and go and don't look back, OK, Ben?"

I'm giving Ben strict instructions about how to say goodbye to me when John collects him for Christmas. I need for it to be as painless as possible, for both of us. I'm an emotional pressure cooker that's going to blow any moment and any charitable feelings I had towards John, any delusional feelings of calm collectedness, of freedom from anger, have passed, seemingly without a trace. Christmas without Ben is here and it fucking sucks.

"OK, Mummy." He nods.

The next day comes all too quickly. Christmas Eve morning and Ben hangs on my neck for much longer than three seconds. John is waiting by the running car, tactfully, perhaps, but probably just eager to get away. I can feel myself starting to cry but hold off the tears by opening my eyes wide and giving Ben a wobbly smile, sending him down the garden path with a pat on his back. Within seconds of seeing John's car turn the corner, Ben's little hand waving cheerfully, his holdall in the boot containing new pyjamas, a carefully wrapped present for John and his old sleeping bag, I'm sobbing out loud. But I must do the right thing. I am doing the right thing. Alternate Christmases are the right thing for children of divorced parents, everything needs to be fair.

I pace around my lovingly decorated living room, touch the crinkly paper chains we made just last week and weep. He doesn't deserve Ben, it's so bloody unfair that he doesn't ever do anything for him and then gets to have him for the most special holiday of the year. It bloody fucking sucks. I tear off the paper chain, shaking needles all over the floor, and kick the tree trunk, showering my feet with more needles. My eye falls on the piece of paper with Ben's emergency phone numbers that John forgot to take. Of course. Such a shit. On the spur of the moment, a very bad moment, I admit, I call John on his mobile.

"Happy now?" I shout into the phone. "You've ruined my life once again." I sob a few more unintelligible things down the line, then realise that I'm speaking into a dead phone. Fuck. I so wanted to be gracious. Like Emma Thompson's character in *Love Actually* when she discovers her husband has been shagging his secretary. She's so together, so brutal. Life is so fucking unfair.

I call Eva and cry down the phone a bit more as she says things like, "Don't worry" and "You'll have Ben next Christmas" and "Think about that". And that perhaps Santa will bring me something nice this year too. I calm down.

"I know, I know," I finally say, my voice raspy from all the shouting. Fiona and Mrs Hartnell must be thinking I'm mad. "I know I'm doing the right thing. It just doesn't feel like it." On the other end of the phone I hear shouting and laughter and someone screaming. I realise I've called in the middle of Eva's family Christmas, which includes her mum and relatives from both sides with scores of cousins all tearing through her immaculate house.

"Merry Christmas, Eva. And good luck with that lot. Let's catch up soon."

She blows me kisses over the phone and hangs up. I love her to death, but I'm slightly resentful that she has a houseful of family, plus her own. It really doesn't seem fair. I make my way disconsolately back to the kitchen and decide to whip up a Christmas Eve morning toddy to stave off the self-pity. Ten minutes later, I'm back on the sofa with two shots of espresso, lots of milk, a big splash of brandy and a generous helping of whipped cream from a can on top. This is usually guaranteed to make me happy, but I doubt that it'll be able to do its full magic today. I light a couple of candles, sip contemplatively, then call Heather. I'll be damned if I don't find someone to speak to all day.

"Hey," I say into the phone, slurping my whipped cream. "Merry Christmas."

"Merry bloody Christmas yourself." She sounds annoyed. Oh good, a fellow misery boots.

I settle back into the sofa. "What's going on?"

"I've got Harvey and his parents and my parents and lots of kids over here. All caterers were booked by the time I had my minor breakdown and decided not to do the food myself, so I'm stuck with warming up tray after tray of Waitrose mini quiches." I hear a clatter and she curses under her breath.

"How about Nick?"

"Who the hell knows. He's pissed off because I initially said, ages ago, that I'd spend Christmas with him and I'm not, although how I could ever have thought I could do that — I must have been drunk when I promised. Anyway, he says this is the last straw."

Ah, so maybe he really was listening when we talked in the car.

"Are you sure?"

"Let's not talk about it, it's all too complicated for a day like today. I think he's just sulking anyway. What're you doing, have you said your goodbyes?" Eva and Heather know all about the three-second rule, which we discussed at length, hunched around cappuccinos during off-peak hours at the café. Heather's first time back, under the slightly anxious eyes of Derek and the few other school mums there. Sod Sarah Flint.

"Yes, it was horrid." I stifle a tiny sob and drain my toddy.

"Are you sure you don't want to be with us?" she asks solicitously.

"No, too many kids. Too much family. But thanks, Heather."

"OK. Take care, darling, I have to run. If you change your mind, let me know."

"I will." I hang up, looking bleakly at the mess around me. I heave myself out of the couch and do what I do best when miserable — the washing, ironing, cleaning, tidying kitchen cupboards. Anything that is meaningless and time-consuming.

But by seven o'clock that night, I've had enough. I wrap up, grab my bag and go out to get some decent food from Marks & Spencer as a pick-me-up. Nothing like a ready meal when you're down. On the way back, struggling up the path with too many shopping bags, I run into Fiona walking the dogs.

"Hey, Caroline, Merry Christmas. How are you?"

I lie.

"Oh, I'm fine. Everything's always fine. And you?"

"Just going down to the church. I do the Christmas-tree lights every year and the children are practising the nativity scene." *Children. Nativity scene.* That's it. That does it. Ben as Joseph and the silver tinsel, watching *The Snowman* together and Ben sitting around a Christmas tree without me, opening his presents on Christmas morning. I crack again. Tears, loads of them.

Fiona doesn't say anything unnecessary or stupid. She watches me in silence, patting my arm every now and then, letting the dogs lick my ankles affectionately.

I eventually manage to stop.

"I'm so sorry. I should have known when I didn't see Ben with you. I do so put my foot in it sometimes. Why don't you come and have a look at the tree anyway? There is nothing quite like a stunning ten-foot-tall Christmas tree beautifully decorated and lit up like a fire to make you smile."

Maybe she's right. I've fended off all efforts to get me to socialise but maybe I need to see some faces around me and some Christmas cheer.

I drop off my bags in the kitchen and follow Fiona to church. Just as we walk in, the ten-footer is being lit and she's right, it's absolutely stunning. We run into the vicar and shake hands and he invites me to the service the next morning. I can't remember the last time I've been to a church service, but, hey, there are worse ways of spending a lonely Christmas morning. I could even stroll along the river afterwards if it's a beautiful day.

As we walk back, the dogs running wild in the sparkly streets, I tell her a little about the past months, Peter and Jack and the pummelling, and she laughs and gasps appropriately.

"God, some year you've had."

We talk about her work — she'll know if she's got her boss's job in the New Year and about Tubby's cruciate ligament, which is on the mend. The stars are out already and the air is crisp and clear. Much better than moping around at home.

"I'm away on Christmas Day, Caroline," she says when we reach my house. "But if you want to join my family, you are very welcome. They're in Devon." She unleashes the dogs into her house.

This is nice, so many Christmas invitations. I feel almost ashamed to have to reject another one.

"Thanks, Fiona, that's very kind, but I'll be OK." I open my door, smell the lingering fragrance of candles, toddy, a clean house. "Have a lovely Christmas."

"You too. You've got my number. Call if you need to talk."

I feel a bit better. I like Fiona, as a neighbour and someone who listens attentively, putting things into perspective by leading such a different life to me. I put on my ready meals (I couldn't make up my mind so I got three different ones, just in case I prefer one over another), then afterwards make some coffee and watch a bit of TV. *Miracle on 34th Street*, or is it 54th? Can't remember. Anyway, it's the remake and not as good as the original. I want more coffee but settle for green tea instead, and a bag of Minstrels. Watch more Christmas cheer on *EastEnders*. Thankfully, everyone in Albert Square is even more miserable than I am.

I want to go to bed now and sleep through Christmas Day and wake up on Boxing Day with a clear head and no memories at all. Total amnesia of all things Christmas. Instead, I make more tea and watch the Christmas special of *The Vicar of Dibley*, which marginally cheers me up. Dawn French inevitably makes me feel good about my weight.

The bell rings. What now? Although, if I'm honest, I welcome any distraction at this point. I open the door to a courier. Poor guy. Who works at Christmas? Apparently he agrees and hands me two packages rather sullenly. From Peter Bishop. Hmm. Not a conventional way of giving gifts at Christmas but still, a nice surprise. I had agonised over his present for a while, then, when things seemed dicey, decided to send him a nice Christmas card instead and couldn't go back to the present after that. But this is nice.

I hurry back into my warm living room and stack up the presents under the tree. Looks pretty good, with the rest of the wrapped gifts. Maybe I should have a feel, though, to make sure it's not something I need to open today? I take the top package and shake it gently. Rustle rustle. Sounds enticing. Number two gives more of a rattling noise. No kittens or water-filled bags of fish. What a relief. I put them back under the tree. But maybe he'll call later to see if I liked the presents? Better open them now, or else that'll be embarrassing. Abandoning all pretence of restraint, I rip them open in quick succession.

Sitting in a heap of paper and ribbon, I admire my spoils. A wonderful amethyst necklace. I'm in awe. He remembered from all that time ago in The Chestnut. And I only just lost my amethyst necklace. I jump up to the mirror and try it on. It looks good. And now the other present, a DVD. I turn it round curiously, before unwrapping it. It says TO MUMMY FROM BEN on the front. Oh God. Do I dare?

I do. I can't get to the TV quick enough, shove the disc into the DVD player and throw myself on to the couch.

Ben's face beams out at me, filling the screen with his huge smile. My eyes start to fill up again, but I smile and move on to the floor, closer to the TV. He's standing outside The Sycamore, in the playground, and I can see Eva and Heather smiling in the background, mouthing "Go on". Ben is looking straight at the camera and I smile at the earnest little face.

"Merry Christmas! Harry and Philip's mummies thought this would be a nice surprise for you." He looks up and over the camera and I see him nod as someone invisible urges him on. "I just wanted to tell you, you are the best mummy in the world and I will miss you loads on Christmas Day. I will stay up for Santa when he comes to deliver my presents and make sure he visits you wherever you are too, OK?" Another big smile. "Now, I want to sing 'Away in a Manger' to you because you like it so much."

Tears stream down my face and I'm so close to the TV now I can almost touch the screen. When he gets to the bit about "all the dear children" he points to himself and says as an aside, "That's me. I'm a dear children, Mummy, aren't I?"

I nod, wipe away my tears and say, "Yes you are."

He finishes all three verses and comes up to the screen to give the camera a kiss.

"Love you lots, Mummy. Happy Christmas. See you soon." And then he looks above again, and says, "Now, can I have the Bionicle, please?"

As the screen fades to black, the only sounds in the room are the whirring of the DVD player and my noisy sobs. But, strangely, I feel better than I have all day. I couldn't have asked for a more wonderful present.

I wake up on Christmas morning tired. Very tired and stuffed up. I stay under the covers for a while, hoping that by some miracle it's the day before New Year's Day and Ben's just outside the door, raring to go. I wait for a little while, not wanting to open my eyes, but, of course, the human time-space continuum of the known world lets me down once more. It's still very much Christmas morning. OK, Gray, hold it together. I'm going to treat this like any other day. Get stuff done that I never get done when Ben is about. Like tidy the kitchen cupboards. Do an exercise video. Wax my legs. Go to church and then walk along the river. Yes, that sounds like the most sensible plan. Thank God, it's a stunning day, clear blue skies, frosty-looking trees. The road below my window is quiet. I'll phone Ben about midday. Yes, Caroline, about midday. Not now, whatever you do.

I get dressed in my favourite woollen sweater and slouchy trousers, wrap myself in various jackets, scarves and a hat, and open the door to a beautifully crisp morning and church bells beginning to ring from afar. As I walk out into the street, a voice hails me from next door.

"Caroline. Love your hat. It's splendid."

Mrs Hartnell in her Sunday best, clearly on her way to church. I would have loved to enjoy the peace and quiet, but Mrs Hartnell is obviously a morning person. We slowly turn the corner and she talks non-stop, about the next Robert De Niro she thinks she's found, about our annoying single guy down the road who keeps roaring down the street at two in the morning, always gunning the engine when he's in front of her house, about her chronic insomnia, about her son in America. Finally, we arrive at the church, crammed with people looking polished and rosy-cheeked. I'm distinctly under-dressed, but hopefully I won't run into that many people I know.

I'm wrong, of course. I find Stephen and Miranda from number twelve near the front pews, with two couples who look suspiciously like their parents. Huh. That's interesting. I wouldn't have pegged them as family people. They smile and wave at me and I nod back. I can also see James and his boyfriend on another pew. I didn't know they were churchgoers too. Not that I am or anything, so perhaps it's only a Christmas Day thing. And there are a few faces I recognise from around the neighbourhood. The woman with the blue jacket in front of me looks like the shop assistant from the newsagent's by The Sycamore. She smiles like she recognises me too, so I decide it must be her. Fiona's dog walker is near the back with her family, but minus the dogs, and scattered around are a few of the playground mums I don't really know but who smile festively back at me. Suddenly I don't feel quite so alone any more. Thankfully only one or two glossy bobs and no hard-core mafia in sight. They've probably got their own church where they sacrifice lambs, or maybe turkeys at this time of the year.

There are loads of children, looking tired but happy and holding dolls or teddies or Lego creations. I feel a pang but push it away quickly and grab a song sheet.

Mrs Hartnell and I get separated, which I'm secretly grateful for, and I sit at the end of a pew in the back, chin buried in my collar. The vicar says things about happiness and peace and thinking about world poverty and urging us to put our own small problems into perspective. Nothing that I haven't heard before, but it's nice, humbling and comforting at the same time. We sing all the carols I remember singing as a child, including "Away in a Manger" (I can't quite get through that one) and "Oh Come, All Ye Faithful", and the children are asked to show the toys Santa got them that year. And it's all really lovely and perfect and quite innocent.

I escape quietly, just after the final blessing, because I don't really want to have to chat and make nice with anyone, and turn towards the river. The sky is almost brittle it's so bright. I wander along the riverbank, dodging the other families in their Christmas Day finery, the children clutching toys that are too new to be broken, and the odd lonely dog walker. I'm OK. There were a few moments when I was worried I might embarrass myself in church, but I pulled through. At least I'm not with anyone I don't love, am not in a hothouse of people who irritate the hell out of me and whom I don't really know. My great-aunt Hetty used to organise the most wonderful Christmas feasts, true fairy-tale events, but after she died I got stuck with endless rounds of Christmas dinners with John's family or with my mother and an assortment of distant relatives. In recent years, John and I were at constant loggerheads, barely speaking.

Now, well, now, it's just me and Ben and that's it. Next year will be nice.

By the time I turn into my street I've talked myself into a much stronger state of mind and I'm chilled and relaxed. A family from down the road has come outside to play, their little boy — I think he's Daniel? — excitedly riding a shiny red scooter, which I presume

Santa delivered this morning. There's a bit of a party going on at number forty-eight — is that Mrs Hartnell's bachelor prat? I hear raucous laughter and a piano player and hurry on quickly, still a bit annoyed by any kind of merriment. I pass Claire's. She's gone for the holidays, down to her mum's in Berkshire, I think, but her windows still sparkle with fairy lights. Must remember to water her plants later on today and maybe unplug those lights. You never know, and I don't want to have to call the fire brigade. But now, most importantly, I must call Ben and wish him a happy Christmas. I quicken my steps and stumble through my front garden, my fingers so stiff from the cold that I drop the key twice before I manage to unlock the door.

Ring ring. Ring ring.

"Yes," a male voice snaps into the phone.

"Hello, John. Happy Christmas."

There's a brief pause as if John's taken aback by the level of civility.

"Hello there," he finally says, coolly.

"Can I speak to Ben?" I say through gritted teeth. There's only so much civility I can do. I can hear John handing the phone over. "Hello, darling," I say trying to sound as happy as possible, cringing as I remember sobbing down the phone to John.

"Hi, Mummy." He sounds happy and overexcited. "Santa brought me a huge Scalextric, it's enormous. Daddy has already set it up and we've been playing it all morning." I make admiring noises down the phone. "Yes, and guess what, there's a green car just like our green car and a silver car just like Daddy's car. Isn't that funny?"

"Yes, that's really funny," I manage.

"And guess what, your car always wins. Isn't that good?" He sounds triumphant. That's my boy.

"And I got a Roboraptor, he's so cool, much bigger than Yoshi's, the new version."

"That's nice." I clench my teeth again. I've also got him one, which I distinctly remember mentioning to John. Bugger. "Thanks so much for your lovely present, Ben. I think you sang 'Away in a Manger' beautifully."

"Yes, it was nice, have a wonderful Christmas, Mummy, and I love you very much."

"I love you too, darling. Look forward to having you back." Tony Blair. Tony Blair. Tony Blair.

"Caroline." John's back on. "Sorry about the Raptor. Forgot to tell my parents."

Hmmm.

"No worries. He'll have two and they can beat the crap out of each other."

Click.

I look at the phone, but I just can't cry any more. Fuck, hopefully this will get less painful over time. I have images of John and his parents and his brothers and Sickly Suzie all playing happy families with my son. And I'm not there. I feel a bit sick to my stomach. There's only one thing to do: I've got to get out again.

Just as I've rewrapped myself in jacket and scarf and hat, the doorbell rings. Expecting no one in particular, I open the door. It's Peter.

And Peter looks a little the worse for wear, like he hasn't slept or washed his hair for days. I'm stunned. He's the only one I certainly *didn't* expect.

"Merry Christmas," I say. That's a good start.

"Merry Christmas. Did you like the presents?" he asks eagerly.

"God yes, so thoughtful, Peter. I loved the DVD."

He takes in my tear-stained face and pulls me into a hug. "I wanted you to have something."

I shake my head, pulling myself together.

"Sorry, but what are you doing here? Aren't you meant to be with your family?"

"I spent a manic few days with them. Three of my little cousins were sick and my mother couldn't cope, so I had to jump into the breach. But I just couldn't let you be by yourself on Christmas Day, Caroline. So go get your passport and pack a bag. We're getting on a plane. And take some warm clothes." He eyes my hat with a frown. "Where we're going it's cold."

CHAPTER
TWENTY-FOUR

Skiing

"You are very good at getting yourself out of trouble. But then again, you get yourself into trouble a lot."

Peter Bishop is sceptically eyeing my skiing technique on the first day of our spur-of-the-moment, post-Christmas/pre-New Year surprise trip. I've been falling down a lot and I'm fumbling with my skis, my gloves, my goggles. Actually, if truth be told, I'm not the best skier in the world. I'm pretty hopeless. I didn't really think about how exactly my bottom would look sticking out of a huge heap of snow when I agreed to go with Peter, having hastily packed an assortment of woollen garments and flimsy nightgowns, plus half my dressing table.

We were a bit late for our flight, so had to hustle through check-in and security until we finally fell into our seats. On the plane (economy but the nicer seats up front, where you can stretch your legs), he pulls out a mini bottle of champagne, two plastic glasses and a bulgy envelope. I'm beginning to like this more and more. A note and two tickets fall out of the envelope. *The Producers*.

"I couldn't possibly," I say delightedly. "You've already given me so much." I squirm, embarrassed at the thought of not having given him anything at all. He shrugs his shoulders, pleased with his gift. I sip my champagne and read the note.

Dear Caroline,
    You mentioned a long time ago that you would love to see this. I hope you enjoy it.
    With love, Peter xx

Hmm. Seems pretty firm. Even. Lots of loops in his writing, which means he's creative and artistic. Strong character and a little bit emotional as well. I can't detect any control-freak tendencies, which is good. And I like the way he writes the word "love". He's obviously taken longer writing that word than any other. Yes, I like this handwriting.

Peter has taken me to Grindelwald, one of the first ski resorts in Europe, which has a beautiful chocolate-box charm to it. Apparently Peter has skied here every year for the past twenty years and, unsurprisingly, he's much better at it than I am. We spend most of the ride from the airport to the hotel discussing his many sporting accomplishments, all of them quite outdoorsy — he skis, surfs and sails, mostly to a fairly high standard. Gosh, I don't know if I can quite keep up with him. I certainly can't match the image of this nice, broad-shouldered man sitting next to me, his hair sticking up at the sides, talking

380

enthusiastically about jibs and paragliding, with my memory of a small, shy, reluctant boy at school.

On the slopes he's not quite as nice as he is off them, bossing me around on the lift about technique and boldness and courage. I think longingly back to the cosy hotel lounge, and the thick duvets I slept so well under last night. *Sans* Peter, alas, but, hey, the trip is still young.

"You're a compulsive achiever," I say to him resentfully, after watching him elegantly swing down a narrow slope on the first morning, skimming a mogul as though it's not there, while I stumble down the hill behind him rather more gracelessly, barely managing to arrive in one piece. We ride the lift back up.

"I'm not a compulsive achiever." He's barely out of breath. "You know, it looks like you've got enough strength in your legs," he casts a critical eye over them, "to manage something more challenging than this, but you need to work on your technique."

Excuse me?

It hasn't snowed for a few days in the resort, so the snow is hard and there are lots of icy patches. We've moved on to the red slopes, even though I've told Peter repeatedly that I'm a blue runner. He ignores me, so here we are. I parallel turn into a wide open basin with lots of snow. He zooms past me. Damn him.

Good, missed the crevice. Great, another flat bit ahead. Peter hangs back and stays behind me, watching my style and keeping up a running commentary as we go down the hill. I think I'd have preferred him to go ahead after all.

"If you have the basics — good technique, strength, a certain measure of luck — then it's best to ski fast. It's an excellent way to focus the mind and rid yourself of all the day-to-day stuff. You focus on staying up and staying alive." He brandishes his ski pole in emphasis. "People ski how they live, don't you think?"

"Do they?" I gasp, only narrowly avoiding another skier who, I'm pleased to see, sucks even more than I do. This beats being at home, moping about Ben, but I probably would have chosen something that shows me in a slightly more advantageous light. "How does life imitate skiing?"

He swings meditatively beside me.

"Well, a lot of people don't ski. Too old or too scared or too poor. It's still a sport for the middle classes. Sad but true. You can get two weeks in the sun for a long weekend in the snow. You not only need the right equipment you need the right conditions and the right attitude. Lots of snow and good snow. Not like here. Watch out — icy narrow steep bit coming up now."

I grit my teeth. Would it be too much to admit that I'm terrified? I'm most definitely going to break my neck today.

Some of my feelings must show in my mutinous face, because Peter stops and turns towards me, forcing me to slow down and almost crash into him. I start to protest in indignation, but he leans forward, steals a quick kiss and then lifts me to him.

"God, I love skiing. The mountains have such energy. I really don't know why people like beach holidays so much — it's just beach wherever you go. Now in the mountains, you get a real injection of life."

His enthusiasm is catching and my heart lifts. I look up at his flushed face and that's all it takes. One moment for me to take my eye off the snow, and whoosh, there I go, flying out of control. Skis akimbo, doing the splits in the most ungainly fashion, feeling like a complete idiot. Upside down on a very steep bit, I slide for about five seconds down the hill, hoping that I stop before I reach a ledge or a cliff, really, and plunge to my death. I close my eyes, thinking of who will look after Ben when I die.

"You OK, Caroline?"

I've skied straight into a huge pile of snow and when I emerge the first thing I see is Peter grinning at me as I fall back, legs apart like some drunken hooker.

"Yes, thank you," I say with as much dignity as I can muster. "Would you be so kind as to help me up?"

"I think you should try to do it yourself."

So that's how he wants to play it. Well then, I will.

I talk myself silently through it. Right, take off the skis. Try to dislodge them without sliding any further. Oh no, I think I'm still on ice. No, sliding further. Right, that's no good and this bastard isn't going to help me. OK. Different manoeuvre. Let go of sticks, bring knees into chest so I'm like a ball. Position myself right way round so I'm not upside down. Done. Undo clasps on skis. Great. Left one done. Now right. Bugger, fucking thing's stuck. Bloody thing. Ice makes it sticky.

"You have to push harder," he shouts from a bit further up.

"Fuck off."

He laughs.

"That's the spirit. You're doing well."

I press the lever thingy as hard as I can, putting my whole weight behind it. Just when I'm about to topple over, it unclasps. I keep hold of the ski starting to slide away from me. Skis off, I can now sit up, but it's so icy I slide further. I can feel my thigh muscles gripping tighter and I want to fart. I think I do. Very loudly, but I don't care. I'm terrified I'm going to fall off that damn cliff. I've got both skis in my hands and the sticks round my wrists and I'm looking, waiting, searching for a patch of snow that will slow me down before I get to the void. A precipice of glorious scenery and certain death, or at least severe head and back injury. Why the hell couldn't my parents have taken me skiing here since I was ten like Peter's did? I look up to see Peter's expression. Am I misreading it or is he looking slightly nervous? Shit. I just keep going, sliding further down. I don't know whether to lie back or sit up and watch where I'm going. Do I want to know I'm about to die? Is it OK that Peter should let me die? Sloosh. And then I stop. I stop dead in the snow and can feel hands reaching underneath my armpits and lifting me up effortlessly.

"There you are. Let me take the skis," Peter's voice says calmly.

I turn round and scowl at Peter, letting out several raspy breaths.

"Why the hell didn't you help me?"

He has the grace to look a bit sheepish.

"We were on that very steep icy bit and you couldn't have got up and put your skis on at that angle with that degree of iciness. So I thought I'd let you slide until you got to snow, but it was a bit longer than I thought. Sorry about that, Caroline." He squeezes my left thigh, which hurts like a son of a bitch. "Strong muscles you have there. And some nerve. Are you really terrified?"

I consider lying, but honestly, what's the point at this stage? I've had my bum sticking out from the snow, I've farted, and I slid spreadeagled for about twenty metres. My reputation as a skier is already ruined.

"Yeah, all right?"

"Don't worry about it so much. With skiing you have to put your brain in your pocket and use your instinct. Your body will tell you what it can and can't do." This is all starting to sound more like one of Anne's yoga talks, a bit deep for what basically consists of pointing your skis downhill and going as fast as you can. "That first slide, the first turn, the first rush of speed, the first glimpse of sun and the exhilarating feeling of zooming down a mountain full of fresh snow."

Now he's starting to sound like a ski brochure. I'm cold now, and can feel the moisture seeping through the seat of my pants. I hope I haven't torn them anywhere. I've had to rent my whole outfit at the classy ski joint next to the hotel; it was bloody expensive and I hope they won't baulk when I show up tomorrow with cuts and bruises and a ruined suit. Peter is still talking and I catch something about the slopes.

"Some only stay on the blue runs and that's OK, but they should go and push themselves on the reds and then the blacks and get themselves an expert guide."

"No blacks for me, thank you very much. I don't even like reds."

"This one's red." He smiles like he's just delivered my biggest Christmas surprise yet.

"But you said it was blue." I'm indignant.

"I lied. I knew you could do it." What? Has he been watching me at all? "If I'd told you it was a red, you would have tensed up, your brain would have said you couldn't and you wouldn't even have tried it. And look what you did! And by the way, just so you know, I did hear you fart."

I blush and mumble something into my collar, putting on my skis the wrong way round.

"No worries, I do it all the time." He's being kind. "Age you know. And prunes in the morning. Bloody things. Don't make me go faster but I shit bricks."

"Bit too much information, thank you."

Finally, I've got my skis sorted and we make our way down the rest of the red, which thankfully now becomes more of a blue until we get to the last bit, which is so steep it looks more like an ice wall.

"Now, just follow me. Parallel along this bit. Very quick and short ones. Only way to do this is fast and focus."

He barks out short orders as we go and I don't mind any more, as long as I get safely down. I focus all my mind and energy and feel absolutely brilliant about myself when I get to the bottom. God, I can't wait to tell Ben when I call him tonight.

"Well done, Ms Gray. Your first red run! Now, enough skiing. Fancy some *glühwein*? Like hot Ribena with a kick, but it's perfect after skiing."

"Yes, I'm done for the day. I don't think I could do that again even a little bit pissed."

Two glasses of *glühwein* later I am feeling very mulled and very frisky. Peter can obviously take his drink better than me. He is now on his fourth and still talking quite coherently, but I'm pretty much a goner.

I'm a glass-a-day person, probably, if I'm forced to count them out during my all-too-infrequent check-ups at the GP, but I don't have much tolerance. I get very mellow very quickly. If I'm in a bad place I cry. But tonight, I'm not. I'm in a great place, on top of a mountain, with a wonderful view and a handsome man. I think I'm grinning like a Cheshire cat, almost purring with contentment. And that's where my second alcohol-related problem comes in. It makes me very brave.

I lean over and kiss Peter, lip balms smudging over each other, and I try to keep my eyes open long enough to see if he looks shocked, disgusted or pleased. He looks amused. I pull away and say, trying not to slur. "Did you like that?"

"Yes, that was very pleasant. A nice way to round off the day."

I grin and then I kiss him again. A bit longer this time. Eyes still open, no arms or hands touching. Just kissing. We're tucked away in a corner, so the disapproving waiter can't frown upon us too much. Our cold noses are too numb to feel each other, but his eyes are closed this time. I pull away again.

"You taste of strawberries." He smacks his lips and I giggle. "Do you want to go now?"

"Don't you like this wonderful view?" He's playful, smiling mischievously.

I play with his hand and look idly out at the mountain range. The sky is cloudless and is making the snow bleach-white, stinging my eyes when I look directly at it. Birds hover overhead, and panda-eyed skiers, some clad in tight black salopettes, others wearing pink duvets with ridiculous multi-tasselled hats, are out in deckchairs, half undressed, soaking in the warmth and light. The smell of food is potent and heady. I can taste the mulled wine in the air, smell the French fries and apple pies, the highly spiced sausages people are eating at a nearby table. Other skiers are talking and laughing and shouting and burping in French and German and Spanish and occasionally with an American accent. No English. This world is as distant from Frencham as Frencham is from Chetley and I have that same exhilarating moment I feel when I've reached the top of the hill in Frencham Park after running for half an hour. Exhausted and exhilarated at the same time, feeling like I'm on top of the world and lucky to be there.

Somehow, sitting here, looking at this view, puts everything into perspective: the court case, my Ben-less Christmas, fighting endlessly with Heather, my mum and John bickering, my first few months at The Sycamore. Really, there're a lot of wonderful things I've got to be deliriously happy about and grateful for, things that I need to store away for darker moments — good friends and Ben doing well and me feeling good. And, of course, as I look back at Peter grinning up at me, a gorgeous man I want to sleep with tonight. Someone I've clicked with even though I haven't really known him for very long. I feel on top of the world. Perhaps it's the view, or maybe the lack of oxygen and the ride down the red slope, making my head spin.

Peter gets up.

"Well, seeing that you've had your fill of the scenery, let's go."

We're not the only ones who want to get off the mountain. The cable car is full. A large Italian ski group crams in with us, chattering to each other animatedly. The upside to being crowded is that I'm squashed very tightly against Peter, although we have two people facing us as well, as if we are all huddled into one conversation. They're both nattering away in Italian, so Peter and I are in our own little universe, almost touching noses again. I rub my body against his, which makes him laugh softly.

"Hey, were you this cheeky in school?"

"God no, I was so dull. Very square. If I'd only known the power of the school uniform, the short skirt, the white blouse half undone, the long socks, the pigtails, then I would have worked it."

There is a glint in Peter's eye now. The Britney thing seems to have egged him on. I swear, it's always the quiet ones that are the most surprising. He leans closer.

"Do you know that time I came round to your house," he whispers, "and you were wearing the face mask?"

"Yes." I shove him playfully and one of the Italians gives me a frown as the lift sways gently. "I've been meaning to ask why the hell you didn't mention it." I whisper too now.

"It was endearing. As was the view. Did you know I could see your nipples?" I blush and giggle like a school-girl. Get a grip, Gray.

"No, I didn't, and it's very ungallant of you to mention it." I try to be dignified but the setting and Peter's body against mine aren't helping my cause.

"And, surely, you weren't wearing any other underwear, were you?"

I blush hot-red now. My face, suffering from wind and sun and mulled wine, feels like it's about to catch fire. I draw myself up, trying to regain my composure.

"I did very much wear underwear that day, I'll have you know."

"Uh-huh," he says, staring pointedly at my chest, where my nipples are clearly visible through at least four layers of thermal material. Damn it. He leans in closer and whispers conspiratorially, "I would love to lick your nipples right now."

"Why, Mr Bishop, that's very bold of you. How forward."

390

The lift comes to a grinding halt. The Italians spill from the doors and as we exit the man who had been standing next to me inside says in faultless English and with only a tiny hint of a lilt, "Have a nice evening."

We race each other out of the lift station, jam our skis and ski boots into the lockers — God, I love taking off those things, my own padded boots feel like slippers — and head through the hotel lobby into the lift. Thankfully we're the only ones this time.

We've stopped laughing and I nuzzle myself into Peter less playfully than before and with more urgency. He starts to kiss me, very gently, on my lips and neck and eyelids and cheeks, and we're talking and kissing at the same time.

"No one to . . ."

Kiss.

". . . overhear us this time."

"No, no one to overhear us. So where . . ."

Kiss.

". . . were we?"

"You wanted to lick . . ."

Kiss.

". . . my nipples. Mind you, you'll have to work hard . . ."

Kiss.

". . . to get through this lot and I'm a bit hot and sweaty."

Kiss.

"I don't mind, I like working for . . ."

Kiss.

". . . my fun."

When we arrive at our floor, we've stopped talking altogether. The lift door starts to close again. But we squeeze through, almost falling out into the hallway. Peter pulls down the straps of my salopettes and starts to unzip me. We're still about five doors away from our rooms.

"Don't you think we should at least wait till we get in your bedroom?" I vainly try to pull his hands off. He's stronger than me.

"You've got at least four layers under that. If I don't start now, we'll never get naked."

I agree. I start to undress him too, unzipping as much as I can before we reach our door.

I slip the key card in the slot as he pulls down my trousers so that I'm now almost naked (except knickers) on my bottom half. I teeter into the room, bound by masses of clothing around my ankles, and he holds me round the waist so I don't fall flat on my face into the room. I can't stop laughing but I can't get undressed fast enough once we're in the room. Peter picks me up as if I'm weightless and puts me down somewhere by the bed. I'm halfway out of my clothes, tied at the arms, unable to see, tied at the legs, unable to move, and can't stop laughing. I can feel his hands on me, stroking my breasts, kissing my spine, touching me between the legs (thank you, Angela, thank you, Angela, thank you, Angela) and can feel myself getting wet. I'm not laughing any more. I'm starting to moan.

I sense him move around and start to lick my nipples.

"Do they taste good?"

"Yes, like strawberries."

I groan, trying to dislodge the salopettes from my ankles, managing with one, not with the other. I must look ridiculous with jumpers over my head and desperately trying to kick off the rest of my ski gear from one leg. Although I love what he's doing, how he's touching, how he's blowing on my — oh fuck, oh fuck, he's blowing on my calves. I love my calves being blown on. And he's kissing me behind the knees. Oh my God, he's starting to explore with his fingers. I'm going to collapse. I mustn't collapse. Oh fuck, have just collapsed.

Peter pulls the jumpers off me so at least I can see him now. He looks like he's going to eat me. Please God, yes! He's still fully dressed, which I think is unfair. One, two, three, four, fuck, he's got five layers on.

Finally he's unwrapped and I run my fingers over his chest. Nice body. Nice chest. Nice arms. Carrying cameras about all day is obviously doing him a world of good. I start to nip him like a cat and lick him, tasting salt and him. I push down his ski pants and leave them round his knees so that he's in the same tied position I was a few minutes ago. See how he likes it.

I stretch my arms out and hold him down while I kiss and lick and tease and nuzzle, until I can feel him getting restless and start to writhe and sit up and want more, and then I take him in my mouth and he suddenly drops back, his hands reaching to mine, holding them tightly as I hold him tightly, until he almost comes. I can hear him say, "Do you want to do this? Really? I want to be inside you."

So I pull back just as I think he's about to explode.

He swivels round and pushes me up against the bed, but instead of kissing me, he lifts my chin and bites my neck, breathing on me, which is frustrating and erotic at the same time. I want him to kiss me and get inside me, but he's holding back, trying to make me as hungry as I can feel he is. I can feel his fingers reaching out to me and teasing me. Pushing inside me, reaching into me, making me so wet I can feel my muscles tensing, drawing him in, wanting him deeper in me. All the time he's looking at me, not kissing me, just looking at me, breathing on me. Each time I go to kiss him, he pulls away, but he's reaching into me deeper now and I feel I'm about to come and he stops.

He stops. Peter Bishop stops. I want to say to him "Why?" but out comes a whimper.

I'm hot and sweaty and throbbing where he's touched me. And muscles that were aching a few minutes ago on the ski lift now feel on fire with energy.

I lean over to him and kiss him again on the lips, longer this time, closing my eyes this time, using my arms and hands this time, allowing him to wrap his arms around me and push himself against me and into me. He fights it, but he lets me push him back and climb on top of him, slowly moving my hips around and over, so that I can feel him against me. He tries to hold my arms then loses control and lets go, then holds my hips, tightly, pushing them hard into his thighs. I can feel him getting larger and harder and see his face looking fierce, angry almost, wanting to sit up and kiss me, and bring me towards him, but I resist until he shouts out and holds me down, so I can't move any more. He closes his eyes and groans for what seems like for ever.

I haven't come but feel as though I've skied down a black at full speed.

His eyes click back open as I lean back and gently move myself off.

He smiles. "My turn."

He pushes me back and starts kissing me on the lips, searching again for the place I was before he stopped. I'm starting to moan and pant and I whisper, "You're not going to stop again are you?"

"Why, do you want me to? I thought you'd like something different."

He continues to stroke but kisses me on the belly button and then slowly down, down to where his fingers are and starts to lick. I can feel myself losing control. I can feel his fingers inside me and his tongue on me and I'm arching my back and . . .

. . . I truly don't think I've ever had better.

That evening, I snuggle up to Peter in front of the fire, after we've both showered together and made love and played a few more times, feeling muscles ache in places I never thought I had, let alone knew had muscles that could ache. We sit peacefully silent, lost in thought.

He kisses me on the hair and suddenly comes out with, "Why are you so afraid of relationships?"

"Why do you say that?"

"I've been watching you, and listening. It sounds like you are very wary."

"Not really, maybe just wary of possessive men, I suppose. John was so controlling. He thought I was having an affair, although I kept saying I wasn't, but he used to have me followed and would endlessly interrogate me. He's not that nice a person, deep down, and for a while I was always thinking I was being watched. That tends to make you a bit paranoid over time. And then, ironically, it turned out that he'd been having flings and things ever since Ben was born. I guess I'm just a bit more cautious now, which is no bad thing."

He listens in silence, just stroking and kissing my hair.

Peter doesn't force himself on me when we're in bed that night, he waits for me to snuggle up to kiss him, to gradually reach my leg over his, and then he turns to me and kisses me very gently on the lips. I feel secure in his arms. And for once, a little less alone.

CHAPTER
TWENTY-FIVE

Introducing Ben to Peter

"Mummy! Mummy!"

My little boy has turned into a Ninja Turtle in the space of seven days. It's eleven o'clock in the morning on New Year's Eve, and John comes up the front path just behind Ben, an overnight bag and several large shopping bags in his hand. Both look tired but happy.

The Ninja Turtle gives me a big hug, taking off his mask as I bend down to kiss and squeeze him and ruffle his hair and pinch his back and generally try to absorb him into me.

"I'm Leonardo today. I can kick your ass." He adopts a strange-looking karate position and punches his leg into the air.

"Hey Leonardo. Happy New Year. Well, almost. Whose ass do you want to kick?" I should reproach him for the ass bit, but I'm too happy to have him back to care.

"No, not *you*, Mummy. I'd kick Patrick's bottom." He scampers into the house happily, toting his bag behind him. John and I stand on the doorstep, rather awkwardly. So many things to say or not to say. I should ask if they had a nice time, but I don't want to know.

But I have to say something, otherwise John might ask me what I did. And that really wouldn't be good.

"Well, then," I say uncertainly. I don't generally ask him in, this is my space and he doesn't belong here, although he did once ask if he could use the bathroom when he dropped Ben off and I thought it was a bit much to suggest he pee in the bushes. Quickly, I call back into the house, "Ben, can you say goodbye to Daddy?"

Ben comes running out and hugs John around the knees. John picks him up and throws him in the air, hugs him back. It's an elaborate ritual, something I'm sure John does to show me what a good father he is. If he were to occasionally show up to things, I'd be the first to believe him.

After a couple of minutes of horsing around, I clear my throat and John lets go of Ben, nods at me and takes off.

Ben's buzzing around the house like a bee.

"Mummy, oh Mummy, the Christmas tree looks different," he shouts, discovering the new decorations that Peter and I put on last night. Peter, being the creative soul he is, has even made a stroppy Christmas-tree fairy that has a real sourpuss expression (uncannily like Karin Blunt's daughter). We had such a nice night, bathing our aching joints and drinking hot chocolate and my special toddies, with the curtains drawn and the fairy lights twinkling on the tree. Peter left earlier this afternoon and the lights are on again now, there's music and there are loads of presents under the tree.

Ben starts digging through the pile and his face lights up as he squeaks with delight like a mouse that has found a huge lump of cheese.

"Are these all for me? When did Santa get here? Did he eat the mince pies and drink the milk? Did he? Did Rudolph have the carrots?" He's dancing around the room like a mad urchin, cackling and laughing.

"They did!" I shout over the din, showing him the plate. Knowing my son, I've come prepared, crumbs and all. Peter thought I was joking when I got out the plate and arranged crumbs and a half-eaten carrot with teeth marks on it, adding an empty mug of milk that I made him drink.

"Can't Santa drink beer this year?" he grumbled.

"No, he can't. Now drink the milk."

Ben looks suitably impressed when he's presented with such flawless evidence.

"Wow, hungry, wasn't he?"

"Yes, very. Now, Leonardo, would you like to open your presents?"

"Yes, please!"

We sit around the tree, and he tears through the boxes and soft parcels to find a Robopet ("Wow, I really wanted one of these, thank you, Santa"), another Roboraptor ("Good, I can get them to fight"), a street car (on the list again), and several games and clothes and soft furry toys and little bits and pieces. Finally, we're done. He beams at me over the mountain of paper, and lunges into my arms.

"I missed you."

"I missed you too, darling," I say, hugging him back, and we sit for a few minutes utterly still, listening to the music and the crackling of the fire. Finally he sidles over to sift through his loot again, putting things together, breaking the leg off one of the figurines my mum included. Well, who gives porcelain to a little kid anyway?

After half an hour pottering around, Ben looks up and says in a businesslike manner, "Right. What are we doing now?"

"Why don't we clear up some of this paper and tonight I thought we could go out and watch some fireworks."

His face lights up.

"Fireworks. Brilliant. When can we go? Can we go now? Can we?"

"No, clearing up first and then lunch. Want to go to Pizza Express? Ninjas like pizza, don't they?"

That's enough to make him spring into action and we buzz around the house, putting things away, arranging toys and putting together his robot thing. I'm high on everything, Ben being home, Peter just having left, and I haven't had time to worry about anything else, really. Coming out of Ben's room, I'm starting to think about the most important thing on my action list. Introducing Ben to Peter. And the fact that I promised Peter we'd all go out together this evening.

It's got to be done right. I pause on the stairs, listening to Ben rummage around his toy chest. I remember John fucking it up big time when he introduced Suzanne to Ben after three months as his "special friend". Ben came home, upset, because Daddy's special friend told him she was his new mummy when he was very happy with the mummy he had. Special indeed.

You can't do that to Ben. He's not stupid and he asks all those difficult questions and more. Best to say, Peter is my boyfriend, but will only be my boyfriend if Ben likes him. Perhaps this is wrong. Perhaps it's giving Ben too much power at this stage? But what if they don't get on? What if Peter isn't up to Ben's energy level? Well, if someone loves me, they have to love Ben.

My plan is that we go to Primrose Hill for the New Year's Eve fireworks and have dinner beforehand at a nice restaurant called Manna. Ben loves that place, because the staff always give him loads of ice cream and spoil him rotten. Peter can drive, so I can have a much needed glass (or two) of something, plus Ben can sit up front and talk to him and I'll sit quietly behind. That's my plan. An hour later, I sit down with Ben at Pizza Express. He's taken a liking to Margaritas with extra tuna so I'm absolved of having to order the Four Cheese. I pick at my pasta as he wolfs down slice after slice. John better be feeding him well. Once he's full and has his first ice cream of the day in front of him, I break the news.

"Now Ben, we're going to see the fireworks with a man called Peter."

"Peter Pan?"

"No, not Peter Pan. His name is Peter Bishop. Do you remember the man who took the pictures of you when you sang 'Away in a Manger' for me?"

Ben looks confused. "No," then quickly, as I'm about to speak, "Yes, I do actually. He's a friend of Harry's mum and he has very messy hair and made me laugh." Good, he made a positive first impression. Sort of.

"Well, he's my boyfriend." So there.

Ben looks at me quizzically. "Boyfriend? Like me and Harry?"

"Well," I begin, "a bit more special maybe." God, this is complicated. And here I was slagging off John for the S-word. Special friend. But what else to say? Perhaps best leave it to percolate for a few minutes. I know Ben's mind is buzzing with questions as he steadily eats his way through the ice cream.

"Does that mean I will have a baby brother soon? Are you having a baby, Mummy?" He looks slightly revolted at the thought.

I'm horrified.

"God, no, I'm not."

I know. I absolutely 100 per cent know that Ben is going to say all of these things and many more to Peter. I can almost hear his mind whirring. Do I prepare Peter or let him use his own instinct? I also know Ben will want to play swords and guns with him. Start attacking him. Oh well, got to find out some time.

Thankfully, he doesn't say much more on the subject for now, and a few hours later Peter arrives early with flowers for me and a present for Ben — a lightsabre. Bribery. Good start. But a dangerous toy and a bad start in that Ben will now expect a present of similar merit and imagination every time.

Ben sits in the front with Peter. No, he can't sit in the driver's seat. But in the passenger seat is OK. Driving north, along the A3, Ben stares at Peter's profile, probably trying to intimidate the poor man. I squint to see Ben's face in the half-light and, yes, he's smiling, so definitely trying to intimidate the poor man. And so it begins.

"Peter?"

"Yes, Ben?"

"Peter, can I ask you something?"

"Yes."

"Are you Mummy's boyfriend?"

"Yes."

"So what does that mean?"

Peter tries not to smile or twitch.

"Well, Ben, that means that I go out with your mummy a lot in the evenings."

"But I go out with Mummy a lot in the evenings and I'm not Mummy's boyfriend."

"That's true. OK, it means we like each other very much."

"But I like Mummy very much and she likes me and I'm not her boyfriend. Are you Mummy's boyfriend because you kiss her on the lips? Does that make you Mummy's boyfriend?"

"Sort of."

"Do all mummies have boyfriends?"

"Well, not if they're married."

"But Jennifer's mummy has a boyfriend. His name is Nicholas. She says her mummy thinks this is OK. And

403

now my mummy has a boyfriend and I have a daddy, so it must be OK, too."

Part of my mind dwells on the fact that Heather seems to have lost her mind, telling her daughter about Nick, and the other part is watching Peter's mind buzzing now, trying to think of something to say, anything, really, that would somehow untangle all of this. But there isn't really anything appropriate for a four-year-old. And if people in their forties still don't get it, how can a four-year-old understand? Peter is struggling, so I decide to rescue him, although I'd have been curious to hear his take on the modern-day dysfunctional family.

"As long as Jennifer's mummy loves her more than anything else in the world, that's all that is important."

Ben doesn't look convinced at all, but he's ready to move on anyway. He looks around at my tummy and then at Peter and says urgently, "Are you going to have a baby with Mummy?"

I knew it, I just knew it. What's he going to do now?

"Not that I know of. Why, is Mummy having a baby?"

"Well her tummy looks a bit bigger today. Look." Ben turns round and points at my stomach. Peter tries to look around at me as well, but has to stop at a traffic light.

"Thank you very much, Ben," I say, seriously displeased with where this conversation is going.

"Well, I don't think so. But I'll have a word with Mummy. Would you like to have a brother or sister?"

"I'd like an older brother."

"That might be a bit difficult, Ben." He's trying not to laugh.

"Jack, you know, Suzie's son, has an older brother and he's lots of fun. Young brothers and sisters are not as much fun. They pooh a lot. Are you going to sleep in Mummy's bed when you stay at our house?"

Knew it.

"I don't know. Do you think I should?"

"Only if Mummy lets you. Her bed isn't very big. And you are too big for my bed and there are only two bedrooms in the house."

I nod mutely, watching helplessly as Ben continues to embarrass me.

"Will you marry Mummy?"

"I'm not currently planning to, no, but it might come up in the future. I'll make sure to let you know."

I cower in the back seat as Ben nods and moves into safer waters, telling Peter which countries he has been to over the past year and that he is a red belt in karate and can he practise his kicks on Peter, and what does Peter do, and where does he live and there is a boy at his school, in his year, called Peter. And did he know that and if not why not?

Peter seems to be able to parry most of Ben's questions and drive without crashing all at the same time.

We finally arrive at the restaurant, Ben having grilled Peter about every excruciating subject he can think of and now desperately trying to think up more. He jumps out of the car and into the arms of the maître d's Italian mamma.

Meanwhile, Peter whispers, "How am I doing?" Which I find quite charming.

"You're doing fine. Just watch your back." I smile evilly, my revenge at Peter's obvious enjoyment of my discomfort, and follow Ben into the restaurant.

Thirty minutes to go to the New Year. Peter, Ben and I are still at Manna sitting over our coffee dregs and the remains of the tiramisu. The excitement of the day has worn Ben out and he's slept through most of dessert, curled up on the bench with his head in my lap. Peter and I have been whispering to each other, talking about everything and anything, smiling and laughing softly. I've just come back from the Ladies', where I sent a Happy New Year text to all my friends, new and old. And now I'm raring to go. I want to make it to the top of the hill and watch the fireworks before twelve.

There's a tussle over the bill, but Peter wins and shoves his card into the waiter's hands before I can even open my purse. He grabs Ben, who mutters something in his sleep and snuggles into his neck, and we plod to the top of the hill, Peter panting a little under Ben's weight. Finally, together with hundreds — thousands it seems — of others we stand at the top, looking out over London, beautiful and sparkly in the crisp, clear night. The London Eye looks stunning from afar, all lit up in red and purple and green and yellow. With just a few minutes to go, I feel my phone vibrating softly inside my coat pocket and I sneak a peek. Messages from Heather, Marie and Fiona, and one from Jack. I can't read any of them, because just at that moment Peter turns to me, Ben wide awake on his shoulders. As we count down to midnight, the fireworks go off and for twenty minutes the sky is filled with colour, noise and smoke, sparks and stars everywhere. I can't take the smile off my face, feeling myself light up with pink and green and red and feeling the occasional gentle buzz of my phone against my chest. I haven't done badly at all this year, moving house, moving on, a new town, a new school, new friends. A new start. And now Peter. Please God, let this be another good year for us.

CHAPTER
TWENTY-SIX

Taking Centre Stage

Shit, only two weeks into the New Year and my mind is completely and utterly fuzzed. If there is such a thing. I am buzzing in all different directions, doing too many things all at once and not being able to really focus on any one thing 100 per cent.

I always try to be particularly organised at the beginning of the year (although by February it's usually gone a bit pear-shaped), painstakingly making lists and setting up project schedules for clients, and now I'm sitting over a cup of coffee in my little office upstairs, with action bullets that extend over two sides of A4 paper. All of them very important and most of them fairly urgent.

I need to finish a marketing plan for Jack by the end of the week (left over from December) and follow up on invoices payable in December, and in one case, November. Pay bills. Do thank-you notes. Take down the decorations. Also, I was going to bite the bullet and start thinking about the roof repairs, which I've put off for months because of lack of money and lack of time and lack of inspiration.

And then I must call and not swear at the credit-card company, who have debited £1,000 from my account in error and charged me interest and a late-payment fee. Another phone call to swear at the guy who sold me the Golf that still won't start, despite paying £300 to get the fucking immobiliser immobilised.

And then Ben. I've got to make sure to squeeze in fifteen minutes each day for concerted maths efforts and I need to stay on top of all his papers, his homework (I'm still a bit annoyed with this, but Marie, Eileen and I have talked and decided to make a real case at the PTA meeting thing) and his academic development this spring (I'm starting to sound like Sarah Flint, which makes me shudder). We need to organise play dates — embarrassingly, I owe quite a few return dates — and Marie and I have signed up for another set of swimming lessons, which I need to follow up on. And I've still got to convince John that football is important for a four-year-old, well, more important than John going to corporate team-building weekends where they run around naked and dive into a frozen lake to prove they're tough enough, one of which coincides with the next weekend he has Ben.

And, lastly, Gary Cooper, the solicitor, who wants me to call him about my looming court case. All of these things are important. And many of them suck.

My inbox pings anxiously. An email from Jack reminding me about that marketing plan. Great, just what I needed. I'm draining my fifth cup of coffee, which is probably a mistake at nine thirty in the morning, it's making me sweaty and tetchy. My eyes are sore from staring at spreadsheets and emails and my back creaks when I arch backwards because I can't afford one of those nice back-care chairs.

I'm having one of those occasional *Fuck, I can't cope any more and am going to explode* moments, which are usually prompted by everyone around me openly assuming that I'm capable of juggling single mother-hood and a successful editorial-consultancy career with ease and aplomb, remaining at all times calm, cool and collected. And it's at that moment, when the gulf between what they think I can do and what I feel actually capable of doing seems too big, insurmount-able even, that I panic. I fold my hands, breathe deeply and look at my list again. Who to call first? Credit-card sharks? Private tutor? Car weasel? What to deal with first? Invoices? Bills? Maybe invoices first, seeing that they're directly related to each other.

It's no use, I've got too much on my mind. And, oh yes, Ben dropped quite a significant bombshell last night, when he returned from the weekend with his dad. Apparently, Ben tells me breathily, Daddy's girlfriend is pregnant, Daddy is getting married and he's giving up work next year. What? What will that mean for us? Well, first things first, looking at the stack of bills: maintenance and possible poverty. Then, having kissy-kissy, platinum-blonde bimbo Suzanne as a stepmum for Ben. Yuck. I call John. His secretary fobs me off at first, but I ask to be put through in a firm voice. One of my New Year's resolutions — be firmer.

"Hi John, had a good weekend with Ben?" I try to be casual, but there's an edge to my voice.

"Yes, thanks, it was g —"

"Ben tells me you're getting married and Suzanne's expecting a baby?"

"What? We're —"

"Congratulations."

"No, Caroline, damn it, can I get a word in edgeways? We're not doing anything like that."

"Oh." I'm deflated. "So he's made that up then?"

"God knows, must be his very lively imagination. You know, Caroline, I think you need to rein him in slightly more on that front. He's just constantly talking, telling me little stories. I'm worried he's got too much going on inside his head, losing touch with reality."

I swell back up again.

"You've got no idea of raising a young boy, John. He's perfectly fine. Actually Ms Silver was very complimentary of his stories and tales the other day, I'll have you know. And now that we're on the subject," well, sort of, "have you thought about taking Ben to football on your weekends? I need to rebook those sessions and if he only gets to go to half, it's not really worth my time and money." Oops, that might not work, seeing that he's paying for most of Ben's things. Must think before opening mouth.

"I'm sorry, Caroline, I can't. Suzanne always has her two coming over on Sundays." I forgot. Her annoying sons Jack and Charlie. "And she goes to all the trouble to make a roast. It's too far to go and make it home on time. And, anyway, sounds like you've got him completely booked up throughout the week, so perhaps he needs a bit of a time out at the weekend." I'm

411

indignant, that's meant to be my line, but before I can launch into another tirade, he says quickly, "Got to go now, Caroline, I'm on a conference call. Call me if there are any more questions."

Not a good phone call, but I've let off a little steam and the jitter in my hands seems to have calmed down. I'm feeling revived enough to tackle the next action point. Ring Jack.

"Jack, hi there, it's Caroline. I'll email you the marketing plan tomorrow. Send me back any tweaks and I'll have a finished paper for you on Friday. OK?" I'm business-like and brisk, just like they tell you in all the entrepreneurial pamphlets, but Jack's laughing. When will that man start taking me seriously?

"Good. Look forward to it. And has Gary called you about the case?"

"Not yet, but I hope to speak to him today."

"Good. Well, I will be there for moral support and to boo the opposition if you want that. Shall I bring eggs and rotten tomatoes?"

"God, no more violence anywhere near me. I'll end up serving a life sentence and then what?" I can hear him laughing as he hangs up.

Next, I try to call Peter but only get his voice-mail. Hmm. I chew the end of my pencil reflectively, then decide to send him a nice, raunchy text before making more calls.

Next week looms all too soon. The night before the court case, one nightmare is chasing another and I wake up on Tuesday morning in a cold, heavy sweat, feeling hungover without having touched a glass of anything in days. I was in court and Sarah and her cronies were there, looking down their noses. I was being sentenced to community service, not in an old people's home but in Sarah Flint's house. For the rest of my life I would have to cook and clean and iron and dust for Sarah fucking Flint. I clutch my bedcovers in terror. This is just too awful. I can't do it.

Ben and I haven't talked much about the court case, although he knows it's been on my mind. I've been trying as much as I can to hide my anxiety from him, but he's like an emotional sponge. When I see him off at the playground the morning of the case, I hug him for a little longer than I usually do and he squeezes me back.

"It will be all right, Mummy. Just say you're sorry right away, OK?"

I nod and pat him on the back as he skips into the Kangaroo Class entrance.

I stand up straight wearily. Somehow I expected other mums in the playground to be staring and pointing and whispering, but nobody is paying attention to me. I'm here so early that I don't really see any familiar faces, but everyone is chatting like they always do, about their days and weeks and weekends and where they're going on holiday, how little Trevor has lost his tooth and now wants a £2 coin instead of a £1 coin and now Jemima wants to go to ballet but there's a waiting list and the teacher has her favourites anyway. And hasn't everyone grown over Christmas and hasn't the year gone quickly already and doesn't the high street look dull now without the Christmas lights. I'm relieved to see these mums are not interested in me. They have their own lives to lead. And not all of them are like Sarah Flint and Karin Blunt and Felicity whatever-her-last-name-is.

I walk out of the playground, still hearing bits of conversation, and I'm feeling better than I have all morning. Maybe this will blow over without too much fuss and I can get back to leading a normal life.

I run into Heather as I walk out of the school gates. You'd think I would still feel a bit resentful towards her about getting me into this mess, but, actually, we're OK. A bit more wary, perhaps, and more honest with each other, but it's not really her fault that people like Sarah and Karin are so evil, plus, and I need to keep reminding myself of that, I haven't actually done anything wrong.

She doesn't say much in the way of a greeting, just hugs me and whispers, "It will be all right."

The tears well up in my eyes.

"Ben said that too."

"Bright boy. And it will, believe me. We're witches, remember?"

"Yeah, but so are they."

"I know, but we're better at it than they are. Come on, let's go. I've got Eva waiting in the car. You've got nothing to worry about, we're in this together."

Eva gives me a sympathetic smile and pats my arm as I clamber awkwardly into Heather's car. We don't speak while Heather reverses and drives down the drive much more carefully than usual, picking her way through the maze of streets towards the courthouse.

When we arrive, I'm ready to throw up, although I've barely got anything in my stomach. Gary Cooper comes out to say hello. God, he's a surprise, isn't he? We've spoken a couple of times last week, but seeing him waiting for me now, I almost forget my nerves. He's tall, a little on the beefy side, but nicely so, with jet-black hair, a broad smile and very sexy eyes. He's looking professional and crisp and hugely sympathetic with that big smile of his. He'll charm the judge to bits. My heart lifts a little.

"Right, hello there." He greets me as Eva and I jump out of the car and Heather screeches off to find parking. "I think this is going to be pretty open and shut, Caroline, please don't worry." He shakes hands with Eva. "Basically," he explains to her, "there are witnesses to say Caroline hit Sarah Flint and she pleaded not guilty at the police station so that she has a chance to defend her character in court. Which was the right thing to do," he says in my direction. "And well, that's it really. It's more a matter of what the magistrate's verdict will be." He sees me blanch. "You're of good character, a good mum and an upstanding citizen." He ticks them off one by one on his fingers. "You have people who will support all of this, and the circumstances surrounding you hitting Sarah Flint were understandable. The court doesn't generally adopt that stance, but they might, they just might, take it into account when sentencing." I turn red at the word "sentencing", tears threatening once more. Eva grabs my arm reassuringly.

"Oh God, will I go to jail?"

"Not jail, God no, but probably a fine or community service. And the cost of the court case. That's the norm. You'll get a warning and if you pummel her again, she could have a restraining order put on you." He pushes back his sleeve, revealing a watch, simple, handsome. "I'll go inside and see where we are. I'll give you a shout when it's your time, OK?" He gives me a reassuring smile, which, weirdly, reminds me of Jack, turns on his heel and disappears quickly into the building.

Heather joins us and Eva tightens her scarf, buttoning up her coat more tightly.

"Brr, cold. Nice, your Barrister."

We traipse into the front hall of the court building and Heather disappears to the loo. Around us, people are milling in all directions, some giving us curious glances as we go by. God, I hope no one recognises me. Can't imagine what would happen if I ran into one of John's associates here. I stare at the clock, willing it to move just a tiny bit faster. It's eleven o'clock. I wonder how long the court case is going to take. God I wish I'd punched her harder. Or not at all, which would have saved me all this trouble.

Eva shuffles her feet nervously and Heather pops back out of one of the brown doors on the side. "I took a peek inside the courtroom and you've got lots of support." I thought she was in the loos. Trust her to have reconnoitred the area already. "Jack, Peter, Harvey."

That gets my attention. "Bloody hell, Peter's here?" This is exactly what I mean, another six degrees of separation and Suzanne's hairdresser will be only too pleased to share the news with her next time he sees her. "Who told Peter?"

"I did," says Heather, smiling smugly. "I thought he should know the whole story, so I told him."

"Shit, Heather, you could have asked."

"He says he would have done the same, but harder." Huh. Interesting. I'm only momentarily distracted by the thought of Peter cheering me on. Five minutes later, a clerk pops his head round the door and ushers us into the courtroom. I walk in, feeling sick, like empty-stomach-with-too-much-coffee sick. Probably because I really haven't eaten anything all day and had about as much caffeine as I can handle.

A sea of faces, some smiling at me but most indifferent. Jack's face comes into focus, looking encouraging, giving me a big grin, and I spot Harvey next to him, nodding sympathetically, and Peter next to him, caring and worried and mouthing "I love you," which is rather sweet and surprising, if not really appropriate.

I'm led to an area which I presume is The Dock.

The magistrate, in his sixties, with a few chins he shouldn't have, looks at me haughtily and asks me to stand. Gary Cooper gets up quickly as the Crown Prosecution solicitor outlines the events. Brief silence. Then, "Right."

The magistrate turns his beady eyes to me. I shrink into my suit, trying to look helpless and forlorn. I don't have to put on much of an act. I'm terrified.

"This is a serious matter, Ms Gray. You attacked Mrs Sarah Flint. I understand there were extenuating circumstances, but this sort of behaviour belongs in the playground not in the outside world. And you are a mother as well, with, I believe," he looks down at his papers, "a four-year-old who looks up to you," he takes off his spectacles to better fix me with his stare, "as an example. This isn't a very good example, is it, Ms Gray?"

I feel four again myself, only the bit that wants to cut off Sarah Flint's head and stick it on a poker is more grown-up than that. I visualise this to calm me.

"No, Your Honour."

He continues, beady eyes still on me, only half convinced that I'm repentant. "But you have a spotless record and I can see from your references that you are of good character. Still," he pauses for effect, "I will not tolerate this sort of behaviour, do you understand?"

I want to slosh him one across his arrogant, patronising face, but that wouldn't do me any good, so I just say demurely, "Yes, Your Honour."

Pause. "Now, will the CPS please call Sarah Flint to the witness stand so we can get this over with?"

Pause. I surreptitiously crane my neck, but the judge sternly orders me to sit back down. The solicitor, looking bored, says, "Mrs Flint isn't here today."

I'm sorry, I don't think I can stay seated. I lift my bottom up, just an inch, to search the room for that telltale shiny bob, actually the row of telltale shiny bobs, seeing that the mafia only travel in packs. My cheering crew is giving me sympathetic smiles and discreet thumbs-ups, but I ignore them, urgently scanning the rest of the room. God, it's true, Sarah hasn't turned up. Why the hell wouldn't she be here with a bottle of champagne, gleefully toasting every moment of her triumph with her cronies? I allow myself a small glimmer of hope. This doesn't look very good, does it? Wasting everyone's time and all? Surely the magistrate can't be impressed by that?

Pause. A pause that lasts an eternity while he looks down at his papers — which I think are references and testimonies Gary has gathered for me. I think I'm going to faint. Please God, don't let my dream come true. But I don't want to go to jail either. I know it's not actually a real possibility, but I feel myself slightly swaying and going dizzy. Just as I think I'm about to pass out, he looks up and prepares to speak again.

"Having looked at the evidence and considering that the aggrieved who took several weeks to report the incident, hasn't even made an appearance at court, and that the assault is minor, I believe there is no case to answer. Case dismissed."

He takes off his spectacles and peers at me sternly. "But I tell you, Ms Gray, if this happens again, it will be taken very seriously. Do you understand?"

"Yes, Your Honour."

I've been told off. In much the same way I tell Ben off. All these past nerve-racking weeks have built up the expectation of a huge explosion, and then when I'm expecting a bang, I just get a pop. This has been such an anticlimax that all my angst and worry and dizziness feel a little ridiculous now and I almost resent Sarah for robbing me of my showdown, my courtroom drama. Until I remember my fear of prison, John, my next six years at this school, and I'm quite pleased I won't be sentenced to cleaning Sarah's floor for the next twelve months.

I leave the courtroom feeling flushed and a bit sheepish. Out in the vast hall, I loiter for a minute, smiling effusively at all the strangers hurrying to and fro.

Heather comes out first, then Eva, then Jack, Harvey and Peter last. They hug me in turn. Gary brings up the rear and I just shake my head at him wordlessly. He smiles.

"Lucky for you that Sarah wasn't there. This was definitely more open and shut than even I could have imagined." I laugh shakily. "Do you know why she didn't show up?"

I shake my head. "No clue, but thank you so much for everything, Gary."

"I didn't really get to do anything. Look, I'd love to stay and celebrate, but I have to run. Hope we meet again sometime in more pleasant circumstances."

He kisses my hand, smiles at Jack, gesturing to his phone, and waves goodbye to the rest.

I can feel Peter bristle. I smile at him, tucking his arm into mine. He feels reassuringly solid next to me. Jack smiles at me.

"That went well! Told you Gary was good." He chuckles. I hug him gratefully, for what seems like the tenth time.

"Thanks so much for hooking me up, Jack, I knew I could count on you." I feel Peter bristle again.

"No worries, that's what *friends*," he emphasises the word meaningfully, "are for. I've got to go, too, though. And don't worry about this any more, just control that temper of yours." He takes off at a trot in the direction of Gary.

"Do you need a lift, Caroline?" Harvey asks solicitously.

"No, I'm fine, thanks. And thank you both for being here."

"God, how could we not?" says Heather. "This whole thing is my fault anyway. I was the one that wanted to go into that ruddy café. If it wasn't for me and you protecting me and getting there first I would be the one in court today — and for much worse, I might add."

I'm so relieved I can afford to be generous.

"No worries, Heather. I didn't have to pummel her."

Eva is thoughtful. "I wonder why she didn't show up, though."

Heather waves her hands dismissively. "Never mind, let's just be pleased she had her hand stuck in her juicer and was prevented from leaving the house." She smiles and tugs Harvey away, Eva trailing behind them.

"You want to catch a ride with me?" Peter asks, as he puts his arm around my shoulder and steers me towards his car. "I've got the day off. And I wish you'd

421

told me before, about all this court stuff. I hope you didn't feel you had to keep it from me? How're you feeling?"

"So much better than I have all week. And yes, I'm so sorry. So many times I almost blurted it out, but things seemed to be going so well and I didn't want to shock you."

I'm so glad this is over, even though, in hindsight, it wasn't actually as big a deal as I thought it was going to be, mainly because Sarah did me a huge favour by not showing up. I grab Peter's hand.

"Let's go."

CHAPTER
TWENTY-SEVEN

Secrets

I spend all evening, all night and most of the next day wondering why Sarah didn't turn up at court. Her triumph, her chance to gloat and glower and smirk. Her opportunity to squash a long-time thorn in her side (Heather), intimidate a newbie (me) and humiliate the third one in the bunch by association (Eva). What could have prevented her from attending such a showdown? Any last-minute feelings of shame? Of decency? I can't think of anything, though, and when I see Sarah that morning across the playground, I look straight past her, smiling graciously at the thin air next to her ear. Putting me through all the anxiety and the nerve-racking fear of the last few weeks. Ruining my reputation at school. Forcing me to explain a visit to the police station and court to my four-year-old son. There's no way I can ever, ever speak to that woman again. But I would like to know why — OK, OK, I won't dwell on it any more.

The days turn into weeks, the weeks turn into months. Nothing, not a word, has been said about me, the pummelling and the court case. I gave Marie, Eileen and Claire a detailed update and we speculated about Sarah's absence, but other than that, and apart from the fact that people gave me smiles, muttering what *seemed* to be "Congratulations" or something, it was almost as if those few weeks didn't actually happen.

Similarly, little has changed in the order of things in the café every morning. The mafia still march in at nine fifteen, in the same tidy line as always. Sarah never looks at us, doesn't nod or give any recognition to any of the other mums, and neither do her hangers-on. She just walks past us. Weirdly, although the court case wasn't really a victory for either side, it seems that the time of beady stares is over and, for the most part, the menace of the mafia has melted away into the shadows for a bit. The absence of whispers whenever Eva, Heather and I walk into the Sycamore Café for our occasional coffee rendezvous is refreshing, and we usually sit with one or two other mums to chat idly about whatever's going on at the school that particular week. The staff are the same as always, although Mitch smiles a little more these days. Eva tells me he's going out with the sparky barista, so, as Heather helpfully points out, "He's getting laid, so of course he's happy." The coffee is the same, the lemon cake is still the special, but they also now offer gluten-free muffins — Marie has talked them into it — and there are fewer *Daily Mails* and more *Times* in the newspaper rack. Ears continue to prick up at Heather's occasional graphic descriptions of love-making, which become more impossible, acrobatic and exotic by the week, but all in all everything seems to be much quieter and calmer in the café and in the playground.

Ben and I have got loads of things going on, especially now that the year's in full swing. We love having people over, parents and kids, Eva and Heather; and some of the other, non-mafia mums have started to invite me to wine tastings and yoga classes and suppers. And I can bring Ben and Peter if I want, no questions asked, no lengthy explanations required on the state of my marriage, divorce, lover, family vision, academic plans, attitude to life. So we do get our fair bit of socialising, and since Heather stirred up a storm in a suburban coffee cup by letting slip that I'm a graphologist at heart, I've had a veritable onslaught of people with various assignments and projects: their own handwriting, that of their son's girlfriend, their husband's, etc. Not that I really needed that much more work, strictly speaking, but I'm pleased to have smoothed over my rocky start in Frencham. And I've already arranged to give a reading in exchange for some piano lessons for Ben, which makes a nice change from sweating over bills and payments. And, lastly, I've utterly and irrevocably fallen in love with Frencham Park over the winter months. It was my oasis during those stressful weeks before Christmas and the New Year and I feel I'm turning my back on a much-loved friend if I don't try to jog there at least twice a week.

This morning is on the wet side, and we have to muster more than our usual quota of self-discipline to make it up the hill. We run through a huddle of majestic hundred-year-old oaks, which seem to nod at us as we pass. There's a tree at the very top of the hill where, in the early days, when I was much less fit than I am now, I had to stop to catch my breath. Now I don't have to stop but I occasionally slow down and pat it, just because it's there. The buds are starting to come out and the birds are singing again, hoping for warmth and longer days to arrive soon. I think we might be in luck. I can smell spring in the air.

I smile to myself, thinking of what the year has brought so far. I've been working hard, mostly for Jack, been seeing more of Peter, with and without Ben. We've taken Ben to see *The Lion King, Stuart Little*, and *The Jungle Book* at Frencham Theatre ("Why don't they have real monkeys on stage, Mummy?"). At the weekends Ben is with John, Peter has taken me to everything "alternative". Alternative theatre, alternative cinema, alternative art galleries. He calls Ben and me the "weapons of mass distraction" because he wants to spend more time with us than he does filming, and has occasionally been reprimanded for being late, which is sweet.

I've left the girls a little behind me, and slow down for them to catch up. All of us are red-faced by now, gasping for breath.

"Fancy coming round to mine tonight? We haven't done a girls' night in for ages. The boys can look after the children."

They nod bravely through their pain, relieved to catch a glimpse of my road in the distance. I think, once I'm out of sight, they just walk home from there.

After the run and a shower, I head into Jack's office to discuss various ongoing projects, hand in my latest assignment and hopefully catch up on a few other bits and pieces. Jack cancelled our lunch in December, so the last time I was here, I remember fondly, was the day I met Peter. God, it seems that so much has happened since then, like I've been on some kind of fast forward and am only now slowing down.

Delilah is at her desk to greet me, baring her teeth in an unmistakable smile when she sees me. Still gorgeous, still wearing an unbelievably short skirt revealing endless legs and still as stick thin as ever.

"Caroline. How've you been?"

"Just fine. And you?"

"I'm great. Go right in, Jack's expecting you."

Jack's sitting behind his desk, flashing me his usual warm smile.

"Ms Gray? Have you recovered from your close call with the law?"

"Yes, thanks again, Jack. I'm still mystified why Sarah Flint didn't turn up in the end. All that uproar, and for nothing. Weird."

"Perhaps she has more to hide than you do?" he suggests. "Anyway, it was good that it fell through, the community service and the fine would have been such a hassle, and all the publicity that would go with it. You know 'Yummy mummy bound over' with a huge photo of you in handcuffs, Ben crying in the background, the witches cackling above. People would eat it up."

427

"God, don't remind me, Jack. Anyway, here's your marketing plan, and I wanted to talk through these other writing samples."

For the next hour Jack and I talk business and I take him through each loop and dropped "y" and "h". At one point I look up and see him watching me, with that funny half-smile he sometimes has. I'm a bit taken aback by the soberness in his eyes.

"Everything OK? I know I've been a bit rushed lately and we haven't had a chance to catch up properly for ages. Sorry if I'm not being a good friend these days."

"Yeah, no worries. Same old, same old." He flicks his pen casually. "I know you've got a lot going on. I'll just take those files from you, that all sounds spot on. Invoice included in the paperwork as usual?"

I nod, not quite convinced but eager to be off. I promised I'd meet Peter for a quick lunch before heading back to Frencham.

He walks me out.

"How are you, apart from having one foot in jail and being incredibly busy? Still with that cameraman guy?"

"Yes, still with that cameraman guy."

"And happy?"

I smile.

"As happy as I can be. Yes I am." We've reached the door and I can hear Delilah's cool staccato barking into the phone. "Look, Jack, give me a shout if you ever just want to chat. Thanks again for being there for me. I'll do the same for you. OK?"

"Thanks, Caroline. But don't go pummelling anyone for me just yet." He pulls me into a hug and I think, as so often before, *if only* . . .

"Lots of loops."

Ten o'clock and my sitting room is slowly getting merry. The girls have arrived like wise men bearing gifts: Chardonnay, chocolate and Coke (diet — twelve cans), a stack of DVDs (just in case) and CDs. M&S frozen nibbles cooking in the oven, we nest in the centre of the sitting room, creating mess, making noise and occasionally jumping up to change the music yet again. We haven't had a girls' night in ages, we are already well into our second bottle of wine, the music is turned way up — I hope Mrs Hartnell is out tonight — and Heather is asking me about Peter's handwriting.

"Yes, lots of loops. It means he's creative. Strong. Determined. The writing shows a lot of emotion and determination. And sensitivity. A bit possessive and jealous, though."

"Oh you don't want possessive and jealous, Caroline," Heather says, nodding her head wisely. "Trust me, I have a lot of experience in that department. Harvey can be such a domineering —"

"Bollocks, Heather," Eva snaps, waving a bag of Minstrels in emphasis. "Load of crap."

We laugh, mainly because Eva very rarely swears.

"Nick's not all that laid-back either," she slurs, Chardonnay in hand, swaying slightly. "You know, Caroline, we were out a few days ago, with the kids. I think you were doing something with Ben and Peter.

429

Anyway, we drove back to Heather's place and got out of the car, the kids all running into the house and as I turn round and say bye to this girl," she gestures to an embarrassed-looking Heather, "who should pop out of the bushes like a seedy Mr Benn but Nick. He was hiding in her bushes."

Heather giggles. "As I was saying, I know possessive guys," she says smugly, tugging the Minstrels bag out of Eva's hand in one swift move. "Back to Peter."

"He was stalking you, Heather. Kind of creepy, really."

I can imagine only too well.

"Oh, it's nothing. I'd forgotten to take my mobile and he was calling me and wondering where I was."

We sit in silence for a moment, sipping wine, eating Minstrels, until Eva breaks the silence with another hiccup.

"I can't quite figure all of this out. Do the kids actually know about Nick, Heather?"

"No, I don't think so."

"Jennifer told Ben that all mummies have boyfriends *and* daddies, because you have a boyfriend and I have a boyfriend."

Heather looks shocked. "Really?"

"Yes, really."

"But she's only five. What did you say to him?"

"I'm hardly one to speak. Ben has a daddy and his mummy has a boyfriend too."

Another silence. Longer this time. More sobering.

"Christ, I'm so pleased I'm not going to go through puberty again," I suddenly say.

430

"Huh, don't think I've come out the other side yet, Caroline." Heather laughs, relieved to move on from her love life.

"No, I think you're right there," Eva agrees emphatically.

Heather rears up again. "God, but you're holier than thou these days. Is there anything you can do wrong?"

"Actually," Eva has her eyes lowered on her wine glass, rubbing the rim, "you're not the only one with problems, Heather, OK? Just because we don't all go around shouting about it doesn't mean any of us are less fragile in our relationships. You talk about Harvey and John being possessive. Well, in my family, it's actually me who's the possessive one. I just can't bear the thought of Harry and Maddy going through what I did, but I'm holding on so tight to what I've got that it's claustrophobic, for both me and Gordon." I pat her hand and she tries to smile. "It's OK, it's just always . . . a balancing act, you have to give a little to get a little." She shakes her head, trying to clear her thoughts. "You know what, girls, we haven't got drunk together in ages. Let's just enjoy tonight, no more talk about men and love and commitment." She jumps and turns the music back up, dancing exuberantly, determinedly, Chardonnay sloshing everywhere.

Later, as I put Eva into a taxi and she slumps on the back seat, Heather holds my sleeve.

"Caroline, I know I'm fairly drunk, but I just wanted to tell you how sorry I am for everything. I know you think I've been a lousy friend." I make a reassuring noise and go to open the car door. "No, wait, I wanted to talk to you."

The taxi driver pokes his head out of the window. "Are you coming, love?"

"Sorry, just a minute. You can turn on the meter if you like." Heather makes a face and pulls me away. "I know why Sarah Flint didn't turn up at court." She looks at me eagerly, but I don't know what to say — Sarah's name cropping up now? At the end of our girls' night in?

"She's a thief."

Now she has my full attention. Of all the things she could have said, I never expected this.

"A thief? What are you talking about?" Out of the corner of my eye, I can see the cabby light up a cigarette and settle himself back in the seat. Eva seems to have gone to sleep.

"Yes, it all came together just before the court case. I felt so bad, I really wanted to help in some way, and then I thought the only way this mess would have a good ending would be if there was some way to keep her from honouring her appointment. Get her to drop the charges. And then it hit me. I'd started noticing some discrepancies in the figures when I was doing the year-end accounts, but I couldn't quite figure out where exactly they were happening. The sums were smallish each time, almost too small to notice really, but all in all, they added up."

She's talking faster now, her hands slicing the air.

"And then Nick mentioned that he'd overheard one of his colleagues saying they'd been hired to redo

Sarah's bathroom but still hadn't been paid yet. Apparently it hadn't been the first time that a cheque bounced either. Somehow, I don't know why, my ears pricked up. Well, I can tell you *exactly* why — I hate that bitch and anything nasty I can get on her would only work in our favour, right? Anyway, I asked around, nothing too obvious, just keeping my ears open, really, and Eric, you know, at The Chestnut, mentioned that he heard Jeremy Flint had been made redundant sometime ago. And remember? That one morning when I thought I saw him in the park? I did think that was weird. But Sarah still kept spending. We saw it all that time — new haircuts, new clothes, and you saw her house. Where would she get the money from? And she's in more than an ideal spot to dip her hand in the till. It must have been her, there couldn't be any other way. But I didn't have any proof. So I waited for her, one night after the PTA meeting, when she was walking back to her car without her two henchwomen. And I confronted her. She denied it vigorously, of course, threatened me, then ignored me. I said I would ask for a full-blown investigation. Go through every record, every receipt. Call in Ms Silver, Mrs Ellison. Finally, she crumbled. Almost had to pity the woman. I think the pressure of it all got to her. Some kind of breakdown, maybe."

Well, what do you know. Sarah Flint has a lot of skeletons in her wardrobe and too many designer clothes that she can't pay for. I'm stunned. There's too much to take in, especially with one too many

Chardonnays sloshing around gently in my churning stomach.

"So how did you get her to drop the charges?" I don't really need to ask.

"Well, let's just say Sarah Flint wasn't too keen to have that particular skeleton aired out for everyone to see." Heather gives me her best evil smile and I have to agree, you almost have to pity the poor woman.

The cabby impatiently flicks his burning cigarette butt out of the window and revs the engine. Eva is stirring in the back. Heather hugs me quickly, breathing Chardonnay on my face, and gives me a kiss.

"You can always count on me." And she jumps into the cab, slams the door so loudly that anyone not kept up by the music still blaring from my windows would most certainly be awake now. I wander slowly up the garden path and into my messy house, blow out the candles and turn off the lights. Well, I didn't think Frencham still had the power to surprise me, but what do I know.

CHAPTER
TWENTY-EIGHT

Doing Your Homework

As Ms Silver promised, Ben has been coming home with homework since the New Year started. Spellings, very basic ones, some sums, the occasional collage to assemble. Nothing huge, but personally I still think it's too early.

With all the Sarah Flint goings-on, I didn't go to any of the monthly PTA meetings she'd been trying so hard to enlist me for earlier, but now is the time to put all differences aside. I gather up Eva and Heather for support (Heather is always good in situations like these; she can argue you out of house and home if given the chance), and my other friends and acquaintances have promised to come as well.

The homework meeting has been set for seven o'clock that night. Ben's safely tucked in front of the TV, with Mrs Hartnell reading the paper, and at five to seven Eva and I are waiting for Heather at the school gates.

Finally, a couple of minutes past the hour, Heather appears, red-faced and panting.

"So sorry, girls, you should have gone in. Now I'll drag you down with me. Let's go."

We start to run through the playground, half chasing each other around the swing sets, giggling maniacally. The reception door is closed.

We make faces at each other, jumping when the metallic voice on the other side says, "Hello?"

"Hi, it's Caroline Gray, Eva Thompson and Heather Charles, for the homework meeting."

"You're a bit late, you know."

Eva suppresses a giggle and we try to look suitably chastened when the buzzer lets us in.

We walk past reception, waving hello to the secretary. She must be doing overtime at this time of year, when everything needs so much organisation and scheduling. Or maybe she's just there to let miscreants like us into the school. It always looks so cosy in there and any day of the week you can find the three of them behind computers, surrounded by piles of paper, files and brown envelopes full of sick notes, dinner money and requests for holidays during term (which is never authorised, so why anyone bothers I don't know), confiscated toys and bags of sweets. Mrs Hopkins, Mrs Cox and Mrs Fitzgibbon, all looking like trendy Mrs Pepperpots. They're the "there-therers" of the school. Whenever anyone in the classrooms is sick, they collect them, call the mums and "there there" the children until the parent arrives. They are very good at it. Mrs Cox is Ben's favourite. She gives him a sweet every time he gets a plaster, whereas he only gets a "there there" from the other two.

Mrs Cox (I think) tut-tuts in mock horror when she see us tiptoeing through the entrance hall, before giving us a thumbs-up and then pointing down a corridor. We troop past dark classrooms as quietly as possible, the hum of the heating system the only sound. It smells vaguely of school dinners.

"Why do I always smell greens, even though I know they almost never have them?" Eva whispers. "Not that the greens in our day looked anything like them. And do you remember the jam roly-poly and the spotted dick in those big metal tubs, cut up into squares?"

Heather sighs appreciatively. "That was good stuff. And remember when Toby Shepherd sneaked into the kitchens and stole a whole tray and sold it in the playground for 50p a chunk?"

"God, yes, he got sent home and a month's detention for that. Today, he'd probably get a business enterprise award for initiative." I smile when I think of the stammering, blundering Toby at the awards dinner. I haven't laid eyes on him since, thank God. I'm sure he's very nice and stuff, but some things just won't ever change.

With a thud, I run into Eva's back and push her forwards into Heather, who's stopped abruptly in front of two large doors. We almost tumble to the floor before Heather grabs the door handle, turning around to glower at us.

"Hey, you two, behave."

We stand to the side, peering carefully through the windows into the main hall, where we had the nativity and the Stroppy Fairy Christmas musical. Gone are the paper chains and Christmas tree, replaced by a colourful montage of papier-mâché trees in flower with furry-carpet squirrels and feather-duster birds and a big yellow tissue-paper sun. I smile. Ben told me just this morning that the competition to have your feather dusters and carpet bits displayed here has been fierce, with lots of bartering and bribery going on in the playground, but the effect is very sweet. You can almost smell the spring and the sunshine, which, always at this point in the year, I'm absolutely desperate for.

I look at the grey chairs and the tables, inhaling the typical school smell — bit of dinner, bit of cleaning, bit of dust and paper — and then, for a quick moment, I have such an intense déjà vu I freeze on the spot. I remember vividly one morning, when the car didn't start and I was late for school, feeling that knot in the pit of my stomach, the anxiety, almost sickness about having to knock on the door and walk into the classroom in front of everyone, getting a late sticker on the register, boys sniggering from the back, girls looking disdainfully down their noses at me. Little bits and pieces flash through my mind in one big, anxious whirlwind: the playground and none of the boys ever wanting to catch me during chase, the few times when I fell out with Eva and Heather and had to pretend I had someone to play with, running from one side of the playground to the other, laughing as though I was going to meet someone, who wasn't there. Being the last one to be picked for hockey and netball teams. Hiding in the library from Rose Johnson. Always, always being in the back of the choir during plays and musicals. There must have been some good times as well, but right now one big wave of miserable moments is flooding over me and, suddenly, I want to cry. I want a Mrs Cox to say "there there" to me. I want to make sure that Ben will be all right, that I'm always doing the right thing by him, taking care of him.

Heather is just about to open the door, when Eva notices my panic-stricken face.

"Good God, Caroline, what's the matter?" she says, putting her arms around me.

"Oh, I don't know. Just being here brought everything back. School, being late, all those anxieties." I take a deep breath, trying to pull myself together. Eva and Heather crowd around me and whisper encouragement. Inside, I can hear chairs scraping against linoleum. I shudder again. After a few seconds, we break apart, and I resolutely wrench open the door, hitting the wall with a huge clang that reverberates loudly through the silent school.

All heads in the hall jerk up. God, it's already full. There are six rows of chairs, about eight on each side, and most are taken. It looks like all the people I've been talking to have shown up, so hopefully we'll get this sorted quickly. I can't see any spares but perhaps we can stand at the back. Mrs Ellison is standing in front of a large screen with the words "HOMEWORK — IS IT NECESSARY?!" in capitals, doubly underlined in red, with a question mark and an exclamation mark to make the question very important. Personally I think it's a bit of overkill.

I walk in first, well, the girls push me in first, then follow quickly. Mrs Ellison carries on talking and smiles at us, but half the mums turn round in unison and stare as though we've all just walked in naked.

Heather does a little wave to everyone and says, "Hi there."

A few of the women giggle, and I see Marie's shoulders shaking, but there's a stony silence in one corner of the room, where I can just about make out the top of Sarah's head, her shiny black hair flicking round and whipping the poor woman sitting behind her across the face.

Now that we've created an actual disturbance, Mrs Ellison stops and smiles at us. "Come in, ladies. Quickly. You haven't missed much. If you would like to take a seat, there are some spaces here at the front."

Our shoes click on the hard floor, like tap dancers, as we slowly make our way across the hall. Mrs Ellison stops again until we find our seats in the front.

Eva and Heather pick up the sheets of A4 paper stapled together, while I accidentally sit on mine. I try to surreptitiously pull it out from underneath my bottom, but the staple catches in my skirt and I have to get up again for Eva to prise it off carefully without tearing the material. I obviously woke up this morning deciding to be twelve.

Everyone is watching us curiously, impatiently, but Mrs Ellison gives us a big grin.

"Sorry, Mrs Ellison," I mumble sheepishly. She chuckles benevolently.

"Now, where was I? Oh yes, I was asking everyone if you can remember the last time you learnt something new." Silence from the audience. Clearly, no one wants

440

to go down the route of public humiliation that I've just taken. Mrs Ellison, obviously used to parental shyness, asks again, patiently. "Right, I'm sure someone has learnt something new this week, this month?"

I can feel Heather itching to put up her hand up, but Eva firmly holds on to her. Looking at her watch and the impassive faces in front of her, Mrs Ellison finally gives up and continues with her lecture.

"Well, it's different for your children. *You* may feel you have stopped learning, but they are still learning. Each moment of the day they are absorbing new information, and we," she sweeps across the room, including herself in the gesture, "are merely here to facilitate that process. But it doesn't start at eight fifty-five in the morning when they enter the playground and end at three twenty when you pick them up, it keeps going throughout their day. Even if you don't think they are learning, per se, they are, absorbing by observing you, their peers, television, family, friends. All of this, let's call it extra-curricular learning," she gives a little smile, "isn't structured and that's where homework comes in. Homework is an essential part of their learning process and it's important in these crucial years to get the foundation right.

"And homework provides an excellent way to involve you, as the parents, in what we are doing for your children at school, for you to know what your child is being taught and to play a role in it. We need your continued involvement to ensure your children do their homework properly and on time and we need to rely on you to provide the right environment at home. I know several of you have come to see me about homework, especially for the little ones. I hope this meeting tonight helps dispel some of your anxieties. Please continue to stay involved. Whenever you like, speak to Mrs Fitzgibbon and ask for an appointment to see your class teacher or me to catch up on your child's development." Mrs Ellison takes a deep breath, either as a dramatic pause or, quite literally, to catch her breath.

"Now, if there aren't any questions so far, I'd like to talk about the level and type of homework we give at The Sycamore. Right, has everyone had a chance to look at the papers you found on your seat and are there any questions?" Silence again. Then a "No" in the back row and a giggle. Confidence is obviously building.

She sighs. "Well, take it home and have a thorough read. It talks through a few more statistics and research findings about homework. OK, at The Sycamore, we slowly build up the amount of homework throughout the year, and it requires different elements of emotional, creative and systematic learning." Step by step, she takes us through the various types of homework, through the forms. With each year I feel slightly more overwhelmed and, finally, I allow my attention to wander, safe in the knowledge that Ben still has a little more time to hone his reading skills. I try to catch Marie's eye across the aisle, but she's looking glassy-eyed in front of her, twirling the ribbon on her skirt. Some people are nodding as Mrs Ellison speaks, probably those whose children are actually in the year

Mrs Ellison is talking about. Suddenly I look up, realising that Mrs Ellison has just asked a question.

"Do you think your children receive too much homework?" She has put aside her notes and looks at us provocatively. This is where it gets interesting. A restless murmur goes through the rows of parents and I sit up straighter.

Heather manages to put up her hand before Eva has a chance to grab her arm. Mrs Ellison looks down and smiles, almost relieved to have elicited a reaction from the crowd.

"Yes, Mrs Charles? You've got Philip in Year 3 and Jennifer in Reception. Correct?"

Heather has to think about this one for a bit. "Yes, I think that's right." A few of the mums laugh. Silence behind us.

Heather stands up, and coughs to clear her voice, turning slightly sideways so that her voice can be heard all the way to the back. She always was good at public speaking.

"I do feel that Philip increasingly receives more time-consuming and complex assignments. I know this is intentional, to some degree, in order to ensure they're suitably equipped for when we're coming up to the time when he'll be trying for new schools. But, and I don't think I'm just speaking for myself, there's a lot of pressure on them already and I'm wondering if there could be a more balanced approach to their workload. I know in the summer months the children would like to use the extra light and warmth to do more outdoor activities, and I think in the winter, when they're less inclined or able to do this, they might be able to handle more. I agree with you on the importance of learning, but there are many different ways to do this and the unstructured ways can be just as effective and character-building as the more structured approach. Personally, and the mums I've spoken to agree, I feel it's just as important to live within a healthy environment, coping with a healthy balance of work and play." Heather sits down.

I lean over and whisper, "I didn't know you'd been speaking to other mums."

She whispers back, "Yeah, well some of us have been doing our homework, Caroline." I smile and nod.

"Yes?" Mrs Ellison says again almost immediately, looking at me.

I haven't put my hand up and, contrary to my promise to Ben, I don't really have anything to add. But perhaps the same rules of an auction house apply here and a nod or twitch means I want to speak. I half rise from my chair, racking my brain for an intelligent comment, but freeze immediately when a soft voice behind me speaks. Sarah Flint.

I sink back down quickly.

"Thank you, Mrs Ellison, for your very interesting speech about the importance of learning and the importance of homework. I'm pleased to see the school take such a firm stance in this case, as the new research on the effectiveness of homework is something the PTA has been keen to see developed and discussed and has, in fact, been paying for over the last year."

Heather whispers in my ear, "She likes the word importance, doesn't she?"

I giggle. Sarah pauses and I feel her frown penetrate just between my shoulder blades.

"It's vital and indeed necessary that, as balanced, law-abiding individuals, we remain responsible for bringing up our children in home environments that are as healthy and happy as possible."

This is unduly heavy stuff and some of the other parents titter at Sarah's pompous stance while Mrs Ellison looks a little confused. But none of the "law-abiding individual" stuff is lost on Eva, Heather or me. Sarah continues.

"It's equally vital, as Mrs Ellison has pointed out, that we provide a healthy learning environment for our children. I know that in some of our more, let's say, *dysfunctional* households, where violence, chaos and unstructured lifestyles prevail, it's slightly more difficult to create and maintain the standards we need for our children to learn and bring their knowledge to The Sycamore. A single parent is perhaps less able, or willing," she coughs delicately, "to uphold that all-important structure, to administer discipline where needed, to make learning an absolute priority. I think those of us who are lucky enough to come from happy, healthy, unified families should do all we can to support those of us who do not." She smiles sanctimoniously and sits down.

I'm outraged and I can tell by the restless whispers in the room that I'm not the only one. I want to get up and fucking slosh the bitch, pull her hair hard, tear it out of her petty, spiteful, arrogant little head. Before I realise it, I'm starting to get up, fist flexing, ready to swing at her and send her flying across the hall. Obviously, I'm not someone who learns from my mistakes.

But Heather holds my left wrist very tight and Eva's hanging on to the other one. I didn't know they were this strong. When it's clear that I'm going to stay seated, Heather gets up, very slowly, very carefully, looking around at each and every parent in the room. Finally, her eye falls on Sarah, who recoils slightly. Heather in a rage is a terrible thing to watch. Even I'm quaking slightly and she's on my side.

Mrs Ellison is looking incredulous and a little bemused by the various undercurrents so clearly fighting their way across the hall, but motions for her to speak.

"Thank you, Sarah. You talk about family unity, healthy environments, about single parents and dysfunctional families." She gives a little hiss in emphasis, and Sarah cowers but stands her ground. "Regardless of each individual situation, we are all in the same boat here, we all want what is best for our children, want them to succeed and fulfil their potential. But I think you missed something very fundamental here, Sarah. You stand in judgement of family structure, but you haven't said much about the basic values we should all share, should all agree on. Simple things like, for example, being against lying, bullying, oh yes, and stealing. If these values aren't at the heart of a household, *dysfunctional* or otherwise, such an environment could be very disruptive to the learning process."

I can see people nodding all around us, but most look slightly confused. Mrs Ellison still smiles, but her smile has lost much of its spontaneity. Sarah scowls at Heather.

"I'm sure I don't quite know what you mean," she hisses venomously. Big mistake. Heather smiles.

"I'll explain. Take my son Philip, for example. He's always getting his maths homework wrong, mainly his additions and subtractions. Most recently, he came home with an assignment and a note. He'd cheated on his maths test, took away *too much*, if you know what I mean, added *too little*."

The air is heavy with hints now and mums around us are muttering. Mrs Ellison is looking even more confused. But Sarah is too far gone to notice, and she smiles triumphantly.

"He cheated," she chants, gesturing. "That just proves my point. Where on earth could he possibly learn the value of cheating? Why don't you spend a little less time talking about values and a little more educating him?"

Heather looks straight at Sarah.

"I did," she says softly. "I said cheating always somehow comes to the light of day and when he's found out, people will call him a liar and a cheat and start avoiding him at school. And that's where we as parents come in. We must, at all times, teach our children and lead by example. And if someone cheats, we've got to find them and put them back on the straight and narrow to make sure they don't do it again."

Heather stops. You could hear a pin drop now, and I think everyone is holding their breath, expecting a punch-up. Or something, anything. All eyes in the room are on the small knot of women standing at the front: Sarah, stone-faced, Karin and Felicity, confused and annoyed, and Heather, well, Heather is for once in control of the situation.

"Oh, and one thing I would like to mention, Mrs Ellison," Heather turns away from Sarah, who continues to stare malevolently at the back of her head. "I've got to have a word with you about the PTA accounts after the meeting. I've been going through them and I'm not sure we'll have enough money this year for the computer room."

The silence in the hall is deafening. No one has a clue what's going on, but they all realise that this moment marks a milestone in the presence of the mafia at school. Some people, like Marie, seem to be slowly putting two and two together, but before anyone comments Heather sits down and looks at me. Her mission is over. I hear a rustle behind me and Sarah has sat down without another word.

Mrs Ellison coughs, shakes her head and nods to Heather.

"Yes, yes, fine, let's talk after the meeting. Well, we don't have much more time, but does anyone else have anything to say on the issue of homework? Questions? Suggestions?" Shyness and boredom have long gone and hands go up all around the room, talking about difficulties, improvements. Not a word out of the mafia.

But I'm not listening any more and I don't think Eva or Heather are either. We are all just waiting for the bell to go and I look at Heather, a bit dewy-eyed, and mouth, "Thank you."

She squeezes my hand and says, "Don't thank me, Caroline. I enjoyed it."

CHAPTER
TWENTY-NINE

Out in the Open

The weekend. And the first official day of spring. It's pretty damp but the air is mild and I've just been for a jog around the park with the girls. Ben is playing football till eleven, trying to win a gold medal, and Peter's meeting me in an hour. We've reconvened, freshly showered, for a well-deserved breakfast at the Sycamore Café, al fresco, to celebrate that it's just about warm enough to do it. If you've got your coat on, that is. There're only two round tables that fit on the pavement, and we've managed to snag one of them. We're on our second helping of coffee and croissants and have papers spread out across the small table. Eva's looking through the property pages, as usual giving us a running commentary on the market in Frencham and its surrounds, and Heather hogs the one sunny chair, covered in crumbs and catching a quick nap. This is truly as good as it gets.

"Fucking hell!"

Heather jerks upwards and almost falls off her chair.

I look around me, slightly embarrassed. Usually swearing loudly and viscerally would cause heads to turn and lots of humming and tutting all around us, but today it is buzzing and everyone seems to be listening to their own conversations.

"What's the matter?" Eva leans over my shoulder to stare at the tabloid I've been reading, one of my few guilty pleasures in life.

MILLIONAIRE BUSINESSMAN COMES OUT

Jack Stone, 45, CEO of Universe International, the world's largest outdoor advertising company, has admitted to his homosexuality. Stone, a renowned and confirmed bachelor, has two homes, one in Hampstead, the other in New York, and has been linked with many beautiful and successful women during his career. His partner is believed to work in law, although he refused to give details.

Stone commented, "My private life is exactly that, private, and does not in any way affect my business. But seeing that you have made it your business to pry into my personal sphere, I'm not ashamed at all to admit that I've been in a long-term relationship with a male partner.

The company's share price has not been affected.

"Well, fuck me," says Heather, without a trace of her usual smug, know-it-all cool. "Who'd have seen that one coming? Jack Stone? He's the last one I'd have put down for it. Did you know, Caroline?"

I'm stunned. And a little bit hurt. How the hell could I have missed that? Jack and I have been friends,

451

colleagues, co-workers for so long, but, somehow, there's this enormous part of his life that he never saw fit to share with me. How he could have kept it a secret is beyond me. But then again, I haven't seen as much of him in the last year and even less over the last few months. I've had so much on with the school and work and Ben and managing to get John at long last to take his son to football and meet some of the other parents, who frustratingly think he's a lovely guy. Peter's taking up all the time I don't set aside for Ben and the house and the school. So I haven't talked to Jack as much as I used to and I feel even worse, because I wasn't there for him when he's always dropped everything to be there for me. Why would he not talk about it to me? And a small part, a very small part, is a tiny bit miffed that things never did work out between us and will clearly never have the chance to.

The girls are still staring at me and I say quickly, "Of course I didn't. Mind you, who knows how much is true here." I scan the article again. "This paper is usually pretty shit."

"Who do you think it is?" Heather's already moved on. We look at the article again, trying to read between the lines.

"God," Eva says suddenly, "I wonder if that partner in law is the guy who represented you, Gary?"

"Ooh, yes," Heather agrees. "He was so lovely."

Eva agrees. "So good-looking. Damn it, it's always the gorgeous ones."

"Yes, he was," I say grudgingly, still chewing over Jack keeping me out of his life. Oh well, he'll have had his reasons. He always does. The girls are looking at me curiously, but, tactfully, change the subject.

"Ok, let's drink up and get ready for this afternoon," Eva says bracingly. "Do we have everything for our picnic? You've got the drinks, Heather?"

"Champagne, juice, water, beer."

"I've got a basketful of food, and you're bringing stuff as well, Caroline? We've got games for the kids?"

Ben was the one who suggested it a few days ago, one morning over mini Shredded Wheat. He'd been in the best mood because Ms Silver gave him two stars the day before for reading and creative storytelling (something quite complicated about a little boy whose mother was half-angel, half-witch and could turn her son into different animals — dogs, spiders, birds, lions — and how the boy ate up all his enemies and was kind to all those who were kind to him) and everyone had clapped when he was finished. Very pleased he was, bouncing off the walls in the kitchen, chattering nineteen to the dozen, returning only occasionally to cram another piece of toast into his mouth, washed down by the puddle of brownish milk left in the bottom of his bowl.

"Mummy, can we go for a picnic in the park like we used to? And I can take my bike and we could ask Harry and Maddy and Philip and Jennifer, and can Peter come too?"

I smile to myself. Nice idea.

"Yes, let's do it, and definitely, Peter can come too."

I surreptitiously remove his nasty cereal bowl and put it in the dishwasher, pottering around the kitchen while Ben is off on another tale from school. Peter has finally sold the house with Dawn and bought a two-bedroom flat nearby. I was a bit freaked out at first, and I certainly don't want him to move in just yet, but I'm relieved that that chapter of his life is finally over. We're still taking all of these relationship things very slowly. Except for sex. It's the best and we're still at that stage where we can't get enough of each other. But I'm not like Heather. I don't need to share every detail.

Over the past few months, Peter's taken the most wonderful films of Ben and me playing in the house, in the park, on the football pitch. I now have a professional video diary of Ben's early years — I really have chosen well. A good cameraman anyway.

We've agreed to meet up on the hill, where you have a gorgeous view down the park. It's the highest point, pretty much, but it has the advantage that very few people make the trek up there. Waitrose has been raided for chicken and salmon slices and gingerbread men and cartons of apple and orange juice as well as cakes and little broccoli florets and salad stuff which the kids won't eat, and breadsticks and yoghurts, which they will.

Ben, Peter and I are the first to arrive. And Ben is whingeing.

"Are we nearly there yet? Are we? Are we?"

"Yes, we are there." I'm doubled over, dumping my bags on the grass. "I swear, if you ask one more time I'll make you walk down and up again. And no, you can't eat any of the food yet, Ben. Wait till the others arrive."

Below, I see Eva trailing behind Gordon, Harry and

Maddy racing up the hill, totally oblivious to the steep angle, trying to trip each other up.

Nothing better to get Ben back up and running. He bolts halfway down the hill, shouting at the top of his voice, "Do you want to play football? Let's play football." They troop off and kick a ball about, occasionally hitting ankles, shins, stomachs and the odd tree. I'm sure there'll be tears in a minute, but hopefully it will be a good five before we hear about someone hurting someone else.

Eva grins as she puffs up the last few steps.

"Hi guys. Chosen the highest point, have you? Sweet of you."

"Sorry darling, but just look at the view. The hard work was worth it." Eva turns and obediently admires the vista, hands on her sides.

The ground's still a bit cold but we spread blanket after blanket to make a nice big space. The air is nice up here and all around us trees sway gently in the breeze. There's one in particular, a willow, which reminds me of the one in Heather's back garden. Well, Toby's back garden now, I guess.

"Wonder how Toby is?"

"He's fine." Peter's voice is muffled behind a huge blanket he's just swung into the air.

"Oh, of course, I forgot you knew him." Eva is intrigued. "Do you ever talk about us?"

"Bloody hell! Couldn't you have picked Everest or something?" Heather's voice rings up the hill, her scowling face slowly coming closer. I see Philip and Jennifer trailing behind her, followed by Harvey.

Heather gives us hugs all round and throws herself on to the blanket. The kids scamper off to join Ben and the twins, looking light-hearted and happy. Actually happy. I haven't seen them like that for a while.

Harvey and Peter start setting up the swingball, which obviously takes two grown men to do, chatting idly about their weekend, Peter's new property and so forth. Those two have taken to each other like ducks to water. Peter can spend hours talking to Harvey and Harvey seems to live vicariously through Peter, always asking about shoots and places to travel and places to go. Peter tells me Harvey slightly regrets having settled for money-making over something more creative.

Eva, Heather and I are sprawled on the blanket, ostensibly setting out food and drink but really just watching our families. The kids are engrossed in their world, occasionally looking up at us, just to make sure we're still here. We watch Peter and Harvey join Gordon in kicking the football around and for a while all we can hear is shouting and heckling, hysterical giggling from five overexcited kids trying to snatch their ball back from the grown-ups.

"Have you heard anything else from Sarah?" I finally break the lazy silence. "I haven't seen much of her over the past few weeks."

"Haven't you heard? She's moving away," Heather says innocently, but I can see she's savouring dropping another one of her bombshells. Eva and I sit up.

"No way. How do you know?"

"Yep, house up for sale and everything. Heard it from Mrs Ellison."

456

"Really, you heard this from her, just like that?"

"Well, actually, she called me a couple of days ago. She said that Sarah was moving, taking her kids out of school and all that, and that the PTA needed a new chair. And that I'd been voted in." She smiles triumphantly, punching the air. This was the real bombshell she'd been dying to deliver.

For a brief moment we're stunned into silence, then, all at once, start shouting questions, laughing, cheering.

"Karin and Felicity voted you in?"

"Oh, course not, are you joking? But now that Sarah's gone, quite a few of the other mums seem glad to have a change, so it seems that Sarah's henchwomen are, for once, in the minority. They were overruled. And" — she spreads her arms dramatically — "I've accepted. So there's a position of treasurer open if either of you are interested? No? Didn't think so. Well, there's plenty of opportunity to stay involved, I'll make sure of that." Another bout of cheering and shouting. Finally Heather says, more seriously, "I have to say, I think it'll be a bit of a thankless task, like working in an office without getting paid, but at least we're on the inside this time and we can choose all the nice people to be as well. And we could actually make a difference, rather than endless scheming and homework committees and so on. After all, our kids go to this school too. There's a lot going on this term. It seems the council has offered more money for some of The Sycamore playing fields and Ellison needs our support to tell them to — what were her words now? Oh yes, 'bugger off'." We fall back on to the blanket, laughing.

457

"This certainly calls for a bottle of something," Heather finally gasps, rooting around her baskets for the champagne.

We drink a toast, spilling champagne everywhere, and Eva suddenly says, "God, she's leaving that gorgeous house. I can't believe it, we may well get a second chance at the house of my dreams!"

We screech, toast again at this final triumph, then settle down to sip slowly, watching the gaggle of kids and men come back to join us on the blanket. Looking at the full hamper and the empty blankets, we hastily spring into action, passing the goodies and opening bottles, fortified by furtive sips from our glasses. The kids arrive and for half an hour mayhem ensues, food and drink disappearing at an alarming rate until Eva finds another two bags full of crisps and biscuits. Hunger and thirst quenched, everyone lounges around while we share the news with the guys. The bones of the story, that is, with many meaningful glances and much clearing of throats. Gordon and Peter applaud Heather appreciatively and Harvey smiles at his wife, the kids busy burrowing into half-empty packets of ginger nuts and Minstrels. Filled to the brim, they scamper off happily, dragging the guys with them for another race around the hill.

Eva, Heather and I lean back on to our elbows, enjoying the rays of spring sunshine.

"So, what's going on with your Harvey vs Nick situation these days?" I finally ask, seeing Harvey toss Harry up in the air as if he was a feather. All the kids are hanging off him and even from here I can see them begging him for a body throw.

"Actually, it looks like the decision is slightly out of my hands, or maybe I could influence it if I really wanted to, but by not doing anything about it I've kind of made my own decision. Nick's definitely decided he can't wait any more, says he's waited almost two years and it doesn't look like I'm ever going to leave my family for him. And he's right, I think. I'm just not ready to get divorced yet. When I said that stuff about happy homes in the homework meeting, it all sounded a bit wishy-washy to me at the time. But, weirdly, saying all that out loud made me realise that I actually did believe what I was saying, or used to at some point anyway. My kids are the world to me and if I move out at some stage, which I hope I won't, I certainly don't want it to be with another man. It may just be to be by myself, who knows."

She looks thoughtful, more thoughtful and composed than I've seen her in ages, but I do her the favour and don't comment.

Eva just nods and says, "Maybe, if you spend a little time away from him, you'll find whether you can or can't live without him."

Heather sighs.

"Not sure. I think I'll hang in there for a while and give it a chance. There's always time to make rash decisions, but once you've made them it's so bloody hard to get things back to the way they were. I'd better be absolutely sure it's what I want. Well, without Nick in the picture, I'll get as far as figuring that one out. Love vs Lust, I guess."

I turn to Eva.

"And you and Gordon? I've been worried about you, I didn't know that things were quite so tense."

"Oh, we're fine, don't worry. I know what the problem is, which is a step ahead of Heather, and I'm sure I'll mellow over time." She doesn't sound anxious, so I just leave it at that and we watch the clouds, lost in our own thoughts.

What about me? My happiest times have always been with Ben, but now increasingly with Peter as well. I love being with him, love his company and his sense of humour, his kindness and energy. The way he holds and kisses me. But I am almost 100 per cent sure I don't want to marry him. I don't really need to. I just want to enjoy this for what it is and I want to give Ben continuity, consistency in our lives, but I can't impose structures and plans and goals, create expectations that might never be fulfilled or hopes that might very well be crushed. It doesn't really sound optimistic, but actually, for someone as organised, structured and, perhaps, predictable as me, it's quite a big step forward. I will be the constant in Ben's life and I'll do everything I can to stay there, be his anchor, help him through the difficult patches, and that's what he really needs. He does need a man in his life too, I still believe that, but I've changed my mind about how that man should be tied to us, to him. He sure as hell doesn't seem to need me to have a new husband and it doesn't look like he's desperate for a new dad.

I look up to find Eva scrutinising me.

"You know, Caroline, I think you're probably the one who's changed most since our schooldays. Don't you think, Heather?"

"Yeah, well, divorce has a way of doing that," I say wryly. "Actually, having children has a way of doing that. I was just thinking about the fact that I've become a romantic who doesn't believe in romance any more. I'm much more realistic about what men are and who I am, what men can do and what, feasibly, I am able to give. I think I've projected on to men what I've wanted them to be rather than realised what they are, and that's where I've gone wrong in the past."

Eva laughs. "Yes, you've changed and I think you've grown up through the realisation that the only person who makes you happy is you. No one else. Not even Ben. *You* make *you* happy."

I like that. I'm not sure that I'll ever be a full, grown-up adult, that I'll ever feel 100 per cent legitimate being a mum, being in a relationship. Every now and then that bewildered girl tagging along after Eva and Heather across the playground in Chetley pokes her head out and makes me realise that I'm only ever a sum of all my experiences. My gaze wanders over to Ben, telling off Peter for cheating, and Gordon crawling round on all fours with Harry and Maddy and, incredibly, Jennifer on his back as well.

It's been such a long year. A good year, but the happy ever after of Frencham's suburban bliss that I'd been hoping for is as much a fairy tale as the stuff Ben makes up at The Sycamore. But as long as I'm aware of that and OK with it, I think I'll muddle through.

"Hey, ladies. Off your butts. Which team do you want to be on?" shouts Peter from below, surrounded by children who are raring to go, wanting to hit something, break something, kick something, punch something, swing something or throw something.

We divide into two teams and we spend the next few hours running about insanely, getting hot and sweaty and laughing and forgetting we're forty until we trip and it takes that little bit longer to get back up.

Ben tries to explain the intricacies of a game the children have just invented, a kind of cross between chess and rounders and football, which none of the parents, all now exhausted, seem to grasp.

Gesturing wildly and using all sorts of expressions and terms that mean absolutely nothing to us, Ben sighs and looks at me, slightly exasperated, exactly how I look at him sometimes when he's got a mental block of some kind.

"Mummy, you just have to pay *attention*. This game is really very simple. You grown-ups always have to make everything so complicated."

Also available in ISIS Large Print:

Life Swap

Jane Green

Amber Winslow has got the kids, the husband, the suburban home — and the feeling that somehow life is passing her by. Vicky Townsley is features editor at Poise! Magazine, she's single, solvent and seriously successful — but she'd ditch it all for marriage, a country home and kids. So when one day Poise! offers one lucky married reader the chance to life swap for a month with a glamorous, single journalist, Amber puts pen to paper . . .

But neither Amber nor Vicky gets quite what they were expecting. And soon they find themselves asking: why does the grass look so much greener from the other side?

ISBN 978-0-7531-7742-6 (hb)
ISBN 978-0-7531-7743-3 (pb)

Babyville

Jane Green

Meet Julia, a wildly successful television producer who appears to have the picture-perfect life. But beneath the surface, things are not as perfect as they seem. Stuck in a loveless relationship with her boyfriend, Mark, Julia thinks a baby is the answer . . . but she may want a baby more than she wants her boyfriend.

Maeve, on the other hand, is allergic to commitment. A feisty, red-haired, high-power career girl, she breaks out in a rash every time she passes a buggy. But when her no-strings-attached nightlife leads to an unexpected pregnancy, her reaction may be just as unexpected . . .

And then there's Samantha — happily married and eager to be the perfect mother. But baby George brings only exhaustion, extra pounds and marital strife to her once tidy life. Is having an affair with a friend's incredibly sexy husband the answer?

ISBN 978-0-7531-7616-0 (hb)
ISBN 978-0-7531-7617-7 (pb)